THE BLOOD MILES

by Andrew Moody

BRIGHTMETTLE

For Emma, who asked for more.

For more information on *The Blood Miles*,
including reviews and a downloadable
group discussion guide, please visit:
thebloodmiles.com

ACKNOWLEDGEMENTS...

This project could not have happened without the help and encouragement of many wonderful friends: my wife Jenny, who told me it was worth a shot; my daughter Emma, who listened and enthusiastically cheered me on throughout the whole process; Peta and Abbey McDonald, Sarah and Rachel Moody, Anne Fries, Jared Turnley and the members of my writing group—Jane Churchland, Belinda Grant and Katherine Canobi—who all offered encouragement and incredibly helpful feedback along the way. I am especially grateful to award-winning author Jasmine Fischer, who gave me timely support and invaluable advice about publishing. Finally, thanks to Doug Norman for sharing his enthusiasm for (and excellent library of) post-apocalyptic literature while I was in the earliest stages of this journey; to Andy Prideaux for helping me recognise Tox-signs; and to Joe Cotton for sharing his firearms expertise in the final leg.

THE WESTERN TERRITORY
(also styled as the Autonomous Zone)
Showing the western approaches to Crux
and the road leading east to Sanctuary City
THE DEAD TOWNS
THE SAVAGE
Gaia
Ockham
Spillan
Law R.
INTERVENTION RANGE
Hatch Pass
Mt Horeb
Amhain
Crux
Wicket Gap
Mt Didasko
Delice
SPILLAN
A - Cemetery
B - Grand Hotel
C - 'Morrow we Die Inn
D - Chris's house
E - Cultivation Quarter
F - Industrial Quarter
G - South redoubt
H - Old station
I - Diner
J - Warehouses
OCKHAM
A - Front gate
B - Library
C - Cafeteria
D - Administration
E - Greenhouses
F - Fishpond
G - Vera's lab
H - Residential halls
WICKET GAP REGION
A - Wicket Pass Rd
B - HORD Camp
C - Canyon Pool
D - Observatory Base
E - Mt Tanak
F - Mt Didasko
G - Law River (mud)
H - River Crossing
I - To Crux
J - To Delice
ADDLE
A - Entrance & St
B - Shallow Dive
C - Scenic Railw
D - Seini's Flat
E - City Watchh
F - City Square
G - Dungeons
H - The Castle

INTERVENTION RANGE
Law R.
Horse Trail
Mt Horch
Amlisin
Crux
Wicket Gap
Mt Didarko
Delice
Green
Ovine
Refinery
Boneyard
Oil Wells

ADDLE
A - Entrance & Street Stalls
B - Shallow Dive
C - Scenic Railway
D - Seini's Flat
E - City Watchhouse
F - City Square & Pillory
G - Dungeons (Gaius)
H - The Castle

ADDLE SURROUNDS
A - Pru & Trevor's place
B - Museum Station
C - Refinery
D - Main Camp Complex
E - Garage
F - Radio Station
G - Stadium
H - Hospital
I - Central Road

To Central City →
Addle
Hesper
Green
Ovine
Refinery
Boneyard
Oil Wells

ADDLE SURROUNDS
A - Pru & Trevor's place
B - Museum Station
C - Refinery
D - Main Camp Complex
E - Garage
F - Radio Station
G - Stadium
H - Hospital
I - Central Road

MAIN MAP KEY
Pipeline
Road
Township
Ruined Township
Summit
Misc. Structure

Archivist's note: This telling is a crosschecked collation of written notes from Citizen Walker. Quotations from the *Roadbook* were added at the subject's request.

VOLUME 1

"You're not listening. This is the way it's got to be. It's the way it was always gonna be—I tried to tell you about it before. But that's not where it's gonna end. You're gonna come back, and you're gonna see something. You're gonna find out that there was a plan all along."

Roadbook; *Chapter 42, "The Envoy"*

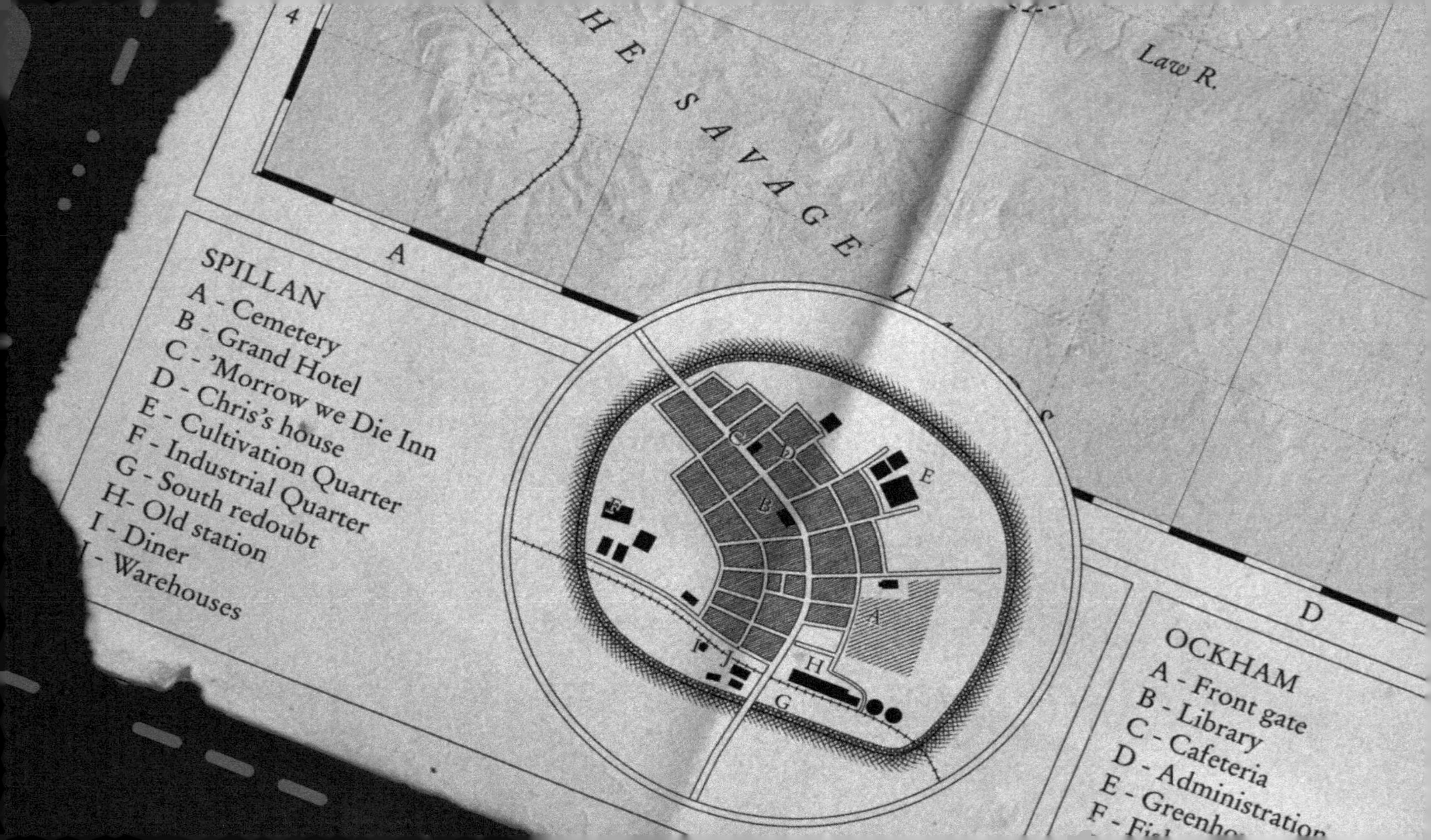

HE SAVAGE L
Law R.
4
A
SPILLAN
A - Cemetery
B - Grand Hotel
C - 'Morrow we Die Inn
D - Chris's house
E - Cultivation Quarter
F - Industrial Quarter
G - South redoubt
H - Old station
I - Diner
J - Warehouses
OCKHAM
A - Front gate
B - Library
C - Cafeteria
D - Administration
E - Greenho
F - Fi
D

CHAPTER 1

It started with Eve, of course. On the day she came to Spillan, it was four o'clock in the afternoon and we were out the back of the town, burying the sister of my best friend, Stick.

The Parson was going on and on like he always did. He was saying how noble Angie was, and how we'd always keep her in our memories, and how sweet and fitting it was to die for your town.

I was standing next to him with a shovel, thinking how sweet and fitting it would be to wham him in the head with it. I hated the way he always tried to dress things up like that. Angie hadn't been a hero—she hadn't chosen to sacrifice herself. She would have died scared. Maybe she'd tried to fight, or bargain, or switch to exile at the last minute. People did all kinds of things—but none of them looked like what the Parson was talking about.

Stick was on the other side of the grave with his hands in his pockets. He'd never been very close to his sister; she'd moved out of home when he was just a kid. But she had been the last of his living relatives. When the wake was over and he went back home to sleep above the machine shop, he'd be there by himself. And he'd know that he was the last of his line. I knew what that felt like too.

Flex, the third of our trio, was next to him, holding the other shovel. He caught my eye and made a mock-pious face. Flex would never be bothered with thoughts like that. He'd just go on being Flex.

The Parson finished his fancy speech and turned to Stick.

"Callan, would you like to say a few words?"

Stick kept looking down. "Yeah. Thanks for coming, everyone ... I'm sure she would've liked you all being here ... Yeah, that's all."

"Thank you, Callan," said the Parson. "These are hard situations. Sometimes, it can take us a little while to express our grief."

He turned and waved his hand at the old bluestone chapel that stood at the top of the cemetery. A second later, the tower bell began sending its tolls out into the motionless air. All the people started going past and shaking Stick's hand and patting him on the back.

Meanwhile, Flex and I started filling in the hole. Flex was making a mess of it; chucking in big spadefuls, which was bad because it was likely to pull the blanket off Angie's face. But I couldn't tell him that with everybody there, so I just said, "You do that end, brother," and got him to concentrate on her feet.

We had just about got her covered when the siren went off, and everybody who was still hanging around went running.

Not the three of us, though. I looked over at Stick.

"Unbelievable," I said. "He picks this moment to run a drill."

"Probably making a point," said Stick.

"Probably. Why don't you just stay here? I can cover for you with Stricton."

"Nah, it's okay," he said. "I'll come. We can finish later."

We put down our shovels and started down the hill toward the red earth rampart that lay beyond the silos. But, just as Flex branched off to go to his post, one of the little kids that the Mayor used for his runners came charging up from across the tracks.

"Boss says he needs you in the South Redoubt, Chris. You too, Stick. He said to say it's not a drill. There's something really bad coming. He said it's Savs."

Then we looked at each other and both started racing toward the wall. Soon we were at the top, running along behind the tyres and barbed wire and dodging around other people headed in the same direction. Some of them were carrying pitchforks and stakes; others had crossbows and Molotovs.

The South Redoubt was a command post—a sunken circle ringed with sandbags that looked down on the south gate and out to the mallee.

Right now, it was a hive of activity, and Mayor Stricton was standing in the centre of it with his legs apart and a field telephone up against his cheek.

"Yeah, more on the South Gate," he was saying. "No, a lot more than that … Someone, shut off that siren … If they breach we'll need everyone firing … Make sure Henry's got his thrower down there …"

When he saw me and Stick coming up, he said, "Good, here's our eyes. Get yourselves set up, boys."

So I went up to the big anti-materiel rifle that was sitting there on its bipod, while Stick grabbed the binoculars and flipped off the lens covers.

"What are we looking at?" I called.

He shoved the telephone at one of his men and came over to us.

"I got a message from Oswald out on patrol—says there's Savs coming up the south road. Says they're driving something big. I need you to stop 'em. I want you to put a round through their engine block."

"Okay," I said. "Have you got some ammo for me?"

"Last of the good ones," said Stricton. "High explosive, tungsten. Make 'em count."

He reached into his pocket and passed them to me—all fat and coppery-green with a white ring near the tip. I'd never even seen one up close—the rounds I had trained with were all lead reloads. These were much heavier—something from another time.

I loaded the first one into the breech and put the other two down on the drop sheet.

"How long have we got?" I said.

"Soon as your spotter sees 'em."

"Nothing yet," said Stick. "Pretty hazy. Visibility out to about six thousand." He was sweeping back and forth, one hand fiddling with his stopwatch as the other grasped the binoculars.

"I want you to set for six hundred," said the Mayor. "You go at six hundred you've still got time to get the other two off if you have to—long as you're fast. Right through the engine block. Driver's gonna be too hard to hit. You remember your specs?"

"Yes sir," I said. I began adjusting the scope from the figures I had memorised. Of course, I had no idea if those specs were right. Nobody had fired tungsten for years—for a generation. If the old rounds didn't work like they were supposed to—or if the velocity-data was wrong—I could be way off.

But there was no other option. I dialled the scope to allow for the fall and tried to imagine how the shot was going to work. At six hundred metres range, travelling at three times the speed of sound, it would take a little over half a second for that bullet to reach the target. That meant I needed to allow, not just for the fall of the bullet but also for the movement of the machine. I would have to aim ahead of it—how far ahead I wouldn't know until Stick gave me its speed.

Then Stick said, "We got 'proachers." He sounded pretty cool, like he usually did, but he had spoken a bit more quickly too.

"Still outside the markers," he said. "Probably about fifty-five hundred."

"What are you seeing, son?" said Stricton.

"Some sort of ATV," said Stick. "Grey panels. Going pretty quick. Got a red X on its side."

"Well, well," said the Mayor. "Haven't seen one of those for a long time."

"What is it?" I asked. I was still trying to find the vehicle with my scope.

"That's a Central Government vehicle. It'll be an Agent driving it."

And now I could see it—a tiny machine, speeding along the south road with big clouds of dust billowing up in its wake.

"Is that what you want me to hit?" I said,

He laughed as he heard the doubt in my voice. "Not worth the trouble, eh? No, not that, son. Look behind it. Wherever you get Agents, you get trouble following."

He was right about the trouble but not about my hesitation. I had my own reasons for not wanting to shoot at an Agent, reasons that I was never going to tell him. I pushed that thought away and tried to find what was following the van.

I didn't have much luck. The scope on my gun had great magnification but too narrow a field of view to be much good for something like this. Wherever I looked, there was just a cloud of churning chaos that made me lose my orientation.

"I can't see anything," I said.

"Me either, brother," said Stick. "All I can see is … Oh, hold on … Oh, Tox! Ram-rig. Really big one. It's not on the road—look off … look off to the left!"

I dipped and swung the scope. There was the little van, still speeding toward us. I went left … and there it was.

It was a huge machine—an old mining truck with armour around its cabin and a big white skull painted on to that. Lower down, a kind of plough or wedge shape had been welded above the wheels.

I'd never seen a live ram-rig, though when I was a kid I had played on the rusted wreck of one that attacked the town in the days when my dad was young.

In those days it had been the Cruelsland clan that had been raiding the towns of the Autonomous Zone. Now the threat came from a host of smaller tribes—some just as ferocious. Travellers and merchants that came to Spillan told stories about attacks on caravans; about villages obliterated; about men butchered and women made into slaves; about children carried off to become new warriors.

But I couldn't think about those things. I needed to be calm.

"Okay … that's four thousand," said Stick. I'm using the front vehicle for speed."

I tried to concentrate on my breathing, but I was also wondering where I should be aiming in that massive grill to hit the engine block.

"Three thousand!" said Stick. "Forty-three seconds."

"Can you give me a per-second?" I said.

He fiddled with the slide rule, which seemed to take a hundred years.

"… About twenty-three metres … That's two thousand by the way"

So I broke it down. If it took half a second to reach the truck, I needed to aim about eleven-and-a-half metres ahead of where the truck would be when I fired the rifle.

"Alright. Count me down in hundreds from one thousand," I said

"Yeah, brother. Just gone eleven hundred … one thousand …"

It was a mind game then. I didn't have enough time to think about anything useful, but plenty of time to mess up my instincts by thinking about what would happen if I couldn't stop that machine.

Images flashed through my mind of it smashing through our south gate. I thought of men in skins and warpaint swarming through our streets, hacking down everyone in their path. I remembered how one survivor from Borough had described hiding in a drain while the Savs cooked people on a big grill.

How could I hope to stop monsters like that with just my rifle? What if I missed?

I tried to remind myself of my training. The Mayor had picked me himself—said I was the best Gunner they'd had for years. And these bullets were giant-killers; they would punch through anything. I just had to get them in the right spot. But how was I going to adjust the scope for that second shot?

"Eight hundred," said Stick.

My mind kept spinning. If it was eleven-and-a-half metres at six hundred, what would it be at four hundred? Maybe ten?

"Seven hundred …"

I moved the cross hair out in front of the moving vehicle. Was that eleven metres?

"Six hundred."

Then I exhaled and squeezed the trigger. The sound was just immense. Dust, stirred by the shockwave rose from the drop sheet. The recoil, even with the muzzle-brake and suspension system, took me by surprise as it always did. But there was no time for thinking now.

"Go again, brother!" shouted Stick. "Hit the top of the ram."

I swore, but I was already pushing the next round into the chamber.

"Five hundred."

I slid back the bolt and sighted the weapon again. It was guesswork now. Was that four-fifty?

"Come on, Gunner, you can do it," said one of the men in the background.

"Four hundred," said Stick.

I fired again … and immediately groaned.

The sound was much too dull—as if it had just been the primer that had gone off. And that gave me another thing to worry about. If the force hadn't been enough to eject the bullet from the barrel, the next round would explode, probably taking my face with it.

Now my hands were shaking as I rushed to reload.

"Three hundred," said Stick.

I tried to aim for three metres in front of the cabin. Hitting the engine wouldn't make any difference—the machine's momentum would still carry it straight through the gates. I knew I would have to kill the driver and hope he or she would turn the wheel.

"Two hundred, " said Stick and I fired the last round. There was no science or maths to it now. I just compressed the trigger as Stick called the number.

The shot was a mess. Even as the butt kicked my shoulder, I knew I'd missed the mark.

But now there was a flash of light through the slot grill over the driver's compartment. Something was burning in there, and something was happening to its steering. The truck was really lurching and swerving.

It skidded. It was turning … It was running past us! Parallel to the wall and slewing from side to side.

As it went by, I could see that its tray had been converted into a kind of armoured fighting-deck, full of wild men waving spears and machetes and spiked clubs.

Up the front, there was one guy who almost seemed like a giant. For a moment, he was close enough that I could see the bones in his hair and all the Tox cysts on his face. He was shouting something and holding up a red banner, and for a moment, I was sure he looked straight at me.

But they were driving away! And it wasn't in an out-of-control kind of way, but a we've-changed-our-minds kind of way. It was so sudden that we all just stood and watched it with our mouths open. Then everyone came to their senses and started firing guns and crossbows after them—which didn't do much—and then cheering and whooping. Big hands were slapping my back and mussing my hair. And when I looked around, Stick was up close, grinning and laughing at me.

"Nice work, brother!"

I felt really light-headed and realised that I had been holding my breath.

"I thought I missed," I said.

"Yeah, me too," he said. "I saw your shot hit the top of the tray, but then something went off in the cabin. Must have deflected!"

"Alright, Walker. Not bad," said the Mayor behind me. And when I turned, the man was nodding at me and giving the first smile I'd ever seen on his face.

"Come with me," he said. "Let's find out what our visitor from Central is doing here."

CHAPTER 2

It was pretty weird walking along the parapet with everyone cheering at us and patting me on the back. I mean, it was nice to be appreciated, but it was too much all at once. Later on, when I had had a chance to think about it, I realised that I didn't trust it. First, they were cheering me for a lucky deflection. Second, if they could switch it on like that, they could switch it off just as fast.

But that came later. Right then, I was mostly trying to keep from falling over.

The south gate was a big metal frame made of I-beams and trench mesh that ran on wheels between concrete walls. As it slid back and we went forward, I could see the van with its battered panels, and red-X silhouette made of crossed syringes.

The driver was standing next to it with her arms crossed. She was middle-aged with short grey hair and a long grey overcoat that parted to reveal a ceramic breastplate and loose combat pants. Over all of it, she wore a diagonal leather strap that supported a sword from her left shoulder.

"You got some nerve, drawin' those Savages up to our gates, Agent," said Stricton. "Who are you and what's your business here?"

"Good day to you, Mayor. My name is Evangeline Veracis, and I'm here with a message for you and the people of Spillan from the Pantarch and the Envoy. Why don't you let me in and I'll share it with you."

Stricton looked at her for a moment, making a ticking noise through his teeth.

"We have pretty strict rules about letting carriers in this town, and those look like Tox scars on your neck. This is a Tox-free town."

The woman laughed. "You can tell your people that, Mayor, but I'd be surprised if you believe it yourself. Still, the choice is yours. If you don't want to hear what I've got to say, I will be on my way."

The Mayor turned to me.

"What do you say, Militiaman? You're the man of the hour."

"I reckon I'd like to hear what she has to say," I said.

"Alright, there you go, Agent. One night. Now, what's your message?"

"Thank you, Mayor. I'll give it to you short and sweet. The Pantarch has ordered a Total Cleanse and Reconstruction for the whole Zone to clean out the 'fection once and for all. All the services are going to be cut and anything and any *one* infected with the Tox is going to be burned out. I've been instructed to warn everyone in the townships that they need to head to Crux before the TCR."

"What's Crux?" I asked.

"Treatment outpost," she said, stretching out an arm. "Due east of here."

"Central's offering treatment, eh?" said Stricton. "What's the catch? How much is it?"

"Treatment's free for citizens."

He laughed and turned to me. "You hear that, Walker? She means they'll treat us if we'll come to heel. Thank you, Agent, but I think we'll go on taking care of ourselves. We like our independence."

She raised her eyebrows. "Taking care of yourself, Mayor? You found a way to do without that pipe that runs under your town?"

"Spare me the propaganda. We've heard your message and we've got the Tox under control … Walker, why don't you show our visitor to the Pacific. I think she can stay there without doing too much harm."

I told her to bring her vehicle in and walked ahead to show her where she could park. But I should have just got in the car with her, because people kept coming up and doing the back-slapping thing and saying what a legend I was, which was embarrassing and made everything really slow.

"You're a popular guy," she said as she locked her vehicle.

"Yeah, sorry about that," I said. "You seem pretty popular too, though. Why were the Savs after you?"

"I told them they should come and get treated. And then they said they'd prefer to stick with raiding towns and eating people."

I laughed. "I reckon you were wasting your time with them."

"You'd be surprised," she said. "I've seen whole tribes show up at Crux. There's more hope for them than places that pretend to be Tox-free."

I turned and looked at her. "So are those scars on your throat really from cysts like the Mayor said?"

"That's right."

"But you had the treatment and got rid of it?"

"Yes and no," she said. "It's complicated. What do you know about the Tox?"

I thought for a moment and gave her the list that they'd given us at school. "That it's a virus … That it produces toxic cysts … That it sends you savage and then kills you … That Central dropped it on us to punish us for rebelling."

"Yeah, half of that's wrong," she said.

We were almost at the Pacific now—an old truck-stop diner and motel perched on the edge of a cracked concrete car park just inside the wall. Hardly anyone went there now—which was why the Mayor had selected it. My own plan had been to simply drop her off and rejoin my friends as quickly as possible.

But she had me intrigued. I stopped a couple of paces back from the door.

"What do you mean?"

"Well, first up, it's not a virus, it's a gene hack. It *started out* as a virus, but the virus was just the carrier. Now the virus is gone but the hack is everywhere. We're just born with it—all of us."

"Then we'd all be savage," I said.

She shook her head and began rummaging in her pack.

"Savagery's just one form it takes. Here—you should read this. It'll explain how it works."

She had pulled a book out of her bag—pale grey leather with the same crossed-syringe symbol that I'd seen on her van.

The sight of it sent a kind of spasm through my neck. I knew if I could see the embossed title on its spine it would say, "Roadbook". I felt a sudden panic, wondering what I would do if she tried to pass it to me.

But she didn't offer me the book. Instead, she pulled something out from a pocket inside the back cover—a red folded card with white writing and rounded edges. "Guide to the Tox," it said up the top.

"Here you go," she said.

"Thanks. I'll take a look later on," I said, pushing it into my back pocket. "I guess I should introduce you to Harry."

I pulled open the aluminium frame door and the diner greeted us with wafts of burnt toast, coffee and cigarettes. Harry Frieden, the proprietor, was sitting in one of the booths, surrounded by piles of books.

"Hello, hello. Who is this? I'd say you aren't my regular customers, but since I don't have any of those, I will say something different. Nice to see you, Chris. Who have you brought … Are you an Agent? Is that what the alarm was about?"

I liked Harry. Before his eccentric ideas had gotten him sacked, he'd taught us reading and writing in year nine. Sometimes I still came down to the Pacific to chat with him or play a game of draughts. But I knew that once he got going, it would be hard to get a word in edgewise and even harder to extract myself.

"Harry, this is Agent Veracis," I said. "She had some Savs chasing her and the Mayor has said she can stay here tonight." Before he could start, I said my farewell, "Nice meeting you, Agent. I hope the rest of your journey goes better … Oh, and don't eat the fish sticks."

"I heard that," said Harry.

I retreated—pausing at the door as I remembered a final question that I had wanted to ask her.

"Hey, what was that you said about the pipe under our town?"

"Water pipe," she said. "Runs all the way from Central. All the towns west of the mountains are on it."

"Huh," I said.

*   *   *

Stick and Flex had almost finished with the backfill by the time I made it back to the cemetery.

"Ooh look, it's Gunner!" said Flex with a grin. "Can we be your friends, Gunner?"

"Shut up," I said. "Give me your shovel."

They stepped back and let me do the last part. I packed in the clay and spread the lighter topsoil that we'd kept aside. It was a good job. If there was a dew, the little mound might even sprout a weed or two.

"How was the Agent?" said Stick as we shouldered our shovels.

"Dunno," I said. "Bit weird. She reckons we've all got the Tox and Central is going to wipe us out unless we get treatment."

"That'd make things simpler," said Stick. "Maybe we should dig some more holes."

"Hey, is she really from Central?" said Flex. "… Do you remember there was that Agent that came around when we were kids, and the Savs got him?"

"Yep," said Stick, looking at me.

"So are you guys coming to the pub?" I said. "Or am I going to have to drink my free drinks alone?"

"We'll help you," said Stick.

The *Morrow-We-Die Inn* on Main street was full of noise and people and yellow light and cheering as we came in the doors. People kept calling me "Gunner" and telling me I was the saviour of the town and buying me drinks.

I managed to pass most of those on to Stick and Flex. But the ones I downed helped me feel a bit less embarrassed about it all. I even tried telling some of the girls what had happened and managed to make it sound like I had known what I was doing.

After that, someone put on some slower music and Sally Menders—who I had always fancied from when we were at school, but who had never paid me any attention—came over and dragged me up for a dance. That was nice, until she put her arms around my neck and something stabbed at the base of my skull.

"Hey, what was that?" I said as I jerked backward.

"What was what?"

I reached around to the back of my neck. "Did you stick a pin in me or …?"

"A pin? … What are you talking about, Chris?" she said.

I looked at her and shook my head.

"I don't know. Sorry, Sally. I gotta go," I said.

I broke away from her and blundered toward the toilets, and then the back door of the hotel. Of course, as soon as I said it, I knew it wasn't a pin—it just wasn't that sort of pain. It might be an infected hair or an insect bite, perhaps even a pimple. But after my conversation with Eve Veracis, my first thought was that it might be something else—something much worse. And if it was that, then Sally Menders was the last person I wanted knowing about it.

My brain was too foggy to think straight as I staggered home. But I was still clear-headed enough to be able to feel the small and tender lump at the nape of my neck. When I got back to the cottage I found a piece of broken mirror and tried to look at it using the bathroom cabinet and an oil lamp. But the light was too dim and my eyes were too blurry, and now I was suddenly really tired.

I kicked off my boots and trousers and fell asleep on the couch.

*   *   *

It was well after sunrise when I woke up. My head was pounding and my mouth felt so dry that I worried it would stick shut if I swallowed. But when I opened my eyes and saw the lamp and the mirror on the floor, I remembered everything.

The mirror still wasn't much help to me—even in the morning light. I thought I could, maybe, see an ominous yellow tinge in the skin when I pulled back the hair, but if it was a Tox cyst, it hadn't come to the surface yet. Maybe it never would, I thought—maybe I'd just have the one cyst deep down there and nobody would ever know.

On the other hand, what if this was just the start? What if the next one came up on my cheek, or forehead, or hand? Then I would be done. They would drag me in and give me the choice—just like they had with Angie; just like they had with so many others.

From there, my mind scattered. If it was the Tox, how had I caught it? From the Agent? (surely it was too quick for that). What if it had already been in my system, like she said?

I suddenly remembered the card she'd given me at the Pacific. It was still in the back pocket of my trousers. I drew it out and unfolded it.

GUIDE TO THE TOX (CONGENITAL PERINEURAL CYSTOSIS)

THE TOX, OR CPC, IS A GENETIC DISORDER THAT IS ENDEMIC TO THE WESTERN TERRITORIES (OR AUTONOMOUS ZONE).

IT GIVES RISE TO TOXIN-FILLED CYSTS THROUGHOUT A SUBJECT'S NERVOUS SYSTEM, ESPECIALLY IN THE BRAIN.

CPC CYSTS CAUSE A WIDE RANGE OF SECONDARY PHYSICAL AND PSYCHOLOGICAL EFFECTS, INCLUDING SENSORY IMPAIRMENT, HOSTILE OR VIOLENT IDEATION, FIXATION AND VARIOUS FORMS OF...

"Blah blah blah," I thought, and chucked it down. Maybe it would make more sense when my head hurt less. I resolved to stop thinking about the thing on my neck and get ready for work.

I went into the kitchen and began to make myself a cup of coffee. But it was too bright in there and the morning light was reflecting off the bits of mirror that my mum had glued onto the wall.

Just before the Council had found out about her cyst, she had suddenly decided to cover all our blank walls with mosaics. For six weeks, she spent all her free time scrounging for bits of broken crockery and mirrors and sticking them up in the hall and kitchen.

I closed one eye and squinted while I finished making my porridge; returned to the lounge to eat it.

The card had landed open on the floorboards so that it caught my eye as I set down my mug.

DO I HAVE THE TOX? it said on the inside flap.
A QUICK SURVEY TO TEST YOURSELF.

I picked it up again and peered at it as I ate.

MANY OF THE MOST COMMON SIGNS OF CPC ARE SUBTLE. READ THROUGH THE FOLLOWING LIST AND SEE HOW MANY ARE TRUE FOR YOU.

- **I SOMETIMES FEEL PLEASURE WHEN I HEAR ABOUT BAD THINGS HAPPENING TO OTHER PEOPLE--EVEN MY FRIENDS.**

- **IF OTHER PEOPLE COULD SEE MY THOUGHTS, THEY WOULD PROBABLY THINK THAT I WAS EVIL.**

- **I CAN SOMETIMES MAKE MYSELF FEEL BETTER BY THINKING AND TALKING ABOUT THE WRONG THINGS OTHER PEOPLE DO ...**

I stopped reading as the remaining questions became a blur. The blood was thumping in my ears, and everything else seemed to have slowed down.

I generally thought of myself as a pretty normal person. But my normal included all of these things. I *did* actually enjoy hearing stories of Savage attacks on other towns. I mean, I knew that they were horrible, but there was something pleasurable about hearing them.

I'd felt a secret satisfaction when Stick was dumped by his girlfriend three weeks before. Of course, I acted like a sympathetic friend—and I was genuinely sorry for him. But underneath, there was also that little feeling … like satisfaction.

And thinking about the first thing led to the second. If I imagined other people being able to see my thoughts, then there would be all kinds of stuff to freak them out. Hadn't I just been thinking about murdering the Parson—bashing out his brains with a spade? If I heard Stick or Flex talking like that out loud, I would have worried that they were going savage. Was that what I was? Was I some sort of secret Savage in my head?

I sagged down on the couch. My head still ached, and now I felt like I'd been punched in the stomach too.

I thought about taking the day off—telling Marj at the Aquaponics joint that I was feeling sick. I was going to be late now, anyway.

But I didn't want to be stuck at home. I wanted to run away. I wanted to go somewhere where I wouldn't have to worry about what was happening to me, or what people would do if they found out about that thing on my neck.

I wanted to see the Agent.

I finished getting ready and charged back down to the Pacific, only to find that I was too late.

"Left at dawn," said Harry from behind the counter. "Grabbed a coffee and that was it. Said she'd seen the people she had to see and had other places to go. Pretty interesting lady, that one. She's given me a lot to think about. You know I met another Agent, long time ago, who …"

But I'd stopped listening.

"Thanks, Harry," I said. I went to open the door, but he leaned forward, holding out something white.

"Not so fast, Mr Walker. She left you a note."

She'd written it on a folded paper napkin with my name on the outside and two sentences on the reverse.

"Go east toward the risen sun and I will find you. Crux is your only hope."

I went to work and made my apologies for being late—Marj was easier on me than I expected. I went about my tasks: feeding the fish, checking the nitrates, cleaning the siphons, and topping up the tanks. But I kept going over the things that the Agent had said; kept thinking about what I'd read on the card she had given me.

Did I believe her? Could I believe that everyone was Tox affected? It went so completely against everything that our town stood for.

And what was I going to do about that thing on my neck? If it was a cyst, I was living with a time bomb. One day, that cyst, or a deeper one that I didn't know about, would rupture and poison me. In the meantime, the Tox would be doing other bad things to my brain and personality: maybe savagery, maybe something else.

I took the flier out of my pocket and turned to the next flap—FAQ:

Q: HOW CAN I HAVE THE TOX IF I DONT HAVE ANY CYSTS?

A: TOX CYSTS CAN GROW ANYWHERE IN A PERSONS NERVOUS SYSTEM (ESPECIALLY IN THE BRAIN) AND THUS MOSTLY OCCUR OUT OF SIGHT.

Q: HOW CAN I HAVE THE TOX IF I AM NOT SAVAGE?

A: VIOLENCE AND SAVAGERY ARE JUST ONE MANIFESTATION OF THE TOX. APART FROM THE SIGNS LISTED IN THE SURVEY ABOVE, OTHER MANIFESTATIONS CAN INCLUDE:

- **FIXATION OR OBSESSION;**
- **EARLY-ONSET SHORTSIGHTEDNESS;**

- ### ACUTE AWARENESS OF SLIGHTS RECEIVED, PAIRED WITH INSENSITIVITY TO WRONGS DONE.

NOTE: TOX-SIGNS FREQUENTLY OCCUR IN CLUSTERS SUCH THAT MEMBERS OF LOCAL COMMUNITIES EXPERIENCE SIMILAR SYMPTOMS.

I just stood there with the hose pouring out onto the concrete floor. I had seen examples of all these things. There was the fixation: I thought of my mum's sudden mosaic obsession; Flex's mad and short-lived business projects.

I knew about the shortsightedness too—it was the reason why gunners and spotters never kept their posts past their mid-twenties. All the adults in Spillan had degenerative eyesight.

Finally, there was that stuff about the "slights and wrongs". People were always falling out and having feuds in our town. My neighbours two doors down had been fighting with each other for ten years because Nancy had trimmed an overhanging branch and thrown it back over Bob's fence. Just the week before, two kids had been arrested for trying to burn down the cinema because it hadn't let them in without shoes—three months before. Even Marj, my boss, was likely to fly into a rage if I didn't call her "Boss".

And of course, it was just then that Marj saw me. She was furious.

"What do you think you're doing? I made allowances for you this morning with what happened yesterday, but this is coming out of your pay. What do you think happens if we bust our water ration?"

"Sorry, Marj," I said, as I shut off the hose. "I got distracted."

"No, really? I'd never have guessed. Get yourself together or look for another job, kiddo. And it's 'Boss', not Marj to you."

But thinking about the water reminded me of something else.

"Boss … where does our water come from?" I said.

"Underground."

"Yeah, but is it like from a bore or ..."

"For 'fection's sake. There's a pipe. Now stop daydreaming and get back to work."

But there was no hope of that now. It was like the Agent had told me the sky was made of plaster, and suddenly I had looked up and noticed a crack in it. If the Agent was right about the Tox and about the water, then maybe she was telling the truth about there being a cure. Maybe a cyst didn't have to mean the end. Maybe I could get inoculated. Maybe the whole town could get inoculated. Maybe we wouldn't have to keep killing and exiling ...

And then the crack widened, and a chunk of the sky fell in on me. Because, if she was right—if everyone had the Tox—then we'd been killing and exiling people for nothing. I thought about Stick's sister lying under the dirt, and my own mother trying not to cry as they took her off to the police station.

I felt like I was going to throw up; like I had been crushed. Then I thought I might kill someone.

I turned off the tap-handle so hard it snapped, and walked out of the greenhouse.

CHAPTER 3

I was sitting on my back step looking at the uncut grass when I heard the side gate creak, and the last person I wanted to see appeared in my driveway.

"You're an elusive fella," said the Mayor. "Marj said you wandered off the job. You doin' okay, son?"

"I dunno what I am, Mayor."

The man gave a chuckle and nodded like he knew all about it. "It can be a shock for a man when he rises up. One minute, you're just Joe average, next you're town hero. Takes some adjustin', but I imagine you'll be okay. Listen, son, I want you to consider something."

"What's that, Mayor?" I said

"I want you to come and work for me direct. Not just as part of the militia, but on my staff. It'll be the same pay, but you'll be doing better work. And you'll be getting the training you need."

I hauled myself out from the black hole of my thoughts. "Training for what?"

"Well, I'm not going to be 'round forever. And the folks trust you— you did good work yesterday with that gun."

I looked at him. What? Was he talking about me becoming Mayor?

"Mayor, there's something I need to tell you …" I said.

But he was on a roll.

"We live on a thin margin of civilisation here, Walker," he said. "If it's not the ferals, it's crop blight or Tox or some young idiot going savage on us.

"People take it for granted. They think that just because we've made it this far, we'll keep going. Some of them want to get fancy notions about spreading out, or stopping the drills. Some of them say we should go easy on the 'fection—let the cysties hang around.

"But the truth is we survived because we've had tough men at the top who know how to keep their heads and take the tough decisions; men who can do their duty under pressure; men who know what it is to pay the price for keeping this town from the Tox—even if it means giving up the people they care about. Do you take my meaning?"

I felt that sick feeling again.

"You're saying that because of my mum," I said.

"I am. But that's not the whole of it. I've had my eye on you for a while and I like what I see. You're a fella who knows how to get on with things. I know you're still only eighteen, but you do your duty, and you've got an independent mind too."

If only the man knew what thoughts had been going on in my head.

"I'm afraid you've picked a bad day for this, Mayor," I said. "I've been doing some hard thinking about all that."

"About what, son?"

"About the Tox … About the cyst rule."

"Yeah? And what have you been thinking?"

"I'm going to go to Crux—the treatment station that Agent was talking about."

Now to be honest, I hadn't been thinking that at all. I had simply been going over the Agent's red card and feeling more convinced. But this crazy idea of me being Mayor—of me sending other people to their deaths while I had this thing on my own neck—made me feel so disgusted that I just blurted it out. I felt as surprised as the look that appeared on the Mayor's face.

Except his surprise immediately turned into anger.

"Why the Tox would you want to do that?" he said.

"I want to see if the cure is real," I said. "I want to see if we've been killing people for nothing."

"Well 'fect me … She got to you, didn't she? I thought if I sent her to Harry, she wouldn't be able to do anyone else any harm. But she got to you. What did she say?"

"She gave me something to read that told me about some of the other signs."

"The cysts are the signs! She was messin' with your head; tryin' to get you to doubt yourself. That's what those Agents do."

"Maybe. I want to find out, anyway. If there's any chance she's right then everyone should know about it. If there really is a cure, I'll come back and report."

"The hell you will! Weren't you listening when I was talking to her, boy? The treatment's for *citizens*. They won't just …"

"She just said it was *free* for citizens. I'll pay for mine somehow."

The Mayor shook his head and made the ticking noise with his teeth. "Well, it looks like I got you all wrong, Walker. I thought you had a good head on your shoulders, but I might as well have been talking to that idiot friend of yours. Those people are our enemies. We're still officially at war with them! You think they're just going to let you waltz in and waltz out?"

"I'm willing to risk it for the sake of the town."

"For the sake of the town. You little plaguebrain—if you came back here preaching that stuff about everyone bein' 'fected, you'd unleash anarchy."

I looked up at him and noticed the white spittle in the corners of his mouth—suddenly wondered if his obsession with purifying the town might just actually be another symptom of the Tox.

"How do you know that there aren't people hiding their cysts?" I said, "I mean under their clothes or under their hair? For all we know, half the town could have it."

"Maybe, and when we find 'em we'll give 'em the same choice we give all the rest."

I opened my mouth to say something, but the man cut me off.

"You know, I think I've had enough of this conversation … I'm glad it came out when it did. Looks like you've saved me from a big mistake. Go if you want. Don't bother coming back."

He turned and left, slamming the wire gate behind him, and I uncurled my fingers from the ends of the splintery floor boards that I had been gripping to keep myself from doing something I would regret.

*   *   *

I told my friends that night. I told them about the thing on my neck, and what I'd learned from the Agent, and about my conversation with the Mayor. Finally, I told them about deciding to go to Crux.

We were sitting on the steps of the old war memorial above the cemetery.

"Don't know why you'd want to trust those guys," said Stick slowly, trying to read the red card in the moonlight. "They threaten to wipe us all out and you want to go and let them inject you with stuff. I mean, I get why you don't want to work for the Mayor. But why go to Central?"

"I don't know what I've got to lose," I said. "I mean, if I've got it—if this thing's a cyst, I'll be dead sooner or later anyway. Either the Council will find out or the thing will burst—or maybe I've got others like the card says ..."

"Still a big gamble, though. Looking at it, I'd reckon fifty-fifty that thing's a cyst. But if you go out there, it's like ninety per cent chance you'll get eaten by Savages or killed for your teeth or something. And even if you make it through to Central ..."

"I just want to go to Crux. That's where the treatment centre is."

"... Okay, even if you make it through to *Crux*, what makes you think you can trust them not to slave you, or do something worse?"

Before I could answer, Flex, lying between us, finished trying to balance a bottle on his chin and raised his head. "How far is Crux?"

"I dunno," I said. "It's not on our map. She just said to go east, and that she'd find me and take me there."

"And will it be all hi-tech like Central?"

"I don't know that either. I just know there's a base there, and that they say it's where you have to go if you want to get treated."

"I wouldn't mind seeing Central," said Flex. "Do you remember that brochure we found behind the bookshelf at school? And how it had that picture of Sanctuary City and the animals and trees everywhere?"

"Yeah, I remember that," I said. "And Mrs Bleaker found us looking at it and said she'd tell our parents and get us expelled if we didn't say who had given it to us?"

"And you told her to go ahead, and she got all embarrassed," said Stick.

"… Hey, maybe if we went to Central, we could pick up some stuff that we could sell back here," said Flex.

Stick laughed. "You guys are Toxed in the head. If Central is as good as the propaganda says, why would they let the likes of you in there? They'd shoot you on sight."

I looked down at the graves.

"Yeah, maybe. I don't know about Central, but I'm gonna try for Crux. If you guys want to come too, that'd be good."

"No thanks, brother," said Stick. "I hope you make it, but I think you're crazy."

"Yeah, I'll come," said Flex.

*   *   *

It took us a few days to get ourselves organized, and it wasn't pretty.

As soon as people found out that I was going, the rumours started. I'd gone crazy with my success and gotten myself a messiah complex. The Mayor had gone off me. I had the Tox and was leaving town before anyone made me.

Just as my reputation had shot up, it suddenly crashed. Some people tried to gently talk sense into me. Others tried to use guilt—who would fire the big gun if the Savages came back?

The Council had an informal discussion about whether they would denounce my "plans to defect"; I heard later that one of them had even put up a motion that I should be imprisoned for my own good.

But none of that happened. Three days later, Flex and I slipped out through the eastern barricade in the morning dark, carrying our backpacks, a rifle and a water skin between us. When the sun came up over the flats, the orange light shone on our faces and cast long shadows back the way we'd come. And for the first time since my conversation with the Mayor, I felt a sort of lightness in my heart.

It didn't last, though. Before long, the glow turned to glare, and the rising heat made the skin prickle inside my shirt.

And Flex talked on and on. He talked about how he had been thinking of travelling to Central for a long time, and how it was nice that we could both go together. He talked about all the stuff we might be able to bring back to Spillan: medicine, food, weapons, clothes—and how we might go about persuading them to let us transport it in one of their skyships.

"You know Central is hundreds of miles away, don't you?" I said.

"Sure, but if Crux is run by Central, then maybe we can get them to give us a lift. Isn't that what the Agent said to you?"

"No. She said that if I went east, she'd find me and bring me to Crux."

"Okay. But she must have a radio or something. She could call down a ship."

"Maybe. I don't know," I said.

But even Flex went quiet as the heat and miles wore on.

Ten kilometres out from Spillan, we came to a spot where the flats went down toward the old riverbed. Most of it was dry—just a few muddy pools under the trees. But as we tried to cross, the cracked crust gave way under us, leaving us up to our knees in stinking mud that sucked and dragged on us as we tried to move forward.

After half an hour, we were totally exhausted and Flex had started muttering to himself. I couldn't quite make out what he was saying, but

I caught the words "stupid caper" and got the impression I was being blamed for it. At some point, he came and took the waterskin off me, which made things lighter for me—but it didn't make him any quicker. He just kept getting slower and slower, and dropping further and further behind.

I tried to encourage him; "Come on, Flex. Keep it up," I called out. "We must be past half way, now"

"Go ahead, brother," he said, "I just need a breather."

I sighed and pushed on.

Looking back, I guess I had always felt a bit superior to Flex. I thought I was smarter than him too. I'd seen so many of his enthusiastic schemes come and go: the rabbit meat business that was going to make him rich; the armoured dune buggy that he had started to build from abandoned cars. The year before, just after we'd finished school, he'd borrowed a whole lot of money from Stick and me to build a commercial whisky still. But he'd abandoned that, like he abandoned all his projects, and never repaid us.

Stick and I put up with him. We laughed at him sometimes, but not behind his back. But as I went over his failures, my patience slowly evaporated. Flex was an idiot, I thought. He was going to give up soon, and if I didn't do something, he was likely to drink half the water while he was deciding to do it.

I stopped and turned back to look at him. He was still in the same spot he'd been when I had last called out to him. Except now he was looking back to face the way we'd come.

"You doing alright?" I called to him.

He twisted round and shook his head. "This is no good, brother. I'm gonna lose a shoe if I keep on like this."

I turned and started walking back toward him.

"Well ... what do you want to do? How about we look for a way round?" I said.

"Nah. Nah, it's okay."

"You thinking of going back?"

Flex shrugged.

"We've just got started," I said.

"I know. That's why. If it's like this now, what's it gonna be like down the track? I can't do it. I shouldn't have come ... Sorry ..."

"Alright," I said. "Stay there and I'll come and get the water skin off you."

"It's okay. I can chuck it to you," said Flex. He swung it by its neck so that it flew in a tumbling arc, landing about five metres off to my left. But even as it was in the air, I could see that it was empty.

I stopped in my tracks. Suddenly, I could feel the sore at the back of my neck throbbing.

"Hey, Flex, what happened to all the water?" I said.

"I dunno," he said. "Maybe you didn't put the cap on properly when we had that last drink."

"What are you talking about? You were the last one to drink. You've been carrying it for the last half hour," I said.

He shrugged. "Maybe there's something wrong with the seal, then ..."

He broke off as he saw the expression on my face.

"You idiot," I said. "You can't even admit it. Why did I let you come?"

I ignored the waterskin and started advancing toward him. Flex went wide-eyed and took a step back.

"Hey, Chris ... what are you doing?"

"What do you think?" I said.

He turned and bolted, and I ran after him.

When I started coming at him, I was just wanting to scare him. But suddenly, I realised I was only half acting. I wanted to knock him down and rub his face in the mud.

"Stop, Chris," he called over his shoulder. "You're going savage!"

"That's right," I shouted.

He had a good lead on me, but I was stronger. Soon, I was close enough to imagine my hands around his neck, pulling him down.

I leapt, but the mud slipped back beneath my feet, so I dropped short. I tried again, but the same thing happened, and I landed on my knees.

And then something bad happened to me. It was like the frustration triggered it. As long as I thought I was in control, I knew I didn't *really* want to hurt him. But when I couldn't get to him, it was like my whole head got full of fire. And suddenly I knew I didn't want to just knock him down; I wanted to bite his neck and gouge his eyes and press him into the mud until he stopped moving.

So I charged at him for the last time, and I really think I would have killed him if I had caught him. I was all teeth and claws and rage. But even as I was preparing for that last jump, my boot snagged a tree root buried in the mud and down I went, face-first into the muck.

He was halfway up the hill by the time I cleared it from my eyes. There was no chance of catching him now, and I didn't even want to. The red fire had gone from my head, and I just felt sick and horrified at myself.

I lay there in the mud, remembering Stick's words from that night in the cemetery: "If Central is as good as the propaganda says, why would they let the likes of you in there?"

But it was too late to turn back now. Flex might not tell anyone but Stick about what had happened, but he might tell everyone. If he really thought I had gone savage, then he might not even think it was being disloyal. We thought of Savages like they weren't human—like they were just the shells of the people they'd been.

So there was no going back to Spillan. I'd simply be sent away or shot from the walls.

And yet, I thought, there was still a ray of hope. If I could just get to Crux—and if the treatment was real—I could still come back as proof that it worked. In that case, Flex's story would make my appearance even more dramatic. The Mayor would be forced to admit there was a cure. The cyst rule would fall.

But how far could I get now that the water was gone?

I got up and made my way back to where Flex had tossed the water skin. There was barely a mouthful in it.

Even as I tilted my head back, however, I noticed something on the horizon—a glint of something silver, just visible above the curve of the river valley. When I shielded my eyes and concentrated, I could see other traces of it—a line that ran right along the ridge.

Could it be the pipeline that the Agent had said supplied all the towns of the AZ—the pipe that went all the way back to Central?

I slogged back through the mud and made my way up to the top of the slope.

It *was* a pipe: a fat zinc-silver snake slithering across the landscape. It was made of bolted segments supported by concrete pylons, and every segment had a logo of waves and the word "*Natura*™" stencilled on its side. There was even a small tap on one of the pylons. Soon, I was clean, refreshed and holding a full waterskin.

Better still, the pipe ran toward the east—not dead east, but near enough to give me hope that it might take me where I needed to go.

As I set off along the line, I took a last look down at the river flat and the shimmering haze of the land beyond. What a stroke of good fortune it was to have found a way around that. Now I had water, a path to follow and shade for my head. Later that afternoon, I even came across some berry bushes and was able to fill my stomach with the sour fruit.

When the sun went down, I stretched out on the sand and was kept warm by the heat radiating off the metal.

But the next day, I was captured.

CHAPTER 4

I was asleep when they grabbed me—dreaming that I was leading the people of Spillan along the pipeline, with Central City shining on the horizon. The Mayor was just saying, "We should have always listened to you, Walker." And the next minute, everyone had charged at me and piled on so I couldn't move or breathe. And then I woke up and realised that there really *were* people on top of me. Someone was kneeling on my chest. Someone else was pulling a hessian bag over my head. Someone was holding down my arms.

Instantly, I was awake, razor-sharp and absolutely clear that I was about to be murdered and eaten. I found myself making a horrible groaning noise as I tried to twist free. I felt my fingernails tear as I clawed the ground.

None of it did any good. Whoever it was had me pinned. I could smell their sweat and hear their grunting as they pressed me into the ground.

"Did you think we wouldn't notice if you came in along the pipeline?" said one of them.

"Gaians think everyone's as stupid as them," said a second voice.

I freed an arm and felt my knuckles graze someone's face. I got a punch in the nose and a boot on my neck in return.

"Get him in the van," said the first voice. Then there was twine pulling tight around my ankles and wrists, and I was being carried and dropped onto the floor of a large vehicle of some kind. There was dirt and patterned rubber under my cheek, and a smell of cigarettes and ozone in the air. Somebody slammed a door, and I felt the pressure pop in my ears as the machine began to move.

"Where are you taking me?" I asked.

"Where do you think?" said the first voice, now coming from the front of the vehicle. "You're coming to Ockham."

"You can help us with our research," said the second voice—now coming from higher up and on my left.

"What's Ockham?" I said.

"Don't pretend to be stupider than you are," said the first voice. "Are you on your own, or have you got some friends somewhere?"

"It's just me. I've just been following the pipeline from Spillan. I'm not trying to sneak in anywhere."

"Yeah, right," said a third voice.

"Just thought you'd take a nice little stroll along our pipe, did you?" said the second voice.

"No, someone told me that … I'm trying to find somewhere where I can get treatment for the Tox."

There was a pause.

"Look through his stuff," said the first voice.

There was a sound of someone moving about, rummaging through my pack.

"Apart from the gun, it's just travelling stuff," said the second voice. "Clothes, flint, a few rounds, dried fruit … dried meat …"

"Dried meat?" said the first voice. "How about that. So you're not from Gaia after all?"

"No, I'm from Spillan, like I said. I'm just looking for …"

"Maybe we should give him the test," said the second voice.

"Go ahead," said the first voice. "Get the book."

I heard the sound of pages being flicked. Through the floor, the engine changed note as the vehicle began climbing a slope.

"Ready, toxface?" said the second voice.

"Ready for what?" I said.

"To decide your fate."

"Quiztime," said the third voice on my right.

"I don't know what you're talking about," I said.

"Prob'ly not," said the second voice. "But that's what we're going to find out … Okay. Here's the first one. Which of the following words is most similar in meaning to 'Irrelevant': A. Ordinary B. Irreverent C. Useless D. Wrong?

"What?" I said, "Why are you asking me …"

"Not right," said the third voice.

"Barrrp," said the second voice.

"No, wait … wait," I said, trying to lift my head. "Ask me again. I just wasn't expecting that sort of question."

"I dunno, toxface, you had your chance. What do you think, boss?"

"Give him another go," said the first voice.

The second voice repeated the question as I tried to force my brain to listen to the words.

"It's either C or D," I said. "No, it's C! 'Useless'!"

"Lucky," said the third voice.

"Yeah," said the second voice. "Okay, here's the second question.

"Some of the children in this class are lazy. No lazy child gets good marks. Which is true: A. No child in this class will get good marks. B. Some children in this class won't get good marks?"

I tried to remember the question.

"Time's a factor," said the voice on my right.

"That's right," said the second voice.

"B," I said.

"He's guessing," said the third voice.

"Maybe," said the second voice. "Alright, let's try one without a multiple choice. If it takes five bakers one hour to make five loaves of bread, how long does it take a hundred bakers to make a hundred loaves?"

"… Can't tell," I said.

"Why not?" said the second voice.

"We don't know the setup," I said. "Are they all sharing the same equipment? If they have to wait for mixers or ovens or bench space or something, it'll take longer."

"Thinks he's smart," said the third voice.

"Yeah, but is he smart or just a smart …"

"Assume the same ratio of equipment as the first example," said the voice from the front of the vehicle.

"Then it's the same time," I said. "It'll take an hour."

There was another silence.

"Get the hood off him," said the first voice.

I blinked and found myself staring up at the grinning face belonging to the owner of the second voice. He was a big man with a round head topped with stubble. He had wire-frame spectacles and a long battered overcoat. Standing over him, I saw a slightly younger man with dark wild hair, a leather jacket, and a bandolier holding what looked like three straight razors.

"Nice work on the questions," said the younger man. "Welcome to Ockham. I'm Liam. That's Bill who's untying you and this is William." I turned to follow his nod and saw the owner of the third voice—a lanky figure with a long, crooked face.

"Why did you grab me?" I said.

"Just doin' our job, mate," said Bill, working the knots loose on my hands.

"We thought you were a Gaian," said Liam. "They're always trying to sneak in and wreck things. We didn't know you were switched on. But if you're a thinker, you belong with us."

"So, who are you guys?"

"We're deep patrol," said Liam. "Ockham sends us out to guard the approaches and to look for stuff." He pointed toward the back of the vehicle where wire crates full of books, magazines and old telecommunications equipment rocked with the motion of the van.

"You should be grateful," said Bill, now untying my feet.

"For you attacking me?" I said.

"Cos of the Tox," said Bill.

"That's right," said Liam. "If you're worried about the Tox, Ockham's the place for you."

"Have you got a cure?"

"Not yet. But we know how to control it. And we've got scientists working on a proper vaccine."

"Civilisation," said William.

"Science," said Bill.

"Same thing," said William.

I looked around at them, wondering whether to trust them. Liam and William looked cyst-free, but when Bill bent down to cut the twine on my feet, I could see a constellation of the blisters in the stubble of his scalp. I wondered if it might be the same for the other two.

"How about if I wanted you to let me go?" I said.

Liam shrugged. "We could do that. "But if you were following the pipe, you would have come to Ockham anyway."

He reached down, pulled me up and directed me to an empty seat next to William. At the same time, I felt the vehicle turning. Through the front window, I could see the silhouettes of tall buildings, distant floodlights and the first colours of morning.

"Is that Ockham?" I said.

"Yep," said Liam.

"Is it a town?"

"No, it's a university," he said. "Used to be a natural sciences institute."

Our vehicle slowed as it approached the razor wire fence that ringed the compound. A guard in a parka and grey scarf unshouldered her rifle and approached us; shone her torch through the windows and gave a hand signal to someone. There was a click and the sound of a barrier sliding back. Soon we were rolling up an avenue flanked by rows of jury-rigged solar arrays, caged water cubes and greenhouses.

At the end of it, we entered a brick-paved quadrangle ringed by a series of glass and steel buildings. We stopped outside the largest of them. "Montag Library", it said on its portico.

"Alright," said Liam. "Let's deal with the junk, and we can get some breakfast. William, take the tech. Bill, show our new friend what to do with the lit."

Bill passed me a heavy wire basket filled with books and magazines of all sizes, and gestured for me to follow him into the dimly lit library. We came past the front desk into a vast open space with a central atrium reaching up through three stories to a skylight roof. Even in the gloom, I could see rows of bookshelves stretching out of sight in every direction.

"How many books are there here?" I said.

"Too many," said Bill. "You wouldn't believe what a tox of a job it was to empty the top stories. Come on."

He led me down a flight of steps, through a basement filled with rows of empty bookshelves. A flickering glow played across the ceiling and, as we came out from between the stacks, I could see that the light was coming from a furnace up the far end of the room. The space around it was scattered with piles of books that cast long shadows onto the concrete.

"Here we go, said Bill, just chuck 'em in one at a time and bring back the basket. I'll meet you back at the V."

"You want me to burn them?" I said.

"That's right. Might have to rip 'em up a bit to get em going."

"Why are you burning books?" I said.

"Heats the water. Get's rid of 'em."

He saw my face and rolled his eyes.

"Here, look at 'em," he said. He grabbed a couple of random titles from the top of the crate. "*A Treatise of Human Nature* … *Language, Truth and Logic.* They're all this stupid pseudo-stuff: sociology, and political studies, and art and history, and plaguey junk like that. That's why we get 'em out of circulation. If we come across anything real, we shelve 'em upstairs."

"What's *real?*" I said.

"Testable stuff. Science. Tech. Not this tox." He opened the furnace door and tossed the books inside.

I watched him walk away and wondered what I'd been dragged into. What sort of University burned books? Harry Frieden used to say that a life without books is like a body without a soul. Of course, even he would have admitted that not all books were equally valuable. But these Ockhamists seemed to have a pretty narrow idea of what made a book worth keeping. Was this another kind of Tox madness?

I didn't know. I did know that I didn't have much choice in the matter. I wasn't about to find out what Bill and his friends might do if I crossed them for the sake of some old books on poetry or something.

I reached into the basket and pulled out a handful to toss into the fire.

And stopped. There, right on the top of the pile, was a book with a pale grey cover embossed with a symbol of crossed syringes.

Roadbook. Complete Handbook and Cognitive Catalyst. Central Issue, it said.

I had almost burned it. Again. Suddenly, I was ten years old, trying to snuff out the flames on a book just like this.

It was too bulky to hide in my clothes, and my pack was still in the vehicle. I thought for a moment, then quickly finished burning the other volumes before making my way back toward the stair. As I came to the last of the empty bookcases, I reached up and laid the book flat on the top shelf so that nobody would see it from the ground.

*   *   *

Five minutes later, I was standing in line with my new friends as we helped ourselves to plates full of eggs and bacon from a kitchen off, what must have once been, the cavernous main hall of the college. At other tables, citizens in overalls, lab coats and patched jackets sat about reading books or talking to one another. They seemed mostly cyst-free, but a few had welts around their temples and ears.

"So," said Liam as we sat down to eat. "Are you ready to tell us your name?"

"Chris Walker," I said.

"Welcome then, Chris Walker. What work can you do?"

"I've been working in a aquaponics setup," I said. "I also helped-out at a garage when I was at school, so I know a bit about fixing engines."

Liam nodded. "Good. Somebody will find you work to do with those skills. We have a big hydroponics system here; kreaponics too."

"What's that?"

"You're eating it. Almost all our meat is tank-grown."

"The bacon?" I said, looking down at my plate. "But it looks real. Smells real too."

"It is real. It's just produced differently."

I looked around at the people on the tables around us.

"So, is everybody here a scientist?"

"No. But they all know how to think—that's why we did the test on you. If you hadn't passed, you wouldn't be sitting here with us."

"Yeah," said William. "You'd be with Vera."

I began to ask who Vera was, but the question was cut short by a sudden series of tones blaring over a speaker.

Immediately, most of the other people in the hall began getting up from their tables and making their way to the door. A few paused to collect metal buckets that were lined up along the wall.

"What's going on," I asked.

"Air raid," said Bill.

"It'll be a kite from Gaia," said Liam. "They use them to drop fuel bombs on us. They don't do much damage if you're quick with the sand, but we've lost a couple of greenhouses and a vehicle or two."

Just as he said it, there was a whump noise and a flash from the open door.

"Guess I better go and make sure they don't get the van," said Bill. "Come and take a look if you like."

I stuffed the last rasher into my mouth and followed him to the door. From the shelter of the portico, I could see people using buckets to smother the flames on a small garden bed situated on the other side of the quadrangle.

I came to the edge of the cover and stuck my head out cautiously. It took me a moment to see it because of the glare and its altitude, but there it was, a tiny box-kite hanging a thousand metres above the town. It had a long banner fluttering ahead of it that read, "Burn the machine," and I could just make out the shape of someone moving about in a basket underneath it. Then, there was a shout from down the avenue as a sheet of flame exploded on the facade of one of the older buildings.

"What's Gaia?" I said to Bill, who was leaning against the brick pillar next to me.

"Ferals. Back-to-naturists. They want to get rid of technology—reckon it was science that caused the Tox—so they keep trying to sabotage us, and we …," he paused to finish lighting a cigarette, "… just want to get 'em out of the gene-pool. Which we will, sooner or later."

After the raid finished, Liam took me to meet one of the Coordinators who ran the place. She was a neat woman with a grey vest, a no-nonsense stare and a poster behind her desk that said, "If you're not part of the solution, you're part of the precipitate." She asked me the same questions that Liam had asked, and told me that she would put me down in hydroponics.

"Do you have any questions you want to ask me?" she said.

I nodded. "When they picked me up, Liam and the others told me that you had ways of controlling the Tox …"

"Yes, we have some researchers working on a cure, but I'm afraid I have no idea how close they are. If you ask around, somebody will …"

"I mean, apart from that. They said you had ways of managing it."

"Oh. Yes, well reason is the answer," she said. "We have weekly lectures that encourage us to think about cooperation and empathy as adaptive principles."

"What does that mean?" I said.

She gave me a patient look. "You fight the Tox simply by thinking about what is most conducive to your own happiness and that of others. And then doing it."

"Okay," I said, suspecting I wasn't going to get any further. "And one other question. Am I free to leave Ockham if I want to?"

"Why would you want to do that?" she said.

"Well … if I wanted to go to Crux or Central or something."

She laughed and then stopped, "… Wait, you're serious? … Central's gone. It doesn't exist any more."

I gave her a puzzled look. "Well, we had an Agent visit us in Spillan last week. And the water pipe must come from somewhere."

"Chris, I'm sure you're aware that not everyone is who they say they are. Just because he said he was an Agent …"

"She," I said.

"… Just because *she* said she was an Agent doesn't mean there is a Central.

"And as for the pipe, let me ask you this; if the water comes from Central, where do you think they get it from?"

"I don't know," I said. "I guess from a river or from underground or something."

"So why does there need to be a city? How do you know the pipes don't just come from the river or the ground?"

I stared at the legs of her desk. "I thought everybody believed in Central," I said at last.

"Not exactly," she said, smiling. "But, in answer to your question, of course, you can leave any time. Now, just wait here and I'll find somebody to take you down to hydroponics."

But as soon as she closed the door, it was like an alarm went off in my mind. There was something off about the way she had smiled at me. Was she going to report me? Was she going to get a gun?

I jumped up from the chair and went to the window, wondering if I should try to climb out and escape. But we were three stories up, and there was no ledge and nothing to hold on to. And what would they do if they caught me on my way out?

And what if I was just imagining it? What if she was just being weirdly polite? And what if these people really were on the edge of a cure?

But then I remembered the razors on Liam's bandolier, and the way Bill and William had joked before they did the test on me.

I got to my feet and made it to the door just as it flew open.

"Hello toxface," said Bill, grinning at me. "You didn't tell us you was a Centralist."

Law R.
C
D
G
OCKHAM
A - Front gate
B - Library
C - Cafeteria
D - Administration
E - Greenhouses
F - Fishpond
G - Vera's lab
H - Residential halls
WICKET GAP
A - Wicket Pass R.
B - HORD Camp
C - Canyon Pool
D - Observator.
E - Mt T.

CHAPTER 5

I don't remember them hitting me. I don't remember them putting me in the cage.

But that was where I woke up. There was straw and cold metal under me and a throbbing pain in the side of my face. Another pain in the back of my head was pulsing like a sound meter with the various noises echoing about. I could hear a dog barking and, much closer, angry voices.

"Lady, if you come near me with that thing, I'll shove it through your eyeball," said a man's voice. "I'm not joking."

I tried to open my eyes. There was a blurry impression of criss-crossed metal bars and a room of concrete and steel. Four metres away, I could see the outline of someone—a woman—in a white coat, standing with her back to me.

"Well, if you won't cooperate," she was saying, "I'll have to subdue you as I did before. But I'd much prefer you submit willingly. Why don't you look at it as a chance to save the animals from testing?"

"If you're looking for volunteers, why don't you test it on yourself or one of your friends?" said the man's voice.

As my eyes began to focus, I realised that the man was in a cage. And that *I* was in a cage. Other smaller cages around the walls held rabbits, rats and cats. A larger cage to my right had a pig in it.

The place smelled of disinfectant, animal waste, and fear.

The woman in the white coat was speaking again. I could see now that she had one hand in her pocket and another resting on a wheeled trolley.

"Well, who would run the experiment if I did it on myself?" she said. "I know you think that this is about the hostility between our towns, but it's much bigger than that. It's about the future of the species. Surely even you Gaians understand that you sometimes have to make sacrifices for the greater good of everybody."

"We let people make their own sacrifices in Gaia," said the man.

"Then why don't you think of it as an opportunity for self-sacrifice? You'll be contributing to ..."

While she was speaking, I'd been trying to sit up—and, in the process, was discovering other places I was sore. I groaned, causing the woman to break off and look around at me.

She gave me a friendly smile of gum and stubby, discoloured teeth and came over to the door of my enclosure.

"Oh, hello, you're awake. I understand that your name is Chris Walker? I'm Dr Vera Eugenia. I'm really pleased that I'll have you helping us with our studies. Your face looks quite sore. Can I get you some analgesics to take away the pain?"

"What ... Why am I in here?" I said.

She began to answer, but the man from Gaia was quicker.

"You're a lab rat. She wants to test her drugs on you. They're going to shoot you up with junk and cook your brain."

I felt my muscles go rigid. My vision suddenly became clear.

Across the room, I could see the man looking at me. He was a gaunt figure sitting cross-legged in his cage; wispy beard, long corded hair and coarse-woven clothes.

"Is that true?" I said.

"No ..." said the doctor.

"Yes. It is," said the man. "If you don't believe me, take a look at Charlie over there. He was normal before she started on him."

He gestured over to one side of the room where, when I tilted my head, I could see another large cell containing a middle-aged man in a dirty singlet and ripped trousers. He was sitting with his knees up, staring blankly at a heap of different coloured buttons.

"That is absolutely *not* the case," said the doctor. She came across the room and positioned her body so that I couldn't see the man who kept interrupting her.

"Mr Pursey was suffering from an advanced form of Tox fixation when he was brought to me. The compounds we have administered to him have relieved him of that …"

"… So he doesn't want anything at all," shouted the man from Gaia.

"Will you be QUIET!" the doctor said.

She turned and walked back across the room, and now I saw that the hand that she'd been keeping in her pocket had some sort of canister in it. Before the man in the cage had time to see it, she brought it up it sprayed a jet of liquid into his face. He lunged at the bars, swore at the woman and collapsed.

"Please learn from this, Mr Walker," she said breathlessly, as she fumbled open the catch on the man's cage and filled a syringe from her trolley. "I would much prefer to do this with my subjects' cooperation and in a gradual fashion, but Mr Wild left me no choice. I hope you and I can have a better working relationship when the time comes."

I watched her and felt the blood hammering in my ears. What kind of mad-house had I been dragged into?

*   *   *

I didn't see her again for the rest of that day.

The man in the other cell slept. I passed my time trying to think of a way to escape.

I noticed that the doors of the cages were kept secure with two mechanisms: an electronic lock that the doctor and her assistant opened with a card of some kind, and also a simple sliding latch that they pulled up after they'd used the card.

I couldn't get at either of these mechanisms from inside my cage—though I realised that I could probably unlock the latch if I had something flat and rigid to slip between the door and the frame. A knife would do it.

But there was no knife. When lunchtime came, an orderly brought me a bowl of cold porridge (without a spoon) and a cup of water. In the afternoon, I heard the siren go off again. It sounded close but muffled—as if it was coming through layers of concrete or dirt.

When they finally dimmed the lights, I tried to find a way to sleep. Somebody had left a pile of sacking in one corner, but it didn't do much to cushion my hip and shoulder against the hard metal of the floor. The best I could manage for most of the night was a fragmentary patchwork of semi-conscious discomfort.

But eventually I did sleep—and dream. I was hiding under a bridge, and there was smoke in the air, and there was something that I couldn't see watching me.

*   *   *

When I awoke, the man from Gaia was back in his cross-legged position with his head down. I said good morning to him and asked him how he was. There was no response. Nor did he answer Doctor Eugenia when she came to make her rounds.

"Well, I'm not sure if you can hear me, Mr Wild, but if I can't communicate with you, I will have to assume that our tests with you are complete and that we no longer have any use for you. Please bear that in mind if you are simply being stubborn."

She waited a long time, but he didn't respond.

"Very well," she said.

"What are you going to do with him?" I said.

"If his brain is gone, there's no point in keeping his body," she said, looking around at me. "We'll euthanise him and feed him into our protein tanks. It will be completely painless."

"How can you do that? He's a person," I said—half horrified for him and half terrified for myself.

"Yes, well, I think that's one for the philosophers," she said. "As far as I'm concerned, if he doesn't have a working mind, he can't care what we do to him."

"But he's sitting up."

She stuck her hands in her pockets and sighed.

"Really, this isn't something I want to talk about right now, Mr Walker. The more pressing issue to discuss is *your* involvement with this project."

"You want to give me that stuff too?" I said, suddenly finding it hard to breathe.

"Yes, but there's no need for you to be alarmed. If you agree to cooperate, we'll be able to start you on a much lower dose. That would be the ideal situation for all of us."

"But eventually I'll end up like him?" I said, pointing to the man from Gaia.

"No, it might not get to that point at all. The goal of the treatment isn't to incapacitate you but to suppress the over-stimulation of your orbitofrontal cortex caused by the Tox."

She paused—I suppose she was waiting for me to ask a question, but I had far too many thoughts flying around my head. She went on anyway.

"We believe that the Tox is primarily a kind of affective disorder that causes runaway emotional reactions. For some people, that means rage. For others, it means obsessive monomania, or grandiosity, and so on.

"The drug we're going to give you tamps down those reactions so you can think clearly without so much emotional noise."

"So, what does cooperating mean?" I said, trying to make sense of what she was saying.

"It mostly means we would ask you questions about how you're feeling and how you perceive things so we can find out how the treatment is affecting you. Otherwise, our only option is to give you a dose that's big enough to allow us to observe changes from the outside."

"I want to think about it for a while."

"Of course. You can let me know when I come back this afternoon."

She turned and pushed her trolley out of the room, and I went back to trying to work out how to break out of my enclosure.

I still thought the best bet was the lock, but I had no idea how to get at it. The only other possibility I could imagine would be to find a weak weld and force out one of the steel grills. I tried a couple of kicks, but nothing gave way. And then, just as I was lining up for a third, somebody spoke.

"You should stop that. If they hear you, they'll come and spray you with water or something."

It was the man from Gaia. He was looking up at me with a pale face and drooping eyelids, but his voice was clear.

I stopped what I was doing and came to the front of my cage.

"You're awake. Did you know the doctor just came by?"

"I heard her," he said. "I didn't feel like talking to her."

"Aren't you … did you hear what she said about …"

"About killing me if I didn't respond? Yeah I heard that too."

I looked at him, wondering at the tone of his voice. It was as if he'd just made a comment about the weather at the end of a long day. He didn't seem angry or afraid or upset—just a bit tired. What had the doctor's injection done to him?

"So, are you going to say something to her?" I said.

"Why?"

"So she doesn't kill you."

"She'll do that anyway."

"Yeah," I said. "Yeah maybe, but not straight away."

"Doesn't make any difference how long it takes."

"But we might find a way to escape. Or, or maybe … She said she'd stop it if they got the right dose."

"We'll still die," he answered. "Even if we get out of here."

I wracked my brain for something to say. It seemed clear to me that the drug had made him depressed. But if he let Vera kill him I would be all on my own.

"Haven't you got friends or family waiting for you back in Gaia?" I said.

But the man had given up on our conversation and returned to the same stationery posture he had been in before. I tried asking him other questions about his hometown and how he had been captured, but he ignored (or didn't hear) them.

And, of course, I had my own thoughts to work through.

*   *   *

I wasn't exactly ready when she returned in the afternoon, but I had my answer worked out.

"I'll cooperate. I'll let you inject me, and I'll answer your questions." I had hoped that my voice would sound strong and casual, but it came out breathy and uneven like I was a kid. I swallowed and went on.

"But I've got three conditions."

The smile that had appeared on her face immediately vanished. "What conditions?"

"First, you don't do anything to Mr Wild.

"Second, I want a mattress and a blanket.

"Third, I want a book from the library. I can tell you where to find it."

She looked up at the ceiling and then at the door. I could hear the rats running back and forth in the straw of their cage.

"Alright," she said. "Alright. I think we can manage those things. We'll do your baseline test straight away and give you the first dose, and then I'll ask one of the orderlies to bring the things you requested."

The baseline test turned out to be a series of questions that ranged from simple problem-solving to moral dilemmas and emotional responses. First, she asked me whether it would be permissible to kill a newborn child to save the lives of three older children (I said, "No"). Then she brought out an ancient music device and played me a recording of rippling piano that sounded, as I said to her, "Like sunlight and … like the sea."

"Have you ever seen the sea?" she asked me, looking slightly annoyed.

"No, but that's what it makes me feel like … What I imagine about the sea."

"Interesting," she said. "Alright, if you would pull up your sleeve and press your shoulder up to the bars I will give you your injection."

*   *   *

The injection made me really sleepy for a few hours. When I woke up there was a thin mattress leaning against the wall of my cage. The grey leather book with the X-mark was on the floor beside it.

I reached across to pick it up, but stopped even as my fingers touched the cover.

My arm was the wrong colour. Or really, it wasn't any colour. It was grey. Everything was grey: the orange conduit on the concrete ceiling, the blue drum of cleaning agent by the rabbit cage, the rainbow patchwork on the trousers of the man from Gaia.

"I'm … I'm colourblind," I said out loud without meaning to.

"It does that," said the man in the other cage without moving from his meditation position. "You'll lose your taste and smell too."

"What else?" I said, trying to control my voice once again.

He was silent for a long time, and I thought he'd gone back to ignoring me. But then suddenly he raised his head and looked at me with a kind of intensity that I hadn't seen before.

"It makes you see through everything," he said. "Everything. Nothing really matters. I came here to rescue the animals, but why? They'll all die anyway—maybe in worse ways than they would here. They'll get arthritis and starve or get eaten by parasites."

He lowered his head but then raised it again as if a new thought had struck him.

"Gaia ... Ockham ... we're all fixated. We latch on to one thing and fight for it—like it's the one thing that will make everything right. They think it's about controlling nature, and we think it's living in harmony with it. But we're both wrong. The world is toxed. We live and suffer, and then we're dead forever, and it doesn't mean anything."

I thought for a moment and remembered something that Harry Frieden had said to me.

"Some people would say that makes everything mean more. If this is all we've got, it means everything."

"People say that," he said, "But it's wrong."

"Why?" I said.

"It only works if you can keep yourself from remembering the truth."

Now he leaned forward with his fingers against the mesh of his cage as if he was coming alive for a moment, as if he was suddenly furious.

"Look, if I told you that Vera was gonna come in here in two minutes and inject you with something that would kill you, and there was nothing you could do about it, do you reckon that would make your final seconds more meaningful or less?"

"But that's just two minutes," I said finally. "It's different for ... "

"It should be *more* true for two minutes," he said. "Less time, more meaning."

*   *   *

I tried to read the book that afternoon, but the damage to my vision and the things the man had been saying were such distractions that I couldn't concentrate. I kept thinking about not being able to see the colours in the dawn sky or taste the purple berries along the pipeline. I thought about never being able to enjoy the prismatic shimmer on the fish scales back in Marj's tanks. When they switched off the lights, I curled up on my mattress and cried until I fell asleep.

*   *   *

Doctor Eugenia returned the next morning with more questions and another injection. She played me a tune, which seemed to have a strong rhythm, and asked me to imagine whether it would be right to eat a dead person to keep from starving (I said, "No," after a long time thinking about it).

"Will this be permanent?" I asked her. "This stuff you're doing to me?"

"It shouldn't be a long term problem," she said.

"Because it'll wear off, or because you'll kill me?"

"She means the second thing," said the man from Gaia. And then she sprayed him with the canister again.

After I had woken up from my post-injection sleep, I sat on my mattress and began to read from the Roadbook. It opened with a description of the Autonomous Zone—the Western Territory, as it was called then before the war; its river systems, fish species and hardwood forests. It itemised the production sectors: the wheat yields, wool clip and grape harvest. It spoke about populations and railways and hospitals and annual rainfall.

And for as long as I was reading the book, my thoughts—which had been constantly buzzing in my head—became still. I thought of thunderstorms and the smell of the rain on the warm earth; I imagined people travelling for miles and miles, free, unmolested, in cars and trains, past sheep and cattle and ripening fields. I thought of what it would have been like to have friends in other towns; to be able to go east to the great City itself.

When I looked up after reaching the end of the chapter, I was surprised to find that my sense of colour had returned.

"Hey," I called to the man from Gaia. "I read this book and it fixed my eyes. Do you want to see if it works for you?"

He let me read to him, but it was like the words that had moved me so much fell dead in the space between our cages.

"So even back then, they were chopping down trees and slaving animals," was all he said.

I don't know if it made any difference to his eyesight, but I soon discovered that even for me, it wasn't a permanent or predictable cure. Over the following days, my sense of colour and smell came and went. The injections made everything grey, but sometimes—not every time—reading the book restored my senses.

And not just my physical senses. Something similar was happening with my feelings too. As time went on, I found it harder to care about things: about the questions; about the music; about my own situation.

But the book could help with this too—mostly by making me angry.

I discovered this as I started reading about the beginnings of the rebellion. At school, our teachers had told us that the war had begun with Central trying to stop the Territory from getting access to new farming technology. It was all about the Pantarch and his personal monopolies.

But the Roadbook talked about how the foreign Corp had started bribing the big farmers to use their illegal gene hacks. The hacks produced massive crop yields and made the wealthy men of the Territory even wealthier, but they also stripped the soil of its nutrients. When their own land failed, the rich men bought up the land of those poorer farmers who had resisted the technology, and used up their soil too.

As I read about all this—about how the money from the Corps and the hacks had corrupted the courts; how the big farmers used their banking connections to choke their smaller competitors—I suddenly realised that I was grinding my teeth. When I got to the point where the scientists started experiments on orphans, all the muscles in my neck became painfully rigid and my clenched knuckles went white.

I had to stop reading to let myself calm down for a while then. But later that same day, when the doctor asked me whether it would be wrong for a town to give more food to families with healthy children who would be better able to become productive citizens, I almost shouted, "Yes, very wrong!"

Yet in the same test session, I found that I could now barely recognise whatever it was she played to me as music. "It's just a kind of scratchy sound," I said.

Unfortunately for me, Vera realised what was going on.

"I'm afraid I'm going to have to take that book from you," she said the next morning. "It's interfering with our results."

"But we made a deal," I said.

"I'll give it back to you when we're done."

"No," I said,

"Well, you know what I can do if I have to."

"It's still 'no'. If your treatment can't survive somebody reading a book, what good is it going to be in the real world?"

She put her hands in her pockets and moved closer to the wire. I moved to the back of the cage. In the background, the siren had started up again. A dull thud passed through the walls.

"Please try to be reasonable, Mr Walker," she said. "Surely you can see that we need to test it under optimal conditions first."

"I'm sticking to our agreement," I said. "If you want me to keep cooperating, you should do the same."

She pulled the canister out of her pocket, but stopped as I did what I had planned to do and pulled up my shirt to cover my nose and mouth. Two more thuds reverberated through the ground.

"Well, I'm sorry, but this is not acceptable. I will have to have you restrained physically."

She swiped her security card past the lock on my cage and called out to her assistant.

I braced myself and prepared to fight.

And then the wall exploded.

CHAPTER 6

My hands clawed at my throat as I struggled to breathe. Although the wire of the cage had caught most of the larger chunks, it hadn't done anything to stop the shockwave that had flattened me against the back wall of my container and forced all the air from my body. When I finally managed to get my lungs working, the air they sucked in was full of fine white cement dust, which immediately made me double over with a fit of coughing.

In between the coughs I could hear shouting, but it seemed to be coming from far away. In a few more seconds I could hear words but now my brain couldn't seem to understand them. It was like my head was full of wool.

By the time I had got my shirt back over my mouth and straightened up, orange emergency lights had come on. Figures were moving through the dust like ghosts: a man in patched overalls with an afro and a sack; a woman carrying a loaded crossbow.

"Hey, this one is still …" she began. "Oh, it's a guy."

She vanished as the afro-man returned bearing something heavy in a sack. Next came a short man with a shaved head and topknot leading a sheep by the scruff of the neck. Two others went past, awkwardly carrying the cage with all the rats in it. As my ears became less dull, I began to hear animals barking and baaing and somewhere, just for a few seconds, somebody screaming.

I came to the front of the cage and could now see the jagged hole that had been blown in the wall. All the other cages in the room seemed to have been opened and emptied—including the one containing the man from Gaia.

"Let me out," I croaked as the short man rushed past me with another sack.

"Just here for the animals, man," he answered.

I tried it with the afro-man and received a similar response.

"Hurry," shouted the woman's voice through the dust, "They're coming."

Desperately, I turned my attention to the door of my cage. I tried kicking it, levering it open to get a hand out, but the hinges and steel of the frame were just too solid. I remembered my discovery about the catch, and cursed that I still didn't have a knife or anything that I could slide through the crack.

Except I did.

I grabbed the book off the mattress and shoved the stiff leather into the gap between the door and frame. Even as I began, there was a pounding coming from the next room and the Gaians—because that's obviously who they were—began racing back toward the hole. Something shining whirled past and embedded itself in the shoulder of the short man, causing him to drop the cat he was carrying. The woman turned and fired her crossbow back at whoever had thrown the thing. In a moment, they had all retreated back into the darkness.

Meanwhile, I held my breath and focused on the catch … and suddenly felt it give way. I fell out, rolled and found myself staring up at Liam's face. He gave a smile, drew a razor from his bandolier … and collapsed at my feet.

As his body fell, the man from Gaia lurched forward out of the dust. He had blood all over his face and a metal bar in his hand.

"You should go," he said, gesturing to the hole in the wall. "There's more of them coming."

Then he was gone. I heard grunts, thuds and more screaming coming from the direction in which he had vanished.

I picked myself up and scrambled into the darkness.

Immediately now, I found myself blundering blindly through a maze of tunnels and passages, and I still don't know how I made it through.

Sometimes, the noises ahead made me think I was following the Gaians; sometimes, I seemed to be walking by myself. At least once I turned away from a passage that carried sounds of (what I guessed were) people chasing me. I found another passage where there was a hiss, like rushing water, and a flight of concrete stairs that led to a larger tunnel with a larger pipe. Finally, I rounded a bend and saw a little patch of flickering light that grew and grew until it became sunlight shining through bushes.

I ran towards it and rolled out of the tunnel, down into a narrow gully choked with bones, fallen trees and a rusted refrigerator. The pipe crossed the depression and rose to disappear over the opposite lip.

When I had collected and steadied myself, I crawled up the slope and began to follow it. It wasn't the main pipe that I had been following before I was captured, but I soon discovered that it rejoined that pipe after about half a kilometre. I found a tap and said a prayer of thanks to whatever luck or providence had saved me and continued my journey.

But I was more careful now. The business with the Ockhamists had cured me of my hope that the water pipe would give me an easy route. It seemed to me now that sticking close to the pipeline would expose me to more danger, so I walked apart from it wherever I could. For a while I travelled only at night, camping out in caves or gullies while the sun was up.

During those long daylight hours, when I wasn't sleeping or foraging for food, I read the Roadbook. Apart from my clothes and the coins in my boot, it was the one possession that I had been able to bring out of Ockham and seemed more valuable to me because of that.

As I read on, I learned more of the history of the conflict between the Autonomous Zone and the Central government.

I read about how the Pantarch had sent in inspectors and negotiators, and how the Territory Council had expelled and imprisoned them. I read about how the Council had used a period of "Formal Re-evaluation" to stall while it conducted a secret military buildup through arms-deals negotiated with the same corporation that had supplied the original gene-tech.

In exchange for their ordnance, the Corp gained greater influence, along with water and land rights. They set to diverting rivers and draining lakes for their massive factory farms. Ultimately these interventions would bring disastrous changes to the weather patterns and soil of the Territory. But that would all take years to show up.

Three years after the Re-evaluation, the Council issued a Declaration of Independence, turning the Territory into the Autonomous Zone, and launching—on the same day—preemptive strikes on Central installations along its borders.

These attacks failed completely. The moment AZ troops began their mobilisation, Central dropped pulse bombs, wiping out all electronic signals. Robbed of communication, the Council began to lose control. Soon the cities of the Territory fell to fighting each other. And in the background, from some secret lab deep in the interior, the Tox quietly slipped free of containment.

As I travelled further, I could see the relics of this history all around me. At night, I travelled through ridged deserts where ancient mobile sprinkler booms sagged over furrows turned to sand. I came to burned-out settlements, abandoned roadblocks and barricades. In one ghost town somebody had built a pile of skulls. In another, a dozen handless skeletons hung between the portico pillars of the town hall.

The pipeline also showed the marks of violence. In some places, it was blackened and dented where it had been attacked and patched. In others, forks, branches and dead ends split away, meandering north and south. Sometimes, it even doubled back and seemed to run west.

And yet I still found functioning taps here and there. I kept myself alive by eating the lizards and snakes that liked to sun themselves on the support pylons. Sometimes, I'd find a berry bush. My senses of taste and colour were still not what they had been before, but I never managed to poison myself.

Meanwhile, the pipeline itself was raising a lot of questions for me. As I read on through the book, the picture I got of Central was so scary that I thought about turning back. When the Council announced its Act of Independence, Central had declared every person within the AZ to be an outlaw and shut down the pipeline, which—with the draining of the rivers and lakes—meant that many towns simply ran out of water. Thousands died before the Pantarch relented.

This all made Central seem brutal. And, of course, there was also the threat that Eve Veracis had given us; of the bigger Cleanse still to come.

But the very existence of the pipeline showed that the Pantarch was the one sustaining the rebel territory. "Independence" was a fantasy. We were all dependent on Central's indulgence. The Pantarch could have finished us off long ago if he'd wanted.

Meanwhile, as these thoughts were going around in my mind, I also had another reason to be unsettled. Someone was tracking me. Now and then, when I was walking in the darkness, I would hear an engine in the distance or see lights moving back and forward in the low country. One morning, after I had finished getting water and was heading back into the hills for shelter, I saw the lights of a vehicle parked on a ridge to the west and a tiny figure standing beside it. I dropped to the ground until it had disappeared, but I worried that the movement of my long shadow might have already given me away.

After that, I travelled even further away from the pipe, keeping to gullies and creek beds. The land rose and fell and the air grew colder. I spent the nights shivering in my clothes. Food became harder to find and the trees I encountered were mostly dead or dying.

Then, I came to a burnt forest and, on the other side of it, found myself staring at a ridge of stony mountains that spread themselves across the horizon. When I looked north, they vanished into blue-grey hills that seemed to go on forever. I had the sense that the same was true to the south as well, but my view in this direction was obscured by one larger mountain that jutted out from the range and towered into the clouds. Far away, I could see a pale ribbon of road winding east up its flank.

That was a low point in my journey. The thought of trying to get over those peaks in the state I was in made my heart sink. And there was worse to come. When I went back to the pipeline, I discovered that it ended in the mountains too, disappearing into a tunnel that was collared with a heavy metal grill.

I cursed and sat down in front of it. I had nothing that could bend the bars or break the padlock, nor did I have the energy to scale the cliffs that rose above the tunnel. Would I have to, after all this time, simply turn back? And if I did go back, how far would I have to go? Right back to the bog where I parted from Flex?

But there was still that road that I had seen to the south. If the pipe couldn't take me through the mountain, maybe the road could get me over. That evening, I took a long drink from the last tap and made my way down through the hills until I found it.

It was three days of hard climbing after that. The track looped back and forth up the side of the mountain and, as I went higher, the cloud closed in on me and it got colder still. The first night on the mountain was almost unbearable—too cold for sleeping and too dark for walking. The second night, I wedged myself into an old wombat burrow and shivered until dawn.

On the third day, a wind picked up. It blew the fog off the lower parts of the mountain so I could look back over the hills as they faded into the distance.

But the upper slopes were still covered—not with fog now, but with dark cumulus clouds that kept flickering and booming. I began to worry about what would happen if I had to pass through that cloud, yet the prospect of storm clouds at least gave me the hope of quenching my thirst. I had found no spring since I left the pipeline and, except for a few berries, had received no moisture at all. I was parched and starving.

Then the slope began to flatten out a bit, as if it was heading toward a shoulder or saddle. There was another switchback, and I found myself at the entrance to a V-shaped valley of shale and boulders. Up ahead, just visible over a rise in the valley floor, I could see a roof of tin and a stone chimney. But directly in front of me, a faded sign on a rusted pole said:

DANGER! HOREB PASS HAS BEEN DESIGNATED A RESTRICTED ZONE BY THE AUTHORITY OF THE PANTARCH. TOX TRACE-SCREENING IN PROGRESS. AUTHORISED PERSONS ONLY.

After everything I had been reading and thinking about, it made me laugh.

"Thank you, Central," I said. "Come and get cured. But first, we're going to kill you."

I wondered what "trace-screening" might mean; what the "DANGER!" might involve. Was it a checkpoint? A minefield? Was it still in effect? The sign was obviously ancient.

Either way, I wasn't going to turn back now. I'd come too far and used up too much of my strength. If the Pantarch wanted to put me out of my misery … well, maybe that would be for the best.

I grabbed hold of the pole, shook it back and forth a few times, and went on.

Looking back now, it just seems stupid of me to have risked this. As I said, I had read enough from the Roadbook to know what Central could do to people who disobeyed its edicts. Even though I could have had no idea about the nature of the danger—and how much trouble I was about to get myself into—I should have known *something* bad would happen.

Guessing that any mines or other hazards would be on the valley floor, I used some of my remaining energy to scramble up one of the side-slopes so that I could travel parallel to the track. It made for slower going, but it made me feel safer as I approached the building. Soon, I had a better view of it and could see that it looked like an old stone hikers' hut that had been adapted for more modern use: solar panels on its roof and a short radio mast anchored to the side of its chimney. A few metres away from its open door I could see a small pool of water fed by a spring.

The sight of that pool stirred such an intense thirst in me that I wanted to race toward it and plunge my face into the water. But someone else was there. A tall man—bald and completely naked—was standing by the pool washing his body. He had a rifle lying by his feet and a pile of gear heaped on a small tarp.

I moved to a position where I could approach under cover and crept closer. Soon I was able to see that he wasn't just washing himself, but shaving too—lathering his legs and scraping away the hair with a long sharp knife. When he stood up, I could see that he'd already finished the rest of his body from his eyebrows down, making him look like a disturbingly proportioned child.

The man finished the tops of his feet and dried them with a rag. Then he rummaged around in his gear and pulled out two fist-sized tins. He put these to one side, bundled up his gear in the tarp and secured it with a long, thin rope.

When that was done, he unscrewed the lids of the tins and began coating himself with the thick white substance that was inside them. I thought it looked like zinc cream. He worked upwards from his feet and legs, paying particular attention to coat a pair of cysts on his stomach.

When he was completely covered, the man spent a while contorting himself, testing for uncovered places. Then he shoved his gun into the loop of ropes that ran around his gear, and began shuffling away up the valley, dragging it all about three or four metres behind him.

I watched him until he passed out of sight and listened until the only thing I could hear was the thunder and the wind blowing down the valley. Then I stood up and threw three stones at the cabin roof. When nobody came out to see what was going on, I charged down the slope and splashed into the pool. The water was icy, but I didn't care. I just drank and drank and felt it bringing me back to life. When I was done, I sat down on a mossy rock and rested my legs.

I was cold now and wanted to see if there was anything in the hut that could help me with that. But I was still worried about the man. Where had he gone? What was the meaning of his strange behaviour? Was he coming back?

I knew that I wouldn't be able to rest until I had at least answered the last question, so I began creeping along the valley after him. After a few hundred metres, I caught sight of him disappearing around a bend.

The way had become narrower now. The sloping sides had turned into cliffs, the gap between them reduced to a stone's throw. But when I reached the next curve, I could see that the walls widened out again to form a roughly circular space, about one hundred metres across.

But there was something strange in the centre of it: a big golden cube, around seven metres across, was rotating slowly in the air above the valley floor.

The zinc-cream man was edging his way around it, obviously keeping as close to the cliffs and as far away from the cube as he could. As I watched him, he turned and gave a tug on the rope to pull his bundle free from a snag. And now I noticed a whole lot of other things scattered on the ground all around him: an aluminium Billy, a few fibreglass tent spars, a mangled pack frame, two plastic bottles, tattered fabric fragments and white things that looked like … no, that *were* … bones.

I took a step back. There was something wrong here—not just strangeness but danger. I could sense it in the base of my stomach and feel it in the static electricity tingle that was crawling through my hair.

But even as I was noticing this, something else was happening: a noise was coming from the cube—a deep grinding hum that grew until it filled the valley and made me want to stuff my fingers in my ears.

Straight away, the zinc-cream man—who was now about halfway

around the circle—dropped his rope and began to run. He was only able to cover a couple of metres before he slipped on the shale. Now he got to his feet and tried to run back the way he had come, only to slip again. The air around him began rippling like heat-shimmer off desert rocks. The noise became even louder—blaring like a truck horn. I wanted to turn and run too, but I was transfixed and horrified by the sight. The zinc-cream man was running again. He was about two-thirds of the way back to the turn where I was standing. Then there was a flash and everything went black.

*   *   *

I lay on my back, opening and closing my eyes. It made no difference.

Where was I? How long had I been lying here? Clearly it was long enough to become dark.

But this was not like the grainy blue darkness of a normal night. This was a rust-tinted black. When I tried pressing my palms hard against my eyes, the darkness bloomed into red clouds … it was more like …

I sat up and began to hyperventilate, unable to accept the thought—trying to push it away from my mind. But it surged back as I remembered what had happened. There had been that cube. And that flash. What if it … what if it had burned out my retinas?

Now I was on my feet. I wanted to run—away from that terrible thought and that terrifying place.

But even as I leaned forward to bolt, a new fear made me stop. I wasn't even sure what direction I was facing now. What if I ran into a cliff? What if I ran forward toward the cube?

I had to control myself. If I let myself go crazy I would die.

But I was blind! What if that man was there? What if that thing … or whatever created it …

I crouched down again and slapped myself with my hands. I couldn't let myself panic. I had to think! I had to listen. I had to work out where

I was.

I fought to steady my breath and counted to ten. Then I reached out my arms and turned in a slow circle.

My fingers contacted the rock face on exactly the opposite side I was expecting. I *had* been turned around. I *had been* about to run in the wrong direction! I cursed myself for my stupidity. Why had I followed the man? What was I supposed to do now?

Again, I tried to calm myself.

I was still alive. My eyesight would return—maybe it would only take a few minutes, or maybe I'd have to wait for a few hours, but it would come good. I just needed to find somewhere to shelter, somewhere to sleep it off.

But where? I was already cold now, and it felt like the air was getting colder.

The answer was the hut, of course. But what would I find in there? What if the man came back?

One thing at a time. I began to grope my way back down the valley, continually feeling for the cliff to reassure myself that I was headed in the right direction.

It was slow and pretty scary. I kept thinking I was being followed and turning around to confront whatever was behind me. A few times, I picked up rocks; one time, tried leaping and striking in the direction that I thought I had heard the noise. But I never connected. I guess the sounds were just echoes of my own footsteps.

Yet, I finally found myself back at the pool. Here again, I had to fight my imagination. The thought of the zinc-cream man creeping up on me as I crouched by the water paralysed me for a while. But my thirst won out in the end. I dropped to my knees and drank and then washed my eyes—which unfortunately made no difference.

Now, I had to think about the hut. The thought of entering it blind scared me, and I cursed myself for not looking inside it earlier. But I was going to get hypothermia if I stayed out here. I sat for a while listening to the door creaking back and forth in the wind and then stood up and felt my way over to it.

Inside, the place smelled of timber and cold stone. I felt floorboards under my feet. Then my fingers found a heavy wooden table. Working back from there I discovered:

- a light switch beside the door;
- a cupboard (empty except for a long-handled shovel);
- a wood stove with a cast iron saucepan;
- a wide bed with a couple of threadbare blankets;
- a bench with a metal basin containing two china cups, three bowls and a spoon;
- a medium-sized safe with a dial in the centre of its door;
- a tatty book with a piece of string attached to its spine on top of the safe;
- a transmitter with a microphone and spring-coil cable;
- three chairs;
- two glazed windows.

But no food. I stifled my disappointment and returned to the safe.

One of my uncle's hobbies, before he had disappeared, was opening old safes like this. I tried to remember what I had seen him do, and began to turn the dial with my ear pressed to the door.

For a moment, I thought I had something: a slight click when the dial went past one point. But I was never able to make anything of it. When I made further rotations—whether fast or slow, clockwise or anti-clockwise—the same sound occurred at the same point.

After that, I set myself to re-exploring the hut from the ground up. First, I got down on my hands and knees and worked across the floor. I looked for loose boards (no luck). I checked under the bed, the stove and the table. All I found were dust, spiderwebs and a small pointed paring knife.

Groping upwards, I came across the light switch again and suddenly wondered where the battery might be stored. In Spillan, such things would typically be kept in a cupboard outside of a house. So I went out into the cold and found it—a tiny lean-to outhouse on the far side of the hut containing a pair of light polymer batteries as well a whole wall of stacked firewood. Now, if I could just find a way to make fire, I would be able to get warm.

In the meantime however, the thought just made me feel colder. The air felt like it was nighttime now and that thought brought a fresh wave of fear. As I worked back around the house, I pictured myself fumbling through the darkness with the zinc-cream man watching me. Then, when I was almost back, the door of the hut banged in the wind and I started back so violently that I fell over.

But everything seemed to be as I had left it. After I had retrieved the knife from the table and finished going around the hut lunging blindly at every corner, I braced the door with the shovel and sat down to think about my next move.

What was I to do now? I'd brought myself to a dead end here with no way forward or back and no way to sustain myself where I was. The only resources I had discovered were the batteries and the firewood and I had no way to make use of either.

But maybe that wasn't completely true. If there was any charge left in the batteries, they might power the light and give me a chance to check my eyes. I found the switch and toggled it a few times, but couldn't detect any change in either heat or light.

It was a different matter when I turned my attention to the radio. When I twisted the left-most knob above the microphone there was a satisfying thunk and a swelling torrent of white noise.

Along with all the kids from Spillan, I had been given a very basic introduction to such transceivers as part of my militia training. I knew the big dial on the right controlled the frequency and proceeded to search for a signal.

And there it was—at the same place it had been when I first discovered it during my training. Amid all the hisses and pops, a calm spot where the noise was quieter. Maybe there was even something buried under the static. What was it? Was it a voice? Singing? When I moved the dial back and forth very slightly, I could feel the noise change, like it was sliding into a groove.

I picked up the microphone, thought for a moment and depressed the button.

"Hello? … Can anyone hear me? … Is this Central?"

There was no answer. I clicked the button to try again but paused and reconsidered. If it was a Central station, did I want them to know about me? I was in a restricted zone. Their technology had just wrecked my vision.

I released the button. And then, almost on a whim, I clicked it again: three times quickly, three times slowly, three times quickly again—the extent of my Morse code.

Nothing changed. I switched the unit off, checked the light switch and the shovel and made my way over to the bed. After I had pulled off my boots and placed the knife where I could grab it, I wrapped myself in the blankets and lay down.

It was a long time before I managed to fall asleep. Though I curled up to retain my body warmth, the cold was more than a match for me. I lay there shivering and hungry while creative (and improbable) schemes formed in my head about how to start a fire or get into the safe.

CHAPTER 7

Something woke me up.

The air had changed. The sharp edge of its cold had gone, replaced by a sweet smell of burning gum leaves and another scent that seemed like, no definitely was, cooking. It was a warm smell: tomato and basil with ...

Someone was in the hut! The realisation blasted all the sleep from my brain and electrified my senses in one frozen second. Now I could hear someone moving around. There was the sound of a chair being moved ... of some utensil being set down on a table ... the quiet pop and hiss of burning hardwood. Outside the wind still rose and fell. The thunder had faded to almost nothing.

I opened my eyes and discovered that I was still blind.

Had whoever it was seen me? Was it possible that I just looked like a pile of blankets?

Trying to move as little as possible, I slid a hand out from under the covers and found the knife on the edge of the mattress where I had left it.

"That won't help you," said a voice. It was a man's voice. Not young, not old. It came from the far end of the room near the stove.

I suddenly felt every follicle on my arms and the back of my neck. But there was no time for fear. I had to project confidence.

With the knife still in my hands, I raised myself on my elbow and pretended to look in the direction of the voice.

"Hey ... Sorry if I've taken your spot," I said, trying to sound like this was an everyday sort of event. "I thought you were ..."

"Yes," said the voice. "But not any more. What are you doing up here?"

"Oh, I've been ... I'm from Spillan. Someone told me there was a treatment station out this way."

"There's no treatment here. If you try to get through the mountains this way, you'll die."

"Yeah. I was afraid that was the way it was. Thanks for the tip. I guess I'll get my stuff and go. Like I said, really sorry to bother you."

I sat up and tried to disentangle myself from the blankets—more difficult because I couldn't see what I was doing and because the tip of the knife kept catching in them.

Finally, I extracted my legs and swung them down. I set my feet wide apart—partly to increase my mobility in case the man attacked me, and partly in the hope that they might encounter my boots and the Roadbook which I knew I had left on the floor.

"You'll die if you travel in that condition too," said the man.

"Oh, yeah, maybe," I said, feeling unsure of what he meant. Was he talking about my lack of warm clothes? My lack of food?

"Still, got to make the best of it." I tried to shuffle my feet a little wider, still trying to locate my possessions.

"Where are you going to go?"

"Back home to Spillan, I guess. I was originally headed for a place called Crux, but I don't know how to get there from here."

"I have marked it for you on this map."

"Oh, thanks. I don't want to trouble you any further than I have, though," I said.

"Your boots and the book are in front of you, not to the sides."

"Yeah, of course," I said, leaning forward to find them. "Still a bit bleary."

There was a pause before he spoke. "If I was planning to attack you, I could have done it by now. I know that you're blind."

I tried to suppress the shudder that went through me and bent down to fumble with my laces.

"Yeah, You're right. Yeah, I … ah, copped a bit of a flash off that cube thing when I was following you before. I mean I can still see, but there are a few black spots. Hopefully it'll come good after …"

"It won't come good. The radiation from that relay paralyses exposed Tox-affected cells so that they die off within twelve hours. You won't recover the sight you have lost."

I suddenly felt a wave of cold wash over me. How did he know that? And if he knew all about the cube, then why had he run like that when the humming started?

"Did you read the sign?" said the man.

"I did, but when I saw you by the pool, I wanted to find out where you were going."

"I am not the man you saw by the pool. But the sign is well before the pool."

"I guess so," I said. "I thought maybe because it was an old sign it would be okay."

"Your first problem was thinking you could find your way through via the pipeline. That was never going to work."

"What do you … How …" I started to ask. Was this just a lucky guess? Or was I following a predictable path that others had taken before? But before I could finish asking my question, I heard the man clear his throat and spit. There was a strangely hollow splash. Something clacked onto the table. Had he just spat into a cup?

"You can stay here for another night," said the man. "There is food in the pan here, and there are rations and a carry sack in the safe that you can take with you … I'll write the combination on the map. There's enough wood in the shed to keep you warm until you go."

"… Thank you," I said, suspecting some sort of trick. "But I don't have anything to pay you."

"I didn't ask you to pay me. You asked for help, and I am giving it. Is there anything else you'd like to ask me before I go?"

"I don't think so …" I said. But what did he mean about me asking for help? Who was this man? I heard him stand up from the chair and walk toward the door.

"Wait," I said. "I lied about my eyes because I was worried you would attack me. But I can't really see anything … Would it … would it be okay if you opened the safe for me?"

The steps halted.

"No," he said. "But I've left something for you in a cup here on the table. If you rub it into your eyes, it will undo the damage … as long as you use it within the twelve hours."

"Thanks … It's not your spit is it?"

"That's right."

"Oh … I think I'd prefer to use my own."

"That won't work. You need something that can change those cells before they die. My spit will do it. But don't wait too long. As I said— twelve hours from exposure."

"Okay," I said. "Hey, if you don't mind me asking, where did you come from?"

But there was no answer. Whoever it had been, he was gone. Outside, the thunder returned, rolling around the margins of the sky.

I gathered one of the blankets around myself and went to close the door before shuffling back to the table.

It was just like the man had said. I could feel the radiant heat of the stove on my face. When my fingers swept the table, they found a folded wad of paper. They also brushed up against a china cup—which I slid away from myself—and a spoon, which I brought closer.

I stood up and found the pan on the stovetop. I still didn't know if I could trust him, but my hunger was so intense. The smell of the cheese and meat overwhelmed me.

In a second, the spoon was in my hand, and then it was in the pan, and then it was in my mouth.

It was some kind of ravioli in a creamy sauce. I don't know whether it was literally the best food I had ever eaten, but that's how it seemed right then. I ate half of the pan standing, with the stove slowly roasting my face and body.

As my hunger subsided, my thoughts turned to the cup sitting on the table. What was I going to do about that?

Did the man really expect me to believe that he had magical spit that could cure my eyes? Did he really think I would use it? It was a repulsive thought. What if the man had the Tox? Or, even if the Agent was right and the Tox didn't work like that, what about all the other infections he might have? It was ridiculous. And it didn't make sense. If what he had said was true, then the cells that had been damaged were the ones right inside my eyeballs—in the part where the image projected. How could anything—let alone spit—heal those?

On the other hand, what did I have to lose? If I couldn't get my vision back, I was already as good as dead. I'd end up walking off a cliff, or being cooked by Savages, or I'd simply starve. What difference would it make then if I had a few germs in my eyes? If it didn't work, I could wash my face in the pool.

And hadn't the man already done so much to help me: given me this food, made this fire, left me a map, allowed me to stay … not killed me.

Suddenly, I knew what I was going to do. Maybe the man was simply tox-crazed. Maybe my eyes would just get better on their own. But I was going to try it. The stakes were so high—and I didn't even know how many hours it had been since I had seen the flash. For all I knew, my time was about to run out.

Before I could change my mind, I reached out and grabbed the cup, pressed the lip of the vessel into my cheek and scooped some of the liquid onto my eye. I did the same on the other side, trying not to retch as I blinked the spittle in with my eyelids.

I wiped it off my cheeks with the back of my sleeve and sat there feeling disgusted and stupid. But it was done. If I was a fool, I was a fool;

the man could have his joke. At least I still had the food and the fire.

Nothing happened. I felt more stupid. Then again, perhaps it was a hopeful sign. If the spit was a trick then maybe the 12 hours claim was too. I decided to go and wash my face.

I was about a third of the way to the stream when my eyes began to itch. At first, I thought I would ignore it; it felt like the sort of thing that would get worse the more you rubbed it—the sort of irritation that needed to be washed away rather than rubbed. But the urge became irresistible. I stopped and ground the heels of my hands into my eyes.

The relief was immediate. And that wasn't all. When I took my hands away, it seemed as if there was a lighter smudge in the black. I turned back toward the hut and saw the door as a bleary yellow smear.

I rubbed again and retraced my steps. By the time I had made it back inside, I was seeing gradations of light and shadow everywhere. As I opened the stove door and blinked, the orange glow resolved into flames.

Quickly now, I grabbed the folded map off the table and held it up near my face. At first, I couldn't read it, but when I stood on a chair near the ceiling light, I could just make out a string of numbers written in the margin: 3-7-12-1-12.

Between my bleary eyes and cold fingers, it took a long time for me to get the door open. Yet finally, just when I was beginning to fear that it was a lie, I heard a click. The heavy door swung free.

It was full of good things. There were shelves with plastic storage tubs containing packets of tea, freeze-dried coffee, sugar and powdered milk. There were Cardboard boxes crammed with silver packets that had things like "Lamb Curry", "Chicken Cacciatore" and "Beef Stroganoff" stencilled on their shrink-wrapped skins.

Down the bottom, under the shelves, I found a new-smelling canvas bag with a flint, water flask, sleeping-roll, aluminium mug and spoon. There was also a small Billy—and, sticking out of it, a bunch of fresh celery.

At first I just swore and stared at everything, not able to take it in. When I had recovered my wits, I pulled it all out and laid it out on the table and stared at it again.

Finally, I made myself a mug of coffee with sugar and took it out to the front step of the hut.

Above the walls of the valley, the morning sun was pouring blood-orange light across the storm clouds over the summit. Higher up, bands of fiery cirrus framed the last stars shining in a blue that was deeper than any I had ever seen.

I just sat there looking up at it all. Everything seemed sharper and more intense—not just more vivid than it had been before Vera's injections, but *ever*. Was it just getting above the dust of the plains? Or had my eyes always been dull?

I made another coffee and washed up. Then I took another look around the hut—paying particular attention to the map and the tatty book from the top of the safe.

It turned out to be a guest ledger, a sort of handwritten record of all those who had passed through before me.

The early entries were stockmen leaving point-form records of names, dates and herd sizes. Then came hikers listing the details of their journeys, or the weather, or going on about the views. After that, there was a long gap in time, followed by some short entries from refugees who wouldn't give their full names or destinations, but spoke of cold, starvation and the burial of children and friends.

Another long break followed, and then there were new records. These came from work teams of Central loyalists who spoke about taking delivery of equipment and beginning "screening tests". There was an excited account from a group who spoke of retreating before a Sav attack, and seeing the cannibals "scythed down like hay by the relay." Then there was a more somber report of a funeral held for team members who had gone into the zone after injecting expired trace-screen.

At last, there were just isolated entries—usually years apart—written by individuals "heading to Central" or just "heading East." Some seemed unaware of the danger up the valley. Others described elaborate precautions to get past the cube. One group described a process of fasting and intense washing. Another man was carrying a large mirror. The final entry was from one Laban Tombs:

> *Trying the east passage this afternoon. I'm going to cover myself with zinc-cream and drag my gear behind me—hopefully the cube won't see me as a threat. Wish me luck!*

"Good luck," I said.

I closed the book and turned my attention to the map. It was a large-scale topographic chart with thin lines that bunched together in the steep places and drifted apart in the flatter regions.

There was a shaded section labelled "Horeb Pass Restricted Zone" and someone had circled a little black square labelled "Shelter Hut" in the middle of it. A short distance away, another square appeared with the words "Stage 1 Detox Relay."

From the circle someone had hand-drawn a series of arrows that led back down the mountain to another road that ran southwards along the side of the range.

Right near the bottom corner of the map, a thread-like track branched east from this road back to the mountains, and the same pen that had marked the circle and arrows had drawn a thicker arrow and written "Crux via Wicket Gap" next to it. In the margin nearby, there was another note: "Keep that knife in your boot—you'll need it."

I spent the rest of the day resting, eating and sitting in the sun. The next morning, I gathered the things that the man had left for me, chose a selection of ration packets, and began my march back down the mountain.

CHAPTER 8

I nearly missed the turnoff. It came on a curve of the old highway and the sign that marked it had been pulled up and dumped in the culvert. The track was narrow, with grass growing between the wheel ruts and scrub on either side.

But I turned and followed it back toward the mountains and the hills rose and closed in around me. When the sun began to sink, I retreated into them and made my fire in the crook of an old creek bed.

There was still no water this side of the mountains. But I had the canteen from the safe and, as long as I carried it in the air and hung it up overnight, it always provided enough for me to drink. If I needed more for cooking, I could walk around, twirling it by its carry loop for twenty or thirty minutes until it filled.

That's what I was doing when I heard the sound of a vehicle coming up the road from the west. It seemed to go past me, stop, and go back.

As soon as I heard that, I abandoned any thought of a cooked dinner and stamped out my fire, praying that the wind would blow the last of its smoke away from the track.

Next morning as I went on, the hills drew closer and became cliffs. Even taller crags and ridgelines appeared up ahead.

I was off the map now, but I guessed there must be some opening up there; Wicket Gap, as the man had labelled it. And before long, I could see it—a narrow cleft in the grey wall of the mountains.

But I still had one more barrier to deal with. As I followed the track up a final rise before the canyon, the breeze shifted, bringing me hints of diesel and woodsmoke. A second later I heard the sound of men's laughter.

I immediately threw myself into the cover of bushes as scenes of Savages flashed through my mind. I thought of the men in the back of that huge truck and the way the man with the bones in his hair had looked up at me.

But they weren't Savages. As I crouched there, a man appeared on the rise to relieve himself. He was wearing some sort of uniform: dark green pants with a wide belt and a singlet of matching colour. He was stocky and muscular, with a crew-cut head and a full beard. When he half-turned to talk to someone behind him, I could see a pump-action shotgun slung over his shoulder.

He zipped up his fly and dropped back out of sight while I wondered what to do next. Was it possible these were soldiers from Central?

When things got quieter, I crept closer. I thought if I could just keep my head lower than the scrub, I might be able to peer into their camp without being seen.

But they were too clever for me. One of my legs snagged a nylon line and the three hubcaps that were anchored to the end of it came clattering out from the bush in which they had been wedged.

Instantly, there was an explosion of deep-throated barking from over the rise. Someone said, "Let him off."

I turned and bolted, shedding my pack as I heard the heavy paws thudding behind me. I crashed through a low bush, leapt and grabbed the branch of a dead tree. As I pulled myself up, I felt something bump up against the sole of my right boot and looked down to see the foam-flecked teeth of the big Alsatian as it prepared to leap again.

But then there was a whistle and someone said, "Oi! Get out of it." The dog gave another bark before bounding back to join its masters.

There were three of them coming toward me now. The bearded man with the shotgun was walking alongside a younger man in grease-smeared overalls who held a oversized torque-wrench. A third man—grey-haired, straight-backed and muscular—strode past them, pulling a pistol from his shoulder holster as he drew close to my tree.

"Well, what have we got here?" he said. "Who are you, kid?"

"Chris," I said, "I'm … trying to get to Wicket Gap. I was told this was the way to go to get to the treatment centre."

"Treatment centre?" he said. "Who told you this was the way to a treatment centre?"

"A guy I met up at the pass in Horeb."

Off to the side, the man with the beard began pulling things from my carry sack.

"Look at this, Chief," he said, holding up my water bottle. "Got a book in there too."

The man with the pistol raised an eyebrow and gestured at the gear.

"Where did you get this stuff?"

"From the man," I said. "I mean … he left it for me. I didn't see him."

"You didn't see him?"

"I was blind."

"But you got better?"

"That's right," I said.

"And did your invisible man tell you his name?"

"No. I … I didn't get a chance to ask him."

The men looked at each other and laughed.

"Kid, I think you better come down so we can have a chat."

"Why? What do you want to know?"

"I want to know where you really got that gear. You see the only folks who carry bottles and books like that are either Agents or Reverts and you don't look like either of those things. So we're thinkin' that maybe you've been murderin' folks and takin' their stuff."

"No. It's like I said …"

"Hop down. It's not a request."

"What about your dog?"

"Buddy'll hold on to him, won't you, Buddy?" he said, calling to the young man in overalls.

"Yes, sir." He stepped forward and grasped the animal's collar, though it continued to make a low growling noise as it stared at me.

I hesitated for a moment and swung down to join them.

"Where are you from, kid?" said the grey-haired man.

"Spillan. But I've been on the road for a while now … Are you guys from Central?"

They laughed again.

"Not exactly, kid. We're with the other side. I'm Lieutenant Bird; this gentleman with the shotgun is Sergeant Beelz, and that's Private Lial holding Luce. We're HORD: Homeland Reaction and Defence."

"Okay," I said. "So, am I under arrest or something?"

The man shook his head. "No, you're not under arrest. We can't let you keep going the way you were going, that's all."

"I was just going to get the treatment," I said.

"You were going to get slaved. Come on up to our camp and we can tell you about it."

I followed them over the rise to a clearing in the scrub. It was a dusty turning circle with a fire pit at its centre surrounded by two large tents and a hulking pickup. The vehicle had a machine gun mounted above its roll cage and the letters HORD on its side. Through the bulldust on the bonnet, I could see a stylised insignia in the shape of a leopard. The place smelled of fuel and smoke, and also faintly of something dead and rotting. I wrinkled my nose and looked around but couldn't see its source. None of the other men seem troubled by it.

The Lieutenant pointed to a stump by the fire while Beelz went into the tent and returned with a kettle and cups. Buddy Lial tied up the still-growling Alsatian to the bull-bar of the pickup.

"I don't think your dog likes me," I said to the Lieutenant.

"Well, he doesn't like Agents or Reverts or their gear."

I looked around at the men; noticed a cyst on Beel's neck and a cluster of the things around Buddy's knuckles. Bird seemed pretty clear, but maybe there was something on his jawline.

"What's a Revert?" I said.

"Reverts are Central-lovers, kid. They go to Crux and get their brains fried and then they wander all over the place makin' trouble for us."

"Like Agents?"

"Agents are a special kinda Revert." He gave me a sharp look as he passed me a coffee cup. "Was it an Agent who sent you this way?"

"It was at first. We had one come to Spillan, and she gave me a leaflet about the Tox. But the other guy … I don't know what he was … Like I said, I didn't see him."

"Yeah, you said you were blind. And yet you seem to be okay now. How'd that all go?"

"I got blinded by this cube thing up at Horeb. And then the guy came and fixed me."

"Did he say where he was from?"

"… Inject you with anything?" said Beelz.

"No … He just spat in a cup and got me to stick it in my eyes."

I saw Beelz and the Lieutenant exchange another glance.

"How about that," said Bird. "Sounds like a regular psycho."

"That's what I thought. But, it worked."

"Well, kid, I haven't heard of that one before. Don't know what to make of it. But I got to tell you it's a good thing you bumped into us." He sipped on his coffee. "Did that Agent or your mystery man tell you what they actually do to folks at Crux?"

"… Or after," said Beelz.

"No … I think I read that there was an injection."

"But did they tell you what the injection does?" said Bird.

"No. Why, what does it do?"

"It does a whole lot of stuff: changes your brain; rewrites your DNA. They'll tell you they have to do it because you're so full of Tox and every cell is affected, but what they really want is to take you over and make you into one of their little lackeys.

"You think you can just go and get a shot. But that's not how it works. First thing they make you do is pledge allegiance. Then they tell you that the only way the cure will really work is if you do what they say."

"So you have to be their messenger boy and go wherever they tell you," said Beelz.

I looked down at the cup in my hand and wondered how much of what they were saying was true. The idea that the treatment was just a trick to control people sounded just like what Mayor Stricton had told me—which was enough to make me suspect it. Neither the Agent nor the man at Horeb had seemed slave-like or robotic.

"Maybe they've got the right," I said.

"Who's got what right?"

"Central."

"To make you a slave? What the hell are you saying, son?"

"Maybe they've got the right to make us pledge. I mean, this all used to be theirs didn't it?"

"Yeah, and we got our freedom." He turned to Beelz and shook his head. "Do you hear this kid? … I'm trying to help him."

"Maybe he can't be helped," said Beelz. "Maybe he's already chimeric."

"Cos of some darn spit? No, I reckon he just doesn't like us telling him what to do …"

"He shouldn't be listening to Central then," said Beelz.

"That's right," said Bird, looking back at me. "He shouldn't."

"You know what Central does when they get their hands on you?"

I shook my head.

"They hook you up to a brain scanner and dig through your past. Whatever you've done—whatever dirty little secrets you've got squirrelled in there"— he reached over and tapped a finger on my forehead— "they'll ferret it out. What do you reckon they'd find in *your* skull, kid?

"Some of the people we pick up out east … they spend years tramping all the way around the country: workin' hard; thinkin' they'll make the Pantarch happy. And then they finally get to the processing station, and Central puts 'em in the scanners and rejects 'em. You should see the look on their faces."

"Well, I can't go back to Spillan," I said. "I left because I've got a thing on my neck, and if I go back with it they'll send me away again, or …"

"You don't have to go back there," said Bird. "You could go to Delice—nobody's gonna put you down for having a cyst there. If you really want treatment, you could try Ockham—they've got a cure."

"Or there's Addle," said Beelz.

"Yep, Addle has the best meds of all of them. That's where our base is. We could take you there."

I looked between them. I couldn't help feeling like there was something staged about the way they had managed that last exchange—as if Addle were the option they were angling for me to pick. I wondered whether the meds of Addle were like the "cure" at Ockham.

"How come I've never heard of you guys before?"

"Because you're from Spillan, and old Stricton likes to pretend he's a one-man army—doesn't like us comin' around in the daylight. But he pays his dues like all the rest—lets us know when he's sending out his people. But we've been keepin' you safe like we do with all the other towns."

"Safe from what? From Savs?"

"Yep, and from Central. Why do you think they haven't rolled in and wiped you out?"

"I heard it was because they were giving us a chance to get treated. So we wouldn't get wiped out with the Cleanse"

The man laughed and flicked the last of his coffee into the fire as he stood up.

"You been reading that book in your bag?"

"A bit."

"Then you should know that they don't have much of a problem killin' people."

This much was true, I conceded. But the idea that men such as these were holding Central back seemed ridiculous to me.

"So what's it going to be?" said Bird. "Addle, Delice or Ockham?"

"What if I just want to keep going?" I said.

The Lieutenant tilted his head. "Well that would be disappointing, kid."

Out of the corner of my eye, I saw Beelz give his commander a smile. "Don't want to say I told you so, boss," he said, "But I told you so. Dope or dice?"

Bird turned to respond but was cut short by an explosion of noise from the Alsatian.

The dog was straining on its collar, dragging against its rope. This time it wasn't looking at me but back toward the track.

"He's hearin' somethin'," said Buddy. "Somethin's comin'."

"Go and take a look," said Bird. "Shut up, Luce."

Lial loped to the edge of camp and peered west. I got to my feet and started looking around for places to run. Between the barks, I could hear the drone of a distant engine.

"I don't like the sound of that motor," said Bird. "What do you see, Buddy?"

"It's one of 'em alright," said the boy.

"Right on cue," said Bird. He shot out an arm and grabbed me by the shirt collar, jerking me off balance and making me collide with the bearded man. "Get him out of sight," he said.

CHAPTER 9

I tried to twist free, but Beelz had already locked a massive arm around my neck and was dragging me backwards through the bushes. I wanted to fight him, but he was just too strong. Instead, I was simply fighting to breathe. The way the man was choking me was cutting off the blood to my head so that my vision shrank away into darkness.

I blacked out completely… returned to consciousness as a stick scraped one of my trailing legs … faded out again. Now I was lying on my back with Beelz's knees on either side of me and one of my own legs folded back painfully under me. The man still had his arm around my throat, and had now also clamped a foul-tasting hand over my mouth. I gagged and tried to pull my head free but again felt the vice close on my neck.

"You shut up and lie still or I'll put you out again," he hissed in my ear.

I stopped struggling. I could hear the engine close by and voices calling out above it.

"You know the rules, Bird," said a woman's voice that was somehow familiar to me. "You've got no business holding him."

"Rules don't apply," said Bird's voice. "If I don't see a coat, he's fair game."

"If he's headed for Crux, he belongs to Central."

"That ain't what he says. He says he doesn't want to join up—says he's just looking for a shot."

"That what he told you? That he didn't want to join Central?"

"Near enough."

"I want to see him for myself."

My foggy mind scrabbled to understand what was going on. Who was this person? Why was she asking about me?

"I don't see any call for that," said Bird.

"How do I know Beelz hasn't got him tied up back there somewhere?"

"How do I know you won't try to snatch him if I bring him out?"

There was a pause before Bird spoke again.

"Give it up, Evie. You ain't gonna win this one."

The woman said something in response, but I was too distracted to focus on it. A string of realisations was forming in my mind as it cleared.

The first, triggered by the Lieutenant's use of the name Evie, was that the voice was that of Evangeline Veracis—the Agent I had met back in Spillan.

The second was that this was my last chance to get away from these men. If I didn't find a way to escape from Beelz right now, I would soon be finding out what the words "dope or dice" meant.

The third realisation was that the thing digging into my thigh was the handle of the knife that I had been keeping in my boot since the hut up in Horeb. I pulled it free and stabbed it into Sergeant Beelz's kneecap as hard as I could.

The man roared and swore as I tore myself loose and began flailing and stumbling through the bushes toward the sound of the engine. I heard a shotgun being racked. Then, there was a massive detonation and the sound of pellets striking metal just ahead of me. I burst into the open, tripped and rolled onto the dust in front of the Agent's van, no more than a metre from the legs of Lieutenant Bird.

I got to my feet as the man drew his pistol.

"Get in, Chris!" shouted Eve. "Quick! They can't hurt you if you're with the V!"

I made it around the corner of the vehicle as the first bullet ricocheted off the bonnet. The second deflected from the windshield as I grabbed the passenger's door. Then, as I dragged myself inside, there was a flash of black and tan as the Alsatian hurled itself after me. It crashed into the door, pushing it closed and projecting its breath, muzzle, teeth and slobber through the half-down window.

I jerked backwards toward the dash and rolled sideways into my seat as Eve jammed her foot on the accelerator. I banged my head on the doorpost as she swerved around Bird. There was another impact on the glass as Buddy Lial swung at me with his torque-wrench. The van rocked again.

Then we were past the other vehicle and out of the clearing. Eve ploughed through a curtain of saplings, roared over a malleefowl mound and drove hard toward the shadowy ravine.

"Hold on," she said. "Soon as we get into the gap we'll be safe."

There was another ping as something hit the rear of the vehicle, another jolt as Eve swerved around a boulder.

I raised an arm to brace myself with the hang-strap but stopped with a groan. A sudden pain had arced across my shoulders.

"You okay?" said Eve, looking over at me as we bounced out of a pothole.

"Think so … I dunno," I said.

"Lean forward so I can see …" she said. "You've been hit … Push yourself back hard into the seat and it'll slow the bleeding. We'll just go a bit further, and there'll be a place where we can stop."

We were in the canyon itself now, boulders and low shrubs flashing by. As the Agent turned the vehicle to follow its curves, the shifting momentum forced me to compensate with my arms and legs. I could feel the blood trickling down my lower back. The pain in my shoulders was like a fire.

"Will they come after us in here?" I said.

"Not likely. This is Envoy territory. They know better than to mess with him."

She turned the vehicle around another bend and came to a wider stretch. Soon, I could see a narrow stream winding along the base of the left hand cliff and small trees and bushes growing from cracks in the rocks. Then the dirt of the valley floor turned to sand, sloping down to the creek. When we reached the next turn, the creek widened to a pool that stretched halfway across the open space. On the far side of it, tiny birds splashed in the water and flittered among the eucalypts and she-oaks growing along the rocky bank.

Eve stopped the vehicle and sat me down on a boulder by the water before peeling back my shirt and injecting me with something to blunt the pain.

"Doesn't look too bad … You've just copped a couple of pellets. Shallow, I think, but I can't really tell."

"Can you get them out?"

"Not by myself. I'll clean you up and give you a temporary dressing. But we'll go and see Prediger. He'll know what to do with you and he's close by."

"Is that the Envoy?"

"Prediger? No. Prediger works for the Envoy. Same as me."

There was a satisfying ripping noise as she peeled off a strip of tape and stuck it over the dressing.

"Thanks for saving me back there," I said. "You came along at just the right time."

She gave a wry-sounding laugh. "Yeah, well I would have gotten to you sooner if you hadn't been so elusive. I've been trying to find you for ages. Didn't you see me?"

I suddenly felt stupid. "I knew someone was following me. I guess I thought it was the guys from Ockham … How did you find me?"

"I only saw you once and then lost you in the hills. I got a report that there'd been some kid up at Horeb. Then they told me to look for you on the Wicket track. I would have kept going, except I saw your gear on the ground back there."

I shuddered, imagining what might have come next after that. "Who were those guys anyway? It sounded like they knew you."

"Bird and Beelz? They're with HORD. It's what's left of the Territory Army from the war. They get their pay from the Corp. I used to be with them in my younger and stupider days … long story. Anyway, they are not your friends. It's a good thing we got you away from them."

"Yeah, I got that feeling."

I looked across the pond. I had a hundred other questions somewhere in the back of my head, but suddenly, I just wanted to sleep. The sun felt good on my bare skin, and whatever Eve had injected into the wound had melted the pain into a warm glow. Over on the far side of the pool, a small honeyeater was taking a bath, hypnotically flashing brilliant yellow patches on its wings as it splashed in the water.

"This is a good place," I said.

"Best spot in the mountains," she said. "Only safe way through, too. Okay, wrap this blanket around you and let's get you back to the V. You can have a snooze as we go."

*   *   *

When I woke up, the sun was in my eyes and my head was lolling against the blanket that Eve had wadded between it and the window. The pain in my shoulders had returned as a dull throb. The engine seemed to be straining, and there was just sky above the windshield.

In the background, Eve was talking to someone.

"Okay, we'll see you in about twenty. Over and out."

"Where are we?" I said.

She passed me a water flask and gestured with her head. "Side of Mount Didasko. Take a look."

I straightened up and instinctively flinched back as I caught sight of the drop. We were half way up a zig-zag track cut into the face of the canyon. On the other side of the ravine, sun-raked cliffs stretched up toward the sky.

"Woah. We're a … long way up."

"Don't worry. Track's solid. I've been up and down a hundred times."

I looked at the Central symbol on the steering wheel and tried to think of something that might keep my mind from visualising our wheels going off the crumbling edge.

"Hey why does everything have the crossed syringes? Is it just because they give you an injection when they give you the cure?"

"They symbolise what happened with the Envoy."

"Who's that?"

She looked over at me. "He's the Pantarch's special representative and the one who came up with the cure. They dropped him into the zone, but HORD caught him. Then they staked him out in an X and injected him with cyst toxin to kill him."

"So he's dead?" I said?

"Was. But they sent in a skyship and crash crew to bring him back. Now he's in Central, running all the ops for the Pantarch … Anyway, they put that X on everything because that was the moment his body metabolised the cure. When you get your shot, it's taken from his blood."

The car rocked and I swallowed hard. I wanted to keep asking her questions—I also wanted to get my mind off the drop—but the thought of distracting her was even scarier.

She solved the dilemma by asking me a question of her own.

"So, did Bird and Beelz try to tell you that we want to brainwash you and turn you into a robot or something?"

"Pretty much," I said. "They said that the cure messes with your DNA and does stuff to your brain … Is that right?"

She tilted her head in a half-nod. "Sort of—like everything those guys say. If you're living in the AZ then the Tox has already damaged every cell in your body. The cure has to alter your DNA to fix you. And, yeah, it has to affect your brain too—that's where the damage is worst."

"Because of the cysts?" I said.

"Yeah, that's right. Did you read that card I gave you?"

I started to answer her, but suddenly I was distracted. We had just come around a projection in the cliff, and now I could see that we were almost at the top. A few kilometres away, a series of solid-looking stone buildings supporting an ancient-looking radio-dish rose above the trees of the cliff edge.

"Is that where your friend lives?" I said.

"Yeah, that's Prediger's place … Prax's too, sort of."

"What's the big dish for?"

"Communication and control. Prax uses it to maintain the network and watch over the whole territory so the Envoy knows what's going on."

The road brought us level with the structure as it reached the top of the cliff. Over my left shoulder, across the other side of the Gap, the ridgelines of Mount Tanak, Horeb and Berit receded into a blue haze.

Then, the road that we were on turned in the opposite direction and began threading its way through lichen-covered boulders and sparse white eucalypts that swayed in the breeze.

"Wind down your window if you like," said Eve.

I did as she said and felt the fresh mountain air flowing past me, smelling of gumleaves and grass. As we went on, patches of sunlight flickered in my eyes. When I closed my eyelids and leant back on the headrest, I became aware of bird calls and the smooth crunching of the gravel under our tyres.

I felt Eve brake and raised my head to see that we had turned into a small shaded parking area next to one of the stone buildings that I had seen from the cliff.

As we came to a stop, a balding man with spectacles and braces was emerging from an arched gateway. He caught sight of us and nodded.

"You must be Chris," he said as he opened the passenger door for me. "My name is Rein Prediger. Eve tells me that you have some injuries to look at."

"Yes, on my back," I said. I turned my body and dropped the blanket to show him where Eve had taped over the wound. The movement sent a deep ache through my shoulder.

"I see. Alright, well let's get you inside and take a proper look there."

He helped me out of the vehicle and led the way through the arch into an arcade of uncut stone that bordered a courtyard of vegetable gardens and buzzing insects. Doors on the outside of the cloister stood open, showing small rooms with beds and tables. Another set of double doors opened into a shadowy hallway from which I could hear distant music.

But Prediger kept leading us on—round the corner of the arcade, then up a low staircase into the main building.

It was hard to see then, after the light outside, but I could sense the mass of the walls, and feel a heavy rug beneath my feet. The place had a smell like incense—mysterious, sharp and sweet at the same time. We came to a smaller door, and the smell changed to disinfectant and soap. I felt Prediger guide me to a chair, heard a click and then shut my eyes as a bright inspection lamp shone down on me.

"Alright, let's take a look at you. If you would lean forward a little..."

I did as he asked, staring down at the grey slate floor as Eve removed the blanket and Prediger began to peel off the tape and dressing. Once again, pain spread like waves of heat across the middle of my back, making beads of sweat spring up on my face.

He paused and lightly pressed on the area above the bandage.

"I can see this is hurting you a bit. Why don't you take your mind off it by telling me what those scoundrels did and said to you?"

So I began telling him about what had happened since I'd first seen Beelz; about all the things that they'd said to me about Central using the promise of a cure to control people, and how they scanned people's brains to expose their secrets.

"And what did you think of all that?" said Prediger.

"Well, I don't really want anyone scanning my brain."

He laughed. "Who would? I assure you that nobody is going to scan your brain when you get to Crux. There *is* a memory scan performed when you reach Central to see if the cure has taken hold in your system, but it isn't so that they can test whether you're good enough to enter, or whatever nonsense they said to you."

"Do I have to go on to Central if I get the cure?" I said. "I mean … I was hoping I could maybe just pay for the treatment myself and then, if it works, go back and tell everyone back home about it."

"Hmm," he said. Suddenly, I felt a stab of pain in the deep tissue next to my shoulder blade. "Well, I'm afraid there's no paying for it yourself. The Pantarch is very strict on that point. And even if it were possible, there's no way you would be able to afford it. The only way they will give you the cure is if you accept the pardon and swear allegiance.

"As to where you go after Crux," he went on, "that would be up to the Envoy. He might send you back to Spillan, or he might order you to go straight on to Central. Generally, he likes to give you some time for the cure to work through your system."

"The blood miles," said Eve.

"Exactly," said Prediger.

I felt his forceps twist and pull, and heard a sticky patter of metal on metal.

"That's one of them," he said, lowering the kidney dish so I could see the peppercorn-sized pellet lying in a small puddle of blood.

"There's another still in there that's too deep and will have to wait for Crux. I can dress it and give you some more painkiller, but it will need attention fairly soon. HORD operatives have the charming habit of coating their ammunition with cyst toxin, which can cause trouble. But if you stay here tonight, Eve will be able to take you on at first light."

I thanked him and waited while he finished numbing and taping the site. In the background, I could hear them talking to each other about other people that Eve had brought through; what they were doing and where they had gone after Crux. It probably would have been a very helpful conversation for me to have listened in on.

But my mind was running around like a rat in a cage.

I realised now, from the answers Prediger had just given me, that the Mayor had been right all along. Central was never going to let me "waltz in and waltz out" as he had put it. They were never going to give me the cure without securing an oath of loyalty. They were never going to accept the four gold sovereigns that I had been carrying in the sole of my boots all the way from Spillan. I was never going to return home as the conquering hero.

Yet even that wasn't the real problem. The main reason why I had been hoping to buy my treatment was to avoid Central asking too many questions about my past. And now it turned out that, not only would I have to pledge myself to the Central government if I wanted to get the cure, I would also, at some point, have to submit to a memory scan, just like Bird had said. And when that happened, they would find out what I had done, and then I would be finished.

CHAPTER 10

Eve and Prediger worked together to ease me into a fresh shirt before leading me out through the door to a spiral staircase of dark grey metal. The room above was a large, ring-shaped observation deck featuring big windows that looked out toward the eastern foothills. In the centre of the ring, storerooms and a wedge-shaped kitchen supported a raised mezzanine where monitors and lights flickered and blinked. The whole structure was built of massive steel beams, filled in with the same perfectly fitted natural stone that I had seen elsewhere.

"That is the base of the main dish," said Prediger as he saw me looking toward the upper level. "I'll take you up to the monitors after you've eaten. I suspect Prax will want to show you a thing or two.

"In the meantime, sit and eat and tell us a bit more about your story. I'm sure Eve is as eager as I am to hear the rest of it."

We took our places at his long wooden table while he went back and forth from the kitchen, bringing out loaves of fresh flatbread, olives, and cheese, along with a pitcher of clear water.

And I began to tell them about all the things that had happened to me, from when I had first met Eve and discovered the thing on my neck, to my adventures in Ockham and the mountains. They were most interested in the part where the man showed up and rescued me at Horeb.

"And he didn't tell you his name?" said Eve.

"No," I said. "Or, where he'd come from. Do you know who it was?"

"Not for sure. But the spit thing makes me think …"

"It sounds like Tobias," said Prediger, setting down a pot of spiced lentil soup.

"Who's that?" I said.

"Tobias Shepherd—the Envoy," said Prediger.

"The guy whose blood's in the cure?

"Yes. Of course, there's more to him than that. But yes."

Then Prediger told me a bit more about the history of the war.

He told me about how the Pantarch had trained up loyalists to establish resistance cells across the Territory—all of which kept failing as the Tox derailed their minds.

He told me about how Central had developed codes of self-discipline and martial arts to combat the disease, and how the program produced a few champions before the loyalists gave up on it.

He talked about how the Pantarch had finally sent his own man into the territory; how the Council's men had caught him and killed him—and how Central had brought him back to life and rebuilt his body and put him in charge of everything.

It all pretty much just washed over me. I caught enough for it to sound familiar when I heard it again later, but I didn't really understand the significance of any of it. Even when Prediger explained that the Envoy had negotiated a full pardon for everyone in the AZ who would swear allegiance (information that would have saved me a *lot* of grief if I'd taken it in) I still didn't really get it. I was too tired, and still too distracted by what I'd heard while they were dressing my wound.

It was almost dark by the time we had finished eating. The sun was edging down behind the base and through the windows I could see the sides of the hills lit up by a wash of yellow light. Below and beyond, the rest of the land faded away into shadow.

"Now, young man," said Prediger, when he had finished clearing the table, "Let's go up and see if our host has anything to show you."

I stood and followed him to the stairs. "I thought you were our host."

"No, no. I'm more like cook and caretaker. This place was built for Prax to maintain the Pantarch's operations in the Territory."

The control station up on the mezzanine featured rings of video screens and control panels. Above, seven small skylights in the low ceiling looked up to the underside of the dish that was now just a silhouette against the starry sky.

Prediger sat me down in front of one of the screen-banks where images of roads, towns, encampments and individuals flickered and cycled. I saw a column of men and women in overalls being marched along a road by guards in dark uniforms. I saw a vast tent-like structure with lights shining through it.

But before I had time to make sense of any of these images, the 12 monitors directly in front of me went black and then flickered back on as a unified display. Suddenly, I was looking at a high-definition aerial shot of a huge truck barreling across a dusty plain. As the camera pulled in, my heart started pounding. The tray of the vehicle was full of ragged men carrying spears and swords. One of them held up a red flag.

I twisted in my chair, wanting to ask Prediger about what I was watching. But he was busy at another terminal. When I turned back, my question was answered. The camera went wide again, and there was the road to Spillan, and there was the Agent's van racing ahead.

And now it was like I was reliving it. I saw the flash as my first shot struck the armoured ram. I waited through the long seconds of the failed round. Then, as the camera zoomed in on the front section of the truck, I saw my last shot tear a chunk out of the top edge of the tray.

Then, two things happened at the same time.

The first was that a kind of overlay suddenly appeared superimposed on the video. Numbers appeared, moving across the top and side of the image. A white square flashed and blinked over the truck—just at the point where the tray went over the driver's cabin. As the truck bounced and swerved, the square moved with it as if it was stuck to the one spot.

A light began to blink in one corner of the screen, and a tiny, but super-bright dot of light appeared in the centre of the square. The square began to move across the roof, and the dot went with it.

Now the truck started swerving, rocking violently as if the driver was trying to get away from it. And I realised that was exactly what *was* happening. The drone, or skyship, or whatever it was that had captured this footage, had fired a beam weapon to force the truck to turn.

"So it wasn't me," I said to myself out loud.

"It wasn't you, Chris Walker," said somebody.

I jerked forward and almost fell out of my chair.

Who had just spoken? The voice was massive—like thunder echoing around the mountains—but it had also somehow sounded close-up—like someone whispering in my ear.

I looked around, but all I could see was Prediger sitting with his back to me, acting as if he hadn't heard a thing.

"Are you Prax?" I said, turning back to the screen.

"I am," said the voice.

"Who are you?"

"I am the Ghost in the machine, the Carrier of the Signal, the Voice of the Pantarch."

As he spoke, the image was replaced by another. Now we were looking at an aerial shot of a ruined town. In the centre of the frame, as the image zoomed in, I could see a man moving about in the shell of what must have once been a really solid building with thick brick walls. But now the roof was gone, and some of the walls were just stubs. The patterned paving that the man was standing on seemed to be the last undamaged part of the structure.

The man picked up a sledgehammer and began to smash the floor. The red freckled skin on his bare back and arms glistened as the hammer rose and fell and rose and fell.

"Do you recognise this man?" said the voice.

For a while, I didn't. The man kept working. He paused to clear away the larger chunks of stone as the pavement broke up.

But when he paused to wipe his neck with a handkerchief, he turned his face up toward the sun. And then it was a face I knew.

"Is that … my … uncle?"

"Yes, it is. You were eight years old when this footage was captured."

"What's he doing?"

"He was attempting to break into an old bank vault."

"He was always hunting for treasure. What happened to him?"

"He died of thirst not long after this. We sent an Agent to try to help him, but he was fixated and would not be turned aside from his goal."

I watched as the man went back to attacking the concrete. It seemed so clear and real—like I could call out to him and he might hear me. I felt a sudden wave of sadness for him, and for my mum, and for all the people I'd seen come and go.

"Why are you showing me this?" I said.

"So that you will understand the nature of things and the futility of the way of life that has been handed down to you. So you can more clearly understand the choice that you are facing."

"Why didn't you force him to stop?" I said. "Why didn't Central or the Envoy or whatever …"

"Because we are not in the business of making slaves."

The screen flashed again, and there was another image. Now it was a green bus speeding along a rutted road through a field of yellow flowers. As the camera tracked around to the side I could see that something had torn away one side of the vehicle. Some of the metal skin had been peeled back and was scraping along the ground.

I could also see people inside the bus. There was the driver—a big man with dark hair, olive skin and a coat that looked like Eve's. In the seats behind him I could see others: another man in a coat with his face turned to look behind; a small woman in overalls with her head down being held by a tall woman in a dark jacket.

"You will have trouble on the road beyond Crux," said Prax. "The men who stopped you in the canyon and the Corp that pays them are desperate to preserve their little kingdom. They and their machines will do whatever they can to stop you. But if you fix your sights on Central, trust the Envoy and travel with friends, you will get through.”

I didn't say anything in response. At that moment, I wasn't sure I would ever go to Central—or even Crux, for that matter.

But the image juddered and scrubbed forward at speed, racing ahead of the bus, along the road—over plains and forests and small villages. It zoomed through a valley and suddenly slowed down over a shantytown of tin and timber. There was smoke drifting up in straight columns and in the distance, above the rickety rooflines, I could see a silhouette of towers and the sun shining on silver water.

“What's this?” I said.

“This is the Beulah refugee camp. The last stop before Central.”

“It looks like a slum.”

“It does. But listen.”

And now I could hear the sounds of the place—the sound of the wind and dogs barking and distant engines and a hammer. But there was singing too. The camera went sideways and tracked down an alley and came out into a clear area between the huts. I could see old people, and people on crutches, and children with waxy skin and dark circles under their eyes. Some of the people had bound up stumps for arms or legs.

But many of them were smiling. In the centre of the space, an elderly woman and a hunchback were dishing out food from a large pot. A ragged couple sat on a step, looking at a book together. There was a man weeping and other people comforting him.

Then the drone ducked under an awning, zoomed over a line of washing and emerged from between the houses to track along a wide dock. I could hear the water lapping and sea birds calling. Across the water, I could see the towers of Sanctuary rising up above tall trees—as if the place was a forest as well as a city.

“Why does Central make people wait before going to the City?”

“They have to be scanned first,” said Prax.

“What kind of scan?” I said, remembering what Bird had said and

Prediger had confirmed.

"A brain scan." said the voice. "If the cure has taken hold it will show up there. Look"

As he spoke, the drone turned and began to follow the shoreline. Its view passed over half-submerged roofless ruins, wrecked boats and a muddy road. Then the ground along the river got a bit higher and the drone tracked around it, pulling back from the water's edge. Suddenly I could see the mouth of a tunnel. It was a massive thing—rust-red and shaped like a square funnel that angled down into the hill toward the river.

On the gravel road that led up to it there was a line of people. They were generally old, I guess, but I could see quite a few kids and people of other ages too. Most of them looked pretty worse-for-wear; some bent over and staggering, though one old couple were laughing like they were sharing a joke.

Then the camera went over their heads, right into the shadow of the funnel, and for about twenty seconds, it was too dark to see anything.

When the camera adjusted, I could see guards in grey uniforms leading an elderly man in a medical robe through a dimly lit chamber toward a tank of dark water. The guards removed the man's gown and helped him recline into the tank. Straight away, moving images began to appear on a large view screen that stood nearby.

At the speed they were playing, they were just impressions or fragments. I saw a little boy tipping over a baby's pram ... the same boy killing a bird ... a teenager carrying a child with an injured leg ... and again, walking away from a weeping girl ... Then there was an older version of the same person walking down a road with a few others ... Older again, now he was sharing food with a beggar in a rickety ghost town ...

"What are they looking for?" I said.

This time, it was Prediger who answered.

"They are cross-checking the surveillance record of his journey against what they are reading off his brain, trying to see if there is any sign of the X-Vector—that's the cure—at work. If there is, it will show up in that dark panel on the right."

"And if it stays dark, does that mean …?"

"It means he's never been treated—he's just been pretending, maybe even to himself. Some people come to Crux and never get treated; some think they can get in to Central by hiding details of their old lives or the extent of their infections."

I sat absolutely still, hearing the blood in my ears as the images continued. I wanted to ask what would happen to the old man in the dark room if he failed the test, but I was afraid of what my voice would do if I tried to say the words.

I didn't find out by watching either. Before the scan was finished, the screens in front of me went dark and then back to the way they were—different views of different places.

"Is that all?" I said.

"Looks like it," said Prediger from behind me. "Come on now, and I'll show you where you can sleep. You will be getting up early, and you should get as much rest as you can.

I got out of the chair and followed him back to the top of the stairs that led down from the mezzanine.

But as I turned to go down, my eye caught a flash from the monitors. Then I had to hold on to the railing as the world began to spin.

Because there on the array was the single image of a kid; a kid scrambling along the side of an old railway line; a kid stooping to collect rocks from the grass between the tracks; a kid running down an embankment toward an old riverbed.

As soon as I saw it, I knew I wouldn't be staying the night. Because that kid was me.

CHAPTER 11

I guess now I need to tell you a bit about what happened to me when I was ten.

By the time I got to the last years of school, I was a bit taller than most of the other kids in Spillan. I had friends and a job, and I could do a few things with guns and engines that got me some respect. But it wasn't always like that. When I was ten, I was short for my age, and some of the kids liked to push me around. The fact that some of them were in the year below me made it doubly humiliating.

So, I wanted some way to become a person that other kids would be afraid of, and I thought I had an idea about how it could happen.

Back in those days, there was a cluster of families camped out in the old riverbed near our town. They came and went a bit and used to bring things to trade that they'd picked up in their travels—even though they were never allowed in through the gates because they had cysties amongst them.

My mum used to go out to them sometimes. She was a midwife and also a nutritionist, and she would give them advice about what they should be buying to help with their scurvy or goitres, and she would help with their babies. It was a pretty brave thing to do when you remember that we all thought the Tox was a virus back then, and I came to see later that people treated her with suspicion because of it.

Anyway, she let me come with her too sometimes, and that's how I got to know some of the boys. They went around in a pack, and all the other kids from the town were scared of them, but they put up with me because of my mum. They even let me come along and see the body of a Savage that they'd killed because he had attacked one of their sisters.

It was after that I asked them to show me how to fight. And that was how I ended up helping them kill the Agent.

They didn't tell me that's what we were going to do until we were all together. Mash, the boy who had vouched for me (and whose baby sister my mum had just helped deliver), just said that Spew—that was their leader—had a job for me to do, and if I did it they would show me how to fight.

So I came along and met them by the old railway line like they said, and there was Spew standing on a pile of sleepers with Mash and a couple of the other boys. They all had their shirts off, so I could see the cysts on their arms and chests. And Spew told me that there was a Central Agent camped out under the bridge, and they were going to kill him and take his stuff.

"But cos he's an Agent, he might have a sword or a gun or something so we're going to need a distraction. That's what you're here for, kid. Mash reckons you can do it. Is he right? I'm only giving you this one chance."

Now, I should have just run off. I was only ten, but I knew what they were asking me to do. I knew that Agents weren't like Savages. I knew that my mum had talked with this Agent and said she quite liked him, and couldn't see why people made such a fuss about them.

But I was weak. And I wanted them to like me. And I wanted people to be afraid of me. So I just nodded and said, "I can do it. What do you want me to do?"

"Can you count to ten?" said Spew. "Then do it slow like this one ... two ... three. And do it three times. Then go over the other side of the tracks and get close and start chucking rocks at him. And then we'll come round and get him from the other side ... Okay?"

"Okay," I said.

"Good. Let's get ready."

That meant fighting each other to work themselves up to what they were about to do. Spew pushed Mash off the sleeper pile and head-butted one of the other boys in the nose. The last of them turned and lifted me by the shirt, only to drop me as Mash pulled him down.

I backed away into the grass after that, while they went on slapping and wrestling each other. Mash, who was bigger than the rest of them, grabbed the two I didn't know and banged their heads together. Then Spew kicked out the back of Mash's legs and all three piled on him before Spew called a stop to it.

"That's enough," he said, releasing his headlock and pulling them off. "Stop it. Time to go. You start counting, kid."

So I began to count as I watched them go off around the curve of the embankment. They were moving differently now that they'd worked themselves up—rolling their shoulders like they were chimpanzees from one of the old nature films we saw at school.

By that time, I was so freaked out that I almost did turn and run. But I worried what they might do to me if they did that to each other, so I finished counting, picked up some stones from between the rails and ran down the slope, to the old river bed.

The Agent was squatting by his fire under the central span of the bridge as I came out through the haze. I saw him look up from his cooking and smile at me. His eyes were watery from the smoke and his teeth looked unnaturally white in contrast to his skin.

"How you doing, young fella?" he said, nodding.

I froze. This was the moment I was supposed to be throwing the rocks at him.

"You want a bit of possum?" he said. "It's just about ready." He held up a stick with a half-blackened carcass on it.

I leapt back like he'd pointed a weapon at me.

"Are you … are you the Agent?" I said.

"Yeah," he said. "But depends what you mean by the word."

I didn't exactly know what I meant.

"Have you got a gun or a knife?"

"Nah. But I gotta sword," he said, nodding over his shoulder to a pile of gear next to his sleeping roll.

Somewhere through the smoke, I could hear the sounds of Spew and the others crunching down the gravel slope. I had to attack. I tried hitting myself in the chest with my clenched fists.

The man looked puzzled for a second and then turned back to his possum. "You 'tryin' to make yourself go savage? You don't want to do that. I knew a fella once who …"

But even as he spoke there was a thudding of feet and a sudden roaring as the older boys charged into view, waving clubs made of tree branches.

I dropped my rocks and fled into the smoke. The sounds of those clubs striking the man would never leave my ears.

But then I came back. The big kids had gone by then—finished their work and taken whatever they wanted. As I crept between the pylons, the smoke from the scattered coals lay around like a heavy fog.

Whatever was left was ruined. The man's pack had been ripped open and his clothes spread over the fire. The cooked possum was a trampled mess covered with ash and sand.

There was a book too—a pale grey leather book with an embossed X on the cover. Someone had spread it out on a half-burned log and when I picked it up and turned it over, I could see that the pages were almost completely gone—just a few brown sheets still legible at the very back next to the cover.

"… hang on to that book, young fella," said a voice from the ground. "It'll tell you what you need to know."

I looked around. The Agent was lying behind me in a wreckage of blood, rags and dust. When I crouched down, I could hear the rattling in his lungs as he tried to breathe.

"I'm sorry," I said. "I'm sorry. They made me do it."

"It's alright," said the man. "… gonna be alright."

"What can I do?"

"Think my water bottle is behind me."

I found the flask and tried to hold it up to the man's mouth. Too much went in at once, and the man was wracked with a terrible bubbling cough that spattered blood on my hands.

"Just a bit in the cap," he said at last.

I tried again. The man swallowed and tried to smile. "… Reckon you're in it now … giving help to an Agent." He coughed again. "What's your name?"

"Chris," I said.

"Know how to read, Chris? … How about you read me something from my book? … They'll come for me soon … Like to hear something while I wait."

"It's all … it's … Something from the end?"

He nodded and coughed—and there was a different note to it now and listening to it made me feel sick and want to cry. I guess somehow even then I could recognise the sound of lungs filling up with blood.

But I took the book and peeled away the ash until I reached a page that I could read.

A Final Note to all Agents in the Field.

Dear Friends,

Many of you may be tempted to be discouraged. Your work will be difficult; you will sometimes feel that you are making no progress, and some of you will lose your lives in the process. Believe me, I know about these things!

But I want you to understand that it is worth it. It is worth it for those you rescue, for the new Territory that will come, for the honour and reputation of Central.

And it is worth it for yourselves. The City that you have not yet seen waits to embrace you as its sons and daughters. I look forward to welcoming each one of you beneath the trees of the Landing and leading you up from the river to present you to the Pantarch. I look forward to seeing you made healthy—with the last traces of the Tox eradicated from your bodies. I look forward to seeing you meet those you brought to Crux.

So don't be discouraged. Don't let anyone tell you that what you are doing is a waste of time. Don't hide what you were, or what you are now. And don't hide what's coming—both the good and the bad.

Stay strong! We will see each other soon.

I wanted to ask who wrote this letter but when I looked up, I could see that the Agent was completely still and that the eye that was still open had become fixed.

CHAPTER 12

Prediger gave me a room that opened onto the courtyard. It had a bed, a sink, a small table and a chair. When he left me, I went out and looked at the fountain and the tiny lights that had come on in the trees. There was a smell of flowers in the air and the sound of singing coming from some other part of the complex.

It would have been a good place to rest if there was any possibility of it. But I knew that there was no rest for me amongst these people. Even without a scan, they already knew what I'd done. So I waited until the place went quiet, and slipped out the way we had come in.

There was a bright half-moon and the air was clear enough up in the mountains for me see by it. Soon, as I followed the track back through the trees, I came across a smaller track branching away to the south-west, and took it.

I had no real plan, no food and no water. I suppose I must have thought of getting back to the pipeline or finding some town where I could live. But really, I wasn't thinking very clearly about anything. All I really had in my head was that Central was on to me and that I needed to escape.

But the stupidity of this *way* of escaping became clear to me pretty quickly. By the time I was halfway down the mountain, the single path I was on began branching this way and that, and signposts to "Didasko Summit"—which I had just come from—seemed to have been defaced or turned to indicate other paths.

Most of the time this didn't affect me—I was headed *down* the mountain, not up. But I could see what some of those detours would mean for Travellers headed in the other direction. One path led over a cliff. Another, which I didn't get too close to, seemed to have human bones scattered around it. Lower down, I had a distant view through the trees of Savages dancing wildly around a campfire—their whoops and screams fading into the night as I pressed on.

And then I had other things to worry about. As the gradient began to level off, the air got colder and darker. Before I knew it, I was in a fog.

Now, my only sense of direction came from guesses about the slope and the location of the moon. But as I went downhill, even that faded away until I was blundering about in near-total darkness.

And then the moaning began.

For a long time, the notes were so low and quiet that I couldn't tell whether they were really there or something my mind was making up. Even when I was sure that I wasn't imagining the sound, it was still something that I felt rather than heard. It made the air colder, the darkness even darker. It spread in from the edge of my mind like ink on wet paper. It made me think of the stories the merchants used to tell about hearing ghosts on Boneyard Road where Central destroyed our army.

The sound drowned out the hopeful thoughts of finding water and a place to stay, replacing them with visions of being caught and tortured by Savages or hunted by Central. It filled my brain with memories of every wrong and stupid thing I had ever done. I saw the faces of Flex, of my mum and, again and again, of the old Agent under the bridge.

As I went on, it got louder and I could sense that it was behind me. The way the sound came and went made me think of an animal moving its head this way and that, searching for something. When I turned and looked behind me, I could see a beam of sickly green light moving back and forth through the mist.

So I ran—blindly through the scrub. Before I'd gone twenty metres, I'd tripped over a bush. I got back up on my feet and immediately stumbled over a rock. As I used my arms to break my fall, there was an explosion of pain from my injured shoulder and I let out a groan.

Then the beam seemed to lock in on my position and I could sense it closing on me. Pretty soon, I could hear the hiss and crunch of machinery alongside the moaning.

I picked myself up and ran on, and for a moment, things got better. I found myself on a stretch of firm, sandy ground. If it went on like this, I thought, I might have a chance.

And then my foot went through the surface.

It was the same as when I had been with Flex; sticky mud under a smooth crust. When I wrenched my foot free, my boot stayed where it was.

I knew I was done for now. The light was too close. The sound was almost unbearable.

Suddenly I wondered whether there might be a drone up above watching me. They had seen everything else, were they seeing this too? Was there a cold glass eye recording my end just like it had recorded my uncle's? Would my final moments be stored away in some archive in Central, or shown to the next visitor to Didasko as a cautionary tale?

But then I remembered the voice in the hut. "You asked for help, and I am giving it," the man had said. And for the first time, I realised what he had been talking about.

"SOS," I said. "SOS!" I shouted it into the fog. Then I tripped and went down once again.

This time, I fell into a patch of spiked grass. I had prickles stabbing into my hands, face and neck. I could feel other clumps on either side of my body. For a moment, I was stuck—wedged in.

I began to try to wriggle free. But the thing that was chasing me was right on me now. I could feel the impact of its feet through the ground; a huge jointed metal leg slammed down into the sedges a few feet from my head.

As the thing bent over me, the noise became unbearable—soul -crushing. I began to imagine I could hear words hidden underneath the pulse: shouted words full of rage and contempt and utter hatred; words that said I was less than nothing, and which stirred up the same feelings in me. I tried to raise my arms to cover my ears but I was paralysed. I could sense the thing right over me like a spider squatting over its prey. Something hard scraped along my back.

And stopped. The sound shut off, leaving my ears hissing in the sudden silence. But as they recovered, I could hear that it wasn't totally quiet. There was another sound coming from the distance. It was singing; a woman's voice—crackly as if it was coming through a crude amplifier. I could hear words about a light coming and darkness fleeing; about the sun coming from the east and setting in the west to come again to bring a dawn that would never end.

The monster answered the song with a roar—a sound that was even louder than that which it had been generating before. But it wasn't directed at me now, and it had a different feel to it. It almost sounded afraid. It began backing away.

Suddenly, I could move again. As the creature retreated, I felt the paralysis and despair lifting off me. I struggled to my knees and saw two white headlights pointed back through the fog at me. And silhouetted against their haze, walking forward with a megaphone in one hand and a sword in the other was Eve.

I don't want to say anything against Eve, but she wasn't a good singer. Her voice was husky, and she couldn't really hold a tune. But as she came on, the monster kept moving backwards. For a moment, it acted like a dog sizing up a bigger threat. It crouched and crabbed sideways; roared again. And then it gave a final moan and just galloped away into the mist.

Eve met me half way and transferred her sword to the hand carrying the megaphone.

"Come on," she said, putting an arm around me. "Let's get you to the V."

"Thank you," I said. "But … I can't go with you."

"Why not?"

"I just can't."

"What are you talking about?"

"When I was looking at the monitors, Prax showed me something—something bad I did. If I …"

She looked back in the direction that the monster had fled.

"For goodness sake, Chris. Just get in the V. We can talk about it in there."

I let her bundle me into the passenger's seat and slam the door after me.

"Now. Tell me," she said as she took her own seat.

"Okay … when I was a little kid, there was another Agent who came to Spillan. He was living under a bridge outside town. And I helped some wild kids murder him because I wanted them to like me."

"And that's what Prax showed you on the monitors?"

"Yeah."

"And you think, what, that it was meant to warn you off or something?"

"Yes."

"Did he say that?"

"No. But why else would he show me?"

"Okay, look. This is pretty standard for Prax. If he knows you're trying to hide something, he'll call you on it. But it isn't to get rid of you. It's to give you a chance to come clean. It's to let you know that he already knows the worst about you."

I looked away and caught sight of my reflection in the window. I looked wrecked.

"Chris, Crux is set up for people with the Tox: the bad and mad. That's what it's there for. If you swear allegiance and submit to treatment, they'll pardon you, no matter what you've done. That's how it works. The moment that Vector enters your bloodstream, you are a citizen of Central. The Envoy will vouch for you and the Pantarch will look on you as one of his own."

I closed my eyes and tried to take it in; tried to believe it.

"But what about that scan they do? Where they go through your memories?"

"They do a scan, but it's not to find out your secrets—they already know all those. It's to check if you've had the cure and if it has made any difference to you."

She started the engine and turned back to me. "Look, I'm gonna get us out of here. Why don't you think about it while we drive toward Crux? If you decide you don't want to get treated by the time we get there, nobody is going to force you. Okay?"

"Okay," I said.

I felt like I'd been through a fight. Everything hurt and my mind was still really hazy. But the idea of a pardon—of Central already knowing the worst about me—was beginning to get through to me. I still didn't know how to hold it all together—I didn't know how to square it with the stuff I had read in the Roadbook about the Pantarch killing people. But I could see that if Central had wanted to get me they could have killed me any time. Instead, Eve had come looking for me and rescued me—twice now. Prediger had fed and treated me. And that guy had come and saved me at Horeb.

It felt like when I'd rubbed the spit into my eyes and begun to see again. Everything was blurry, but there was just a little patch where it was clear. Now, right in the middle of everything, I could see the outline of something that looked like hope.

I watched as the bushes and rocks went past in the headlights. Eve was driving on the hard edge of the bog, following it around a curve.

"What was that thing?" I said to her, "… that machine back there?"

"It was a Desolator. The Corp built them before the war for psychological warfare, but most of them just wander around on their own now."

"Why did it run away from you like that?"

"They don't like singing—especially songs like that. There are others, Hunters, that aren't so easy to scare off. How's that shoulder?

"Pretty bad. I fell on it when I was running away—think I might have pulled off the dressing."

"Yeah, you probably did. Well hang on. We're just coming up to a place we can cross the river and then it's only a couple of hours to Crux."

She eased the car slowly down the bank and gradually accelerated across the cracked mud. I listened to the sound of the tyres squelching and tried not to imagine what would happen if they got bogged.

"This is just like the place I got stuck in when I first left Spillan."

"Not like, same. Same river—the Law. It flows out of Lake Central, but this is all that's left of it by the time it gets here—just a few boggy stretches.

"How did you know to look for me here?"

She laughed. "Trust me, you're not the first one to do a runner after a session with Prax. And there aren't that many places you can go from Didasko if you aren't going on to Crux. I figured you'd either take the track to Delice or end up back in the bog."

"Sorry you have to keep saving me."

"You don't need to apologise. You were running for the right reasons— shows you get it."

"Will they really let me ..."

"If you're ready to swear the oath, Central will give you the cure, wipe your slate and grant you citizenship. That's the deal the Envoy worked out with the Pantarch."

*   *   *

We reached Crux as dawn came up.

The base was nestled in a valley pass where Wicket Gap opened out to the low hills: just a cluster of tents in the centre of an old town. I wondered how it defended itself. Where were its walls and guard towers? Where were its guns?

But the place obviously *was* defended. As we got nearer, we passed the debris of attacks: overturned pickups, burned-out ram-rigs, blackened helmets and body armour. Something had destroyed them. Eve shrugged when I asked her about it.

"Something always just happens to them. They fight each other or get distracted. Maybe a weapon will explode. I guess maybe the skyships get them sometimes."

The track brought us into a dusty parade ground ringed with tents, trucks and stacks of supplies. As Eve parked the car, people converged on us from all sides: soldiers in battle fatigues and orderlies in medical smocks. Some attended Eve, others clustered around me as I tried to climb out of the vehicle. My head swivelled back and forward as I took in their smiles and supporting arms. One nurse, who introduced himself as Bield, shone a light into my eyes and asked me a string of questions: "Can you show me where you were hit. Can you feel that? How many fingers am I holding up? That's great; do you feel okay to walk with us to the clinic or do you need us to carry you?"

When I had managed to convince him that I could walk, Bield and another orderly by the name of Venn got on either side of me and guided me through the camp, pointing out things as we went.

"That's the mess where we all eat together … That's the old library; we've got our communication stuff set up in there … Those guys doing the sword drills over there are the latest batch of recruits—they're about to head out on mission."

The clinic had been set up in what had once been the town courthouse—its original purpose still visible in the shield with its lions above the door and a statue of Justice with her sword and scales in the foyer. Even the judge's bench was still there up the front.

But the rest of the furniture had been replaced with stretchers and trolleys stacked with medical equipment. Down the front, facing away from the bench, there was a plain wooden armchair. Eve was standing next to it talking to a small woman with brown skin and a white doctor's gown.

"Come and sit down on the end of this stretcher, Chris," the woman said. "I am Doctor Esme Klesia. We will have a look at your wound, and then we will explain the treatment and terms that the Pantarch has set out for us here in the Territory."

Bield brought me forward and carefully eased off the shirt that Prediger had given me—now muddy and torn from my adventure in the swamp. Venn switched on a bright inspection light, and Doctor Klesia peeled back what was left of the dressing.

"I'm sorry about the discomfort, Chris," she said as I flinched with the pain. "Your back is quite inflamed by the toxin on that pellet lodged in your shoulder. It looks like it has been pushed a little closer to the surface, but it will still make you very sick if it stays in there.

"So we have a choice. We can either give you the cure—which will counteract the poison—and then dig the pellet out later. Or, I can try to treat the wound first and talk about the cure afterwards.

"Personally, I think the second option would be best because it will mean that you will find it easier to concentrate when we go over the terms. But what would you prefer?

"I think getting it out first sounds good to me too."

"Very good. Alright, why don't you lean forward a little more and we will begin."

I did as she ordered, reassured by feeling her cool hand on my skin as she explored the wound. I might have even found that part soothing, except for the things that she said to me while she was doing it.

"Eve tells me that you ran away from the base last night," she said. "This is quite a common reaction among people who have spent a bit of time with Prax up at Didasko. Was it something he showed you?"

I felt my face flush. "... Um ... I guess so ... Did you want me to say what..."

"No, that's between you and the Pantarch. I really just want to know what changed your mind after that."

"Well, Eve told me that Central would give me a pardon."

"Yes, good." She went back to probing my shoulder blade.

"… And I thought maybe … because it was the Tox that made me do the thing that Prax showed me."

I winced as a sudden pain flared in my back.

"I see. You don't think Tox-affected people are responsible for their actions?"

"… No … Yes … I mean less responsible."

She stepped back and waited for me to raise my head.

"But less responsible is still responsible, isn't it? Tox alters the parts of your nervous system that you allow it to influence and that makes it harder to resist. But we still make choices."

I felt a chill go through my exposed skin. "So are you saying …"

"I am just saying the first part of your answer was right and you should forget about the second. Don't make excuses. Just accept the pardon."

She turned back to my shoulder. I felt a sharp tug and, out of the corner of my eye, saw her holding something up to the inspection light.

"Alright, Chris," she said. "Here it is. I think we have gotten it all but time will tell. As soon as we have finished taping you up we can move on to the treatment if you are ready for it."

And I suddenly found that I *was* ready.

CHAPTER 13

Doctor Klesia picked up a sheaf of papers and waited while the orderlies wrapped me in a gown and led me to the chair at the front of the building. Eve, standing off to one side, gave me a nod as I caught her eye.

"Alright Chris," said the doctor. "I am now going to explain the terms under which the Pantarch, acting through Envoy Shepherd, is prepared to offer you amnesty, full citizenship and treatment for the genetic condition known as the Tox.

"As we go along, I will need to ask you some questions to make it clear that you understand the situation and the offer. None of these preliminary questions commit you to accepting the offer until we reach the end, when I will invite you to make a formal response. Do you understand?"

"Yes."

"Then can I confirm that you are Chris Walker, and that you, until recently, have been a resident of the town of Spillan, situated in the region of resistance to the government of Central—that is, the area commonly known as the Autonomous Zone, or AZ?"

"Yes."

"And do you understand that the Pantarch, as ruler of the Central government, has decreed sanctions against all powers, authorities, institutions, and also individuals, who resist his rightful authority?

"What are sanctions?"

"Judgments or penalties."

"Okay. Yes, then."

"Do you understand that these sanctions apply to you personally, as a citizen of Spillan? And do you acknowledge that you yourself have, until recently, failed to respond to the claims of the Central government?"

"Yes."

"Good. In that case, let me explain the offer:

"Acting in his capacity as the official representative of this region, Envoy Tobias Shepherd has negotiated the following arrangement with the Pantarch:

1. *That he will provide surety and take responsibility for every person within the Autonomous Zone who will yield to his authority and pledge to live henceforth as a loyal and obedient subject of the Central government.*

2. *That those who place themselves under his protection will receive a full pardon for all lawless acts committed within the Autonomous Zone.*

3. *That those who accept the authority and representation of Envoy Shepherd shall be given the full rights of citizens of Central.*

"Do you understand this offer?"

"I think so. What's surety?"

"That's when someone agrees to pay a debt or a penalty on your behalf."

"Okay."

The doctor went on. "To receive this offer, persons within the Autonomous Zone must:

1. *As already mentioned, accept the authority of Envoy Shepherd and pledge themselves to live henceforth as loyal and obedient subjects of the Central government.*

2. *Submit to treatment with blood product supplied by Envoy Shepherd for the Tox.*

3. *Agree to facilitate their ongoing transgenesis by means of various disciplines and tasks assigned by Central Command.*

"Do you understand and agree to these requirements?"

"I don't know what it meant about that ... transgenesis."

"Alright. The Tox comes from damage to your genetic code. Your DNA has been altered and that's why your body now produces poisonous cysts. The treatment we provide here introduces an RNA vector taken from the Envoy's blood which can reverse that damage. That means that, from the moment you receive the treatment, you will become a chimera—a creature of two parts with two different sets of DNA fighting inside you. You will still have the damaged code infected with the Tox, but you will also have the code that has been repaired with the X-Vector from the Envoy.

"Which of those becomes dominant is partly to do with how you act. The tasks that are assigned to you will maximise the influence of the X-Vector and progressively defeat the Tox genes."

"And everybody here has that ... chimera thing?" I said.

"That is correct," said the doctor.

"What does it feel like, when you get it?"

"There are a wide range of experiences. Some people have a strong response initially. Some don't. Many patients describe a sort of peripheral awareness of being connected to Central, which becomes more intense in moments of crisis.

"There can be negative phases too. The more the change progresses, the more you will become aware of the residual effects of the Tox, which can be distressing."

"What does that mean?"

"It means the more the cure works on you, the more you will be aware that you are still sick.

"But the first thing you are likely to experience is relief with regard to your cysts. As soon as the Vector hits your bloodstream, it will give you immunity from the toxin contained in those cysts."

She put the documents back on the bench.

"Do you have any other questions? Do you need a few minutes to think about it?"

I shook my head. "No, I'm ready."

"Good! Then stand up. Place your hand on your heart and repeat the oath of allegiance that I will read out."

Again, I did as I was told; stood, listened and spoke:

I, Christian Walker, formerly of Spillan, do renounce all rebellion and acknowledge the Pantarch as my rightful ruler.

I do accept the pardon offered to me through the representation of Envoy Shepherd and henceforth pledge to obey him in all things.

I yield myself for treatment of the Tox and will undertake to assist the ongoing progress of that treatment through my own actions.

From this hour, over and above all previous allegiances, I shall call myself a citizen of Central and will undertake to fulfil the duties that accompany that citizenship."

"Very good," said the doctor when we were done. "Now sit back down and I will provide you with the treatment."

As I took my seat, I became aware of a hum in the background. When I squinted up toward the ceiling in the direction that it seemed to be coming from, I noticed a faint ripple or shimmer in the air.

"What's that?" I said.

"Probably a drone," said the doctor without looking up. "They like to broadcast it in the Capital whenever anyone takes the oath and gets treatment. They say everyone stops to watch."

The thought made me feel weird. I wondered whether I was supposed to wave or say something. But the doctor had just finished locking a vial into some kind of jet injector and was already tilting my head back to stretch out the side of my neck.

"Chris, by the authority invested in me by the Pantarch and in the name of Envoy Shepherd, I am now administering you with blood product for the treatment of the Tox. From the moment you receive it, your infection will be converted from a fatal disease into a chronic condition. You will also, from this moment, be pardoned and considered a full citizen of Central with all the attendant rights and responsibilities."

She placed the cold metal against my neck. There was a click and a hiss and I felt a slight sting as the air-jet fired micro-droplets of X-Vector through my skin into my carotid. For a moment, nothing changed. And then ... and then suddenly, it felt as if cool water was flowing over my scalp and face, washing back past my ears and down along my body.

I looked around and saw Eve and the orderlies smiling. Then the doctor set the injector back on its tray and took me by complete surprise by grabbing my face and kissing me on both cheeks.

"Welcome, Citizen Walker," she said. "You are one of us now and have the Envoy's blood in your veins."

Archivist's note: This telling is a crosschecked collation of written notes from Citizen Walker with excerpted records of other citizens. In this volume, we have taken the unusual step of including extended sections from the record of Citizen Caleb Dox because of the relevance of his story to this account—and in view of the significance of their parallel discoveries concerning Nimcorp activity in the region of Addle.

VOLUME 2

"We don't understand" they said to him. "Can't the Pantarch just airlift us out? Why do you want us to walk?" "Because there are people between here and Central who need to be told about the cure," he answered. "And because the cure takes time to work. The miles between here and Sanctuary will cost you blood but they will change you. You'll become stronger. And in the end you will come to the City with stories to tell, and its people will welcome you as heroes."

Roadbook; *Chapter 45, "The Blood Miles"*

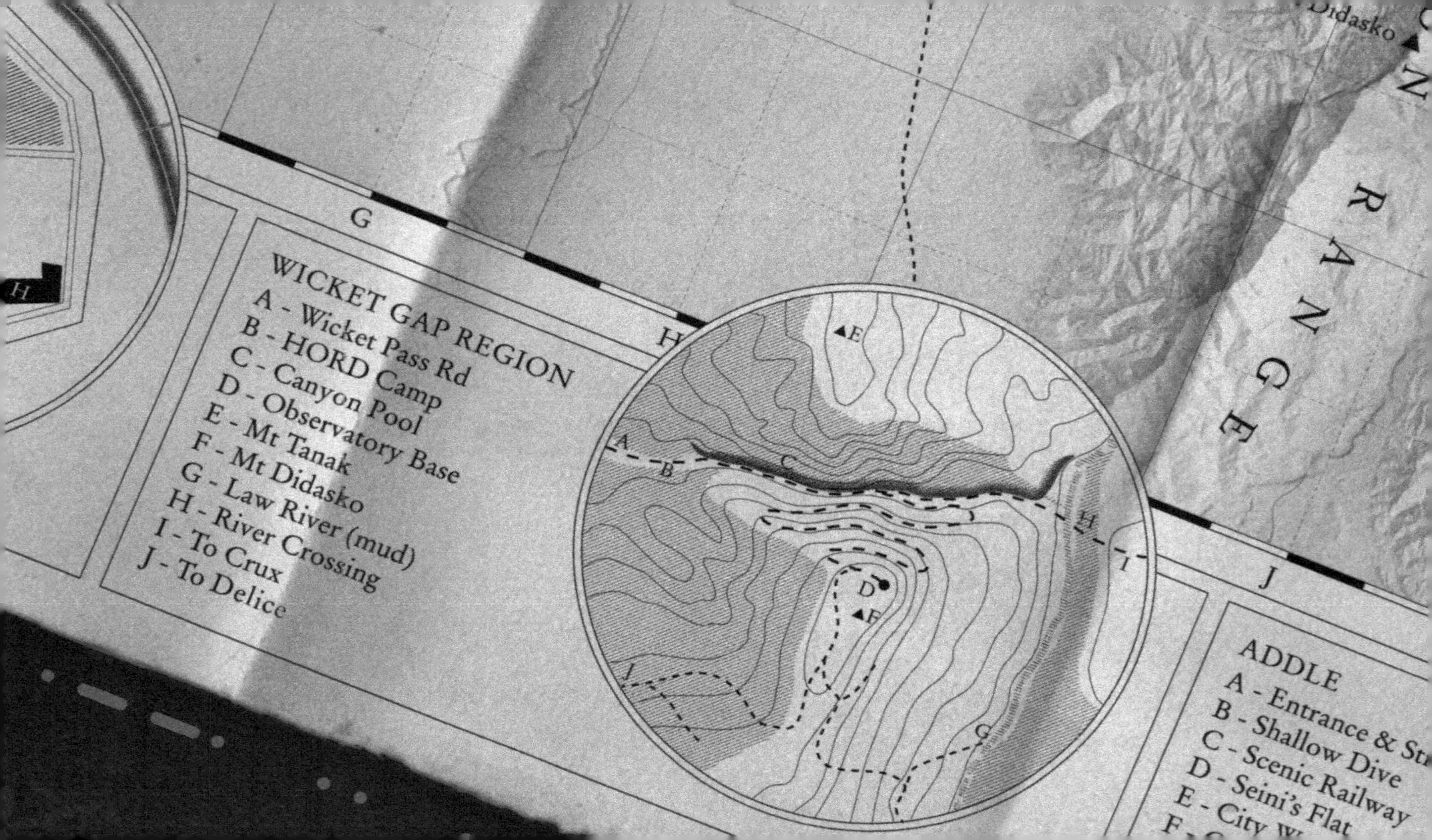
Didasko
N RANGE
G
H
H
I
J
WICKET GAP REGION
A - Wicket Pass Rd
B - HORD Camp
C - Canyon Pool
D - Observatory Base
E - Mt Tanak
F - Mt Didasko
G - Law River (mud)
H - River Crossing
I - To Crux
J - To Delice
E
A
B
C
D
F
G
I
ADDLE
A - Entrance & St
B - Shallow Dive
C - Scenic Railway
D - Seini's Flat
E - City W
F -

CHAPTER 14

(Extract of the Journals of Agent Evangeline Veracis, Vol 3.4)

Chris stayed with us at Crux for around two weeks before moving on. I urged him to hang around longer and Esme also tried very hard to persuade him to stay—at least wait until we could find a few others for him to travel with—but neither of us made much headway.

He was too eager to get going. After finally absorbing the idea that he had been pardoned and made a full citizen, he was just really keen to get on and do something useful. He wanted to put his new skills into practice. We tried to put the brakes on him, tried to warn him that he was asking for trouble by going out on his own. But he insisted that the Envoy would look after him just as he had before; or he'd find some other Travellers on the road.

Our warnings came true, of course—though it wasn't until later that I found out the extent of it. In the meantime, I had other things to think about. I'd been given orders of my own to head back west, and I had a sneaking suspicion it was going to be my last assignment.

And of course, I was right about that too.

CHAPTER 15

It would be nice to be able to say that everything was fine after that; that I got the cure and became a faithful Traveller who walked bravely to Central while doing some good along the way. I pretty much thought that was how it was going to be when I went out.

I guess my story would have been a lot less interesting if it had gone like that. But there were times along the way when I might have wished for a more boring journey.

They kept me at Crux for 14 days, feeding me up and giving me a whole lot of training and instruction. It was pretty intense, but I loved it—even the school stuff.

They told me more about the history of the war and the cure. I learned how the Central underground had spread after the Envoy's mission; how his people had kept being decimated in some places and then suddenly popping up in others—often led by people who seemed really hopeless or a bit crazy.

They explained a whole lot about the Envoy too: how his body had been changed when they rebuilt him so that he was continually connected to Prax; how he worked behind the scenes to direct operations and acted as the Pantarch's mouth and hands for struggling Travellers and failing resistance cells.

The other big thing was learning to use the gear they'd given me. One of the instructors showed me how my coat could deflect blades and projectiles and how I could maximise its protection by learning to crouch down into it. Another taught me how to use the traction grips in my boots to lock my stance.

But the stuff I liked best was the sword training. At first, I was skeptical about it.

"I'm pretty good with a rifle," I said when the weapons master had handed me my *machaira*, "Why don't they just give us guns?"

"Why?" he said, glaring at me and smoothing down his moustache. "Why? First of all, because the Envoy says so, and that should be enough for you. But if you want to know more, it's because there are things out there that can't be shot, and also because the Envoy wants to sharpen you up. Gun's just a weapon. You get to know *this*, and it'll make *you* a weapon. It'll be part of your transgenesis."

And within a few days, I could see what he meant. As I did the drills with the sword, it was like I could really feel the cure changing me— making me stronger and faster; making my senses and reflexes sharper. I imagined going back to Spillan in my new Traveller's coat and my Central-issue combat boots with my sword strapped to my back. There would be no way they would be able to deny that I was healthy. They'd have to listen to me, and I would tell them that the cyst law was wrong, that the Mayor had been exiling and killing people for nothing.

But my orders, when they came through, were to head east for Perseverance.

"It's the standard route," said Eve when she heard. "Perseverance is a sort of proving-leg. They might send you somewhere different after that. Or they might pick you up before you get there and take you to Central. All you can do is trust that they know what they're doing."

I was disappointed—but only a bit. If the Envoy wanted me to go to Perseverance, then he was the boss. I just thought I'd go as quickly as possible, and then maybe I'd get other orders.

They tried to get me to stay. The doctor kept telling me I needed to wait until I could go with a group. Eve said I was acting like a fool and was going to get picked off if I wasn't careful.

But I felt so different. So *strong*.

"I can go faster if I go alone, I said. I'll try to catch up with a group ahead."

Which is how I ended up scrounging for firewood by myself in a forest west of Ovine eight days later.

It was just after I'd finished my training for the evening. I had laid down my sword and left my gear to look for some kindling when I heard something.

It was a kind of pulse in the air, a sound like distant music coming from somewhere beyond the trees. As I edged through the forest, it died away and then came back with the breeze. Other noises came from near by. I heard a horse snorting, a thud of wood on wood, women's voices.

"… No, no, they're both sheared right off, Leah. Rusted through."

"Well, can you take one from the other shaft or something?"

The first voice sounded muffled; the second older.

"I'll have a look, but I don't think I'll be able to get the nuts off."

"Didn't you bring any tools?"

"Well, I didn't expect to be doing wagon repairs, Lea. Besides, it's not just a matter of tools. I would have had to bring spare bolts."

I worked my way between the tree trunks until I could see them. They were at the back edge of the forest, where the treeline gave way to a plain of yellow grass. The older of the two, dressed in a skirt and shawl, was standing by the head of a harnessed draft horse. The owner of the younger voice was somewhere underneath the tray of the wagon. "Yeah … the other bolts are all rusted in, Lea. I think we'll need to walk the rest of the way."

"Alright," said the woman holding the horse. "Why don't you get Cam out and I'll unhitch Jasper. We can tether him up on the concrete near the entrance. We'll be late, but you might still get a spot if there aren't too many people."

The young woman who had been under the wagon said something I couldn't hear as she came into view. She was dressed in work pants and a tartan jacket. As she turned, I caught sight of a tanned face framed by coppery hair tied back in a loose plait. She reached into the wagon, lifted out a folded wheelchair, and bent to assemble it out of sight.

I thought for a second and stepped out of the shadows.

"Excuse me, ladies," I said. "If you need something to help fix that shaft to your wagon, I might be able to help you."

My appearance electrified them. Leah, the older woman, flinched and then straightened, turning to face me with a defiant expression. Her sister—the likeness in their faces made that clear—straightened up, holding a revolver, which she proceeded to cock and point in my direction. As I raised my hands, a third head appeared above the tray—it belonged to a small boy of about ten.

"Lie down, Cam," said the woman with the coppery hair. "Who the hell are you?"

"My name's Chris," I said. "I was looking for firewood and I heard your voices. I reckon I know how you can fix that shaft."

"We'll be fine, thank you," said Leah. "We don't have far to walk, and we will be able to fix it tomorrow. Thank you for your offer, but we'd prefer to get on by ourselves."

"I understand," I said. "And I'm sorry to jump out at you. But it's really simple, and I don't need to come any closer than I am now."

"What's your idea?" said the woman with the revolver, blowing a loose strand of hair away from her face.

"There's an old fence a hundred metres back—mostly burned, but some of the wire is still there. You could loop it through your bolt holes and twist it tight."

"Yes, I don't think we're inclined to follow you into those trees," said Leah.

"You wouldn't need to. I could go and get it for you in a couple of minutes."

"And get your friends. No thanks. You can stay where Mallory can shoot you."

"It's just me. I'm just by myself."

Mallory looked at me steadily over her handgun and spoke to her sister.

"Come on, Lea. Look at his coat. He's a hope-fool."

"All the more reason why he'd have friends with him. Hope-fools travel in groups—it's part of their code."

"It's just me," I said again. "We're usually meant to travel in groups, but I haven't caught up with any others yet."

"I'll go with him," said the girl with the revolver. "And if he tries anything, or if anyone else shows up, I'll just shoot him."

Leah began to say something, but her sister was already making her way around the wagon toward me.

"Start walking, boy," she said. "I'm gonna stay three metres back, and if I think you're about to try something—if you try to get closer, or you try to run off, or if you put your hands down—I'm just going to shoot you, okay?"

"Okay," I said. I turned and began retracing my steps through the forest, wondering what it would take for her to think I was *about* to try something.

"What did you mean by calling me a hope-fool?" I said.

"Just keep your head to the front," she said. "That's what the men from Central call you. Hope-fool travellers because you hope you'll get to Central one day. And fools because you think Central wants you to get there on foot."

"What … What men from Central?"

"They come through every couple of months. Give out food. Take a few people to Central. Did you hear the music back there? That was them—they set up at the old plant."

"Men from Central?"

"That's what I said. Hey, don't keep turning your head like that—I *will* shoot you."

"But … we only travel like this because Central says we have to. Why would they call us fools?"

"You can ask them yourself if you help us with the cart … Is that wire of yours somewhere round?"

"Yes. Just over here, look. If you let me put my hands down, I'll get some for you."

I crouched down by the fallen fence posts and began to disentangle one of the strands. When I had freed a little over a metre, I turned and stretched it out to show her.

"What do you reckon? Enough?"

She nodded, and I began to bend it back and forth, taking advantage of the opportunity to take a proper look at her. She'd called me a boy, but she didn't look like she was any older than me. She had dirty smudges on her fingers and cheeks and eyes that stared straight into mine without blinking.

I looked down at my hands. "Sorry, this is going to take longer than I expected. I didn't realise it was tensile."

"Here. Don't bust your fingers." She reached into the pocket of her jacket and tossed me a pair of pliers.

I snipped the wire using both hands and we began to make our way back. I noticed that there was no talk of me having to keep my hands up or eyes front now.

"I like your horse," I said. "How do you get enough grass for him?"

"Are you from out west?" she said.

"Yeah, from Spillan."

"We still get a bit of rain this side of the mountains. And Ovine's got a little aquifer under it. We pump it up and grow wheat, peas, stuff like that. Animals get the straw."

"Just like in the old days," I said.

"I guess so."

We came out from the trees and Mallory passed the revolver to her elder sister while she and I set to work on the cart—me holding up the shaft while she poked the two ends of the wire down through the adjacent holes so that the beam was tied up to the floor of the tray. When she'd cinched it as tight as she could from below, she twisted the ends together and trimmed off the excess.

"That'll do it," she said, wobbling the shaft. "It's loose as a goose. But it'll take the pull."

"Thank you," said Leah, looking over at me. "We don't have anything to offer you but…"

"He's coming with us," said Mallory. She paused to collapse and stow the wheelchair before taking the gun back from her sister. "Climb up next to Cam," she said to me. "… It's alright, Leah, I can still shoot him if I have to."

I hesitated, looking between the frown of the older sister and the steady face of the younger.

"How far is it?" I said. "My gear is all back at my camp."

"Just a few miles," said Mallory.

Leah stared at me a moment more before shaking her head and climbing up onto the driver's bench. "Okay. Your responsibility, Mal. But you better be ready to do it if you need to."

I settled myself in the corner diagonally opposite Mallory. Between us, the small boy looked at me interestedly as the cart bounced into motion.

"Is it true those coats can stop bullets?" he said.

"That's what they say. I haven't tested it yet, though."

"And have you got a sword?"

"I do … But I left it at my camp." I looked at Mallory. "It sounds like you've seen other Travellers before me."

"Our grandpa was a Traveller. Still got his book at home somewhere. But not much apart from that. We had one come through Ovine last year—said he was on his way to Perseverance, but he ended up going with the Central guys."

"I'm supposed to be headed to Perseverance," I said.

"Well, maybe this is a quicker way."

"You can come with Mal and me," said the boy.

"We're hoping they'll take Cam with them tonight—me too if there's room—so he can get some treatment."

"I've got cysts on my spine," said the boy. "But I don't want to go if it's just me."

"We'll see what they say, like we talked about," she said. "If they'll take both of us, we'll both go. But if they want more money …"

I wanted to ask about that, but the music had suddenly started again—much closer and clearer this time—some kind of fanfare with trumpets sounding over an orchestra.

"That's them getting started," said Mallory. "Have a look up ahead and you'll be able to see the plant."

I tilted my head to peer around Leah's skirt and then looked back to her sister.

"It's a city!"

She laughed at my expression. "Look again."

I squinted at the cluster of slender towers and the pin-prick lights that stood up against the orange sky. It *was* a city. Yet … the scale was wrong. I knew skyscrapers were meant to be much bigger than this. And, now that I looked a bit more carefully, I could see pipes and open frameworks running up and down the outside of these towers.

"It's an old refinery," said Mallory. "They power up the lights with a generator or something."

Leah turned the cart onto a side track that curved around the plant. We passed the shell of an overturned tanker, a half-collapsed Cyclone wire fence and the remnants of a gatehouse bearing the still-legible sign that read "Fata-Morgana Chemicals Ltd."

Beyond the fence and across the cracked concrete that surrounded the plant, a small collection of tents, trucks, wagons and motorcycles spread out beneath the yellow floodlights. Between the vehicles and the entrance to the plant, I could see three men talking animatedly to a woman dressed in a reflective firefighter's suit.

But the men had coats like mine, and two-handed swords like mine slung across their backs. As Leah swung the cart around to join the other vehicles, one of them, a big man with olive skin and a complicated tattoo on his neck, raised his head and nodded to me as we went past.

"Looks like some of your people," said Mallory.

"Yeah, it does," I said. "I might say hello to them. Do you need a hand before I go?"

She shook her head. "We'll be okay now. Thanks for helping with the cart."

"That's okay. Thanks for the lift—and for not shooting me."

"Any time," she said, giving what might have been a wink.

I left them to their tasks and made my way over to the Travellers. The music had quieted down now—still there, but just tones that blurred into each other in the background. I could hear a woman's voice saying, "honoured to have them with us," a sound of cheering and then someone else with a gravelly bass. But now I was getting close to the Travellers and I was more interested in what they were saying.

They were arguing. The oldest of them, a weather-beaten man with bushy eyebrows and bony hands, was holding up his *machaira* by the blade and jabbing the handle in the direction of the woman in the silver overalls.

"If yer truly from the place ye say ye are, then ye should have no objection to our Central-issued weaponry. In fact, it greatly puzzles me that ye bare no such blades of yer own."

The woman tilted her head and cradled the rifle slung around her neck.

"I'm not going to argue with you. The rules are clear. No weapons. If you want to go in, you'll have to leave them with me."

The third member of the group—another young man with freckles and a sandy-coloured beard drew his own sword and held it up.

"How about we just go in and see if you stop us?"

She responded by clicking off the safety catch of her rifle and swinging it around to point at his belly.

"What do you think will happen if you try that?" she said.

"Maybe one of us will get the chop," he said.

The woman rolled her eyes and turned away to intercept Leah as she approached the entrance. In the background, I saw Mallory pushing Cam around the far side of the building.

When I turned back, the three other Travellers were looking at me.

"Who is this apparition?" said the old man. "Is this some associate of yours, Caleb?"

The big man shook his head and stuck out his hand.

"No, I don't know him. But I'm Caleb. This is Fergus and Dil. Are you here to check out this Central show too?"

"I guess I am," I said. "I only just heard about it. Do you reckon it's real? The women who brought me here were talking about having to pay to get taken to Central."

The bloke with the beard, whose name was Dil, laughed at me. "Then that should have been proof enough for you if you'd done any reading. The agreement between the Envoy and the Pantarch is a completed transaction."

"We're here to check it out," said Caleb. "But we all reckon it looks pretty sus. That lady was saying they wouldn't let us in with our swords."

"Shouldn't be a problem for this guy," said Dil.

"Aye," said Fergus, looking at me from under his brow. "Where's yer gear? Where's yer *machaira?*"

"I left it back at my camp. I was looking for firewood when I ..."

Fergus cut me short with an upraised hand.

"If ye have abandoned yer kit, then ye are a fool and will be of no help in this enterprise. "Now," he said, turning his attention to the other two,

"Clearly, we must pursue other routes of ingress if we are to spy out the land. I propose that you, Caleb, set yerself to find a way ..."

As he spoke, the big man glanced at me with a worried expression. He looked like he was about to say something, but I didn't stay to hear it. If they didn't want me, I didn't want them either.

I don't want anyone who reads this to think I was simply a victim here. Maybe Fergus and Dil were too quick to dismiss me—and I guess there was a bit of sting in their response—but I *had* left my gear. And judging them for judging me was convenient, too. It made it easier for me to justify travelling alone.

So I left them and wandered away down the side of the plant in the direction I had seen Mallory and Cam disappearing. They came into view on the far side, waiting beside a pair of hulking all-terrain vehicles that were reverse-parked on the concrete. Both machines had a strange symbol that looked like a tapering spiral staircase on their rear doors.

"Have you been rejected too?" I said.

Mallory turned and smiled. "No, this is where you go to queue for the transport. We're trying to get ahead of the crowd. Why, didn't your friends want you?"

"Pretty much," I said. "Hey, are you sure these guys are really from Central? How do you know they aren't going to ..." But then I looked down at the tense expression on Cam's face. "... How do you know they're going to take you where they say?"

"Because," she said. "Every time they come, they start by showing clips of the people they took away last time. And you can see where they are: they're in restaurants or at the beach. Last year, they took my best friend, Cully, and when they came back, they showed her on this really big sailing boat—it looked like something from the old days—and she was saying how they just look after you, and there's all the food you want."

"But what about them asking you to pay? Why would they do that?"

"They say that's so we'll take it seriously. It's not because they need it but because you only value what you have to pay for."

As she finished speaking, there was a sudden change in the music. The smooth drone became a thumping beat and there was a man speaking words that I couldn't make out.

I looked back at Mallory.

"I think I'm still suspicious."

"You should go in and listen to what they say."

"Okay, I will," I said. "I hope you get where you need to go."

She gave me another smile. "You too."

CHAPTER 16

There were no signs of the other Travellers by the time I got back to the front of the factory. I raised my arms so the woman in the silver suit could pat me down and then made my way past the derelict offices toward the light and sound.

The action was happening in a courtyard in the centre of the complex, where a crowd of about two hundred townsfolk crowded together beneath orange floodlights. Beyond them, standing on a loading dock stacked with loudspeakers, another of the Centralists was holding forth, the top half of his reflective suit rolled down to reveal a clean white t-shirt and a pair of well-muscled arms. A respirator covering his nose and mouth made his voice sound far away and echoey.

"Some of you have heard that Central wants to control you," he said. "Some of you have heard that Central wants to make you into slaves and take away your freedom; that the Pantarch is just looking for a chance to kill everyone.

"Some of you have heard other stories: that the Pantarch wants you to suffer; he wants you to march for miles and eat dry food and get sore feet; he wants to send you through Savage territory; he wants some of you to die!

"My friends, if that's what you've heard, then someone has been telling you lies. Central wants to help you, not punish you! We have food for everyone who wants it. We have transport to take some of you with us. And, if that's not enough, soon you will get a vision of Central. Soon, your eyes will be opened. You will feel the sun on your face. You will breathe deep and you will smell the sweet air of Central.

He gestured across the courtyard and immediately, two other figures in the same suits and masks began to move through the crowd, passing out shining food tins from cardboard boxes. The people all crowded toward them with their arms out.

Meanwhile, someone started projecting a movie on the side of the tank above the man. At first I couldn't tell what it was. There were a whole lot of blurry blobs and lights, and things waving around between the blobs, and there was some really loud music playing. Then it got a bit sharper and I realised that the blobs were people's heads, and the things sticking up were arms, and some people had little flames in their hands like they used to do at concerts in the old days.

Then the picture went blurry again and suddenly there was a young woman in a t-shirt grinning into the camera. And she was bobbing up and down with one arm raised, and she was shouting, "Hey everyone, remember me? It's Dana and I'm at Central, and seriously, you've all got to come here. It's amazing. They give you everything you want, and it's just a big party all the time."

Then everyone in the crowd at the refinery started cheering and jumping up and down like they were at the party too.

But I just stood there, trying to make sense of it. I didn't really believe these people were from Central, but if they weren't, why would they be defending the Pantarch like this?

On top of this, there was, as the man said, a strange, sweet smell in the air. I looked around to try to find the source of it, but all I could see was an old upright fan to one side of the space, blowing air across the crowd.

But even as I wondered about it, I found myself relaxing. It was like there was a golden haze settling over me, like I was sitting against a sun-soaked wall. For a moment, I even imagined that I could see a city shining in the last rays of evening light.

But I was jolted awake by a shout from above.

"Do ye not ask yerselves why these fellows are wearing masks?"

I looked upward in the direction the voice had come from and saw Fergus, the old man who had called me a fool. He was standing on one of the walkways above and was jabbing his *machaira* at us as he spoke.

"Look," he said, pointing down at the fan. "Wake up. Yer all being gassed, ye ninnies! These charlatans are not from Central. They're luring ye to ruin. If they were truly interested in yer welfare, they'd be telling ye to go to Crux and warning ye of the great Cleanse."

But the man on the loading dock just laughed. He looked up at Fergus and back at the crowd.

"Nice to have some of our hope-fool friends along tonight. You know they're so in love with the thought of being martyrs that they can't allow themselves to believe in what Central is offering right now.

"The Pantarch they follow is a monster; he's a tyrant. But the Pantarch who sent *us* gave us good news and an invitation."

"Yer good news is a lie," shouted Fergus. "The real good news is that there is a cure for the Tox."

"They're always going on about the Tox," said the man with the respirator. "You know what we say? Just relax, man. The City is waiting for you; the City where there's food and water and rest, and nobody shouts and waves swords at you."

The crowd had all turned their attention back to him now. When he talked about shouting and waving swords, the people laughed.

But I looked back to the old man. Someone had turned up the music and the microphone so that I could barely hear what he was shouting. What was worse, I could see that one of the men in silver was creeping up behind him, holding a metal bar.

I tried to shout a warning to him but my voice seemed to just vanish into all the other noise. Yet somehow, Fergus saw him coming anyway. As the silver-suit began to swing, he whirled around and deflected the attack. Before I could work out how it had happened, the metal bar was flying away and the man in silver had fallen backwards onto the decking.

Even in my dazed state, I was impressed by that. But there wasn't any time to learn anything from the man's skill because now something else was happening. The big man with the neck tattoo who had introduced himself as Caleb was charging past me with a cloth held against his nose.

"Get outta here, bro!" He shouted. "He's right. They're blowin' chemicals at us."

He reached the fan and threw it down. Behind where it had stood, I could now see an open inspection hatch in the side of one of the vats that surrounded the courtyard.

Seeing that was like a siren going off in my head. I didn't know what it all meant, but I knew I had to find the exit. But where was it? Half my brain was awake and screaming, but the other half was still asleep.

Then, as I was looking around, somebody else bumped into me. It was one of the guys who had been distributing the tins, and he was trying to get to Caleb. As he passed, I saw the flash of a blade in his hand.

That, I could understand. I fell forward and grabbed his shiny legs. It was a pretty clumsy move, but it did the trick and we both went down.

Immediately, he twisted around and started slashing at me, slicing into the skin above my eyebrow. He followed that up with a kick to my nose, and then to my arm so that I let go of his other leg.

But that woke up the other half of my brain, and it didn't wake up happy. If the fog in my head had been caused by the old chemicals, then the pain was like someone putting a match to them. As the silver-suit guy began to get to his feet, my hand found a can on the ground—I don't know how—and smashed it into the knuckles of the hand that he was using to push himself up.

Then he roared and twisted back to slash at me again, but I was already coming at him. I drove the edge of the can into his mouth, so I felt his teeth crunch. As he fell back I crawled on top of him and began hitting him again and again in the nose and cheekbone.

And as I felt the impacts, I got that same hot full feeling that I'd felt at the river with Flex—like everything was simple and everything was on fire. I looked one way and saw Caleb with his sword out, fighting against two of the other silver-suits. On the other side, Fergus and Dil were climbing down from the gantry near the loading bay. Someone fired a gun.

And I thought it was good. Here we were, all fighting together—saving these people from whatever the silver suit guys were wanting to do to them.

But then something struck me on the back and someone screamed, "Savage!"

People were throwing cans at me! Most of the audience had retreated into corners or were rushing out the entrance, but some were helping the silver guys. I saw someone trip Dil as he ran toward the stage. I saw an old woman in flared pants shrieking at Caleb. The group chucking the cans at me was mostly kids.

But behind them, backed up against one of the tanks and staring at me with horror, was Leah.

Seeing her expression brought me back to sanity and jolted my memory: Mallory and her brother. I dropped the tin and charged toward the exit.

*   *   *

I heard the engine start as I ran around the side of the plant. Then I saw Cam in his wheelchair: he was by himself at the rear of the larger of the two vehicles, wheeling himself frantically from side to side and slapping the rear hatch with his open hand.

"Let me in! I want to go with Mal!"

Instead, the taillights of the van winked on and the machine began to roll forward.

I raced after it, sprinting the last twenty metres, and leapt forward as it pulled away. The vehicle had an external frame supporting its roof-rack, and I was able to latch on to this and pull myself up. I tried the handle on the rear hatch. When I found that it was locked, I worked my way around the corner and began kicking one of the mirrored side windows. I got in a couple of good blows and then had to hold on as the driver began slewing the vehicle from side to side.

But they couldn't shake me off. With my hands on the roof rack, I soon realised that if I hung on for the zigs, I could use the zags to give me extra momentum when I kicked. On the fourth swerve, I managed to pop out the rubber seal so the laminate panel pushed inward a crack. I hit it again with my knee and shouted, "Get out, Mal! They're not from Central!"

Then, for a moment, I thought I heard someone call my name, but there was too much noise from the engine and the tyres and from the air rushing past. I lined up for a final kick to remove the window.

And then the silver-suited woman who had patted me down at the gate leaned out of the passenger window and shot me in the side of the rib cage with her rifle.

The impact of the bullet swatted me off the side of the vehicle, like a cricket bat clubbing a mouse. I had three-quarters of a second to wonder why I hadn't hit the ground yet before I suddenly did.

It turned out that the road we had been on had been skirting the edge of a natural embankment. The slope made my initial impact less violent than it might have been, but it kept me tumbling for longer.

When I stopped moving, I was on my back on the side of the slope. Everything hurt. I assumed I was about to die. I had been shot. My organs had to be shredded.

I just looked up at the black sky and wondered how long it would take.

And yet I didn't die. I kept breathing. My racing pulse slowed and steadied. When I finally dared to move a hand to the place where the bullet had struck me, I discovered that my shirt and skin were unholed and unbloodied. The slightest pressure brought intense pain, but it seemed that the damage to my chest had stopped at a cracked rib or two.

The coat had saved my life.

All the same, I wasn't in good shape. Apart from the ribs, my injuries included the still-oozing cut above my eye and a whole lot of deep grazes on my hands and wrists. As I rolled over and began the long process of getting to my feet, I found new bruises and sprains distributed across my neck, shoulders, hips, elbows and knees.

*   *   *

The refinery was dead and deserted by the time I dragged my way back to it. Cam and his wheelchair were gone. The vehicles were gone. The lights and music had been replaced by darkness and silence. I went around the perimeter fence and staggered back along the track that followed the edge of the forest. As I reached my gear, the eastern sky was growing light.

I rested there for the rest of the day while I washed and taped my wounds and gnawed on one of the compressed ration blocks I had been issued at Crux. The next day, I returned to the road and trudged on toward the east.

*   *   *

The landscape changed now. The old road zig-zagged down into a dreary land of half-dead elm avenues, parched paddocks and long abandoned dairy farms that receded into the smog.

I went through the miles alone, camping out in the ruined villages and homesteads. At night, I tried to read the book and do my exercises, but mostly I thought about what a mess of things I had made at the refinery: how I had failed to save Mallory, failed to make friends, failed to bring my sword.

The one thing that I had felt good about at the time—my attack on the guard using the can—now seemed the worst thing of all. It had been savagery. And if it was savagery, then I had to face the fact that I might be getting worse, not better.

Where did that leave me? Had the cure really taken or was I fooling myself? Was I going to be one of those people that Bird talked about; the ones who went along and got rejected at the end?

The darkness of these thoughts made me glad to be by myself. I felt like having to speak to even one other person would be too much to bear.

But there *were* other people out there. Sometimes, when the wind was blowing from the south-east, I would hear the sound of engines in the distance. One evening I saw the smoke of another campfire against the sunset. That made me want to go faster, but my injuries limited my efforts.

The sunsets were pretty much the only thing that still made me happy through those miles. As the smoke and burnt chemical taste increased, it made the sky beige during the day and filled it with fiery red and orange at night. I would stare at it and watch it changing as I ate my rations. Sometimes I would think about the things I'd been through, sometimes, I would think about my friends back in Spillan.

When the wind picked up, I would see spurts of yellow flame sputtering on the horizon and guessed that these were the source of the smoke. One merchant who visited Spillan spoke about uncapped oil wells that had been burning out in the east for years. I guessed that was what I was looking at.

If that was right, it meant I was on Boneyard Road, where Central had obliterated the rebel columns as soon as they had begun to mobilise in the opening hours of the war.

The start of the wreckage confirmed it. At first, it was just a long row of burned-out trucks strung out along the road. A bit further on, the destruction became more intense; I passed lorries with huge wheels that looked like they had been sliced in two. Then I came to an armoured personnel carrier—all rusted and empty, but there was a neat grid of holes in its roof and bones scattered about on the floor.

There was more and more after that: trucks, vans, tanks and guns—some of them had been sliced, some pierced, some overturned, some seemed merely burned and rusted. I went past them as quietly as I could, listening to the wind that whistled through them, and trying not to think of ghosts.

For a while, I could keep my distance from them. The wrecks were in a line along one side of the road, so I could just walk a bit further back through the scrub. But as the evening came on, I came to what must have been a series of staging areas, and the destruction spread out on either side of me. Now I was hemmed in; the track narrowed as it wove between the blackened carcasses.

Then, I began to hear noises again. Some of them, thuds and skitterings, were just animal sounds. But others definitely weren't; distant hammering, shouts, faint engine noises and, sometimes, the same deep pulsing sound that I had experienced in the swamp.

So now I tried to walk even more quietly; stepping around the litter, coughing into a wadded shirt. I began to think of the vehicles as a protection; imagined myself as a lizard hiding in their shadows—too small to be noticed, or at least too insignificant to be interesting to whatever was out there.

When it got too dark to keep going, I crawled under one of the lorries and tried to find some consolation in the Roadbook. But it had been such a long time since I had spent any time with it that I could barely keep my mind on it.

And next morning, I was woken at dawn by a clash of metal and the thrumming of an engine.

CHAPTER 17

I dragged myself out into the morning smog. The sun looked like a huge egg-yolk on a bloody horizon.

The noise that had woken me up was still going, so I began making my way through the wreckage to try to find the source of it. I crawled down between two jeeps, under the shell of a self-propelled gun, through the cabin of an old prime mover. Soon, I could smell the sharp burning-steel smell of welding. The cold blue light flickering up ahead confirmed it.

I was close to it now—close enough to hear voices. As I wormed up the belly of an overturned half-track and squinted through the holes in its sprocket wheels, I could see men: four standing around a burning oil drum, one eating from a bowl, two talking. Another three were off to the side, working on the ruin of an enormous legged machine that sprawled out of view.

The welding light was coming from an open hatch in the thing's shell, and there were cables snaking out of it too—cables that led back across the clearing to where a trailer-sized generator growled and shook. As I watched, there was a new spark-flash from inside the hatch and one of the monster's legs twitched, lifting the shell a few centimetres off the ground.

The men were HORD. Even through the smoke, I could see that they were wearing the same uniforms as Bird and his crew. The vehicles parked in the background had the same machine guns and roll bars.

Then it was like my heart stopped, because I suddenly saw that one of the group *was* from Bird's crew. The man eating from the bowl was Beelz. He had some sort of metal brace around the knee that I'd stabbed. As I stared at him, he glanced up as if he sensed that he was being watched.

I fought down the impulse to jump up and bolt. As long as I stayed flat, the rusty wheels hid me. At least, that was what I told myself.

I slid backwards and began to retrace my steps. I was painfully aware that I was making more noise now, but there was nothing I seemed to be able to do about it. Seeing Beelz made my arms and legs shakey and my breathing too. Then I had another coughing fit and had to bend over and stifle it with my coat.

I was almost back to where I had started now. I was just going to retrieve my gear and get moving before they had any more opportunity to notice me.

But as I began to crawl through the cabin of the truck, I looked up and saw something moving under the lorry. I heard a sound of metal. My pack, just visible in the shadows, was pulled back out of view.

I paused mid-breath. What or who was that? Did they know I was here? If they were looking right now they could see me silhouetted in the cabin. But maybe they were too busy with my stuff.

Once again, forcing myself to move slowly, I slid backwards and dropped to the ground. What should I do? If I went parallel to the road here, I might be able to slip away and come back to it further along. But that would mean abandoning all my gear, my provisions and weapon and book. How long would I last without them?

Then I heard footsteps on the other side of the truck and I just turned and ran.

I didn't even try to go quietly now. My foot seemed to find every loose object. Rusted metal clanged and drummed and squawked as I made my way over it. I squeezed between two APCs, slid beside a line of lorries, skirted a bomb crater. I crawled under a jackknifed semi-trailer and slithered under the shipping container that had half fallen off its bed.

And there, as I pulled myself up, was Bird, waiting for me. He was sitting on an overturned jeep with a rollie in one hand and a pistol in the other.

I thought I was going to pass out.

"Well look at you, kid," he said as he casually brought the weapon up. "I see you went and got yourself all Centralled-up despite my good advice. Some people just can't be helped."

I finished getting to my feet and raised my hands.

"That's right, hands up," he said. "How's it all working out for you kid? You look kind of banged-up. Cuts on your face, bruises round your eyes, dried blood all over your shirt. And shouldn't you have a bit more stuff than that? Where's your sword?"

"If you stop pointing that gun at me, I'll go and see if I can find it," I said.

The man laughed.

"At least you didn't let 'em take your sense of humour. I'll give you that."

I looked left and right, hoping to see some cover or exit. Nothing presented itself.

"What are you going to do to me?" I said.

"Well, here's the thing, kid," he said, tapping the ash off his cigarette. "You owe me. Every time someone goes through that pass up at Wicket they dock the pay of whoever was on duty. So right now, I'm inclined to just put a hole in your head for the satisfaction of it. But that ain't the only option …"

"What else is there?"

The man drew on his cigarette and blew out a stream. "Change sides. Shed your coat. Denounce Central. I get a bounty, and you get to save your life."

"I can't. I took the oath."

Bird shrugged. "Doesn't matter. Plenty of folks have said those words and gone back on them. Looks like it'd be a mercy in your case. No gear, no friends. Hell, kid, you're half-way there already."

He blew another stream of smoke, and I took the opportunity to glance back down at the place I'd just crawled out of—wondering if there was any chance of making a dive for it. Maybe I could turn my back so that my coat would catch the bullets, but my legs would be completely exposed as soon as I started crawling.

"Kid, you try to look back in that direction again and I'm likely to shoot you straight off," he said. "Try a little focus."

I looked back at him and remembered the last time I had seen him. I remembered how he had told me that Central was going to mess with my brain, and how Beelz had talked about "doping or dicing" me. And then I suddenly remembered something else he had said—something that I had thought about a lot in the days since that first encounter; something that made me feel angry, even in the midst of my fear.

"When I saw you last time, you said that Mayor Strictland repays you by telling you when he's sending people out."

He looked amused and gave a shrug.

"Yeah, that sounds like something I would have said. What about it?"

"What did you mean by it?"

"Just what I said. Strictland sends 'em out. We pick 'em up."

"But what people?"

He gave a grin. "The cysties—the ones you're all too good for."

I felt the anger surge through me, pulsing at the base of my skull.

"And what do you do with them?"

He shrugged. "Seems to me you should be concentrating on what's going to happen with you."

"I know what's going to happen. You're going to kill me or slave me."

Bird shook his head.

"Like I said, doesn't have to be that way. It's not too late to make a deal. Hey, maybe you can even come and work for HORD. How about that? Take off that coat and you could be the one holding the gun."

"Why would I ever trust you?"

"Well, I haven't shot you yet, have I? But face it, kid, you don't have a lot of choice."

I glanced up at the sky above the man's head.

The man laughed. "You hopin' for air support? Give it up, kid. If they thought you were worth the trouble, they'd have already sent it. Maybe if you'd stuck to the road, but out here, you're ours."

But even as he spoke, I felt something tapping the leather at the back of my boot.

CHAPTER 18

(Extract of the transcribed Records of Caleb Dox, Vol 1.23)

After Fergus and Dil went off, I was by myself for a while. But I didn't like that much—cos when you're by yourself you can't train properly, and your singin' doesn't work as well either. So I kept lookin' for other people on the road up ahead and behind me, but I couldn't see anybody.

But then, when I was going down into this big valley, I saw someone way up ahead. It was a bit smoky so I couldn't get a good look at him, but I thought maybe it was that guy we had met at the place with all the pipes and lights. So I tried to catch up with him. And later on, when it got dark, I made a campfire so he'd see me.

But it still took me a few days to get to him, and before that, we'd got to this big junkyard with all these busted tanks and trucks and stuff, and it was kind of smoky too—so I was thinkin' I might just go past him if he was scared of me or hidin' or somethin'.

So I had the feelin' that I should probably slow right down and start checkin' in the junk. But I also had this other feelin' that I needed to catch up with him and that somethin' bad was gonna happen if I didn't. So I kept goin' fast and slow. And then I'd go fast and worry that I'd missed him and go back and check the bits I'd skipped.

That was really tirin'. And then it got too dark to keep goin', so I found a place to sleep. But I kept havin' weird dreams about giant spiders grabbin' me and draggin' me off the road into the junkyard.

So eventually, I just got up—but I must have gotten a bit of sleep because the sun was just startin' to come up too. I got goin' again, and then after a while, I heard some noises in the distance—like guys buildin' somethin'. And I climbed up on the roof of one of the carriers to see what it was, and there were flashes of light up ahead—looked like weldin' or somethin'—but I couldn't see where it was comin' from.

But then I saw the guy. Just as I was about to jump down and keep goin' I saw him crawling in through the cabin of a truck and goin' toward the flashing. And I couldn't see him very clearly because of the smoke, and cos the light wasn't very bright, but I was pretty sure he didn't have a sword with him.

And then I *really* got that feeling that somethin' bad was about to happen, so I sent up a signal and just started runnin'. I went along the road until I came to round about where he must have come from, and found his gear under a flipped tip-truck.

So I grabbed his sword and started after him. But he thought I was comin' to get him and started runnin' too! And I wanted to shout out to him, but I could tell that we were close to the guys doin' the weldin', so I just kept followin' him.

Anyway, he kept on goin' and I did too. Then he got to this big shipping crate and started to crawl under it, and I followed him. But by the time I was half-way, I could see it was gonna be too tight for me to get through, so I thought I'd come back out and try to climb over the top. But just then, I heard some people talkin' and, when I put my head down, I could see that Chris was standin' right there on the other side, and worked out that somebody was threatenin' him.

CHAPTER 19

Whatever was tapping on my heel did it again—harder this time. It was weird because my attention was all on Bird, but there was this thing going on at my feet.

"So what's it gonna be," said Bird. "Are you gonna see reason, or am I gonna have to put one through your scone?"

I dropped my head and looked down—tried to make it look like I was about to give in. As I stared between my feet, I could see it. It was something made of wood, something smooth and round, coming out from under the steel edge of the container just behind me. It was the handle of my *machaira*.

Bird clicked his fingers. "Hey, what did I tell you about looking down there?"

But suddenly, I wasn't scared of him. The thought that someone was down there, passing me a sword seemed so insane that for a second, I felt like laughing.

I looked up at Bird. "Okay, I've made my decision," I said.

"Yeah? And what is it?" he said.

Without answering him, I turned my back to him and dropped down into a crouch. He fired once at my head, but it was bent forward, and my collar deflected the slug. He fired again, but now I was coming back up with the sword in my hand. As I spun, the bullet hit the back of my left shoulder just before the *machaira* bit into the bone of his forearm.

For a moment, we both looked at it—like neither of us could believe what had just happened.

Then I wrenched my sword back, and time restarted. Bird grabbed his arm and shouted a curse as his pistol hit the ground. I twisted back toward the shipping container and dove for the gap; one arm forward, scrabbling in the dust, and one arm behind, still holding the sword.

Somebody grabbed hold of my shoulders and yanked me through to the other side.

There was too much shadow for me to get a good look at his face but I recognised his shape straight away. It was Caleb, the big man with tattoos from the refinery. He lifted me up and put me down on my feet, then looked at me like he was counting my arms and legs.

"Hey bro," he said. "Let's get out of here."

I nodded and hurried to follow him as he began working his way back through the wreckage. He was going faster than I could go, but I wanted him to go faster. I kept looking behind, expecting Beelz or Buddy Lial to come charging through the smoke.

But we reached the road without being attacked. Then Caleb turned back to the west, which confused me and, for a few seconds, made me afraid that maybe this was some elaborate trick. But then I saw the place where I had spent the night, and I realised that he had brought me back for my gear.

"Go for it, bro," he said as he stood back, looking left and right. "I'll let you know if anyone comes after us."

I raced forward and began gathering my stuff, my hands shaking as I packed my sleeping roll.

"Do you think they will?" I said.

"Nah, probably not now that we're together and on the road—reckon that'll make 'em think twice. But we'll give 'em a good fight if they try."

He waited for me to hoist my pack and helped me sheath my *machaira*.

"You good to go?" he said.

"Yeah, I think so," I said.

We walked quickly together in silence for a long while after that. As the light grew brighter, the mechanical sounds faded into the distance. Then I began to feel like we were safe—which gave my body permission to feel exhausted—but I kept pushing myself to keep going. Then I had another coughing fit and had to plead for a break.

"Sure bro," he said. "Take a seat. Hey, you want some water?"

He passed me his flask and then pulled a ration block from one of his pockets.

"Have some food too," that'll help you feel better. "You look like you got some pain there."

"Yeah," I said. "I got shot in the side by one of the people with the shiny suits back at the refinery. The coat caught it, but I think it cracked some ribs.

"But what about you?" I said. "I thought you were travelling around with those two other guys."

"Fergus and Dil. Yeah, they let me ride with 'em for a while, but it didn't work out so they dropped me off back on the road, and I've been tryin' to catch up with you."

I looked round at him. "So that was you with the campfire?"

"Yeah, bro. I was tryin' to get your attention!"

I laughed and winced. "I thought you were Savages or something."

"Yeah, I been called that before."

I laughed again and then stopped as I remembered how my own savagery had been on display back at the refinery.

"Well, thanks for coming to my rescue."

"Hey, all I did was pass you your sword, bro."

"Well, I'd be dead without it." I bit off part of the ration block he'd passed me and stopped.

"Hey, your rations taste different to mine," I said.

"Yeah, bro, they're all a bit different. That's so we'll share 'em."

"What? I didn't know that."

"Yeah, that's how it works. Do you reckon it tastes better or worse?"

"Better," I said. "A lot better."

He gave me a grin. "That's what I always reckon. But I think maybe it's just that it's different from what you're used to."

"Huh," I said.

It was strange having somebody walking along with me and, for a while, it felt awkward. I had gotten out of the habit of conversation, but still thought I should be making an effort—which basically meant me asking a whole lot of questions. Caleb obviously didn't feel the need to do the same, but he happily answered mine, which was how I found out a whole lot of things about him all at once.

He told me that he had spent his earliest years northeast of Gaia, where his extended family survived on their greenhouses, chickens and pigs. He grew up with his sisters and cousins foraging for treasures in the ruined homesteads and villages of the hill country.

Caleb's people had been part of a loyalist cell further east in the old days and still kept some of its traditions in their songs and stories. He had been told from his earliest years that the Pantarch was the rightful ruler of the AZ, and that all the disasters that had come to it had come because of the rebellion.

But their loyalty didn't go much beyond that. They kept to themselves and lived on mostly peaceful terms with the people of Gaia and Ockham.

And then his sister disappeared.

"We had these guys travelin' round in trucks with a work crew," he said. "They'd do things like diggin' wells or help buildin' stuff. And they'd do it all for free—said they were doin' it for the Pantarch, and that if you did enough to help rebuild the AZ, Central would let you in. But when they left one year, my sis was gone. And some people said that she had gone with them because of a boy. But I was thinkin' she believed 'em about gettin' to Central."

"So what did you do?"

"I tried to track 'em down—wandered around for about a year, lookin' for her and not findin' anything. I went to a whole lot of weird places and talked to a whole lot of strange people. And then I finally ended up in Delice workin' as muscle for the Mayor. That was pretty bad because they used to pay half our wages with booze.

"But one night, when I was out drinkin' with some of the guys, I heard people singin' in the distance, and they were singin' one of the old songs my aunties used to sing. So I walked off and followed them, and they led me up that place in the mountains where Prediger lives. And then Eve came and took me to Crux."

So it was singing that had saved him, and it was singing that he still liked best. Caleb had the same idea as Eve about Central songs keeping away attackers. He also thought they could help with the changes.

"You see?" he said as he tried to teach me the harmonies of some song he'd learned from his childhood. "You can feel 'em doin' you good. We used to just sing 'em when we were muckin' around back home, and I never thought about what they meant. But now I reckon they must have come from Crux cos they talk about the same stuff."

Later on, as we ate our dinner, he told me about how his songs had been a sore point with Fergus and Dil.

"They didn't like 'em," he said. "They reckoned it was okay to sing stuff if it was in the Roadbook, but they didn't want me singin' the stuff from home."

"Was that why you split up?" I said.

"Yeah, kind of," he said. "Other stuff too. They said I had too many weird ideas—reckoned I needed to go and get straightened out at some training camp they'd been to."

"What kind of ideas?"

"Oh, stuff like how it works when you send a signal to Central. Somebody told me that when you put your fingers together, the stuff in your blood makes a circuit. But Fergus reckoned that was stupid and that you could just talk, and Central would hear you.

"And I told 'em that I thought you could get signals back sometimes— like when I was chasin' after you—but Fergus and Dil both said I was just imagin' it, and that I was goin' crazy."

"That sounds pretty harsh," I said.

But Caleb's ideas sounded weird to me, too. I didn't know about receiving signals, but the circuit idea didn't make a lot of sense. On the other hand, hadn't the Envoy come to me after I'd tapped out an SOS on an actual radio?

But mostly I was happy to have a friend. Caleb was the most open-hearted and straightforward person I had ever met, and his optimism was a powerful antidote to the sense of gloom that had been hanging over me since the refinery.

I thought everything would be better now we were together. I imagined that we would stay together right up to Perseverance—maybe even to Sanctuary.

But we weren't clear of trouble yet.

CHAPTER 20

The next day, when we came to the end of the wreckage, the smoke grew thicker, making it harder for us to walk quickly (or sing). Up ahead, the hills at the end of the valley appeared as gloomy silhouettes lit by the red glow of the oil-fires.

Further on, the path led us into a maze of rocky valleys that twisted and turned all over the place; soon it was so dark that we weren't really sure what time of day it was anymore.

Then, voices started coming at us out of the smoke. At first they were too far-off for us to hear what they were saying—though sometimes we could hear shouting and screaming and laughter. But as we went on, they seemed to come closer, and we started to hear bits of words and sentences. It made us draw our swords and bunch together in the centre of the path.

We kept going for a long time like that. Sometimes the voices seemed to be a long way off and sometimes they seemed closer. When the road began to climb more steeply, they went quiet for a while, and we thought that we'd gotten past them. But I think that was when they noticed us.

"Murderer," said a voice from one side that sounded like a woman's voice, "That's a murderer you're walking with."

"Murderer, murderer," hissed other voices from the other side—some sounding like men's voices, some women's.

"So fine in his nice coat," said a man's voice. "But what's underneath?"

"We know. Ask him. Ask him," said the other voices.

I looked over at Caleb. He was holding his sword in front of him but stooping like he was walking into a headwind.

"I thought the last part was creepy," I said.

"Yeah, bro. I reckon this is worse."

"Are you doing okay?"

"Um ..."

"Ask him about his cysts," said a voice behind me.

I spun around, but there was just the smoke and gloom.

"Watch out that he doesn't kill you," said a voice to the right.

"Don't go to sleep," said a voice to the left.

"He's a Savage," whispered the voice behind.

And now, suddenly it occurred to me that they were talking to Caleb—and that he was looking like that because he knew that they were telling the truth about me.

"He's a faker," said a voice.

"And a hypocrite," said another.

"Can't stay on the path."

"Can't be trusted."

I felt my gullet rise and turned to Caleb, determined to confess what these voices were obviously about to reveal, but he spoke first.

"Bro, I don't know how they know this stuff about me. But if you don't want to keep going together, that's okay."

"What? I thought they were talking about me."

"Nah, all that stuff about havin' cysts and bein' a killer. That's me. I did some bad stuff when I was back in Delice."

Before either of us could say anything more, there was a sort of muffled shout from up ahead—a different sort of sound from what we'd been hearing—and then a frightened animal noise as something charged at us out of the gloom. I raised my *machaira,* ready to impale it, but Caleb caught my blade with his own and lifted it out of the way.

"It's a sheep, bro. See if you can grab it."

I lunged for it as the animal passed me, felt my fingertips catch in the greasy crust of its fleece. Then the momentum of its charge pulled me off balance, causing me to crash down onto my side. The sheep gave a terrified baa and tried to get free, dragging me for a couple of metres.

Straight away, the voices closed in, laughing and hissing.

"What a hero."

"Can't even keep his feet."

But I still had my sword. I saw a shadow and swung out at it. Something swore at me. But the sound came from further away—like I had forced it back.

I got to my feet and called out to Caleb, still clutching the struggling ewe by the scruff of its neck.

"Over here, bro. There's another one here."

I found him wrestling a panicked ram that was alternating between trying to twist free and butt him with its horns. I tried to work out how I could help him, but before I could think of anything, he had the creature off the ground and hoisted over his shoulders.

"Now what?" I said.

"Dunno, bro."

"Now you can come with me, brothers. That's what."

As we looked up, an old guy in a Traveller's coat stepped out of the gloom ahead of us. He had a thick walking stick in his hand, a battered hat, and a little flock of sheep and lambs that clustered around his legs.

"Who are you?" I said, still holding up my sword.

"Name's Clem Berger, brother. We're all on the same side here. Thanks for catching Milly—she's a bit jumpy, that one. And look at you, brother, with Baz on your back. That's a mighty effort. Don't think I've ever seen anyone manage that before."

Caleb set the ram down and offered a hand to the old man.

"Hi, I'm Caleb. Are you really with Central?"

"That I am, brother. Envoy man to the end."

"Which direction are you headed?" I said.

"Same way you are tonight, I reckon. If you fellas would care to give me a hand getting the animals through this next bit, there's a nice place where we can camp up on the top of the rise."

Caleb and I exchanged a nod and went on with him, flanking the flock to keep the sheep from straying. I noticed that now we were with Clem, the whispering had dropped to a background mutter that was barely distinguishable above the sounds of our steps. When we had gone on a bit further, I asked Clem about them.

"Yes, they're a bit of an enigma, brother. Some of 'em are Tox-crazies. Some of 'em sound like Corp machines. And some of 'em are what's left of convoys where the leaders went feral. Now they just lurk in the shadows and hiss at everyone."

"So they're like Travellers?" said Caleb.

"Maybe some of them still are, but they don't generally like to come out and have a proper conversation, so you can't really tell what's going on with them."

"We both thought they were talking about us," I said.

"Well, we're all guilty men, brother. They don't have to fling too much before they hit something."

As the ground levelled off, the smoke began to thin out. When I looked back, the last of the sunset was lighting up the smog as an orange blaze, outshining even the oil fires that were now visible behind us on the ridge.

"Looks pretty, doesn't it?" said Clem.

"Yeah," said Caleb. "Funny how the smoke makes the sun look good."

"Quite right, brother. I reckon there's something deep about that. But I've got something even better to show you. Once we've got things sorted out, I'll give you a squiz."

We had just reached a slight depression ringed by sheoaks and sliprails. On the far side, a fire pit surrounded by sawn stumps provided a broad view of grey-blue plains vanishing away into the east. After we had helped Clem get the animals into their pen, he made us sit and tell our stories while he lit the fire.

"Well, you've cleared a tough bit now," he said when we were done. "Boneyard's a killer, and the smoke's pretty rough too. You'll probably have it a bit easier now for a day or two.

"But there's some other stuff to look out for up ahead. There's a big Corp settlement that you'll have to go through, and that can give you a bit of trouble. You're gonna have to stick close to the Envoy."

"What kind of trouble?" said Caleb.

"All kinds. Mostly they'll try to sell you stuff."

"We should be okay, then," I said. "We don't have any money."

He looked up at me and grinned. "Good for you, brother. But that's not really what they want."

"Why, what do they want?"

"They want to keep you and make you a part of their machine."

"Like slaves?" said Caleb.

"Yep, slaves or worse—they got some pretty crook stuff goin' on."

"Can we just go around it, then?" I said.

"Well, that's not really the official way, brother. Some blokes manage it, but I wouldn't recommend it. You'll avoid some trouble, but there's other things that'll be very happy to have a go at you if you go off-track like that."

"What about Perseverance?" I said, "Is that far?"

"That's just a bit on from the settlement. Once you see the yellow fields you're there.

He finished with the fire and disappeared into the trees for a moment. When he returned, he was rummaging in a canvas bag.

"Alright, brothers, here's something to lift your spirits."

He pulled out some kind of gadget made of red moulded plastic. It had two bits sticking out that looked like eyestalks and a white disc protruding from the top.

"Hey, that's one of those stereo-pic things," said Caleb. "I saw one of those when I was a kid. It had pictures from the islands and stuff."

"I bet you've never seen what's on this one."

Caleb took it from him and held it up to his eyes.

"Woah! Hey, is that … is that?"

"Sure is brother. That's Central: Sanctuary City—home of the Pantarch and the Envoy. Fill your eyeballs with that, and the bad stuff up ahead will go past you like a dream—maybe a bad dream, but a dream."

Caleb started clicking the lever but stopped and held it out to me.

"Hey, Chris, you should take a look at this!"

"You finish, Caleb," I said. "I can look when you're done."

As he went back to it, I caught sight of Clem nodding and smiling.

"You fellas stick together and you'll do okay."

Caleb worked his way around the disc and passed it over. Of course, it didn't really do justice to the City. The colours were a bit washed out— and they were just still images, even though they were sort of 3D. But they did give you a bit of a sense of the light, and the space, and the way the streets and houses worked with the trees. It gave me the same feeling I'd had when I first read the Roadbook in Ockham, except more intensely. I think it was the first time I began to see that the place where we were headed wasn't just better and safer but absolutely good in itself.

Not all the pictures were from inside Sanctuary. One showed views of it across fields. Another showed people out on the water in boats, silhouetted against a sunset light that shone on the distant towers—a similar view to one I had seen at Prediger's place. There was even one shot taken from a long way off with the City under the shadow of massive billowing clouds. As I looked at that one, I could almost smell the rain and the wet earth; almost feel the water flowing around my feet; almost see wild fish darting through the light and shadow.

Those images stayed with me for a long time.

*   *   *

But it was back to present reality when we packed and returned to the road the following morning. As we said goodbye to Clem and left the hills, the trees became stumps and stubble and the sky went flat grey.

We passed ruined farms, the bleached bones of sheep and cattle, and the husks of homesteads—all strung out along a branch of the pipeline that seemed to have stopped working. When I bent down to look into a tap, a sudden swirl of wind blew sand up into my eyes.

"Looks like Prax shut the water off on them," I said, remembering what had happened after the war. "Pretty harsh."

"You reckon it was Prax?" said Caleb.

"Isn't he the one who manages all that stuff?"

"Yeah, but people do stuff to it too. When we lived up north, the Gaians used to reckon that the Ockhamists were always tryin' to damage it or destroy it. And one time, there was a big fight because Gaia cut into Ockham's branch and dumped a whole lot of old weedkiller into it. Don't know if it did anything, but it made the Ockhamists crazy. And then they blew up a bit of Gaia's branch, and that shut the whole thing down for a while."

"Wow, okay," I said. "Well, good thing we've got our bottles anyway, I guess."

But it wasn't long before we discovered where the water had really gone.

Refinery
H
J
K
M
ADDLE
A - Entrance & Street Stalls
B - Shallow Dive
C - Scenic Railway
D - Seini's Flat
E - City Watchhouse
F - City Square & Pillory
G - Dungeons (Gaius)
H - The Castle
ADDLE SURROU[ND]
A - Pru & Trevor's pl[ace]
B - Museum Station
C - Refinery
D - Main Car[...]
E - Gas[...]

CHAPTER 21

We had just finished passing through the bones of another deserted town when we suddenly came on it—a green wall of thirty-foot stalks that curved away to the left and right.

"That's a crop," I said, "A full-on crop. How can there be a crop out here? Is this Central territory or something?"

"I don't know, bro," said Caleb. "Let's have a look."

He ran back a hundred metres and began scrambling up the half-collapsed roof truss of a petrol station we had just passed. Soon, he was balancing up the top, shielding his eyes with his hand and staring all around.

"Goes for miles. I can see sprinklers too."

I followed him up and stared out at it, amazed. The green went on as far as I could see. Where it met the sky, there was a line of spindly structures wrapped in clouds of water-vapour. When the breeze changed direction for a moment, there was a sudden smell of wet earth and plants.

"Wonder what they're growing," I said. "Looks sort of like bamboo."

"Nah, it's sugarcane," said Caleb.

"Wow," I said.

"Yeah," said Caleb.

To understand the impact it made on us, you need to realise what agriculture was like west of the mountains back then. Nobody could afford to spray water on open fields where most of it would evaporate into the sky. We grew everything in greenhouses and vats, making the most of what came through the pipeline and what we could recycle.

"Where do we go now?" I said at last. "I don't like the idea of trying to get through that."

"Me either, bro. But check the tyre tracks. Maybe there's a way."

I looked at where he was pointing. Up close to the green barrier, where the cracked asphalt seemed to completely vanish into the greenery, two faint wheel ruts branched away, following the curve to the south.

Half a kilometre down that track we found that Caleb was right. There *was* a way through—the ruts turned and became a wider road driving straight through the cane. As we went forward, the plants closed in around us like a green canyon, full of rustling and creaking.

Most of those noises were caused by the wind. But not much of that wind got down to where we were. The lower parts of the stalks were choked by a whole lot of wispy stuff that made the air feel heavy and dead.

It also blocked the view. Occasionally, where there was a sideways track, we could see down between the rows. But most of the time there was too much of the wispy stuff for that—and that was a bit unnerving because it meant we couldn't see what was making the *other* noises—the thuds, creaks and hisses.

Caleb's response was what it always was.

"Let's sing, bro."

It lifted our spirits for a while—and maybe it made a difference to the noises—but we weren't able to keep it up for long. The thick air made deep breaths impossible and seemed to swallow up the sound that came out of our lungs.

"Gotta stop, brother," I said. "Getting too tired."

A bit later, we came to a place where a wider road crossed the one we were on. This road was paved with asphalt, and there were vehicles on it too. Caleb and I had just enough time to throw ourselves down before a pair of tankers charged past us—big machines with the word "Nimcorp" painted on their silver tanks. There was also a logo that looked like a staircase or a spring. It looked familiar to me, but I was too distracted by the trucks themselves.

"Did that look strange to you?" I said to Caleb.

"Yeah. They were too close together … and they didn't have cabins."

He was right about the first thing. The two machines were travelling at high speed, but they were as close as if they had been connected by a tow bar.

But it wasn't exactly true that they had *no* cabins. Each of them had a sort of black dome thing above the engine wedge. But it was nowhere near big enough for a person to sit in. And it gave me the creeps.

We waited until the noise had faded to silence and then darted across the asphalt to continue with our own track. Later, when it got dark, we turned and made our camp on a path that ran beside a narrow canal. It was closer to the cane than either of us would have liked, but it made us feel safer to be off the road. We did our training, read the Roadbook and tried to sleep in our bedrolls as the strange noises rustled and clunked in the dark.

At first light, we were woken by the sound of one of the sprinkler booms crawling along the path toward us. We raced to pack our sleeping gear and hid ourselves in the stalks, but there were no guards, or even field workers going along with it—just the fat wheels rolling past as the spray soaked our hair and trickled down our necks.

That was the closest thing I had ever experienced to a real rain shower and, under different circumstances, I might have even enjoyed it. As it was, I was too worried for that. The general feeling of dampness made me irritable too.

"Why do you reckon they don't give us maps?" I said to Caleb as we returned to the track. "I mean, don't you reckon it would make more sense if we knew where we were and what we were up against?"

"I think that's meant to be part of the training," he said. "We just follow the road they put us on and learn what to do as we go."

"But why not give us a map and show us where it goes? I mean, how do we even know we're still on the right road? Maybe we weren't supposed to go off to the side when we reached the crop? Maybe we were supposed to bash our way through."

I knew I was being unreasonable, but I couldn't help myself.

Caleb looked around at me and nodded.

"Yeah, I don't know, bro. But I reckon this'd have to be part of that Corp place that Clem was talkin' about—I mean, those trucks and stuff."

"Maybe," I said.

"We just have to trust Central. But I'll send a signal."

He put his fingers together in his usual way and started talking.

"Hey Prax, this is Caleb Dox reporting in with a message for the Envoy. I'm with Chris here on the way to Perseverance, and we're in this big sugarcane crop, and we're not sure we're still on the right road. If you could ask the Pantarch to send us a sign or somethin', that'd be really good. Okay, thanks."

I watched him and felt sort of annoyed, but I knew he was right.

And pretty soon, we did get a sign—even though it wasn't the sort of sign I wanted.

It looked like the top of a tent when we first saw it. We came around a slight bend in the track and it was up ahead of us, rising above the cane. It was huge and sort of coppery-coloured, and it had these poles poking through which were holding it up.

As we drew closer we could hear distant music. Closer still and we began to smell smoke and cooking meat. Finally, after one more bend, we came to the gate.

It was a porch made of galvanised steel set into a high concrete wall. The wall curved away to the left and right of us, and its top was the bottom edge of the big tent.

At the back of the porch, there was a metal panel, about three metres wide, that I guessed was a door. Just beside that there was a viewscreen, some cameras, a round hole about the size of a handspan and two little turrets with machine gun barrels sticking out of them.

On the other side of the panel there was a sign:

WELCOME TO ADDLE:
NO FIGHTING, NO CANNIBALS,
NO TROPHY-HUNTERS, NO SAVAGES,
NO UNSHEATHED BLADES.

ENTRY 1 CREDIT.

I felt a sudden hammering in my ribcage and lungs—like something was crushing me, stopping me from breathing.

But Caleb just looked puzzled.

"Hey, I wonder how you get in if you don't have any credits," he said. He took a step forward but stopped as I grabbed his arm.

"What are you doing? This is Addle," I said, hearing my voice come out sort of breathy and strange. "This is where the HORD guys were wanting to take me before Eve rescued me."

Caleb looked at me, then looked back at the gate. He rubbed the back of his neck.

"But … this is where the road goes, bro. It's like Clem said."

"Yeah, but he said that it was bad."

"But he still said we had to go through."

"But he didn't know about my history with HORD. What if Bird's in there now, watching us through one of those cameras? And look—those swivel things are *machine guns!* We shouldn't even be standing here. Come on."

I started backing down the track. Caleb followed me for a few metres and stopped.

"Where we gonna go if we don't keep going, bro?" he said.

"We can go round. This whole place is a huge circle. We can just go back to that canal and follow it round until we get to the other side. Clem said some people go that way."

"But he said it was dangerous, cos other things would try to get you."

"Yeah, but it's dangerous this way too. Every time I run into those guys they nearly kill me."

He looked at me for a long time and then down at the ground. For a moment, I thought he was going to agree. But he finally shook his head.

"I reckon we gotta stay on the path. I got one of those feelin's."

"Why would the Envoy want to send us into a HORD base?"

"I dunno. Maybe there's people who need to hear about the cure."

"But what if they slave you … or something worse, like Clem said?"

"We just gotta trust the Envoy, bro. If you go off path, how do you know you'll be able to get back to it?"

I opened my mouth to say something else but stopped. There was that familiar heat building in the back of my neck and I knew that if I kept going I was going to say or do something I'd regret. Instead, I bit my cheek hard and grabbed onto the straps of my backpack. There was another long silence.

"I can't do it," I said at last. "You go if you want to—maybe it'll be different for you, but they know who I am."

"But who's gonna watch your back, bro?"

"I'll just … I'll just stick to the track and go as quick as I can."

Caleb looked at the ground and then looked back at me, put a hand on my shoulder.

"Okay, bro … You take care. I'll look out for you on the other side."

"Thanks, brother. You too."

I watched him walk back to the gate area. I heard a metallic-sounding voice but I was too far away—or maybe my heart was making to much noise in my ears—to hear what it said.

Then, the gate opened with a couple of clicks and thuds. Caleb gave me a final wave, and he was gone.

And then the pressure that had been building in me burst. As the last hisses and clicks faded away into the background, I pulled my *machaira* from its sheath and started hacking furiously at the cane again and again until I was surrounded by clusters of fallen stalks. For a brief moment, I imagined hacking my own path all the way around the town. But then, suddenly, the fury left me, and I dropped down, exhausted.

I finally made it back to the canal track around midday and began following it around its curve. When I had gone far enough to be invisible from the road, I got some relief by swimming in the canal to cool off.

After that, I began to feel a bit more optimistic. I knew it had been better with Caleb, but I had survived on my own before and I was sure I would be okay for this short journey. It would just take me a day or two to get around the ring and then I would meet up with Caleb again.

But part of me knew I was fooling myself. I felt guilty about leaving my friend to face Addle on his own. And I worried about the "other things" that Clem had warned me about.

When the light began to go, I tried to walk faster. I didn't want to be in the way of the sprinkler again and was hoping to find some sort of shelter or cross-track that would allow me to get away from the water.

Instead, something else found me.

I heard it before I saw it. Its voice was a sort of a quiet, mangled noise that sounded halfway between a yowling cat and a hammer drill. At first, I thought it was some sort of bird, then I thought it couldn't be that because the oscillation sounded too mechanical. And then I stopped trying to work out what it sounded like, because it had appeared above the cane behind me.

It was taller, but less bulky, than the machine that chased me near Didasko. It had a black bulbous head, six long jointed legs, and two clawed arms. As it walked forward, its head was swinging backwards and forwards as if it was looking for something.

I froze, trying to work out whether I was better off hiding or running. Had it seen me? Was it the sort of thing that was interested in me? Maybe it was just an agricultural machine.

But then it stopped still and tilted its head in a way that made me sure it was looking straight at me. It started to come in my direction. So I ran.

It was faster than me. After ten seconds, I could feel the thudding of its feet through the ground. After twenty, I could hear its legs rustling against the cane.

Then, a tiny concrete pump house appeared on the other side of the canal. I jumped across the water, landed badly, and fell.

Almost immediately, the machine was above me, trying to grab at my face with its pincers.

I rolled aside and launched myself at the building. I managed to reach it … ducked around the nearest corner … discovered a half-open door … shoved my way into the darkness. Ignoring the spider webs that stuck to my face and hands, I started groping about for something to shove against the door. I found a heavy plastic fuel tank on one side of the room and a grease-covered pump on the other side. But I couldn't move either of them.

Finally, I felt a square of tread plate right in the centre of the floor. Thinking that it must be a drain cover—and that I might be able to lever it up and use it as a door brace—I got my fingers under it and lifted. The panel turned out to be hinged, but the cold air and echoes underneath told me that this was more than a simple sump. I reached down with my free hand and found a metal rung.

Just then, a terrible screeching sound came from above, almost stopping my heart. I looked up to see the source of it and saw a triangle of sky that hadn't been there before. The monster had begun to peel back the roof.

I still didn't know exactly what was below me, but there was no time to find out. I slid my feet into the shaft, found another rung and pulled the trapdoor down after me.

CHAPTER 22

(Extract of the transcribed Records of Caleb Dox, Vol 1.25)

So I went up to the gate, and there was this video screen there and cameras and guns stickin' out of the wall. And then some lady started talkin' to me.

"Unidentified visitor. Step forward and insert arm to receive RF chip, credit and access."

"What's that mean?" I said.

But she just said it again, so I guess she was a recordin' or somethin'.

"Unidentified visitor. Step forward and insert arm to receive RF chip, credit and access."

I looked around, tryin' to work out what she was talkin' about, but then the video screen came on and showed a picture—not a video, but like a cartoon, of a guy puttin' his arm into this hole next to the screen.

And then the lady said, "Place arm inside the hatch as far as it can go with palm facing upwards. Subdermal implantation is instant and painless.

"This RF chip will allow you to buy, sell, earn and borrow during your stay in Addle."

And then the guy in the cartoon pulled his arm out, and he was lookin' happy and he had this little lump in his wrist, and it was givin' off wiggly lines.

So I got it that they wanted me to stick my arm in the hole—cos there was a real one there, just like in the video. And then I wasn't sure if I wanted to do it—and I thought of maybe just givin' up and goin' round with Chris. But I looked up and saw him givin' me this weird look, so I thought I better do what I said I was gonna do.

So I stuck my arm in, and there was this sort of 'shookh' noise—and it was like they stabbed me with somethin'. And I said, "Hey, I thought you said it wasn't gonna hurt!"

But the lady just said, "RF chip now inserted. You may approach gate and enter. You now have two Credits."

Then I yanked my arm out and looked at it. And there was a spot of blood and a little hole, and when I tried to feel for what they stuck in me it was really sore.

But I reckoned there was no goin' back now, so I went up to the door. And it slid back, and there was a bit of space and another door. And then when I went in, *it* opened up too and I was inside.

Now, lookin' back, it doesn't seem that special what I saw when that door opened. I mean, once you've seen Central, everythin' else looks like a bunch of sticks or somethin'. But at the time, it kind of freaked me out a bit cos it was twenty times what I'd seen at Delice, and that was the biggest place I'd been to up till then.

It was like the pictures of the olden times. It was all a bit yellow cos of the light comin' in through the big tent. Then there were these old shops with painted signs, and there was a little road with stones on it and grass and trees, and a whole bunch of people walkin' round in fancy clothes—I mean big dresses and top hats and stuff—though some of 'em had ordinary gear too.

And they had all these little stalls and carts and stuff. And people were sellin' clothes and plants and machines from before. And I could hear music comin' from somewhere.

But the thing that I really noticed was all the food smells. Some of the stalls were cookin' these pastry things in oil, and they smelled good. And some others were cooking barbecue stuff with meat on 'em, and they smelled good too—and the air was all a bit smoky—which I guess was because the tent thing was keepin' it in.

I just stood there for ages lookin' at everythin'. But then I thought, "I better not get sucked into this cos Chris'll be waitin' for me." So I started walkin' down the road past all the stalls and all the stuff. And then I went round the curve a bit and I could see a girl singin' on a stage with a bunch of guys playin' fiddles and little guitar things, and more shops. And there was one of those big wheels that kids used to ride on—and it was goin', and people were ridin' on it.

And what was weird was that everyone was lookin' pretty healthy. I mean, you could see that some people had cysts on their faces and hands and stuff, but they didn't look all big and red like they did back in Delice. So I was thinkin' maybe Clem was wrong. Maybe this place wasn't so bad. And that made me think of Chris and started me worryin' that I hadn't been able to talk him into comin' with me.

Anyway, I was kind of distracted by that, but then this guy with wild-lookin' hair, who was runnin' a sausage cart, called out to me and said, "Hey, new guy. Want a sausage?"

"No thanks," I said, "I'm just passin' through on my way to Central."

And he said, "So I see. But you still gotta eat, don't you? Can't flee the great Cleanse on an empty stomach."

"Hey, you know about the Cleanse?" I said. "Are you with Central?"

And he just laughed and said, "Very far from it, my friend. But you ain't the first of your kind to come this way."

So I said, "But if you know about the Cleanse, why haven't you gone to Crux and gotten the treatment."

And he pointed to his cart and said, "Cos I've got these sausages to sell … you want to buy one?"

And I said, "I got no money."

"Sure you do," he said. "If you've just come in through that gate, you'll have one credit right there on that chip in your arm. That's enough for a sausage in bread. I'll even throw in some onion and sauce. Smell good, don't they?"

And they did smell good. But I still didn't get how he could know about the Cleanse and be so casual. So I tried to ask him about it, but he shook his head and said, "Tell you what, my friend. Buy a sausage and you can ask me all the questions you like."

So I looked down at what he was sellin', and there were these big bits of soft white bread, and the sausages were all sizzlin' away on the grill.

"What's in 'em?" I said—cos you got to be careful with meat like that.

"Beef and breadcrumbs," he said. "They make 'em right here on the farms around the ring."

"And if I have one, we can talk about Central and stuff?" I said.

"Sure," he said.

So I held out my arm, and he put a scanner thing over it and got me a sausage. And I have to say it was pretty good, but I didn't start eatin' until I'd asked him about the Tox.

And he said, "Yeah, we don't worry about the Tox too much here; got it under control—mostly anyway. We manage our own affairs without Central sticking its nose in, and that's the way we like it."

"But what about the Cleanse?" I said, "It's gonna kill you if you haven't got the cure."

"Yeah, well so you folks keep saying," he said. "Maybe you're right. But maybe it's just a bluff. Or maybe it'll come but I'll be outta here. Corp has a nice little retirement island down south if you can get the credits together."

But I said, "Nuh, man. You won't be able to get away from the Cleanse like that. It says in the Roadbook that it's gonna go everywhere."

"That right?" he said. "Well, I'll take my chances."

"Don't you want to get properly cured?" I said.

"Maybe I do," he said. "But, I hope you don't mind me saying that you guys don't look a hundred per cent cured."

"That's how it works," I said. "It takes time. You shoulda seen me before I went to Crux."

But he just shrugged. "Okay," he said. "Maybe that's true, but if I can't see it, I can't see it. Besides, it's not just the cure is it? They make you take that oath and turn yourself into a vagrant."

"We're Travellers," I said. "Not vagrants."

"Yeah, potatoes, tomatoes," the guy said. "Point is, it's not a very attractive deal."

So I just looked at him. It was really confusin' cos it was like he knew everythin' I was gonna say, and it just washed off him. And you know, he seemed pretty happy, and he had a bit of a cyst underneath his ear, but it wasn't too bad.

So I just finished my sausage and said thanks. And the guy grinned and said, "Any time. And since you've been a good customer, I'll give you a bit of free advice."

"What's that?" I said.

"Be careful about who you say that stuff to," he said.

"What, about the Cleanse?" I said.

"Yeah," he said. "And about the Tox and Central and all that. There's quite a few folks round here don't like to listen to it. You take a look at the town square and you'll see what I mean."

"Why, what's there?" I said.

But then the guy suddenly started lookin' at somethin' over my shoulder and gettin' this worried look on his face. And then he said I should take off quick.

So I turned around to see what he was lookin' at, and these freaky lookin' people dressed up like cats were comin' through the crowd. And some of 'em had like vests made out of fur and fake ears. And some of 'em had gloves with claws on em and, like whiskers drawn on their faces. And there was a girl leadin' 'em, and she was a bit younger than me and she had these big boots and a collar that was meant to be a mane or somethin'.

"Hey, who are those guys?" I said to the sausage guy.

And he didn't look up at me because he was tryin' to pack up his stall really quick, but he said, "That's the lions. They like to make trouble and they don't like your kind. If you know what's good for you, you'll get out of here."

But it was kinda too late for that, cos the girl with the mane was already lookin' at me and had started headin' over to us.

"Ooh, look," she called out. "Looks like we've got ourselves a doggie."

Then the guy with the sausage cart said somethin' else, but I didn't hear it cos the people in the cat gear were all comin' over and spreadin' out in a kind of half-circle with the girl in the middle, and I was lookin' at 'em all and wonderin' whether they were about to attack me.

"You're a big doggie, aren't you?" said the girl.

"I don't know what you're talkin' about, lady," I said.

"I'm talking about you being a good loyal doggie—just doing what your masters tell you to do," she said. "They must like it that they've got a big strong boy like you being their slave. Did they tell you to come in here?"

Now I didn't like that stuff she was sayin'—especially the stuff about bein' a slave—but I got the feelin' that she was sayin' it to pick a fight, so I just kept quiet and kept lookin' at 'em all while she kept on goin'.

But then I suddenly noticed that there was a kid who looked like he was a bit younger than the rest of 'em, and he didn't have much lion stuff—just a couple of fake ears stickin' up from his hair and a bunch of whiskers drawn on his freckles. But he was wearin' a Traveller's pack on his back. So I pointed to it and said, "Where did you get that?"

And the girl laughed and said, "We took it from a doggie like you."

"Why did you do that?" I said.

And she said, "Well, he hurt our feelings. He told us we were sick, and we don't like it when people say things like that. So we ate him up."

I looked at her and thought she was probably just tryin' to scare me—I mean, I'd seen a few real people-eaters out in the west, and I didn't think she looked like one; and also, I thought, no city would let that sort of thing happen out in the open like that. So I just said, "I thought the sign on the gate said no cannibals?"

Well, she didn't like that—kinda hissed at me—and said, "Tell him, Tau," to the kid with the pack.

And the kid looked like he was tryin' to look fierce and said, "It's only cannibalism if you're the same species."

Then the girl said, "That's right." And then she looked back at me and said, "So tell me, doggie. Do *you* think we're sick too?"

"We're all sick," I said. "Everyone's got the Tox. Haven't you been hearin' from the Agents?"

Then she hissed again and said, "We've got a nice big wall and a nice big tent to keep those nasty things out. We don't like Agents, and we don't like their books. And if doggies like you try to bring them in, we maul them. In fact, why don't you open that pack of yours so we can see what's inside?"

And then one of the guys with the clawed gloves tried to grab at my pack, but I was ready for him and stepped sideways so he fell over.

But, straight away, all the others started comin' in closer. And so I thought, "Okay, here we go," and I put my hand up to draw my sword.

But just as I was doin' it. Somebody who was standin' behind me grabbed my hand and clicked a gun next to my ear and said, "Don't do that, Traveller."

And then all the lion people stopped, cos the gun was pointin' at them. And I stopped too, but for a different reason. I stopped because I recognised the voice.

"Leave it in its scabbard," she said. And then she said, "Simha, call off your gang. If you have complaints against this man, you make them through the proper channels."

But Simha, who was also the girl with the mane, made a kind of growling noise.

"It's not a gang," she said. "You know the right word for what we are. And who do you think you are to come between me and my prey?"

"I'm an officer of the Council charged with preserving order," said the person behind me. "Step back."

"Or what?" said Simha.

"Or you'll find out that the law applies to everyone," said the voice. "Even to girls who call themselves lions while exploiting their family connections."

Then the mane-girl stared back at her for a minute and made a sort of hand signal, and they all went past us on either side, leanin' in and hissing and growling at me, and sayin' things like, "next time, doggie."

But I didn't care a bit because I was too excited. And as soon as they were gone, I turned around to look at the person who had rescued me. And there she was—lookin' the same but older and wearin' a dark blue uniform and a really serious expression.

I gave her a big smile and said, "Hey, good to see you, sis." But she held out a hand and said, "Keep your distance, please, sir. I have to caution you that it's a serious offence to draw that weapon within the city walls, and that it could result in fines, imprisonment or pillory. Do you understand?"

And that made me feel really weird for a second, but I guessed why she was doin' it with all the people around, so I put my arms down and said, "Yeah, I guess so."

And she said, "Good," and put her gun back in its holster. Then she came a bit closer and reached up and pushed the handle of my sword down, like she was makin' a point.

"Make sure it stays there," she said out loud. But then she whispered, "Not here. Meet me at the Shallow Dive in a couple of hours."

And then she turned around and walked away.

CHAPTER 23

About five or six metres down, the shaft finished in a wide concrete passage that smelled of cold air and concrete dust. It was totally dark, and quiet too, though I could still hear the machine clanging about up above. I didn't know whether that thing would be able to find the hatch, or be able to do anything about it if it did. But I *did* know I wanted to get as far away as I could from it, so I took my best guess at a direction and began walking, holding out my arms to feel the walls on either side.

I went on for a long while and passed five or six openings before the tunnel ended in a heavy metal door. The door was only slightly open and jammed fast, but I was able to squeeze through and pull my gear after me. After that, I discovered that the room on the other side was half collapsed, and when I tried going on, slipped sideways on a chunk of concrete and almost impaled my kidneys on a couple of reo bars.

I decided to turn back then. But just as I began to retrace my steps, I heard something. Music. Somewhere, up ahead in the darkness, someone was playing a piano.

I stayed there listening to it for a long time, wondering what to do. I didn't really want to meet anyone in a place like that. But the tune seemed familiar—and it didn't seem to be the sort of thing that Savages or HORDsmen would be playing.

So, I started to pick my way forward, moving slowly and carefully toward the sound. Soon, I could see a faint glow up ahead. A bit further, and it became a patch of yellow light that was bright enough to reveal the masonry and the tilted ceiling above me. Finally, as the space forced me to crawl forward, I could see the light for what it was; a piece of patterned tablecloth stretched across a jagged crack.

I could hear singing now too—croaky whispered words that I couldn't make out. But the tune was one I'd heard at Crux.

I edged forward and found I was looking down through the fabric into a sort of lounge room. I could see a couple of padded chairs surrounded by piles of books, a small table holding framed photographs and an electric lamp. Further away, on the edge of the light, two hazy shapes swayed in front of what I guessed was the piano.

They finished their song and stood up—a middle-aged man and woman by what I could see of their outlines. The man went and sat down on the nearest armchair. The woman went to a door at the back of the room that I hadn't noticed before. As she opened it, a slight breeze billowed the tablecloth and filled my nostrils with a warm cooking smell.

She was saying something, but I couldn't make it out—both of them seemed to have these husky voices that made me wonder if there was something wrong with them.

But as I leaned forward to evesdrop, the chunk of concrete I was resting on broke loose so I fell forward, head first through the tablecloth, through the crack, and into the room.

The concrete hit the floor. I landed behind the sofa—wedged in with the fabric around my neck.

Somebody gave a scream. Then everything went quiet.

"Sorry," I called out. "Sorry, I didn't mean to do that."

They showed up as half-lit silhouettes on the edge of my vision. I got an impression of two pale faces, hair-curlers, a grey beard and an unpolished *machaira*. As I twisted my head to get a better look at them, I could see that both of them were wearing Traveller's coats over pyjamas.

"Keep back, Pru," said the man in a thin raspy voice as he pointed his sword at me. "Who are you? What are you doing here?"

"I'm sorry," I said again. "I was attacked by something, and then I found a tunnel and … I heard your music."

"Where are you from?" he said.

But the woman spoke up before I could answer.

"Oh, stuff and nonsense, Trev. You can see he's a Traveller. Put your sword away and help me move the couch. Look at the state he's in."

In a moment, they had made enough space to allow me to haul myself to my feet.

"Aren't you a sight," said the woman. "What's that all over you?"

I looked down at the grey film covering my arms.

"I think it's mostly dust and spider's webs," I said. "The pump room where I found the hatch was full of them."

"Well, let's get you cleaned up and then you can join us for a nice cup of tea and some apple pie. Trev, why don't you show our guest where the showers are, and I'll go and finish getting things ready."

The man looked uncertain for a moment, then gave a sort of shrug and put his sword on the piano. "Alright, come on then," he said, and beckoned for me to follow him out through the door. He led me down a long passage that was painted black and covered with chalk drawings of houses and animals and quotes from the Roadbook:

Fix your eyes East ... What the road takes from you, I will return.
Whatever the road destroys, I will rebuild.

Other doors appeared left and right. They were mostly closed but through one, I could see stainless steel benches and a wooden table. The cooking smell coming from it made me feel starved.

But we weren't stopping there. After a corner and another door Trev ushered me into a big bathroom lined with white tiles, sinks, shower stalls and a wall-length mirror.

"You weren't followed here, were you?" he said quietly.

"I don't think so," I said. "I went through a manhole in the floor of the pump house and closed it after me. But I don't know how smart the thing that was chasing me was."

"Was it a Reaper?" he said.

"I don't know what that is," I said.

"Big tall thing with six legs," he said.

"I think that sounds right."

He seemed to relax a bit and gave me a smile. "That's all right, then. They'll have a go at you sometimes but they're not too bright.

"Now, there are towels by the sink and soap in the stalls. You can leave your gear outside the curtain. I'll find you something clean to put on. Take as long as you like, the water won't run out."

"Thank you," I said, feeling very confused. "… Is this a Central base?"

"Ah, well, not officially," he said. "But it sort of is."

He left me to peel off my filthy clothes and work out the mechanism that controlled the flow and mixture of hot and cold water.

After I had lathered myself with soap and combed the cobwebs from my hair, I just stood there in the stream with the warmth soothing the aches and bruises. When I was finally done, my muscles felt weak, and my fingers were wrinkled from soaking.

I dried myself, put on the flannel pyjamas that Trevor had left for me and felt very strange.

Pru and Trev were waiting for me at a kitchen table spread with cups, saucers, jugs and a teapot. As she saw me enter, Pru took up a knife and began dividing a pie that was sitting in the very centre of it all.

"Take a seat, Chris," she said. "Would you like a bit of cream with your apple pie?"

I sat between them, overwhelmed. The pie-crust was thick and buttery. The tea had a clean, strong taste that seemed to refresh me with every sip.

"This is incredible," I said. "But where does it all come from? How do you have apples? Do they grow them up there with the sugarcane?"

"Oh no, dear," she said. "They manage to grow the basics, but they can't do anything like that. This is all from before."

"Before the war?" I said.

"Not that far back," she said. "It's from Hesper. This is from the deep storage reserve in their bomb shelter. We've been living off it for years."

"And not just us," said Trevor.

"Sorry, what's Hesper?" I said.

"Oh, it's the city that used to be here," said Pru.

"Is it the same as Addle?"

She made a humph noise. "No, dear. Addle is a pretend village run by the Corp. Hesper was a proper city."

"Until the Corp got their hooks into it," said Trevor, pouring himself another cup of tea.

"That's right," said Pru. "But let's not talk about that. Tell us about how it is that we come to have the pleasure of your company."

"I was travelling with a friend, and when we got to Addle he thought we should go through, but I had heard that it was a HORD base, so I wanted to go around. So we split up. And then I got chased by that thing … the …"

"Reaper," said Trevor. "You made the right choice, though."

"Indeed you did," said Pru. "Better to be chased by a Reaper than to try to go through that wretched place."

"Why?" I said, suddenly feeling a stab of fear. "What happens if you try to go through Addle?"

"Oh," she said, looking at my face. "Well, maybe nothing. Some people make it through alright if they keep to themselves."

"If they're lucky," said Trev.

"Yes, but I wouldn't worry about your friend," she said. "Things can get a bit unpleasant sometimes, but the Envoy does have a few people living in there."

"But what do they do to you?" I said. I had put down my fork. The apple pie suddenly seemed too thick to swallow.

"Well…" she said, "They'll try to persuade you to settle down. Mostly, they're subtle about it, but if you make a fuss and start talking about the Tox and about the Envoy, they might get a bit nasty. They might arrest you or send you to the work camps."

I pushed the plate away and got to my feet. "I need to go back. Thank you for your hospitality. Is there another way I can …"

"Steady on, steady on," said Trevor. "There's nothing you can do tonight. Tell you what. If you stick around until tomorrow, we can drive down and see the Professor and the others down at the Museum. They've got a video room that's hooked up to Addle's security cameras. We can take a look and see if there's any sign of trouble."

I stood there, covered in confusion. How could I sit here in pyjamas eating pie while the friend who had come to save my life was in danger? I cursed myself as a coward for not going with him in the first place.

But they were right. What could I hope to do in the middle of the night?

"I don't know what I should do," I said.

"You should stay here tonight and make your decisions when you've had a rest," said Pru. "Come on. I'll show you where you can sleep."

The room she showed me was part bedroom, part store room; two beds hemmed in by boxes of clothes, piles of boardgames, squash rackets, musical instruments and old computer consoles. There was a faint smell of naphthalene in the air.

"This was our boys' room when they were still with us," she said. "It's a bit cluttered now, but I think you'll find the bed comfortable enough."

She was right about that.

I slid between the sheets and let the exhaustion drag me under.

CHAPTER 24

(Extract of the transcribed Records of Caleb Dox, Vol 1.26)

So I went to the Dive place, like Seini said. It was this old-style-looking place with lots of wood and dim lighting and plants in big pots and a piano and booths along one side of the wall.

And there was a young guy with specs up behind the bar—looked like he was doing his bills or somethin'—so I went up and asked him if I could just sit down in one of the booths to wait for someone, and he said sure, and asked what he could get me to drink. I explained that I was just passin' through and didn't have any money now, but he just gave me a smile and said, "That's okay, you can earn some in about two minutes."

So I said, "What do you mean?"

And he said, "See that little booth over there with the curtain and the vid screen? If you sit in there, they'll show you an advertisement, and that will earn you two credits."

So I went and did it. It was some ad for cosmetic Tox-cream, and they made me do a sort of singalong, which was pretty easy. And then, when I went to the bar, the guy checked my credit and said it was okay, so I bought myself a sarsparilla with ice in it, which was pretty good.

While I was drinkin' that, I asked the guy why people didn't watch ads all the time if it was that easy to make money.

He said that they wouldn't let you do it more than a few times, but you could do other things that would earn you more points.

"Like what?" I said.

And then he gave me this laminated card, which had all these different things you could do to earn credits.

Some of it was stuff you could do in the video booth; like there was one thing called "say what we say," where they made you repeat stuff—

the bar guy said it could be weird stuff like, "one plus one equals three," or "dogs and cats are the same species."

But there was other stuff you could do at the registry office. Like you could leave your Roadbook with them while you were in Addle, and they'd give you five points for that.

And they had another thing called "Bestlife" where they'd give you six credits if you went and answered questions, and let somebody type up a plan for what you'd do if you stayed in Addle.

And the guy was explaining that to me, and I said, "Do you mean what kind of work you'd do?"

And he said, "Sure, but also whether you want to work at all."

"How would that work?" I said.

And he explained that you could do this thing called "going red", where you'd go into debt—so you'd have negative credits—and the city would still let you buy stuff. But when you got to a certain number, they'd take you off to the work camps to work until you paid it off.

"How long does that take?" I said.

"Hard to say. Most people don't come back," he said.

"Why would anyone do it, then?" I said.

"I guess some people like to get things up front and pay later."

I was gonna ask him more about that, but then we both got distracted because there was this young kid with red hair and baggy clothes hangin' around one of the big pot plants near the booths and lookin' really shifty.

And the barman said, "What's that in your hand, Bernie?"

The kid said, "Nothing," and held up his hands, but the guy didn't believe him.

"You know what I said would happen if I saw you bringing a lighter in here, don't you?" he said.

"I don't have one, Gus. Look," said the kid.

"Out," said Gus. "And don't come back for the rest of the week, or it'll be permanent."

The kid went to the door and looked out. But then he sort of turned and looked back at the bar guy.

"If I go, they'll catch me," he said.

"Who?" said the barman.

"You know."

"Alright, you can hang out the back for twenty minutes and run some stuff through the washer for me."

Then the bar guy opened the door behind the bar and let the kid through.

"What was that about?" I said.

"That's Bernie. We used to get him to do a bit of work—washing and cleaning and so on," he said. "He's a pretty good kid. But he's got a fix on fire, and sometimes he'd creep up behind customers and light up a bit of their hair. So I had to let him go."

"I can see that would have been a problem," I said. And then I said, "Hey when I came through the gate before, I met this guy sellin' sausages, and he reckoned that you guys had Tox-stuff like that under control."

And he nodded and said, "That's sort of true. But it's been getting a bit worse in the last few years—especially with the riots. We're even getting a bit of savagery now."

"You got riots?" I said.

But then I heard the door open and stopped listenin' cos it was Seini. And this time, she was in civilian clothes, and she had a big smile. And she came over and said, "Look at you, little brother. You got all big."

And I said, "Well, I had lots of time while I was lookin' for you."

"Well, now you found me. Come and tell me about everything."

So she got us both a drink, and we went and sat in one of the booths. And I told her about what had happened to me, and she told me what had happened with her.

And it turned out I was right. She said that she'd left our village and gone with those work guys because they told her they could get her into Central. But after workin' with 'em for a few months, she realised that the thing was a con. When she started making a fuss about it, the crew turned on her and dumped her without any food or water out in the dead lands west of Addle.

She almost died after that—except she found the big cane plantation and followed one of the roads up to the town. Then she almost died again when a Savage tried to jump her right outside the gate. But she fought him off and came in. And somebody saw the security video of her fightin' and offered her a job with the city watch.

"And that's what I've been doing ever since," she said. "It's a good living if you know how to handle yourself and the pay is good. You should join too, Caleb. I could get you in."

But I said, "We can't stay here, sis. The big Cleanse is comin'. You need to get treated, and we need to go to Central."

But she said, "I'm done with all that, Caleb. They conned me once; I'm not going to be conned again."

"But that wasn't Central that conned you," I said.

"Yeah, maybe not," she said. "But how do you know the guys you met aren't just another scam?" And before I could argue with her, she said, "Look, Ca, what I've got here works. It's not perfect, but it works. There's food and water. There's work. I'm earning money—I've almost saved enough for retirement. You can't expect me to chuck that all away."

"But you're workin' for HORD," I said, "They go round killin' people!"

"No, HORD's different," she said. "They're based outside Addle. I'm working for the city."

"But doesn't HORD run the city?" I said.

"No," she said. "I mean, we all work for the Corp somehow. But we do our own stuff in here, and HORD's meant to keep out of it."

So I was just listenin' to her, and it was like when I was talkin' to the sausage guy. Cos she was all clean and healthy, and wearin' nice clothes, and the place we were in had all these drinks and food—and I'd seen the market with all the stuff there—and it was like I didn't know how to get through to her.

So I just said, "I know this all looks good and stuff, Sei, but don't you reckon there's somethin' fishy about it? I mean, when I came in, I didn't know what was goin' on with all the shops. And there's this big tent thing over the top."

And then she laughed and said, "You haven't worked it out, have you? Come on, I'll show you something."

So we went out of the Dive place and across the alleyway and up a bunch of steps made of stone, and then up some other steps made out of metal until we got to this big platform thing with a tiny wooden house on one side of it. And it had like a roof made of planks and a window with "tickets" written on it. And there was a sort of archway that went right through the house to a little train track that was stuck up on a big framework. And everything was orange, cos the sunset was comin' through the tent.

And Seini said, "Do you recognise it now? Look over there."

And where she was pointing, there was this buildin' like a castle, and it had little towers and windows with pointy tops and there was light coming out of its windows. And then I did recognise it.

"Hey, this is that World place!" I said. "That's the Scenic Railway."

And Seini laughed and said, "Yeah, Story World. From that guidebook thing we found. All the bits are still here: WildWest Town, Fairytale Town, Mermaid Town. The Corp made it into a real town and put the tent over it and everything."

And I said, "Wow, I used to love that book. Remember how you used to think the different bits went together—like you wanted to be a pirate mermaid?"

And Seini said, "That was you! I was just playing along because you kept talking about being a cowboy knight!"

And then we both laughed. Except then I felt a bit confused too, cos this was like the place where we always wanted to go when we were kids—and now Seini was *livin' in it*—except Clem had told me it was a bad place. And I felt like I needed to get out of it cos I was worried about Chris, except Seini was here, and I didn't want to go without her.

And all this time, Seini was watchin' my face and givin' me this big grin. And she said, "When I realised what it was, I kept thinking, I wish I could show Ca this place. And now you're here! And I can show you everything when I get my next day off!"

But I said, "So if this is Story World, are you a real cop? Or is it just acting?"

"It's for real," she said. "It's not a park anymore! It's a real town."

"Okay," I said, "but when I came in there were all these people in old clothes, like they used to have in the pictures. And what about that chick who was … bein' a lion? Is she for real, cos she was talkin' about killin' and eatin' people?"

"Those are just Alts," she said. "That's how they cope—they don't like the world, so they pretend it's different. But the rest of it's real."

"So she doesn't eat people?" I said.

"Not yet," she said. "But they do mug people and steal their stuff sometimes. They get away with it cos Sharon—that's the girl who leads 'em—is the Mayor's daughter."

So we just stood there for a long time after that, lookin' at everythin'. I couldn't think of what to say to her—and I kind of thought I should be happy for her.

But there was something about it all that made me feel sad, too. It was like everybody there thought Addle was like Central, and they didn't need to go anywhere or worry about anythin'.

So I just said, "I reckon I'd miss bein' able to see the sky, livin' here."

And she said, "You get used to it. And the light from the tent makes everything look nice."

And she was right about that. All the other lights were comin' on now in the streets and sort of glowin', cos there was a bit of a haze. And a bit further off, I could see the edge of an open space with lots of pavement and fancy stone buildings around it. And I asked Seini what that was, and she said, "That's the city hall. Used to be a bank."

"Yeah, but I mean where you can see the people standin' round."

"That's just the town square," she said. "Hey, come and I'll show you where I live."

We started to go back down the stairs. But then somethin' started making a noise in her pocket, so she stopped and pulled out an electronic tablet thing which had glowin' writin' on it. And she said, "I'm gonna have to go back to the station. Some of the Reds are trying to set fire to the trucks down at the depot."

"Do you want me to come?" I said.

"Nah," she said. "See that tall building over there—the place with like four storeys and a fancy roof? I live in the top floor. Go around the back and up the fire escape and I'll be back soon as I can. Here's my keys."

"Okay," I said. "It's good to see you, sis."

"Good to see you too," she said. And then she ran off.

But I went down to take a look at the city square. And as soon as I got there, I could see that there was somethin' dodgy goin' on. Cos just near the big building, there was this platform-thing with a gallows and also a pillory where they lock up your hands and neck so people can chuck stuff at you.

And there were two guys standin' round the pillory—and one of 'em had a leather jacket, and one of 'em had something that looked like a Traveller's coat except it was kind of greeny-brown instead of grey.

And there was somebody in the pillory, too. I couldn't see him, but as I got closer I could hear him speakin', and I could tell it was Fergus. And he was arguin' with the other guys and sayin', "What are ye talking about, ye numbskull? What difference will all that make when the Cleanse comes? Reds, Savers, HORD, Corpsmen. They're all heading for the same end while yer Scorcher pals keep shoutin' about money. Why do ye think the Envoy sent ye here? To make Addle more equitable? This whole place is doomed! All of it! Why can't ye get that in yer head?"

"That's not right," said the guy in the Traveller's coat. "The Envoy isn't going to destroy the Territory; he's going to restore it."

And then I realised that it was Dil—the guy who had been travellin' with Fergus and me before—except now he'd shaved off his beard and just had a moustache. And his coat was a different colour, and he had a whole lot of badges on the front of it.

And now I was closer, I could see Fergus too. And he looked in pretty bad shape, and had all muck in his hair and on his clothes.

And he was shakin' his head and glarin' at Dil, and he said, "Ye should go away and read the Roadbook again. Ye'll find it says that the reconstruction comes *after* the destruction, and it's the Envoy's job to do the rebuild. Your job is to warn these people so they don't get taken down with the rest of it.

"Look at ye—how quickly ye've accommodated yerself to this madhouse. No gear. No weapons. Do ye think yer on holidays? Do ye think that this is yer home and the people here are yer friends?"

"We're fighting the system," said the man with the leather jacket. "If you're against the Corp, you should be with us Scorchers instead of bothering the Alts."

"Fighting the system?" said Fergus. "Yer *part* of the system! Ye can fight the Corp until yer blue in the face, but if yer still a rebel against Central, yer still on the same side as the Corp."

Then they were all talkin' at once for a second, but Fergus put his head down and then lifted it up again.

"Ye weary me with yer foolishness," he said. "Dil, go off and make nice with yer revolutionary friends. Or, better still, come back tomorrow and chuck a bit of fruit at me? I'm sure that'll make ye more popular."

"Alright," said Dil. "We'll go. But remember, we came to help you."

"Seems to me ye came to lecture me from yer superior wisdom," said Fergus. "Away with ye."

Then they turned to go, and Dil saw me and looked at me like he was gonna say something but just nodded and went past.

And Fergus looked up and saw me and shook his head.

"You too, lad?" he said. "Didn' I tell ye to get yerself to Amhain?"

"Yeah, you did," I said. "But I decided to just keep goin'."

"Well, at least ye've kept yer kit and sword," he said.

I gave him a drink from my water flask and offered him a bit of a ration block, but he didn't want any of it.

"How did you end up in this thing?" I said.

"Why do ye ask?" he said. "Are ye tryin' to avoid the same fate?"

"No," I said, "I'm just tryin' to work out what's goin' on. I only got here today, and it's the weirdest place I've ever seen."

"Ye got that right, lad," he said. "This is a rebel place, and its people are Tox-crazed. They act like madmen, and if ye tell 'em so, yer likely to get attacked."

"Is that what happened to you?" I said.

"Aye, near enough," he said.

"I've been tryin' to tell people about the cure," I said. "But none of 'em reckon they need it."

"That's right, laddie. The Tox makes 'em blind and deaf. And it's getting worse. Won't be long before this whole place goes back to savagery. Smell the smoke; this place is going to burn. The fog and fury is getting thicker by the day. They won't hear a word of sense."

"Are you sayin' we should just get out and leave 'em?"

"Nay, lad. That's not what I'm sayin'. I'm sayin' it's hopeless without assistance. Ye just have to keep shoutin' the Roadbook at 'em and wait till Prax sends ye some help."

Now I wanted to ask him about that. But, before I could, there was like a big roaring noise from over on the other side of the square. And when I turned to look, I saw that it was that animal gang back again.

Then that girl that Seini called "Simha", but who was really called "Sharon", saw Fergus and me, and she pointed at us and said, "Doggies! Good doggies. So faithful to their master. Let's find out what's inside them. Come on, Lions!"

And then they all started runnin' over and tryin' to make it look like they were kind of boundin'.

So I drew my sword and stood up on the platform so they couldn't get to Fergus and said, "You aren't lions. Lions don't talk and stuff. You're just people with the Tox. You need to get help from the Envoy."

And Fergus said, "Good lad. Let 'em have it. I'll call on the Envoy."

But what I said made 'em really mad, because they started comin' on faster and faster and makin' weird snarlin' noises. And then most of 'em stopped in front of the platform, but the kid with the backpack came forward and tried to claw at my leg—even though he didn't have claws like the others.

But I moved my leg and, at the same time, sliced off one of his fake ears. And then they went kind of crazy and all started comin' at us. And some of 'em went around the sides of the platform and started climbin' up and comin' in at different angles.

So then I got really worried because I thought they'd be able to come around behind me and get at Fergus. So I said, "Fergus, I don't know how to stop 'em without hurtin' 'em or killin' 'em."

"Ye need to hamstring 'em, lad. Tis the only way to hold 'em off."

And then I was even more scared, cos I knew I didn't have the skill for that. And how was I gonna get to the legs of the ones that were climbin' up in front of me?

But right then, just as I was tryin' to work out what to do, and not comin' up with anythin', all the lights went out.

CHAPTER 25

In the last dream I remembered from that night, I was in the forest near the refinery and Mayor Stricton was stalking me through the dead trees carrying a stove-top moka pot.

"Wake up and smell the coffee, son," he was saying—which doesn't sound scary but was about the most creepy thing I'd ever heard when I was in my dream. "Wake up … and smell … the coffee!" And now it wasn't a moka pot in his hand but Caleb's head.

I sat up with my heart thumping, not sure where I was or why I was in this soft bed. There was a long strip of light off to one side of my vision and a really good smell in the air.

And then I realised that the smell was coffee and the light was the crack of the open door into the corridor, and I remembered where I was … and what the old woman and the old man had said about Addle. And I remembered my worries about Caleb.

I switched on the lamp and got changed—the clothes that I had peeled off before taking the shower were washed and folded and at the end of the bed. When I finished checking and repacking my gear, I opened the door and made my way down the passage to where the coffee smell mingled with background sounds of dance-hall jazz.

It was all coming from the kitchen, of course. Trevor and Prudence looked up from their books and mugs as I entered.

"Morning, sleepy head," said Pru. "You've had a good old rest. Would you like some cereal or shall I make you some scrambled eggs?"

I looked at the food packets lined-up on the table—They were made of stiff silver plastic with bright labels depicting grains and fruits.

"What are they?" I said.

"Oh, mostly types of muesli; toasted, fruit and nut, some with flakes. They were freeze dried years ago of course, so some of them have lost a bit of their flavour, but they were kept cool down in the vaults so none of them are off or anything."

"I'm not sure … I want to see about …"

"Try the one with flakes," said Trevor. "Coffee? Milk? Sugar?"

I took the cup that Trevor passed me; then watched as he poured a small pile of the flake and fruit mixture into my bowl.

"Oh, for heavens sake," said Pru. "Give him more than that, there's no shortage."

It was like the pie from the night before; full of new flavours and smells. Some of it seemed strange, but the newness of it all—and the very idea that it was unlimited was overwhelming—like stumbling into a diamond mine where everything glittered.

After the cereal, there was scrambled eggs and bacon together with toast spread with tinned butter. And then more coffee and jam for my third piece of toast. I kept saying, "I should stop, I need to get going," and then they'd say something like, "Just have a bit of this. We shouldn't let it go to waste" or "You need to keep your strength up."

"How are you two not really fat?" I said.

"Well, of course, we don't always have quite as much as this," said Pru. "And there's the gym …"

"And we still do our sword drills, don't we?" said Trevor.

"That's right," she said, "Though there's not so much use for them down here and at this stage of our lives."

"Do you ever go up—outside, I mean?" I said.

"Not if we can help it!" said Pru, laughing and then coughing.

"Sometimes," said her husband. "When we need to feel the wind."

"What about going to Central?" I said.

"Ah," said Trevor, "The thing is …"

"It's not so simple to do," said Pru.

"Pru and I think we can do more good here …" said Trevor.

"Yes. Would you like some more coffee, dear?" Said Pru.

"What do you mean about it not being simple?" I said.

"Well," said Pru, looking at Trevor and putting down the coffee jug, "We've already told you a bit about Addle and how you want to stay away from there. The trouble is that going around it isn't a lot better."

"Maybe worse," said Trevor.

"Yes, maybe," she said. "You were lucky to find us when you did."

"Because of the Reaper?" I said.

"Not just those," said Trevor. "If you'd kept going there's the camps. And the Hunters—which are a bit like Reapers but worse."

"The point is, dear," said Pru, offering me more toast, "You're better off here with us."

"Safest place by far," said Trevor.

I looked at them and thought how obvious they were—trying not to sound too eager; trying not to lay it on too thick.

"I really want to find out about my friend before I decide what to do next," I said. "You said there was somewhere where we could see what's happening in Addle."

"Yes, of course," said Trevor. He looked at Pru and shrugged. "When you've finished we'll head down to the platform."

"Thank you," I said. "I think I'm ready now. I'll just get my things."

"Oh, just leave them here." said Pru. "You'll have to come back this way if you're going to Addle."

"She's right," said Trev. "No point in lugging your gear about if you don't have to. Besides we might be able to top up your pack with a few items before you head off."

"I think I just want my stuff with me," I said. "I had a couple of bad experiences when I left it behind."

I got up from the table feeling like I was being ungrateful or heartless. There was something sad about them; something that made me sorry for them. But it also made me wary—I had the feeling that the longer I stayed, the harder they would make it for me to get away.

I went and gathered my things and straightened the bed covers in the room. When I returned to the corridor, Pru was waiting for me with an armful of silver packets.

"Here are a few things just in case you don't come back this way. I know your rations are enough, but I don't think the Envoy would mind you having a few nice things."

I thanked her and stowed them in my backpack. Then Trevor led me down the passage to a door I hadn't seen before. Beyond that there was a bare concrete stairwell and lights that flickered on and off as we went down through the levels.

We ended up at another door. Then there was a big echoing space with a faint breeze and a smell of burnt-out electrical motors. When Trevor switched on the lights I could see we were in an underground train station lined with tiles and faded posters advertising deodorant, life insurance and other things I couldn't make out. As I looked down the platform, I could see overturned vending machines; enamel bench seats and a big sign saying "Park Station". Just in front of this, a tiny yellow and black train carriage sat on the tracks, tethered to the wall by an orange extension cable.

"We have to run it off batteries," said Trevor as he unplugged the flex and began coiling it up around his forearm. "The lines are still connected but they'd probably notice the power drain if we switched them on. Hop on—there's a couple of seats up front."

A minute later I was sitting beside him watching the train's headlight illuminate the passing segments of the tunnel.

"Won't take us too long," he said, leaning close to me so I could hear him over the whine of the engine. "Only a couple of stops before we get to Museum—not that we'll actually be stopping, of course."

"This place is amazing, Trevor," I said. "How did you end up here?"

"Ha, well it's a bit of a long story," he said, scratching his whiskers with his free hand. "But to give you the short version, Pru and I were travelling with a group that got to Addle and fell apart. They arrested our leader and persuaded him to give up his coat and sword for a whole lot of credits. Then most of the others followed. It was a bad business.

"After that Pru and I decided to get out while we still could. We tried going round the perimeter—like you've been trying to do—but when we got to the camps some guards saw us and we had to run. Then, the others—who you'll meet in a few minutes—found us when we were hiding out in the old city and took us to Museum.

"We were only going to hang about for a few days and then move on, but we found out that Pru was pregnant so we decided to stay until she'd had the baby.

"And then one thing led to another, I fixed up this train and found Park Station and then we decided to stay a bit longer until the kids were old enough to travel. Then we stayed because we wanted to keep the boys safe. And then, after they left, we felt like we had to stay so they'd find us here if they came back."

"Sounds like you've been here a long time," I said.

"Almost twenty-five years, now," he said.

"Do you think you'll get back on the road again one day?"

He glanced at me for moment and gave a sad looking smile.

"I'd like to think so. Maybe we'll get a signal from Prax, or the Envoy will send us a message. But you know it get's harder the longer you stay in one place and neither of us are in the best of health now."

We were quiet for a while then. We passed through another abandoned station, then a bit where the tunnel had cracked a bit and the rails bounced us around. But Trevor didn't seem worried by any of it.

"I think I met the Envoy once," I said after a while. "Up at a pass in the mountains."

"Well that's something," said Trevor. "What did he look like?"

"I didn't see him because I was blind," I said. "But he saved my life. He gave me food and told me how to get to Crux."

"Just showed up, did he?"

"Well that's what I thought at first," I said. "But later I realised that he'd answered my signal. They had a radio in the hut up there and I did an SOS thing on the handset. I didn't even think about it at the time, but he said he'd come because I asked for help."

"Well that's something," he said again. "That's definitely something."

He adjusted the lever and I felt the carriage slow slightly.

"We're not far off now," he said. "Now, I asked Pru to let them know we're coming so it should be fine, but don't be too surprised if some of them are a bit jumpy."

"In what way?"

"It's nothing you need to worry about. And you come from Spillan, which they'll like. But I wouldn't be too quick to say that you're thinking of going to Addle. Not straight up anyway."

"Who are they? Are they Travellers?"

"Well they're a mixed bunch. Some of them are Travellers."

Up ahead now we could see a faint yellow light, growing bigger as Trevor slowed us down again. Soon I could see the edge of another platform and two figures standing on it. One had a Traveller's coat and a rifle over his shoulder.

The other, a young woman, had a leather jacket, shaved head and a sub machine gun. She swung it up as the train came to a stop and glared at us as Trevor opened the door.

"What the Tox, Trev? Why haven't you got him blindfolded?"

Trevor held up his hands and stepped out of the carriage.

"Morning Rose. Johnny," he said. "This young fella is Chris. He's from Spillan and he's just wanting to check the security cameras. He's not going to make trouble."

"That's not the point," said Rose. "What if he gets caught? What if they interrogate him and ask him where he's been? He should have a bag over his head."

The other man, Johnny, a few years older than me with a long face, smoothed back his hair and gave me a wink.

"Too late for that, Rosie. If he found his way to Trev and Pru's he already knows about the tunnels."

"Trev shouldn't have brought him here then."

I caught her eye. "If you want to put a blindfold on me that's okay. I'm not here to find out your secrets."

"What are you here for, then?" she said.

Trevor spoke up before I got a chance. "Chris was travelling with a friend who made the mistake of trying to go through Addle. We just want to see if there is any sign of him on the security feed."

She looked at me suspiciously for a moment.

"So you haven't been in there yourself?"

"Addle?" I said, "No. I heard that it was a HORD base so I've been trying to go round."

She snorted. "Good decision, bad reason. Okay, show me your legs."

"What?"

"Lift up the bottom of your dacks so we can see your ankles."

I did as I was told while Johnny shone a torch on my feet.

"Alright," she said, "Bring him up. I'll go and tell the Prof you're coming."

She turned and clattered away up one of the long travelling stairs that stood in the background.

"What was that about?" I said. "Why did she want to see my legs?"

"Checking to see if you had a tracker," said Johnny. "Making sure you were telling the truth about not having been to Addle. Come on up."

He turned and led the way up the same metal staircase that Rose was still climbing. I followed, looking at the plate-sized target design he had stitched on the back of his coat.

"What's your patch mean?" I said.

"City Militia," he said. "You know about Hesper?"

"Pru and Trevor told me there was a city before Addle."

"That's right—the real city. It was one of the last sanctuaries after the AZ went to the dogs. At the moment we're right under where the square used to be, right next to the museum—not that you'd know if you went up top."

"What happened to it?"

"The Corp," he said, twisting around to look at me. "They killed it. First they sent in spies and saboteurs to stir up trouble and interfere with the water supply. Then they gave weapons to all the factions so they'd murder each other.

"Eventually the place just fell apart and the Corp came in and claimed what was left. They took the survivors and stuffed them into that stupid tent and they bulldozed the parkland and outer suburbs to make the ring farms. And then they started cutting off the water to the surrounding villages so they could keep it for themselves."

"I think we went through those when we were coming in from the west," I said. "Didn't look like there was much left."

"No, there's nothing. Rose and I came from the last one they killed. The Corp started charging us for our own water ration and then cut us off when we couldn't pay.

"That's the Corp," said Trevor, puffing behind me. "They never saw a good thing they didn't want to steal or sell. They're still doing it up top—got their slaves sifting through the ruins looking for valuables."

"That's right," said Johnny, "But they don't know about the really valuable stuff. We've got that down here."

"What's that?" I said.

"Aha," he said, holding up a hand. "Listen."

We were almost at the top now and could see a dimly lit roof and the columns of some grand space opening out above us. But as we paused I could hear music echoing about in the curved ceiling. It was classical music, different from the stuff that Vera had played me in Ockham, but it had its own beauty. There was a solitary violin that kept climbing up and up. Then there was a swelling orchestra.

"Come on," said Johnny, "There's more."

We followed him up the last steps, and then I had to stop and hold on to the railing because there *was* more—a lot more.

It was too much to take in. First there was the hall itself. It was enormous—a tall vault supported by massive classical columns—all lit by a hundred reading lamps and flood lights and complicated chandeliers (though most of these weren't lit).

But the "more" that Johnny was talking about was the mountain of stuff that filled the hall: giant paintings of battles, mountains and hunts leaning up against the columns; pianos, cellos and harps and other musical instruments I'd never seen before; statues of naked men, and women in robes; fancy furniture; tables and shelves stacked with film reels and music discs and old-fashioned machines to play them on. Up in a gallery that ran around the outside of the columns I could see rows of book shelves, more chairs and tables and lamps.

"What ... what is this?" I said.

"Used to be the main train station," said Johnny. "Now it's where we've been putting all the stuff we rescue. Come on, we'll introduce you to the Prof."

He led the way forward through the maze—past tall vases decorated with pictures of heroes and gods; past stuffed animals and suits of armour; past painted globes and strange brass contraptions.

I wanted to ask about them; what they were all for and what it all meant. But the music was fading away now and an amplified voice was echoing around the hall.

"My friends, if we are ever tempted to believe the lies of the Corporation concerning what came before, we need only listen to a track like that to be disabused. There was once a city where life had meaning; where people lived with a vision of a shared destiny. There were once villages and farms tilled by generations of families united by bonds of love and duty.

"Music such as this cries out in lament for that lost world. It commands us to lift our eyes. It demands we do more than survive—more than merely escape."

The voice coming over the speakers was husky but sort of full and round. The way he formed his words seemed to fit the place we were in.

And now that we were halfway down the hall, we could see the man himself. Part of the upstairs gallery had been enclosed with windows and I could see a man pacing about. On the walls behind him, I could see rows of clocks and dials lit by a yellow light.

The man wasn't much more than a silhouette at first, but I could see that he was wearing some sort of suit and holding a microphone. As he turned, he seemed to catch sight of us. He held up a hand.

"Now," he was saying, "I think we have time for just one more caller. Who have we here?"

There was a loud fuzz and crackle. Then there was a younger male voice speaking in a whisper.

"Can you hear me, Professor? Am I on?"

"You are indeed, my friend," said the man, "but you are a little muffled. Where are you calling from?"

"I'm in Addle. I think the signal gets mucked up by the tent. But also I have to talk quietly because I'd get into trouble if people knew what I was doing."

"I completely understand. And I appreciate your courage. How might I help you?"

"Well, I was going to ask about fighting the Tox. You said that our only hope is to be courageous and to be self-disciplined and willing to suffer. But I heard that in the old days they had treatments for it. Can't we get hold of those?"

"Thank you for this question, my friend. Here is what I know.

"First, you are correct that there *was* a general treatment in the old days. The Hesper city fathers had a very effective suppressor-agent that they put in the water. If you are living in Addle, you yourself have had some of it because they have been eking out the last of a cache of the stuff they discovered years ago. That's why Addle, despite all its ... well you know what I think of the place ... has been as stable as it has for so long.

"But that stockpile is gone now. They've tried making their own version and it isn't working—that's why things are getting worse in there. So until somebody cracks the recipe or they find another store of the stuff, I'm afraid we are on our own and have to fight it on our own. And that means all those things about courage and suffering are going to be true.

"And it will be harder for you in there because Addle has developed whole industries built to encourage self-indulgence. It wants to weaken your character so it can put you in its debt and turn you into a slave. Tell me, my friend, are you in the red?"

The other man began to answer that he was, but I couldn't hear the rest of the conversation because Johnny had led us off into an enclosed staircase next to the main hall. By the time we stepped out on to the gallery, the man with the husky voice was thanking the caller and introducing the final recording. This time it was a chorus that seemed to explode out at us.

Johnny opened the door to the room with the glass windows. It must have been the control room when the station was still a station. Below the clocks and dials, there were rows of levers and banks of small cathode-ray monitors. Rose was working her way along these, switching them on.

The Professor was standing in front of the windows with his eyes closed, conducting the music. When he heard us enter, he stopped and turned it down before coming around to face us.

"Trevor," he said. "Always a pleasure to see you. I hope you are well. And this must be the young man that your charming wife mentioned on the telephone."

"Chris," I said.

"Delighted to meet you, Chris," he said, holding out his hand. "Aldus Channing at your service. I understand that you are hoping to use our link to the Addle security system to locate a friend."

"Yes, please," I said. "Trev and Pru told me about what they do in there and I'm trying to find out if my friend is okay."

"I understand your concern and salute your loyalty to your friend," he said. "Rose and Johnny can show you what you need to know."

He gave a final smile and looked around at us.

"And if anyone needs me I will be in the library."

He left the room and I looked back to see that Johnny had moved to take over from Rose at the screens. She was slouching against one of the desks, lighting a cigarette.

"Come on," said Johnny.

I went over to him. There was a smell of dust, ozone and hot resin as I got closer.

"Start over here," he said. "This bank shows the main gates, including the one you would have entered through if you were on the road from Crux ... Over here we have the west promenade where the market is. See, you can flick between different views along the way.

"Then we have the town square—a few different angles there too— and the rest are various views of different streets ... and the portables ... and the tenements—if there's any trouble it's usually over there. In fact, look, you can see some smoke coming up ... and there's a police van in the background ... Doesn't seem to be much happening with any Travellers though."

I tried to follow him, squinting at the figures walking about in the grainy images. Did that person have a coat? No it was some other kind of jacket. There was a big man—but was it Caleb? I didn't think so.

I reached out and flicked the switcher on the monitor that showed the town square: cafés with awnings; people dressed in old-fashioned clothes; police strolling past a man with a pushcart.

"What's that?" I said.

"That's the pillory. Sometimes they chain people there as a punishment—it's a bit of a sport for them. Occasionally they'll put a Traveller in there—not today though."

"Looks all clear," said Trevor, peering over my shoulder. "Maybe he's gotten through already."

"Yeah," I said. I suddenly realised that there had been a sort of knot in my stomach all morning and that it was finally untwisting.

"But what about these screens over here?" I said, pointing to a small cluster to the right.

"You don't need to worry about them," said Johnny. "Those aren't Addle—they show the camps and farms."

"Oh, okay," I said. I began to turn away to check the other screens for a last time, but something stopped me. It was like something had set off an alarm in my head for a second, but I didn't know what had caused it. When I looked back at the end screens, there didn't seem to be anything remarkable on any of them. One showed some sort of factory where people in overalls were feeding bundles of sugarcane into a shredding machine. Another showed a crossroad bordered by some kind of crop that was rippling with the wind. Then there was an open space with a flagpole and a small hut. And finally, a truck parked next to an open loading platform.

"See something?" said Johnny.

"I thought I did," I said. "But I don't know…"

Yet, as I spoke there was movement on the last screen. A woman wearing overalls was coming out of the truck, pushing a trolley stacked with sacks.

She was short, middle-aged. I couldn't see her face, but I knew straight away that she had been the cause of the alert, because now there was a sudden pounding in my ears. I opened my mouth to speak and there was no air.

And now the woman was gone.

I pointed to the screen and looked at Johnny.

"That one," I said. "Can … Can you make it zoom in?" My voice sounded like it was cracking—like it was coming from a long way away.

"No," said Rose.

"Actually, we *can*," said Johnny, "but we don't like to do it because we don't want the real security people wondering who's messing about with their gear … What are you wanting to look at?"

"Her, I said," as I pointed to the woman who had just come back into view.

"Ah, that's not a Traveller," said Johnny.

"No, I know," I said.

"So who is it?" said Rose.

"I think … I think that's my mum."

There was a half-second silence, then Rose swore, lunged past me and depressed one of the buttons below the screen. Immediately the view narrowed in to the rear of the truck—just as the woman reappeared pushing a new load. She looked down as she eased the trolley off the small step that was created by the height difference between the truck and the dock.

Then she raised her head.

She looked different; older and thinner, and her hair had gone grey. But there was no doubt.

"That's her," I said, barely managing to speak. "How do I get there?"

CHAPTER 26

(Extract of the transcribed Records of Caleb Dox, Vol 1.27a)

So I was feelin' pretty bad when I woke up. My face and neck were all hot, and it was like one of my arms had been stung with wasps or somethin'. And I couldn't open my eyes. And when I tried to move my arm to find out what was goin' on, somethin' was stoppin' it from movin'.

That made me pretty wild for a second. I started rollin' about tryin' to yank my arm free. But then somebody put a hand on my wrist and said, "It's okay, Ca. Use your other hand for now."

And it was Seini, so I settled down a bit and said, "Where am I? What's goin' on?"

And Seini said, "You're at the Watch-house clinic. You were in a fight and you got cut up a bit."

"Oh yeah," I said, cos I kind of remembered. "It was those lion people. But why can't I open my eyes?"

"It's okay," said Seini, "One side of your face is all swollen, and it's got tape on it. The other eye is just stuck down with gunk. Hold on, and I'll see if I can clean it up."

Then she got a cloth with warm water and wiped my eyelids until I could open my eyes, and then I could see that my arm was handcuffed to the side of the bed. And I wanted to ask her about that, but I suddenly remembered about Fergus, so I said, "Hey, what happened to the old guy? There was a guy in the stocks…"

And Seini said, "Don't worry about him. He'll be okay. But listen, Ca. I gotta talk to you, and I've only got a few minutes."

So I shut up and looked at her, cos even though she was a bit fuzzy she looked really serious, and she told me that the reason why I'd been cuffed was that one of the lion kids had got killed and they thought I did it.

"Why?" I said.

And she said, "Because when we got to you, you were lying there with blood all over your sword, and the kid had had his throat cut. And Simha says you drew your sword and attacked them."

Well that made me feel really worried—especially because I suddenly found out that I didn't have any memory of anything that had happened after the lights went out.

"But they attacked *us,*" I said—cos I could remember that.

And I told her that I did draw my sword and cut off that kid's fake ear, "But I was about to put it away, cos I couldn't use it without hurtin' 'em … But I can't remember what happened."

"Okay," she said. "Don't tell them about the ear. Look, Ca, in a minute, they're going to come in, and they are gonna charge you. Just tell them the lions came and attacked you, and that you can't remember what happened, and that you don't want to answer their questions without a lawyer. Don't let them pressure you into anything or try any tricks on you. They'll try to get at you while you're still sorting yourself out—might try to offer you a deal or something."

"What kind of deal?" I said.

"Something like, if you admit you did it, they'll go easy on you—maybe you'll just have to do a bit of time in the camps or …"

But before she could finish, the cops came in like she said they would. They were wearin' dark suits with holsters. And one was a man, and he was like middle-aged with bad skin and a busted nose. And the other was a woman, and she was a bit younger and she had blond hair and pink lipstick.

And the man said, "Okay, Seini. Out you go. We'll take it from here."

So Seini got up and squeezed my hand and said, "Just remember what I told you, Ca."

And I said, "Sure, Seini," but really I was worried I wouldn't remember any of it because everything was sore and my brain was all foggy.

Meanwhile, the two cops were gettin' set up. The lady had the same kind of tablet thing that Seini had, and she was doin' somethin' with it. And the guy was watchin' her and lightin' one of those cigarettes that smell like cloves and blowin' out smoke and lookin' at me.

"Seems pretty clear," said the lady.

"Totally clear," said the guy. And then he looked at me and said, "Less than one day in town and you're pulling out your sword and chopping kids in the neck. Did you think people wouldn't notice or something?"

"I didn't kill anyone. I took out my sword because they were comin' to attack Fergus."

"And then what happened?" asked the woman

"Someone switched off the lights."

"And then you pounced," said the man.

"No ... I don't remember after that," I said.

And the guy looked at the lady and laughed and said. "Can't remember? Well, that's very convenient. But I don't think it's gonna help you here.

"I should tell you at this point that we are recording this conversation. I am detective Nigel Gull. This is detective Tina Swike and we are now charging you with the murder of Thomas Privy, aged 16, of Addle City. Anything you say from this point on may be used in your trial. Do you understand what I have just explained?"

"I guess so. But I don't know the kid you're talking about."

"Well that didn't stop you chopping off his ear, did it?" said the lady.

And I guess I looked surprised or sick or somethin' cos then they both laughed, and the guy said, "We've got you right here on the security feed. Show him, Swike"

And the lady cop flipped the tablet thing around and there was a video on it. At first, I couldn't see it properly cos my eyes were still a bit blurry, but I could tell it was showing me and Fergus and Simha's gang, when they were all comin' at us and gettin' crazy.

And then she pushed a button or somethin' and it all slowed down, and I could see the kid with the backpack grabbin' at my legs, and me steppin' away and slicin' off his ear.

"Looks like you missed that time," Gull said. "But as soon as the lights went out, you had another try."

"Or maybe you were scared and just started slashing about—not knowing what you were doing," said Swike. "That's the way I'd go if I were you."

"It wasn't like that," I said. "It wasn't either of those things. I was tryin' to scare 'em off. I wasn't tryin' to hurt 'em. If you ask Fergus, he'll tell you that. I was askin' him what to do cos I didn't want to cut 'em."

"Yeah, he's not going to be able to answer any questions for a while," said Swike.

"And even if he did, it wouldn't help you," said Gull. "Maybe you didn't want to hurt anyone, but you did. Maybe you were just slashing about like Swike says."

"No," I said.

"What do you mean 'no'?" he said. "You said you don't remember."

"I mean, I wouldn't have just been slashin' about."

"Listen," said Gull. "We've got you right here on the camera, with your sword out, attacking the victim just before the lights go out. Next thing, someone calls the Watch, and when they get there, they find the kid with his throat cut and you with blood all over your sword. Have a think about how that's going to play when you go to trial."

I got pretty scared when he said that. But I remembered what Seini told me.

"I reckon I shouldn't talk to you anymore without a lawyer," I said.

"You can play it like that," said Gull. "And you'll get convicted and sent out to the camps for life. Or you can play it our way."

"What's that?" I said.

"You apologise and admit you did it under the influence of Central.

Tell everyone that you were misled and that the Central Gov made you crazy. And then we forget about the charges."

"And nothing bad happens to your sister, either," said Swike.

I started to tell Gull I wasn't gonna do any of that. But then I realised what Swike was saying and I suddenly felt really cold. "What do you mean?" I said. "She's got nothing to do with it. She wasn't even there."

"Really?" said Swike. "Because somebody cut those lights."

"And that's not all," said Gull. "We've got another video with the two of you that shows her pointing a gun at Simha down at the market."

"That was just cos they were about to attack me," I said.

"So, just like at the town square?" said Swike.

Now I was feelin' really bad, and it was like the bed I was on was startin' to spin. But then I remembered what Seini said about 'em tryin' to trick me, so I said, "I'm ... still not gonna say I did it. I'm not gonna blame Central."

Then Swike laughed and told me I was a great brother. And Gull blew a whole lot of smoke at me and said, "You sure about that? This is a one-time offer. Once we charge you and you're in the system, it'll be too late. This is your last chance to make it go away."

"No," I said. "I'm gonna stick with Central and trust the Envoy."

"Alright," said Gull. "Get out of bed then. We're taking you downstairs to the cells." And before I had a chance to do anythin' else, he tipped up the side of the mattress so I fell out onto the floor. And that banged up my arm, but what was worse was I realised that they'd taken off all my gear, and I was just in one of those gown things and it was all twisted round.

Then Swike laughed again and said I should get some clothes on.

*   *   *

After that, they took me downstairs to the station room, which was this big hall with arched windows where all the cops had their desks and where they brought in the people they were arrestin' and questioning and stuff.

And it was all really full that mornin', cos that fire that Seini had gone off to had been the start of a bit of a riot. So there were people with swollen eyes, and blood-noses, and torn clothes. And some of 'em were just dressed in normal clothes or overalls. And some of 'em were in old-fashioned gear. And some looked like robots and chimney sweeps and stuff. And there was a cowboy and a girl dressed like a fairy, and they were shouting at each other and tryin' to fight, except the cops were holdin' 'em back.

So Gull and Swike were kind of pushin' and pullin' me through the crowd and between the desks. And I was still really sore where my arm was bandaged cos it kept gettin' bumped. And I still couldn't really see out of one eye, and the other wasn't seein' that well either—which is why I didn't see Simha until we were almost right next to her.

She was sittin' at a desk talkin' to another lady cop—I guessed she was makin' a witness statement—and there was so much noise that I thought maybe we'd just be able to slip by her.

But just when we were almost past, she suddenly looked up and saw me. And before anyone could do anything, she got up and jumped at me. And she was makin' that roarin' sound, and clawin' at my face and tryin' to bite my neck—except she mostly just got my collar.

I could only do a bit to stop her cos my hands were cuffed, but Gull and Swike and the cop who'd been talkin' to her managed to drag her off me. And some people were laughin' and cheerin', and Simha was screamin' at me and callin' me a dog and a murderer, and sayin' that she was gonna tear out my throat and eat my heart.

And I said, "It wasn't me, lady."

Then they took me to one of the interview rooms and got my details and fingerprints. They took my photograph, and Swike said I'd be given a lawyer and they were gonna remand me in custody until the Chief of the Watch or a judge decided whether to grant me bail.

I didn't mind all that stuff. When I was workin' for the Mayor back in Delice, we sometimes tried to do it properly and make it look like we were gonna treat everyone fairly, but most of the time, we just roughed people up and tried to get 'em to confess. But these were like real cops, and they made notes and recorded what I said on their tablet things. And I was rememberin' what Seini had said to me about me joinin' 'em, and I thought maybe it wouldn't have been so bad.

But it didn't stay like that.

After we got out of the interview room, they put the cuffs back on me and took me to another stairwell and made me go ahead, and Gull was just behind me, and Swike was behind him and she said, "You know you could still avoid all this if you just confess."

"That's right," said Gull, "Why don't you do yourself a favour before we lock you up? You think they're gonna go easy on you down there in the cells cos you've got bandages on?"

And I said, "But I thought you said it would be too late once you processed me."

And then Gull kicked me in the back of my knee and gave me a shove, so I slipped on the stairs and came down on my back.

"Want to get smart, do you?" he said. "You think you can come in here and do whatever you like and nothing'll stick to you because you're wearing that coat? Think you can just start chopping up kids and the Pantarch'll protect you?"

"No," I said. "If I did what you reckon I did, I deserve to get locked up or whatever you wanna do to me. But I'm a citizen of Central and I'm gonna appeal to the Envoy."

"Wake up," said Swike. "You're under our tent here. Central's drones can't see you."

But I said, "Nah, I reckon the Envoy sees everything—even in here."

Then they both grabbed me and looked like they were about to push me down the next flight of stairs, but Seini came around the corner and said that the Chief wanted to talk to me, so they had to hand me over.

And Seini took me back up the stairs, and I said, "What's happenin', Sei?" And she said she was gettin' me out.

"So does that mean they're droppin' the charge?" I said.

"No," said Seini. "It means I'm trying to get you bail. You understand how that works?"

"Yeah, 'course," I said.

"They wouldn't normally do it for a case like this," she said, "But I'm vouching for you, so the Chief said she'd consider it. But she wants to talk to you first. So you got to be really good. And you gotta convince her that you aren't gonna get into any more trouble. Can you do that?"

"Yeah … I reckon I can."

"Because if you get into any more fights or do something they don't like, they'll just take my money and put you back in the cells."

"Yeah, I get it," I said.

So she took me back up the stairs to see her Chief, whose name was Paula Diritto.

And the Chief told me to sit down in a chair on the other side of her desk, and she told Seini to go out and close the door behind her.

And then she just left me sittin' there for like ten minutes while she was writin' and stuff. And I guessed it was like some kind of test to see if I was gonna go psycho, so I just tried to sit there really quiet.

But while I was sittin' there, I started lookin' at the pictures on her wall. And there was one of her in her uniform. And there was one with her with a guy and a couple of kids. And there was one with her and a guy in a suit and another lady cop. And the guy was givin' the other lady cop a piece of paper in a frame or somethin'.

"Hey, that's Seini," I said out loud.

Then she stopped and looked up at the picture and said, "Yes, it is. She's receiving a certificate from Mayor Fortuna for being Employee of the Year."

"That's good," I said.

"Yes, it is," she said again. "But right now, you should be thinking about what Seini is doing for you. Do you know what she is risking to get you out?"

"She said she was trying to get bail," I said. "So, I guess that means a stack of money."

"A very big stack," said the Chief. "All her money and more besides. She's going to have to dip into the red for you."

"I didn't know that," I said. "I wouldn't have wanted her to do that."

"Well, I haven't approved it yet. Do you want me to say 'no' and send you back downstairs?"

"Yeah. If she's gonna lose all her money. I don't want her to have to go red."

"She won't lose it if you can behave yourself."

I nodded. But I was a bit confused about what she was wantin' from me, so I just waited for her to talk.

Then she said, "The evidence makes it look like you're a thug, Caleb. My detectives have sent me videos of you pulling out your sword and attacking the boy. You also seemed to be on good terms with Fergus Dort, who was in the stocks for provoking the same group. I think your lawyer is going to have to do something spectacular to convince the judge that you aren't the perpetrator."

And she looked at me hard and said, "Have you got anything to say about that?"

"I know it doesn't look good," I said. "And I don't know what happened cos I can't remember anything after the lights went out. But I wouldn't have done that to that kid. And when I cut off that ear, I was just trying to scare him a bit."

"Maybe so," she said. "And maybe that's what I thought when I saw the video."

Then she stopped and clicked her pen a few times and looked up at me.

"I'm going to let you out, Caleb. Your arresting officers aren't going to like it, but I'm going to do it for Seini's sake."

"Thank you, Chief," I said.

"Don't thank me," she said. "If you want to show your gratitude, keep out of trouble. I'll concede there are some mysteries about this case, but the *prima facie* is still clear. If you start acting up and make me look bad, I am going to take it out on you, and Seini is going to be up to her neck in red."

"Okay, Chief," I said.

"Do we have an understanding?"

"Yes, Chief."

"Alright. Now, go out and someone will fit you with an ankle tracker. Seini will tell you what it does. If we find that you've been tampering with it, you'll breach your bail."

And then she stopped and said, "But that's not going to happen to you because you care about your sister, right?"

"Yes, Chief," I said.

"Good."

CHAPTER 27

Nobody knew exactly where the camera was that had showed my mum. Trevor thought it might be at the biofuel plant where they processed and distilled the cane. Rose reckoned it looked like part of the main camp. Johnny didn't have an opinion, but he was the one who offered to take me to an exit and set me on my way.

"It'll be a bit of a hike down the tunnel," he said. "But I can get you pretty close to that distillery."

The others said their goodbyes in their own ways. Rose gave me a nod and warned me not to get caught. The Professor called down from the gallery to wish me all the best. Trevor, last of all, put a hand on my shoulder and told me to take care of myself.

"I want you to know that you'll always be welcome back with Pru and me," he said.

We left him next to his train and crossed to another tunnel that branched away into the dark. There was no train and no lighting here, but Johnny had a faded yellow flashlight to show the way.

"Old fuel-cell job," he said. "Not super bright, but it'll go for ages. They knew how to make 'em in the day."

Johnny was a talker. He told me about how in the old days, this tunnel had been the zoo line and that families used to come out to see the animals or picnic in the parklands that surrounded it. He said sometimes the animals would escape: once, a troop of baboons had come into this tunnel and made it all the way back to Museum. He talked about how musicians used to play in the concourses, and how the same tunnels had become bomb shelters in the civil war.

I didn't really want to listen to him. I was too distracted by what I had seen. I kept thinking about my mum and kept wondering what had happened to her; how I was going to find her and get her out.

And yet some part of my brain must have been paying attention because suddenly I found myself asking him a question.

"Why are you here?" I said.

"I'm helping you," he said.

"No, I mean, why do you stay here instead of going on toward Central?"

"Oh," he said, "Well, because it's all that's left. And because it's worth fighting for. And because if we don't do something, they'll destroy it all."

He waited for me to say something in response. When I didn't, he went on:

"If you haven't been to Addle, you've no idea what they're capable of. It's a madhouse, and it sends everyone who goes there mad too, if you stay long enough. We're just trying to provide a bit of sanity."

I thought about it for a while and said, "You don't reckon we should be looking forward instead of back? I mean, Hesper isn't Central, and by the sounds of it …" But Johnny cut me off.

"You know that if you manage to get your mum, you'll need to bring her back here, don't you?"

"What do you mean?" I said.

"If she's in the camps, she won't be able to go beyond the perimeter of the camps zone."

"Why?"

"Because she'll be wearing a tracker round her ankle, and if it detects that she's left the area, it'll go off and fire a whole lot of toxin into her leg."

"What?" I said.

"'Fraid so," he said. "I told you it was a bad place. Even when you get away you can't really get away."

"Well, if I bring her back to you guys, can you cut it off her?"

He gave a strange laugh. "Wish we could. But if you try to mess with them they tend to go off. Look"

He paused mid-stride and pointed the flashlight down at his feet, simultaneously hitching up the cuff of his trousers to reveal a slim black anklet.

I stared at it, horrified.

"How come you've got one?"

"Got it at Addle. We all did."

"But I thought you were all against that place."

"Now you know why."

He turned and began walking on. Even though he was just a silhouette to me as he went ahead, I could sense a change in his movements. I guessed I had stirred something up, but I couldn't let it go now.

"So my mum will have one like that too," I said.

"That's right."

"And if I try to take her away, it'll ..."

"Shoot toxin into her."

"Tox toxin?"

"Yep. Same chemicals that the cysts produce."

Now we both went on in silence for a long while. The tunnel turned and felt like it was sloping up. We came to another turn, then a small doorway set back into the curved wall.

"This is us," said Johnny. "I am going to have to blindfold you for this bit, and you'll have to crawl for a while at the end. Might scratch up your knees, but you should be okay."

"Alright," I said.

He pulled out a handkerchief from his pocket and began to tie it around my head.

"Now, if you make it back, what you'll need to do is head for the big radio mast on the hill—you'll be able to see it in the distance when we come up. If you go into the building at the bottom of that tower and wander around the entrance area it'll trigger one of the cameras and let us know you're there."

I heard him open the door and allowed him to guide me through into another stairwell. After a long climb, another door and another staircase (this one made of metal), he got me to crouch-walk and then crawl under a bunch of cables and pipes. At the end of it all, we passed through something more like a normal building and out into the open air. Johnny led me a little further, spun me around a few times, and took off the blindfold.

When my eyes had adjusted to the hazy sun, I could see that he had brought me out to a kind of no-man's land where an asphalt road divided a cornfield from a row of abandoned warehouses. Further down the road, I could see more fields, then burned-out apartments, smashed office towers and newer-looking industrial buildings under columns of steam. Further back and off to the right, I could see a solitary radio mast with a flared truss tapering to a point.

"Is that the one?" I said, pointing at it.

"That's it," said Johnny. "The camps and factories are straight ahead, though. If you go along here, you'll start seeing them on your left pretty soon. Keep your head down and listen for patrols, and you might be okay."

"Thanks," I said. "I really appreciate you helping me like this."

He gave me a grin. "Well, honestly, it's nice to have a bit of variation in the routine."

He held out his hand, wished me luck, and then I was alone again.

*   *   *

I came to the place where they processed the sugarcane first; semi-enclosed sheds of sheet metal, with men and women in red overalls hauling cut cane into the open mouths of milling machines. Other workers watched over conveyor belts or drove forklifts back and forth.

They looked pretty tired. The people loading the machine kept having little pauses and then looking up as if they were worried that someone would see them. One woman watching a conveyor belt actually nodded off to sleep.

She didn't get to rest very long, though. A guard in a green uniform suddenly showed up and shoved some kind of batton into the back of her neck. The shock—I guess it was like a cattle prod—made her jerk and throw herself off her stool. When she tried to get to her feet, the guard shocked her again in the chest before walking away.

It sickened me watching that. But I didn't see any sign of my mum here, and I had a sense that I wouldn't. These sheds all looked like recent construction; the loading dock that I had seen in the video seemed older.

So I moved on. I passed fields of broccoli and potatoes tilled by the same sort of workers and the same sort of guards. Later came silos, barns and a long shed that stunk of chickens. Then more fields.

I had to go slowly to avoid being seen. Sometimes, I would have to retrace my steps and go back hundreds of metres from the road to find cover.

I was doing that—walking parallel to the road behind a line of old warehouses—when I heard a siren go off in the distance. By the time I found a place to watch the road, I could see that it must have been the knock-off signal because all the workers and crews that I had passed had begun to stream along the same road I had been on.

I waited for them to pass and followed them until we came to their camp. It was a big compound enclosed by barbed wire fences and guard towers. It smelled of cooking food and open sewers.

As dusk came on, I managed to hide myself in an overgrown drainage ditch about eighty metres from the gate. I couldn't see too much, but there were bright lights that illuminated key parts of the compound; vehicles, barracks and administration buildings.

In the centre of it all, the workers were waiting around—hundreds and hundreds of them, each holding an aluminium mug and bowl. When a single tone sounded over the loudspeakers, they formed themselves up by the door of one of the larger buildings and slowly filed out of sight.

I stared at them closely as they went past my field of view. None of them looked like her. They weren't the right size or shape, and hardly any of them even looked old enough.

*   *   *

When it was a bit darker, I made a circuit of the camp, hoping to get a glimpse of that loading dock. I didn't have any luck, but I reassured myself that there were large areas blocked from view. I was also encouraged to see that some of the buildings looked old—as if the camp had been built around an existing factory.

But I still wasn't sure what to do next. If she was working in the kitchens or administration—which was my best guess—how long would I have to wait before I caught sight of her around the gate? How long *should* I wait if I didn't see her? How long could I risk hanging around? And the biggest question of all, what would I do if I *did* see her?

When I finally got to sleep, it was like my brain kept going in the background. My dreams kept replaying the last days of my mum's life in Spillan: the moment when I'd first seen the cyst on her shoulder; the moment when the Mayor's men showed up at our house; the moment when they pulled me away from her at the gate.

"Can't afford you gettin' 'fected too, son."

*   *   *

Next morning, I watched and waited as the prisoners began moving off to their worksites. Some marched out following mounted guards. Others waited to be loaded into trucks. A few went out unescorted by themselves or in small groups. I saw a few individuals riding out on bicycles—one of them I recognised.

It wasn't my mum. It was Mallory, the girl I had met back at the refinery. She was on her own, standing next to a bicycle and waiting for one of the last columns to file past. Her hair was short now and she was wearing grease-smeared camp overalls, but there was no mistaking her.

Despite everything, I felt a sort of thrill when I saw her. She was still alive. Maybe I could rescue her. Maybe she would be able to help me find my mum.

She mounted her bike and rode away. When the gates closed, I waited a long time and then circled around until I found her trail.

For a while I was able to follow her tyre marks. Then her tracks finished and the path turned into an overgrown concrete pavement that led to a curving asphalt road bordered by smashed shops and bleached plastic barricades. When I stopped and listened, I could hear sounds of heavy machinery to the right and a faint hammering coming from the other direction.

I tried the machinery first. It turned out to be an excavator working with a salvage crew at the wreckage of a shopping centre. Through the dust I could see a line of workers dragging things out of the debris: a television, some sort of hand-held kitchen appliance, a bent reading lamp, a life-sized baby doll.

There was something strange about this work unit. The other workers I had seen looked tired or distracted—though sometimes they would talk or even joke with each other. But these people worked with absolute concentration. When they found a prize, they would straighten, pivot, and carry the object to a skip before immediately returning to the place they had left. There was no conversation, no eye contact. I couldn't even see any guards watching over them. It gave me a weird feeling.

I went back the way I had come. When I reached the path, I found that the hammering had been replaced by other noises; a squeak like a rusty hinge, a ping of some tool on concrete, scraping castors.

The sounds grew louder as I followed them around the curve. I passed an old service station, skirted a carwash choked with ivy.

Just next to that, there was a sort of laneway that led to an open gate and a car yard, where thirty or forty vans sat in parallel rows on the cracked concrete paving.

They looked like they'd been there for a long time, judging by the condition of their tyres and paintwork. Some of them had been green, and some had been blue, but they had all faded to dull, milky versions of their old colours.

And Mallory was there, halfway down the nearest line, standing next to a vehicle with a raised hood. She had a wheeled trolley stacked with tools and car parts, and she was in the process of topping up the oil. As I watched her, she replaced the cap and moved on to the battery.

She seemed to be the only person in the place. The office and workshop in the background looked dark and empty.

"Need a hand?" I said as I stepped forward.

She jerked upwards and flung herself behind the trolley so that it was between her and me. By the time she looked in my direction, she had a long screwdriver in her right hand.

"What do you …?" she began, then broke off as her face changed from anger to recognition.

"Well, well. If it isn't Chris the Traveller," she said.

"That's me."

"I thought they shot you."

"They did," I said, pointing to the spot, "Right here, but my coat caught it. Who were you expecting?"

"Someone else," she said, shaking her head. "What are you doing here?"

"Long story," I said. "But I was watching for someone near your camp this morning and saw you come out. I thought I'd come and see if I could help you."

"Why, have you got some more fencing wire for me?"

"No. I mean …" I lowered my voice, "To escape."

She gave a smile. "At least you're consistent. Do you try to rescue everyone, or is it just me?"

"Don't you want to get away from here?" I said.

"When I'm ready," she said. "Not yet. Hey, if you want to be useful, why don't you come over here and help me get this old battery out? The nuts are always a dog of a job."

I put down my gear and came over. There was a crust around the terminal and a smell of kerosene—dark patches of it around the bolt. Bright edges of metal showed where a shifting spanner had failed to hold.

"I see nobody thought to disconnect the batteries before the end of the world," I said.

"Yeah, what were they thinking?"

I looked through the trolley and found a stumpy screwdriver and a hammer, then set about loosening the nut with tangential taps to its edges—first as if I was tightening it, then loosening.

"So this is your job, is it?" I said, "To get these going again?"

"That's the deal."

"So, you aren't a prisoner?"

"Nope." I sensed her lean closer to see what I was doing. "Good trick by the way. Where did you learn that?"

"One of my uncles had a garage," I said. "What about you?"

"My dad," she said. "He was the town mechanic and the town doctor too."

"So, do you know about fixing people too?"

"Only the bits I helped him with. But if you need help with a gangrenous toe or a sucking chest wound, then I'm your girl."

"I'll bear that in mind."

I finished removing the terminals, and Mallory hooked up the connectors to a pair of jumper leads that led from the trolley.

"How about you try the key for me and we'll see if the starter will go?" she said

I slid into the cabin and turned the key. Lights came on around the dials. I turned it further, and the starter clicked and whirred.

"Okay, that's good," she said, "Now wait. I'll just switch the distributor cable ... Okay, try again."

I tried and the engine coughed and then caught. I instinctively pumped the gas.

"Woah, woah, woah, I'm doing that ... Okay, that'll do. Turn her off."

I climbed out and stood beside her as she bent over the engine.

"Now what?"

"Now I think it's time for a cup of tea."

She passed me a cloth to wipe off the grease and led the way back to the office. It had chequerboard linoleum, aluminium fittings and cracked vinyl chairs that reminded me of Harry Frieden's place back in Spillan. There was a small kitchen bench along the back wall where Mallory had set up her own supplies.

"So, are you going to tell me why you're here?" I said.

She struck a match and lit a small fuel stove that was sitting in the sink. "Why don't you tell me why *you're* here first," she said. "Who were you watching for?"

"My mum," I said. "She's out here somewhere."

She looked up, face lit by the yellow flame. "Your mum? Seriously? Your mum is in the camp?"

"I'm not sure exactly where she is," I said. "I thought she was dead until yesterday, but then some people showed me a security feed, and she was on it. They were pretty vague about where the camera was. But they said it would be in the camps district somewhere."

"Wow, Chris. I'm really sorry to hear that. How did she end up all the way out here?"

"That's another long story," I said.

I watched as she filled a kettle from a white plastic water drum on the bench and rummaged in the cupboard for a second cup.

"What's your tea like?" I said.

"Well, I'm not sure it's actually tea, but it's not too bad if you put sugar with it."

I picked up my gear and fished out one of the silver packets that Pru had given me.

"Try this."

She ripped open the seal and sniffed the contents. I watched as her eyes went wide.

"Where on earth did you get that?"

"Same folks who showed me the video. There's condensed milk and chocolate too, if you'd like some."

"Um, *yes*! I thought you guys were meant to live on compressed nutrient blocks or something."

"On the road, yes, mostly. But that doesn't mean Central is against us having other stuff. When I met the Envoy, he cooked me ravioli. Prediger gave me lentil soup and flatbread."

"You expect me to believe that you met the Envoy?"

I shrugged. "Well, I can't prove it."

"Didn't give you any of his magic pills, did he?"

"What do you mean?"

She sighed. "Let's just make the tea first."

We sat side by side on the front step of the office, sipping our tea and nibbling squares of Pru's chocolate.

"So, did you go back to the refinery?" she said at last. "After you got shot, I mean. Did you see Cam or Leah?"

"It was all empty by the time I got back," I said. "But I'm sure they were fine. I met one of the other Travellers later, and he told me that the only people who were badly hurt were a couple of the silver-suit guys.

"What about you? Is this where they brought you?"

She shook her head and broke off another square.

"No. I think maybe that was the idea, but their van carked it, and I fixed it for them, so they took me to Addle instead. I only came here later after I heard about the meds."

She caught sight of my puzzled expression and nodded.

"Do you remember why Cam and I were trying to come here?"

"Because the silver suit guys reckoned they had meds to fix him," I said. "But that was a con, right? They were just trying to get people to come here and become slaves."

"Pretty much. And you told me so … so, well done, or something. But look. It wasn't completely wrong. I met a guy in Addle who said that there used to be a Central base out here when it was a city, and that when the Corp was setting up Addle, they found a whole bunch of Tox suppressant and stuck it in the water."

"I heard about that," I said. "I also heard that it ran out."

"That's right. And they haven't been able to get any more because they don't know where the Central base was."

"Okay," I said. "And you do?"

"The guy I was talking to did. He said it was hidden in an old lightbulb factory somewhere on the east side of the city past the radio mast."

"So what's your plan?"

"I keep going until I get these vans all working, and then they pay me—which I don't care about—and give me a pass to salvage, which I do care about."

"So, they don't know what you're looking for?"

"I just told them I was looking for stuff to take back to Ovine."

I drank the last of my tea and shook the drops onto the weeds by our feet.

"Why do you think they'll let you go?" I said. "I mean, aren't these the same guys that were trying to trick you back at the refinery?"

"Well they want their vehicles. And at least one of them likes me. And I reckon if I get the feeling that there's something suspicious, I'll just take off."

"What about that thing?" I said, pointing to the black ankle band, just visible under the cuff of her overalls.

"It's just a tracker. I'll cut it off."

"I heard those things hit you with toxin if you try to remove them."

Mallory broke off another piece of chocolate. "I think you are underestimating my resourcefulness."

"I just don't trust HORD."

"Me either," she said. "That's why I'm not trusting in them. I'm trusting in me."

I thought about the reflex reaction I'd seen when I had approached her and wondered how much of her confidence was real and how much of it was for show. But she spoke again before I managed to think of a way to ask her about that.

"It's sweet that you are concerned, Chris. But I know what I'm doing. I'm going to find those meds and go back home and get Cam on his feet. But if you'd like to help me, I have a proposal."

"What kind of proposal?"

"You could go and see if you can find that place for me—I know it's a bit risky, but I guess you must be able to keep out of sight, or you wouldn't be here. And, while you're doing that for me, I'll take some of that chocolate and give it to someone who can do a records search for your mum."

She watched her words sink in and gave me a smile that looked like triumph. I smiled back. I felt like a weight was lifting off me. It was a great plan. It might solve all my worries.

"You really are resourceful, aren't you?"

"I most certainly am."

CHAPTER 28

(Extract of the transcribed Records of Caleb Dox, Vol 1.28)

After I talked to the Chief, Seini took me back to her place and I pretty much just slept all the rest of that day and night. Seini went back to work, and I remember her comin' in late, but that was about it.

But the next morning when she got up, she reheated some sweet and sour pork that she'd bought for me the night before. And then she opened up these door-window things she had, and we sat on her couch lookin' out at her balcony with the light comin' in. And that was pretty good. And the pork was pretty good too.

Then I asked her about what was gonna happen next, and she told me that we were gonna do some investigation and try to find out what really happened, because there was definitely somethin' fishy about it.

"Like what?" I said.

"Like the lights," she said. "Somebody cut the main power cable, which means that there was somebody else at the square with a blade."

"Those detectives said they thought it was you."

"They were just tryin' to bluff you," she said. "Nobody'd believe that. I was at the riot with the others. We were all together when we rolled back through the square and found the lights off and you and that kid lying there."

"That's good," I said. Cos that made me feel much better. I didn't care so much what happened to me, but the thought of them doin' stuff to my sister made me really sick.

And then Seini told me that there was somethin' else that was suspicious about what they'd found—and that was that the kid had been searched.

"The stuff from his backpack was all over the place," she said.

"Somebody had even cut his laces and pulled his boots off."

"Was there anything interestin' in his stuff?" I said.

"Not that I saw," she said. "I saw a knife, a bit of food, some papers. But I had only just started looking at him when someone shone a light on you—and then I was a bit distracted."

"Hey, that means it wasn't me," I said. "Cos I wouldn't have done that."

"I know, Ca. But it's not enough. They'll just say you were working with someone and that maybe you wanted to rob the kid."

"But I was, like, unconscious!" I said.

"That's still not enough. Maybe they'll say you were just pretending or that you went unconscious after—I don't know. But we need to get some more evidence."

"What about Fergus?" I said. "He was right there … But I don't know where he went."

"Neither do I, yet," she said. "We'll find out. In the meantime, there's somewhere else we need to check out."

"Where's that?"

"The place where the kid was staying," she said. Then she gave me a grin and said, "It's somewhere you'll like."

She made me put on a disguise before we went out because they'd already showed a picture of me on the Addle vid channel, and we didn't want people recognising me.

So she gave me this black cloak and a leather mask. And I didn't want to put it on cos I didn't want to cover up my coat—like I was ashamed or somethin'. But I didn't want people givin' us trouble after what the Chief said, so I just said, "Won't it make me stand out if I look like a villain?"

And she said, "You'll look more like a villain to people if you go out dressed like a Traveller, Ca. This way, they'll just think you're a big Alt."

So I put the stuff on like she wanted me to and we went down to a part of Addle that was at the back of Fairytale town, which had all these little streets and shops, and some of 'em looked okay, but lots of them were like slums with washin' hangin' out and bad smells and stuff.

And then we came to the end of a street that was behind the castle. And there was an archway with a big iron gate. And the archway had these old signs with fancy writin' over 'em—and a big one said, "Dungeons" and then there was another one underneath that said, "Abandon all hope ye who enter here."

I recognised that straightaway cos when we were kids and had the guidebook from Story World, I always used to look at the pictures of this place cos it freaked me out.

"Hey, this is where the waxworks used to be," I said. "With all the torture stuff."

"That's right," said Seini. "Still is."

And she was right, cos now we were in the entry bit, and there was the cage with the skeleton in it, and over near the big wide stairs that went down there was the waxwork guy with a hood and an axe who was holdin' up a head. Except someone had stuck googly-eye things on its eyes and a curly whistle in his mouth.

I thought that was pretty funny, and I was gonna say somethin' to Seini about it, but then I heard people singin'—and it was one of the old songs that Seini and me learned when we were kids—I mean one of the old Central songs. So I asked Seini about that, and she told me that the place was a sort of orphanage run by Travellers.

"It's called the 'Far East Children's Shelter'," she said. "The Council lets them run it so the town doesn't have to look after the kids whose parents go off to the camps."

As soon as she said that, I started to take off the mask and cloak, and while I was doin' that, a couple of kids came up the stairs carryin' big brooms and eatin' big hunks of bread. And Seini said, "Is Gaius down there?" And the kids gave us a suspicious look, but the bigger one said, "Yeah."

So we went down and saw some other archways and another waxwork with some guy stretchin' another guy on a wheel thing, except someone had put a feather duster in the first guy's hand so it looked like he was ticklin' the other guy.

Then the stair ended in this big room with all these kids sittin' at tables and eatin' and muckin' around. And up one end of the room, an old guy was handin' out bread, and like a middle-aged lady was pourin' 'em tea from a big teapot. And they both had Traveller's coats on.

And Seini went up to the old guy and said, "Hello, Gaius. I'm officer Seini Dox and this is my brother Caleb. We were wondering if we could have a few words with you?"

And he gave her a bit of a smile and said, "Seems to me that ye already are, officer."

But before she could answer, I said, "Hey, you sound like Fergus," Cos he did. And he sort of looked like him too.

And then he stared at me for a second and said, "And how do ye know my brother?"

"I was travellin' with him for a while," I said. "And then the other night I was with him in the square and we got attacked."

"Ah, I see," he said. "Then I suppose ye must be the young man they arrested?"

"Yeah, that's right," I said. "I'm out on bail, and Seini and me are tryin' to find out what really happened, cos I didn't do it."

"Well, that is good to hear," he said. "But I'm afraid Fergus can't help ye at the moment, if that's why ye are here. They made quite a mess of him. We're still waiting to see if he'll recover."

"Actually," said Seini," We *would* like to talk to Fergus, but we really came to ask about the boy who died. We understood that you had him staying here."

"Well not for a while," he said, "But I am happy to help ye in any way I can. Let's adjourn to my office where there will be fewer small ears to distress." Then he asked the lady—who was his daughter, Phoebe—to look after things while he was gone and took us to his office—which used to be the Wizards Laboratory—and was like a cave with all stuff in jars and weird bottles and lanterns.

"Please excuse all the paraphernalia," said Gaius. "We only keep it here because the city Council has made it a condition of our occupancy."

"I like it," I said. "But I reckon the waxworks would scare the kids."

"Aye. That's the reason why they make us keep them. They're making their point that we are scary Pantarchists. But I must confess, I don't mind working in a laboratory."

Then he sat down behind the desk—which had all dragons and stuff carved on the legs—and we sat on the chairs that were in front of it, and Seini started asking about the kid and how long he'd been livin' there.

And Gaius said, "Well bear in mind that Thomas hasn't been with us for more than two months. Bren still returns to us, but Thomas moved out after he took up with that gang."

"I'm sorry," said Seini, "who's Bren?"

And Gaius looked a bit surprised and said, "Thomas's brother. Did the other policemen not tell ye about this?"

"There's a bit of a complicated situation, I'm afraid," said Seini. "The other detectives aren't really talking to us. Do you think we could speak to Bren?"

"Aye, if he turns up," he said

"Are you saying Bren has gone missing too?" said Seini.

"That is what I am saying," he said.

"Are you worried about him?" she asked.

"It's not unusual for the children here to disappear for a day or two. Should we be worried on his behalf?"

"I don't know yet," she said. "Do you know if they had any enemies? Was there anybody who might want to hurt them?"

"Not Bren," he said. "But Thomas was getting himself into a few fights. I remember Phoebe telling me that it had something to do with their sister Eliza getting sent to the camps. That happened just before the boys came to stay with us."

"I see," said Seini. "Would you have a photograph of Bren so we can look out for him?"

"Unfortunately the other officers took it," he said. "I think I might have another one somewhere, but I would have to dig around."

Then Seini asked if we could take a look at the place where Bren's stuff was, but Gaius said we'd need a warrant.

"No offence, officer, but ye must understand that these children have had a difficult relationship with the authorities. They have good reason not to want government officials rummaging through their possessions. I think ye would be better served if ye talked to yer colleagues. They already took a look at his bunk."

And we said we understood his point, and Gaius took us back down to where the kids were eatin' after that and waited for 'em to finish. One of the kids was readin' a bit out of the Roadbook, and then they had a last song, and I joined in cos it was another of those old ones.

Then all the kids went off in different directions, and we went and asked Phoebe about the fights,

"Poor Tommie," she said. "He was so full of anger."

"Who was he angry at?" said Seini.

"Oh, everyone; other children, Gaius and me, the city for taking Eliza away. He was fighting with the Scorchers too—Eliza was involved with them, and I think he blamed them for what happened to her."

"What did happen to her?" said Seini. "Was it something more than the camps?"

"Aye," said Phoebe. "There was some accident and she was killed. I don't know the details. But it was after that that Tommie went a bit wild."

That was about all she knew, so we said thanks to her and they both walked with us back up the stairs. And Gaius said that I had a good singin' voice, and that if I ever wanted to come back for another visit, I'd be welcome.

And I said I'd like that and asked if I could talk to him about a few questions I had too.

And he said, "Certainly. Do ye mean about your case?"

"I mean about bein' a Traveller and livin' here," I said. "Cos I'm kind of confused about everything."

"Ye'd be welcome," he said. "Why don't ye come and help us wash dishes and peel potatoes some time? That'll give us a nice opportunity for conversation."

Oil Wells
M
N
Q
ADDLE SURROUNDS
A - Pru & Trevor's place
B - Museum Station
C - Refinery
D - Main Camp Complex
E - Garage
F - Radio Station
G - Stadium
H - Hospital
I - Central Road
MAIN MAP KEY
Pipeline
Road
Township
Ruined Township
Summit
Misc. Structure
A
B
C
D
E
F
G
H
I
Due

CHAPTER 29

My plan was to head straight to the radio station so I could find Johnny and ask him to help me locate the lightbulb factory. But like everything in that part of my journey, it didn't go the way I planned.

First, it took me longer than I expected to work my way back around the camp. I wanted to keep away from the road, but my attempt to find a path through the suburbs got me completely lost.

The result of that was that I didn't get close to the tower until mid-afternoon, and when I did I was too tired and distracted to pay proper attention. That's why, as I came up the hill, I didn't stop to wonder about the faint smell of burnt plastic and cooking, at least until I reached the car park and found the body.

It had been a guard. There was still enough of his jacket and boots to tell me that much. Someone had killed him, dragged his body behind an old rubbish enclosure and set him on fire. From the smell (I was paying attention now!), they'd poured some kind of fuel over him to get him going.

I quietly drew my sword and turned around with all my senses twitching. Whoever had done this had done it pretty recently. They might still be around.

And they could be anywhere. The rusted hulks scattered in the parking bays and the trees that surrounded them were all excellent hiding places. A few metres away, I could see the stairway that would take me up to the building Johnny had mentioned. But who knew what might be waiting for me up there?

Then something moved the bushes just behind the body and my nerves sent my flying. As I landed, I tripped on one of the overgrown kerbs and went down.

But it was only Johnny and Rose, laughing at me as I tried to disentangle my sword.

"Nice move," said Rose.

"Like ballet," said Johnny.

I got to my feet and came over to them.

"What happened here?" I said.

"Savages," said Rose. "Killed the guard and butchered his horse—you can see what's left of it if you go a bit further on."

"Are they still around?" I said.

"Nah," said Johnny. "Gone back down to the farms."

I looked at them. They seemed completely undisturbed by it all. But everything about it disturbed me.

"I thought you didn't get Savages this far east of the mountains," I said.

"The Corp gives 'em juice," said Rose, "To keep their trucks going."

"Then why did they … ?" I pointed back in the direction of the body.

"Bite the hand?" said Johnny with a shrug. "Yeah, it's pretty weird. It looked like they were searching for something up in the radio station, which is why we found out about 'em when they triggered the camera. But who knows what *this* is about—maybe they were just feeling like a bit of horse."

"It's good, though," said Rose.

"That it is," said Johnny. "Savs attacking HORD is fine by us. Funny too. You should have seen the look on his face when they speared him. Even with the lousy video, you could see the whites of his eyes.."

"Anyway," he said, turning to me, "What brings you back here? Did you find your mum?"

"Not yet," I said, "But I found somebody who can help me, and she told me about something else."

Then I told them about Mallory and what she had said about the old light bulb factory. And they looked at each other and Johnny smiled.

"What?" I said. "Do you know the place she was talking about?"

"Well, we know it," he said. "It's less than a k from here."

"But there ain't no secret base," said Rose.

"Nope. It's just a bunch of old machinery and some skeletons."

I felt my shoulders sink a little.

"Can you take me there anyway?" I said. "I reckon I should at least be able to say I had a look."

"Yeah, sure," said Johnny, giving me a shrug.

The old Salis Light Factory turned out to be a big red-brick building surrounded by half-collapsed tenement flats and pockmarked storehouses. The factory itself was three stories high with tall (mostly broken) windows that ended in arches made of darker masonry.

Inside, the place was a maze of destruction and disorder. Some parts of the factory floor were simply a mess; conveyor belts, chains, and machines mouldering under rust and dust. There were overturned hoppers of glass tubes, aluminium mouldings and tiny filament springs that crunched under our feet.

But in other places, the damage was more obviously the result of armed conflict; half-burned barricades, gaping holes and radial blast patterns in the brickwork.

"Who was fighting?" I said.

Johnny shrugged. "They didn't leave much behind to tell the story. Maybe it was just another bit of what was going on everywhere, or maybe it was the workers trying to stop the crazies from outside. But if you come down to the basement, you can see where they had their final stand."

I still hadn't seen any of the skeletons that Johnny had mentioned, but as we came out of the stairwell and he shone his torch around, they appeared: some were propped up against the brick piers; some were lying face down; some were more like mummies—still in their clothes and with the skin dried onto their skulls. But most were burned to bones. Where they still had their weapons, these were half-burned too.

"Are these the defenders or the attackers?" I said.

"Attackers. The others were on the other side of that barricade over there. But someone must have done something with their bodies."

He led the way through a breach in a wall made of crates, overturned benches and spools of sheet metal.

The space beyond was just a corner of the basement, but the rubbish strewn all around the place showed what had happened—the shell casings and empty ammunition boxes, the rusted food tins, filthy bandages and the cardboard sheets soaked with long dried blood.

The place smelled of mildew and decay.

I looked around, remembering how it had been in the command post as that Savage ram-rig had come charging at our gates. That had been bad enough; what must it have been like in a place like this? Why had they let themselves get trapped down here?

"Well, I guess I see what you mean about there being no secret base," I said.

But even as I said it, I noticed something sticking out from under the edge of one of the sheets of cardboard. It was flattened and barely visible, but it looked like a Traveller's backpack.

"Hey, shine your torch down here," I said.

Dust particles swirled into the air as I peeled back the layers of cardboard. Everything was stiff and stuck together from the blood. But my intuitions were right—it *was* a Traveller's pack. And other things too: the cover of a Roadbook, two half-eaten ration-blocks, a rusted *machaira.*

In one of the pockets of the pack, I found a sheet of moulded plastic ampules with tiny needles and some kind of fluid in them. When I took them closer to Johnny's light we could make out small letters pressed into their sides:

X-VECTOR - BOOSTER SYRETTE.

"What's that?" said Rose.

"That's the cure," said Johnny. "Want one?"

"Dunno," she said. "What's it do?"

"It stops the Tox killing you," I said. "And it changes your brain. But you shouldn't take it unless you're going to swear allegiance and do the training."

"Why not?" she said.

"It can do bad things to you: make you blind or deaf, stuff like that."

"Let's split 'em," said Johnny.

I folded the sheet back and forth until the little joints snapped.

Meanwhile, Rose pulled out her own flashlight and began looking closely at what remained of the barricade. In the background, I saw her reach in and pull out another ammunition box.

"There's stuff in this one," she said.

"What have you got?" I said.

"All kinds of stuff. Another of those books. More food blocks. Some goggle things. A bottle of pills."

"Can I see those?" I said.

She passed it over, and I held it up to Johnny's light. The bottle was made of blue glass. It contained a handful of white tablets and a half peeled-off label:

PROLEPTIX TOX SUPPR...

ADULT DOSE: TAKE ONE TABLET MONT...

CHILDREN: HALF A TABLET MONTHLY OR AS...

"Is that what you're looking for?" said Johnny.

"I don't know," I said. "She was talking about drums of the stuff—the stuff they were putting in the water supply. I'm not sure, but I think this might be something from before—I mean the stuff the Envoy was handing out before they made the X-Vector.

"The miracle pills?" said Johnny.

"Maybe," I said.

"What's with all the Xs?" said Rose. She was sitting down on a big spool-reel with the goggles on, moving her head left and right.

"They're crossed syringes," I said, remembering Eve's response. "They symbolise what happened to the Envoy when HORD caught him and injected cyst toxin into him. That's how we got the cure; his body made it as the stuff killed him."

"Huh. Too bad for him," she said.

"Yeah, except they brought him back. Now the Pantarch has him running everything from Central."

But something was happening to Rose. Even as I spoke, I saw her stiffen and turn her head.

"What the Tox?" she said. "What the Tox?"

"Hey, Rose," said Johnny. "Are you okay?" He bounded over to her and tried to pull the goggles off her head, but she pushed his hands away.

"Get off me," she said. "I want to ..." She began to stand up and fell sideways.

We got the things off her and laid her out on my sleeping roll. She was breathing normally by now, but she wouldn't wake up.

Johnny and I took turns looking at the goggles—Johnny even put them on—but we didn't find anything that could explain what had happened. No lights or sounds, not even any buttons that I could see.

"It must have been these though, right?" I said.

"S'pose so," said Johnny. "What else could it have been? I mean, we would have seen if she'd taken one of the pills or the syrettes."

I asked if he wanted to try carrying her back to the museum so they could look after her there, but he shook his head.

"Not tonight. It'll be dark by now. We'd just trip over and drop her, or run into those Savages. Better to camp down here."

While he stayed watching over her, I cleared a wider space on the floor, lit a small fire and harvested some water with my flask. Soon, we were sitting on either side of the flames, eating a reconstituted ration block.

"Good old Central rations," said Johnny. "It's been a long time since I ate one of these, but this is better than I remember."

I thought about telling him Caleb's theory about Central giving us all slightly different formulas, but there was something more important I wanted to ask him about.

"So you and Rose. You're good friends, right?"

He gave me a strange look, "That's right, since we were kids. Why, do you fancy her?"

"That's not why I'm asking. I just don't understand why you haven't told her about the cure and the Envoy and everything."

Johnny was quiet for a long time, staring at the fire.

"When you come away from Crux, you think you're going to save everyone," he said. "You've had the injection, and you can *feel* it working in you. And you're with everyone else, and you all think the same, and you sing together and do your training together.

"And then you come back home, and nobody has time to listen because they're all worried about their debts, or they're trying to make their water ration stretch just a little bit more, or they're sick, or they've already been taken off to the camps or gotten ankle trackers to keep them in line."

"And it's like all those grand ideas about Central just get choked out of you. They just don't seem real anymore."

As I listened to what he was saying, I thought about my own desire to get sent back to Spillan. Would I have been any different if Central had sent me back there, or would I have just settled back into the same life I'd had before—doing my duty, drinking with my friends, hating the Mayor?

"I don't really know what to say to you, brother," I said. "If they'd done all that stuff to my town, I reckon I would be wanting to spend all my time fighting them too. But I've got an idea."

"What's that?"

I drew my sword and reached around the fire to point to his ankle.

"Why don't you take one of those boosters, and we cut that thing off you right now?"

He gave a choked sort of laugh.

"I reckon those things might have expired."

"Well, technically you shouldn't need it," I said. "I mean, the cure is meant to keep protecting you from the toxin for your whole life. I just reckon the booster would make it easier."

"Easier for *you*, maybe," he said. "But you're not the one who's gonna get that stuff fired into your leg."

"I know," I said. "But I've got a feeling that if we cut that thing off, it would make a difference to you."

He laughed again. "Well, you might be right. Let me think about it. Maybe in the morning."

"Okay," I said.

But when I woke up in the morning, they were both already gone.

CHAPTER 30

(Extract of the transcribed Records of Caleb Dox, Vol 1.29)

After we went to see Gaius and Phoebe, I reckoned we should go and talk to the Scorchers, but Seini thought that was a bad idea cos they were dangerous, and she reckoned that if I went to the parts of the city where they were, I'd probably end up breachin' my bail.

"But what if I know somebody who's with 'em?" I said. "Cos before Fergus and me got attacked, there was a guy, Dil, who we used to travel with, and I think he'd joined up with 'em."

"Do you know where to find him?"

"Not really. But maybe Gaius or Phoebe would, cos he was a Traveller."

So the next day, I went back to the orphanage and talked to Gaius and Phoebe while we peeled the potatoes. And they didn't know Dil, but they told me that some guy had called a meeting for all the Centralists at this old amphitheatre, and maybe I could see him there.

"But you should wear your mask," Phoebe said.

"Wouldn't that be weird if we're all Centralists?" I said.

"Aye, but they won't all be real Centralists," said Gaius.

"And there'll be other people wearing masks too," said Phoebe. "But the main reason you should is that they'll probably be talking about you."

"Why are they gonna do that?" I said.

"Because the Mayor's planning to change the laws," said Gaius. "And it's yerself and Fergus that he's using fer his pretext. That's what the meeting is about."

"What kind of changes?" I said. And they said they didn't know, but it would be something to control Travellers because everyone was sayin' we were violent now.

So that made me feel a bit sick, and I didn't know what to say, so I asked if Fergus was gonna be okay. And Gaius said he wasn't sure, but some of the claw wounds were pretty deep, and the fever wasn't a good sign.

"We'll know which way he's headed in the next few days," said Phoebe. "Were you close to him out on the road?"

"Sort of," I said. "I tried goin' along with him for a while, but he told me I wasn't keepin' up and that I needed to get some more trainin'."

"Tried to send you to Amhain, did he?" said Gaius.

"Yeah, you know about that place?" I said.

"Aye," he said. "And it's a good place. If you're in a fight, it's the Amhain boys you want by your side."

"Yeah, I saw him fight," I said. "That's why I wanted to join up with them."

"But sometimes," he said, "they forget to stop fighting. Ye might have seen that in him too if he sent ye away."

"Yeah," I said. "And that's one of the things I wanted to ask you about. Fergus always said that we had to start by tellin' everyone that they were in trouble with the Pantarch. But the Travellers I met before him said that the first thing to tell people was that the Pantarch wanted to help 'em."

"Aye, and what's yer question?" he said.

"Well, which one's right?" I said. "And what should we be sayin' to people here?"

"Maybe they're both right," he said.

"How do you mean?"

"Well, Fergus is right to want us to warn people," he said. "Ye talk to some of these young Travellers and ye get the impression that the only problems we have are caused by the Corp. But that's wrong. The Corp is a wicked entity, but it's the Tox and the Cleanse that are the real threat to us in the long run."

"Yeah, that's what Fergus was sayin'," I said.

"Aye, and he's correct. But sometimes Fergus leaves out a few things too."

"Like what?" I said.

"Well, the pipeline, for example. If ye're going to warn folks that the Envoy is at war with 'em, ye mustn't neglect to remind them that he's also been giving 'em the water that keeps them alive. The Pantarch has been strangely generous to his enemies.

"Any good thing ye get in this territory is a gift of Central. The Corp would have us believe that they are our benefactors, but they're just giving what they stole. It's the Pantarch we should all be thankin'."

Then I looked at the potato I was peelin' and thought about what he was sayin'.

"Fergus reckoned that you had to say the bad news before the good news or people wouldn't understand the cure."

"Aye, correct again," he said. "But if ye've read the Roadbook, ye'll notice it doesn't begin with bad news, does it? It tells ye all about how things were before the war."

"Oh!" I said, "So it's like Fergus forgets the first bit and those other guys leave out the middle bit," I said.

"Aye, that's one way to put it," he said. "Both are important. Ye leave out the start, and ye'll make the Pantarch sound like a tyrant. Ye leave out the middle, and they'll think he's optional."

CHAPTER 31

(Extract of the transcribed Records of Caleb Dox, Vol 1.30)

I told Seini that I wanted to go to the meeting, but she thought it was a bad idea.

"It's too risky," she said. "That amphitheatre is right near where the trouble is. And what if someone recognises you?"

"Yeah, but I'll have my disguise, and they'll be Centralists so, even if they find out, they'll understand, I reckon."

"I wouldn't bet on that," she said.

"But how will we get to talk to the Scorchers then?" I said.

Then she got up from the couch and walked around the room, and said, "Okay, but I'm coming too. And you have to stick with me."

"That suits me," I said.

So after it got dark, I put on my cloak and mask and Seini put on a disguise too, which was like a coat with a big collar and a triangle hat and a hankie under her eyes, so she was like one of those guys that used to rob people in wagons.

And then we went down to the old amphitheatre—which was where they used to put on plays when it was Story World, except now there was a whole lot of rubbish lying around it.

And when we got there, I could see about forty people sittin' around on the steps and a few of them had normal Traveller's gear with coats and swords—and a couple even had their packs with 'em. But most of the people had other clothes—coats and cloaks and stuff—though it was pretty hard to see too much cos of the shadows.

But there was a lighter bit down the bottom cos there was a thing like a streetlight there. And there was a guy standing and talkin' under it. And he was wearin' somethin' that looked like a Traveller's coat, except it had all gold and silver patterns on it.

"I wonder who that guy is," I said to Seini.

"That's Desmond Seever," said Seini. "He's the guy that represents Central to the City Council."

"Why doesn't he have a normal coat?" I said.

"You tell me," she said. "You're the Centralist."

But I didn't know, so I just tried listenin'. And he was talkin' about how his friend, Mayor Fortuna, was worried about all the violence that Travellers had been doin'. But he said that he'd been tellin' the Mayor that it was just a few people who were like that and that most Travellers felt bad about it.

And he said that the Mayor said he wanted to believe that was true, but he also had to consider the safety of the people of Addle, and that other people on the City Council were wantin' to ban Travellers or round 'em up.

So the Seever guy said he'd called the meetin' so we could show the Mayor that we were on his side.

And then somebody shouted out, "What do you mean, 'on his side'?"

"I mean, we don't want to disturb people or hurt them," he said, "And I am proposing that we find some definite way to show that ..."

"Like what?" said the person who had shouted out.

"Please," said Seever, "I don't think we'll be able to make much progress if we just shout out. But you are asking a good question. I have my own thoughts, but perhaps other people have others. Would anyone like to come down and address our gathering?"

And then some people near the front put up their hands, and the guy invited one of them to come up—and it was a lady with fancy specs and all different colours on her coat. And she said that we should pass a resolution that anyone who drew a sword in Addle wasn't a real citizen of Central. And she kept sayin', "Not in our name, not in our name."

And then there was another lady who had a coat that looked like it was homespun. And she said that we should do more than that. She reckoned we should ask the Mayor to take away everyone's sword before they came into the city so there couldn't be any more tragedies like what happened with Thomas.

And then she pulled out a bit of a newspaper and read some stuff that was meant to be from an eyewitness—and it said how I'd been laughin' and sayin' they were all sick and that I was gonna fix 'em by choppin' 'em up.

And then some of the people made a groanin' noise, which made me feel really bad, cos it was like they all believed it. And I wanted to get up and tell 'em it wasn't true. But Seini grabbed hold of my arm and held me down.

"Don't get distracted. We're here to look for your friend, remember? Have you seen any sign of him?"

So I tried to stop thinkin' about what the lady was sayin' and went back to lookin' around.

Meanwhile, the guy who had been callin' out before started shoutin' again. And he was sayin' that they were bein' conned.

"You're all pawns of the Corp." He was sayin'. "They want us to give up our swords so we can't fight back. That was the first thing they tried to do when they took over Hesper."

And when he said Hesper, a whole lot of the people started booin'. And someone near us chucked something in the direction of where the guy was talkin'.

Then Seever tried to calm everybody down. And he was sayin' that we all needed to listen to each other and that sometimes the only way to win a fight was to surrender, and p'raps that meant we should consider what the lady was sayin' about givin' up our weapons so everyone would know we didn't mean 'em any harm.

And then someone shouted "you first!" cos you could see that Seever was wearin' a sword on his back. So he reached back and pulled it out, but it was just a handle—except it had all gold and jewels on it.

Then some people were cheerin', and other people were booin' and shoutin' stuff I couldn't understand. And two guys in masks stood up at the back and chucked a couple of eggs down at Seever, and one hit him on the arm.

And then a whole lot of other people stood up and started screamin' stuff back at the people who chucked the eggs, and someone chucked a rock—which ended up hittin' the step just next to me.

And then Seini started pullin' out her tablet thing and told me I should get out of there. "This is about to turn, Ca, and you need to not be here."

"What about you?" I said. "I'm not goin' and leavin' you to get yourself hurt."

"I know how to look after myself," she said. "Besides, I just sent an emergency signal. The Watch'll be here soon."

As she was talkin', I could see some guys with balaclavas were tryin' to set fire to a pile of rubbish up the top, on the other side of the circle. And one of the guys who'd chucked the eggs had pulled out a slingshot and was aimin' it down the front.

Everythin' was gettin' more and more confusin'. Everyone was standin' up and shoutin' stuff, and I still couldn't understand what they were talkin' about. And Seini was sayin'. "Go! If the Watch catches you here, they'll lock you up!"

So I felt kind of confused—cos I didn't want to leave Seini, but I remembered what her boss said about her losin' all her money for me. So I got up and went and grabbed the slingshot off the guy with the mask and threw it away. Then I kept goin'.

I thought the best thing to do would be to go back to Seini's place through the lanes, cos' I could hear the sirens comin' now and I didn't want 'em to grab me. But I'd only gone like half a block when I heard a scream from behind me, and it was some lady shoutin' "help, help" and "leave me alone." So, of course, I went back to see what was goin' on, cos you couldn't run away if a lady was bein' attacked.

Anyway, the noise was comin' from an alley—which was pretty dark—and when I went into it there was some guy grabbin' hold of a lady by the hair and pushin' her up against a wall. So I came and pulled him off her and lifted him up by the back of his collar.

"Maybe I should be liftin' you up by your hair," I said. "Then you'd know what it feels like."

"That's right," said the lady. Which was weird, cos she didn't sound scared or anythin'. And when I turned my head to take a look at her, she was pointin' a pistol up to my face and holdin' out a pair of handcuffs.

"Thanks for comin' to save me, Dox," she said. "Now, how about you put him down and slip these on. No sudden moves."

So I let him go, and put on the cuffs. And then the guy took off my mask and put a bag over my head.

"What are you gonna do to me?" I said.

"That depends," she said. "There's someone who wants to ask you some questions."

"Hey, you guys aren't Scorchers are you?" I said. "Cos if you are, I've been wantin' to ask you questions too."

Then it was like everyone went quiet, and someone else—like a different guy with a deeper voice—said, "And what did you want to ask us?"

So I twisted round—even though they tried to stop me—and said, "I wanted to ask whether you knew who killed that kid that they're blamin' me for. Cos I heard that you guys were fightin' with him."

And then the lady said, "Ha!" and the guy with the deep voice said, "Nice try. What did you do with the stick?"

"What stick?" I said.

"The data stick you got off him after you knifed him," he said. "Have you still got it?"

"I don't know anythin' about a data stick," I said. "And I didn't knife him."

"You can't expect us to believe that," he said. "They caught you red-handed."

"Literally," said the lady.

While we were talkin', the sirens were gettin' closer and one of 'em was really loud, and like it was slowin' down. So they all pushed me into a nook or a doorway or somethin', and we were all quiet until the noise went past.

Then I said, "Where did this data stick come from?"

"From his sister," said the guy who was doin' the talkin'. "She sent it to Tom before they killed her, and he was meant to pass it on to us."

"Except he didn't," said the lady.

"Yeah," said the main guy. "And then you killed him."

Now I was about to just say I didn't kill him, but then I thought maybe I could find out more if I sort of played along for a bit. So I just said, "Why do you want it so much?"

"Have you seen what's on it?" he said.

"Not yet," I said. "What's on it?"

"We don't know," he said, "But Eliza said it was something big—something that was going to blow up the whole system."

"That sounds good to me," I said. "But I still don't have it."

Then the main guy swore, and somebody—I think it was the other guy—kicked me in the back of my knees so I dropped down.

And the lady said, "Maybe we should take him back with us."

"Yeah, maybe," said the main guy. "Search him first."

And then they started going through my pockets and feelin' round my clothes and everythin'. But before they'd finished, the sirens started comin' back, so they grabbed me and began draggin' me down the alley—and I kept trippin' over and almost fallin' cos I had the bag over my head.

And the sirens were gettin' closer and closer, and so the Scorchers were wantin' me to go faster and faster.

And then we got to some steps and I really did fall down, and as they were gettin' me up, one of 'em saw the tracker round my ankle and they all freaked out.

Then the big guy said, "Cut it off him." And then *I* freaked out, cos I knew that if they did that it was gonna break my bail. And I was shoutin' at 'em to stop and tryin' to do stuff, but it wasn't much good with the cuffs and the bag over my head and the noise from the sirens, which sounded really close.

And then one of 'em whacked the tracker with somethin' like a brick, and *it* started makin' a siren noise too. And then a second after that, it was like it bit me—and it was like someone had lit my leg on fire, and it hurt so much that I thought I was goin' to throw up. And they kept tellin' me to get up or they were gonna shoot me, but it was like I couldn't properly hear 'em cos of my leg. And then I could hear other people shoutin'. And someone fired a gun, and the Scorchers just ran.

CHAPTER 32

Mallory was bending over the tyre press when I found her.

"Did you find the light factory?" she said without turning to face me.

"I did," I said. "I even found some meds."

She released the treadle and looked around at me with an amazed expression on her face.

"Really?"

"Yeah," I said, "But don't get too excited. It's a pretty small bottle."

She took it from my hand and held it out to read what was left of its label.

"Well, it isn't what I was expecting, but it is something."

"I know," I said. "I couldn't find any sign of vats or anything like that."

"But it *was* a Central base, right?"

"Mostly it was just a factory. But there was a place in the basement where some Centralists had made some kind of last stand."

She rotated the bottle, letting the pills clink against the glass.

"There's nine in there," I said. "If they still work, they'd give him a year and a half."

She nodded and gave me a smile.

"Okay … okay. That's a start. Thanks, Chris. Let's have some of your tea."

I followed her back to the kitchen and watched as she peeled off her work gloves to light the stove.

"I asked about your mum," she said.

I looked up from her fingers to her face. "Did you find out anything?"

"Not really. There were only four women in the system over forty, but we couldn't find any Maras or Walkers. I got my friend to do a general search with those names too, but we couldn't find anything."

"I wonder what I should do," I said. "I can't just forget I saw her."

Mallory turned back to the water cube. "There's still one more place she could be."

"Where's that?"

"There's the admin centre. It's in an old hospital a few k's down the road. I haven't been there, but it's where the guards have to go if they get in trouble. Sometimes they send workers down there too."

"Okay. That sounds worth checking out," I said.

"Yeah, probably. The only thing is …" She placed the kettle on the burner and looked up at me. "The only thing is that the workers who go there never come back."

"Why?"

"I don't know. But you should be careful."

There was something in her voice that I hadn't heard before. Something in the way she was looking at me too.

But it was just for a second. She crouched down to get the tea and the cups from the cupboard under the sink.

"So, your mum," she said, "Was she a Traveller too? Why did she leave Spillan?"

"That's sort of a long story."

"We've got time."

So I told her.

I told her about the cyst rule and how we thought the Tox was something we could keep out.

I told her about how the people from the Mayor's office had come down to the school to talk to us about it—how they told us that it was really important to tell the doctor if we saw anything like a cyst on anyone in our family—and that we needed to tell him as soon as possible so that they could look after them.

"They kind of made it sound like, if we told them early enough, the doc would be able to treat them or something—though you know, looking back, they never actually said that … But I was too young to see what they were up to. And I was still stupid enough to trust the guys in charge."

"And did your mum have a cyst?" said Mallory. We were sitting side by side on the step with our tea by now.

"Yeah. Just below her shoulder. I'd only seen it a week before, and it had made me really worried for her—though I hadn't said anything to her about it. But when they said that it was important to tell them before it was too late, I thought … well, I pretty much went straight up to talk to the doctor as soon as the class finished."

I stopped talking—partly because I was having trouble making my voice sound normal, but also because I was suddenly aware of Mallory looking at me again.

"… Anyway," I said at last, "That's why she had to leave. They gave her the choice, and she picked exile."

"What will you do if you find her?" she said.

"I'm not sure. We found these little X-Vector booster shots up at the light factory. If she'll let me treat her with one of those, then maybe we can just keep going east. But if not … well, there's my friends in the old city. Maybe I could take her there."

"How about you?" I said.

She looked out over the vans. "Same plan as before. I'll finish the job and go searching."

"Are you sure about that?" I said.

"What do you mean?" she said.

"I mean, are you sure you still want to do that? I had a pretty good look around, and that bottle was all I could find. I don't think it's very likely you'll come across any more of them, and even if you did, it's only ever going to be a temporary fix for him."

"You think I should give up and go home?"

"I'm just saying, maybe you should think about the cure they give you at Crux. If Central stopped handing out those pills and started telling everyone to get the injection, there must be a reason."

"Will the cure make my brother walk?"

"Probably not—I know it's not like the pills—but it'll stop his cysts *killing him.* And it's permanent. And ... it *does* undo cyst damage. Just not like those things do ..."

She tipped up her mug and got to her feet.

"I've got to get back to work."

"Why? Because I suggested you get more up-to-date meds?"

"Because you're trying to tell me I've been wasting my time. And because you just reminded me that we're headed in different directions.

She was right both ways, I thought. But her sudden coldness felt like a slap.

She went back inside and returned, pulling on her gloves.

"I was just trying to help, Mal."

She looked down at me. "Yeah, well, sometimes trying to help makes things worse."

I can't remember what I was going to say to that because there was a sudden change in her posture. She waved a hand to cut me off.

"Get out of sight," she said quietly. "Someone's coming. Grab your stuff. There's a back door near the bathrooms."

She stepped past me onto the step, blocking my view while I slid backwards and crouch-ran to fetch my gear. In a matter of seconds, I had reached the small corridor that had once led to the men's and ladies' bathrooms. Then I was pushing against the buckled plywood of the rear exit, looking out through a five-centimetre gap at a pile of oil drums and dried grass.

But the door was caught. I could feel its frame warping and cracking as I tried to shove it open. Maybe it was the rubbish, or maybe it was just that the door had sagged onto the step, but it was stuck fast down below.

I thought about kicking it free, but I had no idea how much noise that might create. Then I noticed a rusty pry bar leaning against the wall next to one of the toilets and thought I might use it to lever the door up and out from below.

I slipped into the stall to grab it, but before I had a chance to try my luck, I heard voices coming from the front of the shop.

"Havin' a break, Mal?" said a man's voice. It was a harsh middle-aged sort of voice.

"Just having a cuppa, Frank," said Mallory's voice. "Going back to work now."

"No hurry. Just came over to see how my favourite mechanic was going."

"Not bad, thanks. I should have another three done by the end of the week. The ones in this line are in pretty good shape. I think they were probably more shielded from the sun than the ones in front."

"Did you get my flowers?"

"I don't know. Somebody left a bunch on the step yesterday. Yellow ones. Sorry, I've never been that into them."

"More into engines than girly stuff, eh? That's cool. I like that. Still, you're pretty girly in other ways, and I like that too."

"Okay, thanks … Still, I better get back to it."

"Not so fast, Mally. I reckon I wouldn't mind a cuppa too."

"Go ahead, Frank. Stuff's all there. Clean cups under the sink." Her voice was quieter now like she was walking away.

Then the man gave a laugh that made all my nerves go electric and started that pulse in the back of my neck.

Mal said something that I couldn't hear. And the guy laughed again and said that he knew she was bluffing and that he thought it was time she did something for all the special treatment she was getting.

Then there was a scuffling sound, and I heard Mallory say "Let me go."

And after that, I don't remember what either of them said, because there was a roaring in my ears and I was running out of the cubicle and down the corridor with the pry bar in my hands.

I was almost at the front door before the guy heard me coming. He had Mal around the waist and was trying to drag her back toward the door, so it was a half-turn for him to see me. I saw his eyes go wide as he pushed her away and turned to face me.

But he was too late. My first strike smashed his collarbone. The second broke the outer bone in his forearm as he tried to intercept the swing that would have taken out his skull.

I can't remember what he looked like. I can remember that he had a HORD uniform. I remember the fear in his eyes and the way he sounded like a wounded animal as he tried to back away. I remember the satisfaction I felt as I heard his bones crack.

And I remember with absolute clarity that I was going to kill him. I was going to bury the pry hook in his temple and feel the blood on my face. In that moment, there was nothing that I wanted more. I felt like I was full of fire; like a drum stretched tight and waiting for the blow.

But someone was shouting at me. I could hear another voice, but it was as if it was coming from a long way away. The tiny part of me that was still able to think registered it and said there would be time to deal with it when we had finished with this animal.

Yet, even as I was making my backswing, something caught my arm, making me lose balance for a second. I broke free, righted myself and spun around, ready to smash whatever had attacked me. And then I saw Mallory lying on the ground with her arms raised to fend me off.

"Chris! Stop it! Don't!"

And all the fire turned to ice. As my mind went clear, I realised what I had done and almost done. Mallory had a long scrape on her arm where the edge of my hook had caught her: a line of pale skin with blood just beginning to well up.

Behind me, I could hear the guy limping away, footsteps scraping on the loose stones.

"Leave him, Chris. You'll just make things worse," she said.

"But," I said.

"No," she said.

"But if he gets away …" I said.

"Just don't."

I threw away the pry bar and dropped down beside her. Then I got straight back up.

"Stay there. I'll get a dressing."

I raced to retrieve my backpack and found the first aid kit they had given me back at Crux. By the time I returned from the corridor, she had made her way over to the water cube and was washing the scrape.

"Here's some disinfectant and gauze-tape," I said. "Is it bad?"

She took the stuff without looking at me and began to smear the area with the antiseptic cream. The injury was on the outside of her right arm which meant that she had to twist her arm up to get it and had to use her left hand to work on it.

"Here, I'll get the bandage started for you," I said.

But she pulled away from me.

"Stay away."

"Are you … okay?"

She laughed. "No. But not because of this. This is just a scrape."

"I'm really sorry … I was just … I thought he was trying to …"

"Of course, he was. And now something worse is going to happen. What do you think he's going to tell them when he gets back to the camp?"

"I could still … Why don't you leave? You could come with me. I've got food and water and …"

"I'm not going to do that."

"Why?"

She began smoothing down the adhesive with her fingers.

"Same reasons as before. And because I don't want you going savage on me."

"I'm not…"

"You think I don't know what that was?" She looked at me straight in the eyes. "You should go, Chris. I need time to work out what to do. And you need to get away from here. They'll be hunting for you."

I nodded and gathered my things.

"Do you want me to leave you some food?"

"No. And here, take your tea and first-aid stuff too. The fewer signs that we were friends, the better."

"Okay," I said. "I'm really sorry, Mal. And I hope… I hope everything works out for you."

"Yeah, you too."

I sealed up my backpack and went out the door with my head down.

CHAPTER 33

At first, I just ran through the back lots and ruins, trying to get away from whoever might be coming after me, and even more than that, trying to get away from what had just happened with Mal and the guard.

My thoughts were a total mess. One minute, I was angry with Mal for turning on me when I'd only been trying to help her. Then, I was worried and full of guilt about making things worse for her. Then I was ashamed at losing control, which led to frustration with myself and anger at Central—because, what difference had the cure even made to me? Then I was cursing myself for trying to go around Addle and calling myself a fool for thinking I could ever rescue anyone.

So I kept running until my lungs were burning and my legs were shaking. When I couldn't go any further, I sat down on a rusted-out station wagon and tried to work out what to do next. Part of me wanted to look for the east road and just keep travelling. Maybe I would find Caleb before Perseverance, or maybe I'd just keep to myself and avoid trouble.

But I couldn't go on yet. My mum was still out there somewhere and I would never forgive myself if I didn't do everything I could to find her. I had to look for that Admin centre that Mallory had told me about.

And then I caught a break. I came to an old sports stadium and managed to climb up one of its stands until I reached the roof. As I stood looking around, I located the radio tower, the camp, and then the office buildings where I'd seen the zombie workers with the bulldozer. From there, I worked out where Mal's place was and finally spotted a big cream-brick building rising up on the far side of a low wooded hill.

Even though its upper windows were broken, I was certain that it was the place. It had a ruined neon + sign on the near side that showed it had once been a hospital, and there was a newish tarpaulin roped down over one edge of the roof. It looked used. And it was close—only about a k away. My blind running had brought me almost to it. As I looked down into the shadows, I could even see the traces of a path that would take me there—a cracked concrete highway and a tunnel running through the hill.

I thought hard about going that way, of course. I'd heard too many stories where people went into old mines or train tunnels and ended up being eaten by cannibals. But when I got closer and found that I could see through to the other side, I decided to risk it.

The tunnel exit brought me to within a couple of hundred metres from the hospital—close enough to smell its smoke and hear the sounds of its machinery. As I looked down at it, I caught a flash of colour from some vehicle on the far side of the trees.

I found cover in an old bus terminal and waited for dark.

Long after the sun had gone down, I made my way forward. As I got closer, I saw that the hospital had a series of wings. Some of them—like the section I'd seen from the stadium—were dark and abandoned. Other sections had light in their windows and yellow floodlights shining on their walls.

But I came in at the back—three stories of empty windows rising above an overgrown carpark. I ran under the entry porch, passed a shot-up ambulance and slipped through the wrecked aluminium doors.

At first, it was mostly just a ruin: a half-burned reception desk; glass fragments and peeling linoleum, then came rooms of overturned equipment and rusted bed frames. At one point, it looked like someone had tried to build a barricade out of cupboards and trolleys, but it had been pushed aside.

Then I came round a corner and suddenly found myself looking at a sliding fire door with light shining around its edges.

It was pretty tough to get it open—the old rollers were stiff, and it was more complicated because I was trying to do it without making any noise. But when I finally managed to squeeze through, I could smell fresh paint and feel clean linoleum under my feet. The glowing "Exit" sign above the door that I had just opened gave me enough light to see a passage leading off to my right.

I followed it and found other doors. Two were locked. The next opened into a storeroom stacked with cleaning equipment. Then, there was an elevator and a door to a stairwell. As I stuck my head through that one, I could hear voices and footsteps coming down from above—which sent me into a panic and made me lunge for the next door.

Now, I was in a carpeted office. It was faintly lit by the light of a sleeping computer and smelled of cigarettes and mint.

I guessed it was an interview room of some kind. Opposite the desk with the computer was a lounge chair surrounded by small cameras on black metal stands.

I went behind the desk and looked at the screen. I didn't really know much about computers, but I knew they were the sort of thing where people kept records. For a moment I entertained a vague idea that I might use it to find out something about my mum.

Instead, as I touched the keyboard, the screen changed to show three little picture-panels—each with the same woman in exactly the same pose in different spots. In one, she was wearing a white shirt and sitting in the chair with the cameras around it. In the other two, she was wearing different clothes and sitting in other spots: on a balcony looking over a beach; at a table in a restaurant.

There was something about those pictures that made me feel strange, but I had too many other things to think about. As soon as I was sure the people in the stairwell weren't coming for me, I slipped back out into the corridor.

At the next bend, there was more light. When I peered around the corner, I could see that it was another lobby.

But this one was completely different from the entrance where I'd come in—polished floors and rows of chrome chairs along the walls. The receptionist's desk looked like it was made of black marble and there was a gold logo on the wall behind it—two Rs back-to-back with a plus sign between them.

Some of the light here was from floodlights outside the front doors. Most of it was coming from two other doors on the opposite side of the entrance area. I stopped to listen for a moment and ran across the tiles toward them. They were mostly frosted glass, but I could see that there were also some unetched bits, which I thought I might be able look through. But as soon as I got close, the doors just slid open by themselves.

Straight away, I was hit by a smell of chemicals that reminded me of the doctor's office back in Spillan. As my eyes adjusted, I could see a large white room lined with stainless steel trolleys and blinking consoles.

On my left, two chairs that looked like they were from a dentist's surgery faced the side wall. Behind and between them, a melon-sized pod made of white enamel hung off an articulated armature that was bolted to the ceiling. The pod itself had other arms and tubes dangling down from it, making it look like a dead spider.

All of it—and especially that last thing—gave me the creeps. I turned to retrace my steps, but as I was right in the centre of the space, I heard the front doors slide open. A rush of cold air hit me and a woman's voice said, "Who the hell are you?" And I just ran.

I raced back the way I'd come; past the office and the elevator and stairwell. I was almost at the fire door before I heard the alarm go off—a buzzing sound like someone had taken an electric school bell and filled it with gravel. It wasn't really loud, but it felt like it was rattling my teeth and going straight through my bones. I squeezed through the gap and ran on—around the barricade and out through the wards. I tripped and cut my hand as I went out the doors, but I didn't feel a thing.

Then I was out in the car park and running up the slope to the highway that went through the tunnel, with shouts and revving engines and flashing lights flashing behind me. I wasn't sure if they were following me or just rushing around and looking for me, but what I was really worried about was the thought of the Hunter machines that Pru and Trevor had mentioned. What would I do if I had to deal with one of those?

Yet I made it to the tunnel without being caught, and the receding were still mostly what I would expect from humans. As I ran into the darkness I even began to hope that I might get away. There would be cover on the other side—trees, ruins, the stadium—maybe I could find somewhere to wait until the fuss had died down and try again.

I slowed to avoid injuring myself on the obstacles that I remembered from when I went through before: the shopping trolley … the wrecked car … I felt charcoal from the old campfire crunch under my feet.

After that, I knew it would be clear to the other side, and I felt a thrill of hope and relief. The noise of pursuit was definitely louder, but there was no way they would be able to catch me before I was through. I began to pick up speed again, looking up ahead to see the black of the tunnel give way to the blue-grey night.

But instead, there was something else: something massive and square and which filled up the space ahead of me; something that radiated heat and smelled of diesel and unwashed bodies.

I froze. A huge spasm went through me. There was no way. It couldn't be.

Then someone behind me shone a searchlight up the tunnel, and lit it up—an armoured grill painted with a big white skull. Around it, white eyes and yellow teeth … and a huge man with bones in his hair.

Something flickered in my mind—something beside the recognition and the terror—but there was no time to think about what it meant. I was already running back toward the light and the guards who had been chasing me.

CHAPTER 34

When I opened my eyes, I was lying on concrete and everything hurt. I was in a room with cinder-block walls on three sides and a locked frame of galvanised steel and chainlink on the forth. There was a pile of blankets in one corner and a brass tap trickling into a stinking gully trap halfway down the right-hand wall.

Beyond the chainlink, a dormant generator sat beneath a plinking fluorescent light. A few metres past that, glass-panel doors admitted a weaker glow and the distant sound of an electric motor.

I sat up painfully and checked myself. I had bruises on both sides of my body and swollen lumps on my jaw and forehead. My sword and gear were gone, but I still had my coat.

How had I got here? For a long while, my mind was just blank. Then I remembered the tunnel … I remembered the Savages … I remembered running back toward the guards, and them catching me, and throwing me down, and kicking me.

I dragged myself over to the gully trap and caught some of the water in my hand. It smelled like rust and left a metallic taste in my mouth.

When I had taken the edge off my thirst, I crawled to the front of my cell and took a look at the wire barrier and its supports. There was going to be no escape that way. The posts were bolted into the concrete of the floor and ceiling. The door section was secured with a fat chain and a fatter padlock.

I was exhausted now, and my head was pounding, so I retreated to the blankets in the corner. But they weren't blankets at all; they were Traveller's coats—three of them—and they looked like they had dried blood on them.

I felt like I was going to throw up then. What was going to happen to me? I needed to think!

But I couldn't think. And I was so tired.

*   *   *

When I woke up again there were new sounds; footsteps … the rattle of a chain … somebody clicking their fingers in front of my face … and then a creaky voice that sounded like a hundred kinds of throat cancer.

"Oi. Hey, wake up, loser. We need to have a chat."

I opened my eyes and tried to raise my head. There was a wheelchair parked in front of me—a pair of white, blue-veined ankles stuck into aged leather shoes resting on the footrests.

"You admiring my Mercurys?" said the voice. "They're a good shoe alright. Vulcanised laminate soles—last you forever. Not bad for kicking in teeth too."

I squinted up to see an aged and pock-marked face framed with thick spectacles. Below that, leather suspenders tracked down a flannel shirt to support dark pinstripe trousers. A pocket calculator stuck out of the breast pocket.

In the background, two guards in uniforms—one tall, one short— were busy doing something with trolleys, boxes, tripods and cables just outside the wire.

The man in the wheelchair bent down and snapped his fingers again in front of my face.

"Oi. Over here, buddy. Here's how it works. I'm gonna ask you a question. If you answer it, you earn yourself something nice. If you don't, we do something else. Does that make sense?"

I looked up at him again without answering. He held up something wrapped in foil.

"Okay. I'm gonna take that as 'yes'. Alright. First question, playing for a bit of the chockie, which we found amongst your stuff. What's your name?"

"Chr…" I said, biting off my words. The thought had suddenly struck me that if they had my mum, I didn't want to make it easier for them to connect the dots by telling them my surname.

The man in the wheelchair raised his eyebrows.

"Chr… eh?" he said. "That's a pretty funny name. What, did your mum and dad have a speech impediment? How about a second name?"

I shook my head.

"No? Okay." The man turned to his men. "How are we going with that amp back there, boys? All good?"

He looked back at me.

"Alright, Chr…, I'm gonna go off and eat your chockie and leave you on your lonesome for a while. If you change your mind, you can wave at the camera and sooner or later, somebody'll see you. Switch her on, boys."

"All the way?" said the bigger of the two guards.

"No, Kev, not all the way," said the man in the wheelchair. "We want him to be able to talk at the end of it. Start him on 4."

There was a deep crackle and pop, and a tiny red light began to glow from one of the tripods.

"Okay, we're off. See you later on," said the old man. "Wheel me out, Stumpy."

The shorter of the guards came into the cell and looked at me blankly from deep-set eyes as he grasped the handles of the wheelchair and backed it out into the plant room. The big guard followed, locking the gate behind him. As the three retreated through the double doors, I had a brief view of a short corridor ending at an open elevator.

And then it was quiet. I looked at the pile of equipment that the guards had set up, expecting a noise to start coming from it, but there was nothing—just the sound of the lift, the fluorescent light, and the water trickling from the tap.

And yet, as I lay back down again, there *was* something—the feeling in the air had changed. I had a sense of something pulsing just outside my auditory range. When I tried to focus on it, it slipped away from me, so I couldn't be sure it was really there. But the act of listening for it made me feel a bit sick—it was like the feeling I had once when I had a deep splinter in my finger and tried to dig it out: the close staring, the digging into my own flesh and the sensation of the needle ripping and dragging.

I sat up again. Suddenly, sleep seemed impossible.

*   *   *

A few hours later, the short, hollow-eyed guard appeared with a tin bowl. As he pushed it under the chainlink barrier I saw that he was missing all the fingers on his left hand, and remembered how the man in the wheelchair had called him Stumpy. He gave me the same empty look he'd given me before and left in silence.

When he was gone, I went over and examined the bowl. It was a sort of pale yellow slurry that smelled like burnt corn with the consistency of thin chunky porridge. I tried to eat a mouthful but the taste and texture made me gag. If it was corn, it was mostly cob. I tipped it down the drain

and slid the empty bowl back under the barrier.

CHAPTER 35

(Extract of the transcribed Records of Caleb Dox, Vol 1.31)

When I woke up in the cell, my leg wasn't hurtin' anymore, and for a moment, I felt okay. But then I reached down and felt that the ankle thing was gone and remembered what had happened and that I was in prison now until the trial. And that Seini was gonna lose all her money.

And suddenly, I felt like someone had pulled out all my guts and chopped 'em up into little bits.

When Seini came in to see me before work, I tried to say sorry, but she wouldn't let me.

"I don't want to talk about that, Ca," she said. "I'm really angry, but I know it wasn't your fault. But if you keep apologising, I'll get really annoyed at you, and that won't do either of us any good. What we've got to do is focus on finding who did it and getting you out."

"But you'll still be in the red," I said. "I don't want you to have to ..."

"Stop it, Ca," she said. "I mean it. There's only one thing you can do that would make a difference, and I know you aren't gonna do that. So just leave it alone, okay?"

"Okay," I said. "What can I do then?"

"You can tell me everything that happened with the Scorchers."

So I told her about it all, and when I was done, she said, "Okay, that's good. That was smart how you led them on. Now we know it wasn't them, and that it probably had something to do with that memory stick."

"So who do you think did it?" I said. "Do you think it was someone workin' for the Mayor?"—I said that pretty quietly cos, although they had me in a cell by myself, there were other cells and guards around.

"I don't know," she said. "But if it was something to do with the camps, it's more likely to be HORD. And there's something else, too. They found

Thomas's brother, Bren. Someone murdered him too."

"When?" I said.

"They found him yesterday at the bottom of the Scenic Railway. Someone had cut his throat.

"But that means they didn't get what they wanted off Thomas. If it's that data thing, they were still lookin' for it. Maybe they still are."

*   *   *

A couple of hours after Seini left, I got a visit from an old guy in a suit and fancy specs who said he'd been appointed to be my lawyer and that the City had set a trial date.

"Okay," I said. "But Seini and I are still tryin' to work out who did it. Can't we ask 'em to wait a bit?"

And he said that that wasn't how it worked.

"What can we do then?" I said.

"I understand that you have already been presented with an offer from your arresting officers."

"Yeah, but they wanted me to say I did it and blame Central. And I didn't. And I'm not gonna do that."

"Well, I'm not going to be able to get you off with all this evidence against you."

So I told him about how someone had cut the power to the lights, and that couldn't have been me, and I told him about what the Scorchers said about Eliza and the data stick. But he just shook his head at it all.

"I'm afraid none of that is going to do you much good, my boy. Once they show those videos of you, everyone will think you did it. They might think you had accomplices, but that won't help your cause."

After he left, I was on my own for most of the day, just thinkin' about everything—and everything I was thinkin' was sort of bad—like how all the Travellers had been actin' at that meetin'. And how nobody in Addle wanted to know anything about gettin' cured. And how I'd messed it up for Seini so she was gonna have trouble gettin' out of debt.

CHAPTER 36

It was Kev who woke me up. I'd gone to sleep at the front of the cell, leaning against the chainlink, which made it easy for him to kick me without opening the door.

When I lifted my head, the man in the wheelchair was looking down at me through the wire. Everything was stiff and sore and there was a dull throbbing in my ears.

"Wakey wakey, Chr… You look a bit uncomfortable there. We should get you a bit of Bandicoot Oil. Good for the muscles. You rub it in and it fixes you right up. 'Course they don't make it anymore, but I've got a bit."

I sat up and skidded back from the wire.

The man in the wheelchair kept talking.

"I heard you chucked out your dinner. You're gonna get pretty hungry if you keep doing that. 'Course, all you have to do is tell me your name and I'll get you something a bit nicer …"

I shook my head.

"No? … Sure? Maybe you need another day. What do you reckon, Kev? Let's try him on six."

"It's Craig," I said. "My name is Craig Jones."

The man pursed his lips and shook his head.

"I thought you fellas were supposed to tell the truth," he said. "Isn't that what it says in your little book?"

"I *am* telling the truth. That's my name."

"No, Chr… It isn't. You think I don't know who you are? You think I don't know about your little adventures with our Lieutenant Bird?"

I felt like he'd punched me in the chest.

"If you know who I am, why are you asking me?" I said.

"I'm not talking to you now … Make it eight, Kev."

The guard fiddled with the control box on top of the speaker and immediately I felt a pressure change. The throbbing in my ears turned into a sort of erratic hammering.

Kev took hold of the wheelchair and began to turn it back toward the door.

"My name's Chris Walker," I said.

"Too late for that," said the old man.

The guard pushed him through the doors, and I was by myself again.

But it wasn't the same as before. The un-sound was something almost physical now—like a presence that was watching me, a thing that hated me and wanted to crush me and stop my breathing. Almost immediately, I recognised it as the same thing I had encountered in the swamp near Didasko. There wasn't any of the audible moaning that I'd heard from the Desolator, but the effect was the same.

Except this time, I couldn't run from it. The whole cell was thick with it. It filled up my head so that whatever I thought of became poisoned with it. Sometimes it was like a fog that made everything hazy. Sometimes it felt like I was being drowned in a pool of filthy water.

And, bit by bit, it found its way into the cracks and crevices of my mind. It flooded my brain and made bad memories break loose and bob to the surface: the old Agent under the bridge, my savagery toward Flex, the expression on Mallory's face, my betrayal of my mum.

And there in the middle of them—all shiny and new—was my attempted lie. The old man had been right about that: the Roadbook *did* warn us to be scrupulous about the truth—it was one of the main ways our transformation could be promoted or corrupted. Lies and truth-telling, it said, altered the mental pathways on which they travelled. If it was truth, those pathways would become clear and reliable: they could become main highways reaching new areas of development and feeder roads for increased regions of understanding. But lies would produce a maze of dead ends and potholes. And the more a lie was told, the more it would resist revision. A person's mind would become a patchwork of impassable dead zones and confusion. Finally, a person might not even know when they were lying.

Was this what had already happened to me, I wondered? Had that lie about my name been the product of greater lies that I couldn't see anymore? Was this why I'd ended up out here instead of going straight through Addle with Caleb? Had I been fooling myself all this time? Was I already lost beyond recovery?

In an effort to get as far away from the speaker as possible, I finally retreated to the pile of Travellers' coats. I had tried to avoid them up until then because of what they seemed to represent, with their burn marks and blood.

But I sat down on them now, with my chin on my knees and my arms wrapped around my ears.

A bit later—I don't know how long because I had lost all sense of time by then—Stumpy came and pushed another bowl under the wire. It was the same mixture that I had rejected before, but this time I was so hungry that I forced it down.

CHAPTER 37

I have no idea how long it was before the wheelchair guy came to see me again. The time was a haze and I have never had any desire to check the drone footage.

Part of the reason for my confusion was the fact that I could never really sleep while that machine was blasting me. There was something like dozing I guess, but like everything else, it was shot through with that same texture.

But then the noise stopped and he was there again. He had some kind of electronic device, and he was clinking it on the middle bar of the barrier.

"Wake up, buddy … Time for a chat."

"What do you want?" I said

"I want you to be happy. I want to be able to turn off the grind and for you to be able to walk out of here."

I closed my eyes and savoured the silence for a moment.

I was still sitting on the pile of coats in the back corner. I lifted up one of the sleeves sticking out of the pile.

"Like you did with them?"

"Yeah … yeah … Well, one of them, anyway. One of them topped himself. Another of 'em wouldn't give in until we pruned him. But Kev is the model for you, aren't you, Kev?" He twisted his head to look at the guard, who nodded without smiling.

"Kev saw the way the wind was blowing and gave it up. Took off his coat. Did a little speech for us. Come on over and I'll show you."

I hesitated, not wanting to get any closer to him than I had to, but he tapped the bar again.

"Come on. Unless you want me to just go away and let you find out what 9's like."

I shuffled forward until I was a couple of feet back from the chainlink. The old man held up the device he was holding so that I could see the moving image that had begun to play on its surface.

The video was taken from the room outside my cell. The door was open and the guard called Kev was standing just in front of it—gaunt, unshaven and dressed in a Traveller's coat.

"Alright buddy," said the wheelchair guy's voice, sounding tinny through the little speakers. "You're on. Go for it."

Kev looked down at a piece of paper in his hands and began reading.

My name is Kevin Turner, and I am making this recording of my own free will to formally renounce my allegiance to the dictatorial power of the Central Government based in the city of Sanctuary, and of the Pantarch and his representatives.

When I took my oath at the Tox treatment centre at Crux, I believed that the Pantarch's representatives would take care of me and help me to reach Central-controlled territory. Instead, I found that I was abandoned and had to make my own way with very little food or guidance.

My conclusion is that the offer I received at Crux wasn't sincere or genuine— and I believe that I am not alone in this conclusion. I don't know why the people at Crux are doing what they are doing, or if they really represent the Pantarch, but I can't trust them anymore.

I would like to express my gratitude to Nimcorp—and especially Administrator Devlin—for looking after me while I was making this important decision, and for welcoming me into the Nimcorp family. I look forward to participating in the Corp's plans for the Autonomous Zone which, I sincerely believe, will be good for everyone.

With that said, all that remains is for me to remove my Travellers' coat and renounce my oath, which I now believe was made on the basis of false information.

The man bent down to place the script on the ground. Then there was a cut and he reappeared, just in the process of removing his coat. He held it out in front of him by the collar and let it fall out of the frame. The screen went dark.

"Good work, Kev," said the Administrator. "I always like seeing that. I thought that was a really nice touch about the Nimcorp family."

"Well, you wrote it," said the guard.

"Yeah, I guess that's true. Still, you were spot on with the delivery. And I like how you did the coat-drop at the end too—very dramatic. You should've been an actor."

He turned back to me.

"So here's how it is, Chris. You're a wanted man. The moment I ran your face through our system, I found out all about your adventures—how you got away from Bird and his boys at Wicket and how you gave him that chop on Boneyard Road. You're a bit notorious.

"Now, because of that, what I should be doing is handing you over to our friends in the mobile response division—Bird's people. I don't know what they'd do with you, but I'm sure it wouldn't be anything you'd like.

"But I don't want to do that. First, Bird and me aren't the best of friends, and I don't want to give him the satisfaction. Second, I get a bigger bounty if I can get you to turn, like you saw our Kev do just then.

"So that's what we're gonna work on. You're gonna be stuck in here until you chuck it in and do the speech. We're gonna crank the box up to nine—I'd do ten, but that'd scramble your brain—and we're just gonna wait. It's not gonna be very nice for you, but you can stop it any time. You won't even have to write your script."

He paused and looked down at me.

"Make sense?"

I shook my head.

"What bit don't you get?" he said.

"I mean, I won't do it," I said.

"Why not?"

"Because you guys keep trying to do bad things to me and Central keeps rescuing me."

"Buddy. Hope you don't mind me saying this, but you don't look rescued. You look like rubbish. In fact, you looked like rubbish on the security footage even before the boys caught you and worked you over.

"Seriously. Central doesn't care about you, or you wouldn't be stuck in here. Maybe they don't know you're here. Maybe you've been a bad boy and they've given you the flick. But nobody's coming for you. You're just gonna sit here with that noise blasting at ya until you crack. If you had any sense, you'd do yourself a favour and pack it in now."

I shook my head and bit hard on the inside of my lip. I tried to look defiant, but I felt more like I was about to fall to pieces—like I'd already "cracked".

The Administrator watched me for a few seconds and laughed.

"Won't be long, buddy. Okay, Kev. Handcuff him to that pipe near the drain. People tend to hang themselves when they're on nine for a while, and we don't want to have to be watching him all the time."

CHAPTER 38

Nine *was* worse.

I'd anticipated some sort of pain—like a headache or nosebleed—but the first physical reaction was in my stomach. I felt queasy and unsettled—as if I'd eaten something bad or done something wrong that I couldn't quite remember.

But as before, the feeling soon found memories to stick to. It coated them and grew around them. Before long, I couldn't tell the difference between the memory and the growths. I thought I had betrayed Mallory, and she had been beaten and tortured to death. I'd let Caleb down by leaving him, and he'd given up and gone back to the bottle. I knew for certain that I'd come too late for my mum—she was already a mindless shell. Wherever I turned, my thoughts accused me, and every sound and sight in my cell brought new guilt.

I wanted to retreat into darkness and silence. I wanted to sleep. But there was no escape there. When I found a way to support my shackled arm and slip away for a few moments, new visions of death and misery crowded in on me. Spillan had been attacked, and there had been no gunner to save them. My friends were all dead.

So, time went by without any real sense of night and day. The flickering strip light was an endless present that became another torture. I guessed days were going by because Stumpy kept bringing me food, but for all I knew this was part of the way they were messing with my mind (and I found out later that *was* what they were doing). All I knew was that the space between these visits sometimes seemed like minutes and sometimes like weeks.

I thought of refusing the food they gave me and starving myself into unconsciousness. But I found that I simply didn't have the strength. My willpower was almost gone.

I knew then that I wouldn't be able to hold out much longer. As my memories degraded and became infected, the things that had sustained me in my journey became more unreal: Eve … Dr Klesia … Crux … the meal I'd eaten at Prediger's house … my time with Caleb … the pictures that Clem Berger had showed us. They all became like shadows. I might be able to remember them once or twice, but then they'd fade—as if the act of recalling them used them up.

At some point, the Administrator came and looked in on me again. I heard him without really listening—like I was at the bottom of a well or at the end of a tunnel. But I got the gist of it: I'd been conned by the people at Crux; life would get much better if I switched sides. After I shook my head, he told Kev to give me a bit of a touch-up, which ended in another fractured rib, bruised kidneys and a sprained wrist.

I sank pretty low after that—thought of giving in just to get it over and done with. But the idea of becoming like Kev seemed even worse than what I was going through now. Eventually, I thought of another plan: after my next meal, I would surrender and then, when they uncuffed me to make my statement, I'd curse them and charge head first at something hard—perhaps the wall on the other side of the generator room—to try to kill myself.

Yet when Stumpy brought me my meal, there was a surprise. As I lifted the bowl from the concrete, I felt wet paper stuck to the underside of the enamel. When I peeled it off, I found that it wasn't just any piece of paper but a page from the Roadbook.

It wasn't easy to read it. Sitting up was painful after the beating, and the only way to hide what I was doing from the camera was to put my back toward the light. But it was a passage that I knew better than any other:

Your work will be difficult; you will sometimes feel that you are making no progress, and some of you will lose your lives in the process. Believe me, I know about these things!

But I want you to understand that it is worth it. It is worth it for those you rescue, for the new Territory that will come, for the honour and reputation of Central.

And it is worth it for yourselves. The City that you have not yet seen waits to embrace you as its sons and daughters. I look forward to welcoming each one of you beneath the trees of the Landing and leading you up from the river to present you to the Pantarch. I look forward to seeing you made healthy—with the last traces of the Tox eradicated from your bodies. I look forward to seeing you meet those you brought to Crux.

I paused and wiped my eyes with the back of my wrist and wondered how it had happened? Was it just an accident? Had someone put the wet bowl down on some old papers and this had gotten stuck to it?

But the next bowl Stumpy brought me came with another page.

It was another bit from the last chapters of the Roadbook; where Prax shows what the Cleanse will look like:

… As we looked down on it all, a line of brilliant blue fire was moving across the mountains and valleys. It turned the stubble black, and the shanties went up in flame. I saw utes full of Savages trying to drive away from the line, only to disappear as it overtook them. In another spot, I saw men wreathed in blue light falling to the ground and clawing at their skin.

"Is this the end?" I asked him.

"It is the end," he said, "But also the beginning. Keep watching."

He made it go faster now. I saw great storm clouds billowing up from the East, and soaking rain began to fall across the whole expanse of the Territory. It went on for a long time and became very dark. But when the light came in under the cloud, the sun was clear and bright, and the dawn that shone over the land showed patches of green on the blackened plains and trees that I thought must have been dead. Suddenly I could feel the cool wind. There was a scent of wet earth and eucalyptus. Everywhere I looked, life was coming back. Water was beginning to flow in the riverbeds. There were people in the towns. Animals appeared on the plains.

I read that one again too and, when I was finished, carefully eased it into one of the side pockets of my coat so it could dry. Then, I pulled out the first page from the other side and began to memorise it.

It took me a long time. Even when I thought I had it in my head, I kept getting bits wrong.

But while I was doing it, the time simply seemed to slide by me, and even the noise didn't seem so bad. It wasn't like the silence when the Administrator came around and they switched off the machine—but it became bearable, like it had fallen into the background.

Much later, Stumpy returned to bring the next bowl and collect the one I'd finished. I tried calling out to him, but he gave a tiny shake of his head and pointed sideways to the camera with one of his remaining fingers.

The bowl he left for me this time had another page stuck to the bottom—a passage where one of Tobias' crew was explaining how distress could be a catalyst for transgenesis. I didn't really understand it, but I stowed it in my drying-pocket for later.

When I had finished revising my memorisation of the other pages, I tried to eat the swill. It was still a near-impossible act of will to get it down. But this time, I discovered that someone had submerged chunks of ration-block in the slop.

Before I'd been captured, my rations had often seemed flavourless to me—especially after I'd eaten the stuff at Pru and Trevor's hideout. But now, as I bit into them, I felt like I was eating the greatest food ever made. I know that probably sounds weird. And I know I've said similar things about the meals I had at Horeb and Didasko. But this *reminded me* of those meals.

Then, as I was finishing, someone switched off the noisemaker. When I turned, Stumpy was back at the wire, fidgeting nervously.

"We've only got about three minutes while the camera guy gets his food."

His voice was hoarse and scratchy—like it was painful for him to get his words out.

"Are you a Traveller?" I said.

He held up his fingerless hand. "Was," he said. "Till they did this."

"What are they gonna do to me?" I said.

"More of this"—he pointed to the equipment—"Devlin doesn't want to do too much to you physically until after they've videoed your confession."

"And after that?"

"Don't know. It'll depend on how he's feeling, probably."

I strained, trying to think what to say or ask. Should I ask him about my mum? Or about escape? But the camera was still on—what if they returned from lunch and played it back?

"What's your name," I said.

"Lenny," he said. "Len Timens."

"Thank you," I said.

He switched the machine back on, and the un-noise hammered me again.

CHAPTER 39

(Extract of the transcribed Records of Caleb Dox, Vol 1.35)

So, the trial started five days after they put me in prison.

Chief Diritto came down with some of the guards and put handcuffs and ankle chains on me. And she said, "I'm sorry that we have to do it this way, Dox, but I was pretty clear about staying out of trouble, wasn't I?"

And I said, "Yes you were, Chief. I just wish Seini didn't have to bear the consequences."

"I thought I was pretty clear about that too," she said. "But I imagine you could still make it better for her if you pleaded guilty."

Then they took me out to the back of the Watch-house where they had a van waiting, and they all got in with me and we drove over to the courthouse, which turned out to be the old puppet theatre near the front gate.

When we got close, there was a big crowd of people outside the building, and they all started booin', and some of 'em were chuckin' stuff at the van. And I could see that the ladies from the amphitheatre were there, and one of 'em had a big sign on a stick that said, "Not in our name." And other people had signs too that said, "No mercy for kid killers," and "Central Kills! Kill Central!"

Then the Chief made 'em stop the van right outside the front door, and the guards who were already there and the guards from the van made like a corridor for the Chief and me, and we went through it—and it was really loud, and someone got me in the back of the head with an egg, and the Chief got splattered with some red stuff that I guess was meant to look like blood.

Once we got into the courthouse, it was a bit quieter. Some of 'em started hissin' and booin', but the judge—who turned out to just be the

Mayor with a wig on—banged his hammer and said he'd chuck 'em out if they made a ruckus.

He was up the front at this big desk where the puppet thing used to be, and they had a bit of a stage in front of that with a chair on one side for me to sit on. And my lawyer and the prosecutor guy were on smaller desks in front of that.

Then the Mayor made us all sit down, and he read out the charges, which were murder and affray, and asked how I wanted to plead, and I said, "Not guilty." And he said that before he entered that plea, he wanted me to understand that he thought that this was a pretty open-and-shut case, and that it would go better for me if I pleaded guilty.

He also said that they'd recently changed the law in Addle so that cases involving Central were gonna be guilty until proven innocent because Centralists had caused so much trouble.

And then he asked if I still wanted to plead not guilty, and I said, "Yes," and then he said, "Okay then," and we got started.

Then the lawyers got up and gave speeches.

Mine went first, and he said that the evidence against me might look bad, but everyone should remember that the lights were out and nobody saw what happened—and that was about all he said.

After that, the prosecutor got up. And he was this fat guy with kind of shiny cheeks, and he said that everyone was gonna see that there was no doubt in this case and that the thing everyone should all really be thinkin' about is how to send a strong message to Central that this atrocity wouldn't be tolerated.

Then he went on to talk about how Thomas had had a really hard life, and nobody looked after him, and he'd finally found a family to care for him and then "this ruffian"—and he was pointing to me—"decided to put an end to that because he couldn't take a bit of teasing."

When he finished, the judge said it was time for 'em to present their evidence, and the prosecutor started by calling "Sharon Fortuna"—who was Simha—and she came in and sat in another chair that they put on the other side of the stage and kept glarin' at me like she was about to attack.

And the lawyer said, "Miss Fortuna, thank you for agreeing to testify today. Could you begin by telling us why you are dressed as you are?"

Except she didn't answer—she just kept starin' at me. Then he asked again and kind of looked at the judge. And the judge said, "Come on, Shaz." Then, when she still didn't answer, he said, "She'll only answer if you call her Simha."

So the prosecutor tried asking again like that, and she said about how her clothes and claws and stuff were like a reflection of who she was inside—which was a lion.

And the lawyer asked her how people treated her when she was wearin' her lion stuff.

And she said, "Most people know you have to treat wild animals with respect."

"But not everyone?" said the lawyer.

"No, not everyone," She said. "Sometimes we have to teach them ..."

But he interrupted her before she finished saying that. "Could you give us any examples of people who have failed to respect your condition?"

"You, just now," she said. "It's not a condition. It's a nature."

And he said, "I do apologise. Can I rephrase ..."

But she interrupted him and said, "You're still doing it. When you look me in the eye like that, it's a sign of attack."

So he kind of looked away and tried again.

"Simha, is there any particular group that you feel fails to treat you with respect?"

"People like him," she said, pointing at me and growling.

"Centralists?" he said.

"Yeah," she said. "The Pantarch's Dogs."

"How does this disrespect manifest itself?" he said.

"You mean apart from killing our cubs?" she said.

"Yes, apart from that," he said.

"They say we're sick, and they look at us in the eyes like we're humans," she said.

"And was Mr Dox guilty of this?" he said.

She said, "Yeah."

Then he brought in a video screen and showed the video of when I first met them near the sausage cart. And he asked her to say what had happened—cos it was sort of fuzzy, and there wasn't any sound—and she said how I'd shouted out at them and called them sickos and been laughin' at 'em and threatenin' 'em.

And then she said that Seini had come over and pulled her gun and that she'd called 'em freaks and told 'em all to get away from her brother or she'd shoot 'em.

While she was talkin' about me, it was like I started boilin' inside cos of all the lies, but I knew I shouldn't shout out. But when she said that about Seini, I couldn't help myself.

"That's not true," I said. "Seini didn't say any of that. Ask the sausage guy. He'll tell you what happened."

But the judge told me to shut up or he'd have me gagged.

Then the prosecutor asked Simha if the other members of her gang would back up what she was saying, and she said they would.

So he went on and showed the other video of where I was with Fergus when the lion gang came along. And he asked her what was happenin' there, and she said how they were just goin' past and I'd shouted out at them and told 'em I was gonna chop 'em up because of what had happened to Fergus.

Then they got to the bit where I cut off Tom's lion ear, and they slowed it down and played it a few times. And then the prosecutor asked her what I'd been saying when that happened, and she said that Fergus was tellin' me to let 'em have it (which was true) and that I'd laughed and said I was gonna have fun slicin' 'em up (which wasn't).

I tried to call out and tell 'em that—even if they gagged me—cos it made me feel really sick in my guts that everyone thought I'd said that.

But nobody could hear me, cos all the people in the court started makin' a big noise and shoutin' out that they should hang me or chop me up. And some of the lion-guys were there, and they were all growlin', and one of 'em tried to charge at me, except the guards caught him.

That took a long time to die down. And then my lawyer got up to ask Simha a few questions, and he said that it looked like the videos showed the lions comin' up to me instead of the other way round, and said that it looked like maybe I'd been actin' out of self-defence.

Then the prosecutor said, "Objection", cos my lawyer wasn't askin' a question, and the judge said, "Sustained", and told him to move on.

And then my lawyer asked Simha if she or any of her gang had ever got in trouble for assaultin' people before.

But the prosecutor said, "Objection", cos it was me on trial, not Simha and she was bein' retraumatised by bein' asked these questions, and the Mayor said, "Sustained", and said that it was time to wrap it up for the day because he had another meeting to go to and that we'd start up again tomorrow.

Then everyone stood up and started goin' off, and my lawyer came over and asked if I wanted to change my plea cos it was lookin' bad. And I said I'd think about it and let him know the next morning.

But when I got back to the cell and tried to think, my thoughts were just spinnin' round and round. I kept thinkin' about all the stuff Simha said, and how the Mayor hadn't let my lawyer talk, and how even the Travellers were against me and believin' the lies.

I kept thinkin' about Seini, and how she'd been so close to retirin' and how they were tryin' to make out that she was helpin' me attack the lions.

The only good thing that happened to me that day was that Phoebe came round to see me in the afternoon.

She brought me some bikkies. And cos the guard knew her from when he was a kid, he brought her a chair so she could sit down outside the bars. And I told her about everythin' that had been goin' on, and she just nodded and listened.

"Do ye feel like ye've been abandoned, Caleb?" she said when I was finished.

"I dunno," I said. "But I guess I thought that it would go better if I was tryin' to follow the Envoy. I mean, Chris and I had an argument about it, and he went around Addle—and he's probably past Perseverance by now."

"Ye wouldn't have met yer sister if ye'd done that," she said.

"I know," I said, "And that was really good. But I couldn't do anythin' to get her to come with me, and now I've made everythin' worse for her."

Then she thought for a while and said. "Did anyone ever tell ye why they put my uncle in the stocks?"

"Was it cos he did somethin' to the lions?" I said.

"Aye, there was some of that. They came at him, and he carved up their costumes a bit.

"But his real crime—what he was doin' when they tried to attack him—was damaging the tent."

"You mean the big tent over the city?" I said.

"Aye, that one," Phoebe said. "He was planning to work his way around the perimeter and cut away the main anchor points with his sword."

"Why did he want to do that?" I said.

"So people would remember that there's a world outside it," she said. "Addle is such a thing of smoke and mirrors. It's all show—all distraction. All the fancy dress and credits and protests—it's not that none of it matters, but it's not the main thing we should be thinking about."

"Yeah, that sounds like Fergus," I said.

And she laughed and said, "Aye, except he'd say *none* of it matters except the cure. And I dare say he'd put it a bit more strongly."

"But how does that help me with Seini?" I said.

"Och, I don't know," she said. "But the point is not to forget where ye really are. Don't let these circumstances fool ye. The Envoy knows exactly what's going on in here. Ye've not been left alone. I don't know why these things have happened to ye, and I don't know what's going to happen. But yer still a Traveller."

And when I thought about what she was sayin', it was sort of helpful. And I thought, if all that bad stuff happened to the Envoy, and it turned out okay, maybe that could still happen to me too. So I said, "Thanks, Phoebe. How's Fergus goin' anyway?"

"Oh, not well," she said. "Gaius is tending him, but his injuries aren't really healing. If the Envoy sees fit to arrange yer release, ye should come and see him. His journey'll be over soon."

And when she said that, I suddenly felt like cryin'—and I was a bit embarrassed about it, cos Fergus was her uncle, and I didn't even know him that well.

Then she got up to go, but just as the guard was comin' to take her out, she stopped and got something out of the pocket of her coat. And it was a photo.

"Oh, I almost forgot—Gaius found that photo of Thomas with Bren and Eliza."

So I took it and had a look. And the girl, who was Thomas's sister, had a leather jacket and Mohawk, and Thomas was lookin' really serious, and there was another boy with freckles givin' a grin and makin' a V sign with his fingers.

I thought about how they were all dead and how the last thing Thomas had seen was me wavin' a sword at him.

But just as I started to hand the photo back to Phoebe, I suddenly realised that I recognised the other boy's face too—cos it was the kid from the Shallow Dive who Gus called Bernie. And then suddenly it was like a shock went through me, because I remembered what he had said that night about people bein' after him.

"Is that Bren?" I said.

"Aye," she said. "Ye heard they killed him too, I suppose?"

"Yeah," I said. "But I saw him somewhere else before it all happened. Hey, Phoebe, do you reckon you could take a message to Seini for me?"

CHAPTER 40

"How are you liking number nine, buddy? You ready to chuck it in?"

I slid the latest dry page back into my breast pocket and painfully turned myself around.

The Administrator was parked in the open doorway. Kev was switching off the machine.

I closed my eyes and bowed my head. I wanted him to think I was in a stupor. I certainly didn't want them to know that my mind felt the clearest it had been since I'd split up with Caleb.

I felt like I was constantly noticing things now. Right now, I was noticing the smooth texture of the sudden silence and thinking about how strange it was that the mere absence of something could be so wonderful. Was it just the relief that I was feeling, or was silence itself a good thing? Or was it more like that the world was full of good things but ordinary noises kept me from sensing it?

But the Administrator was talking to me again. I only tuned in at the end.

"Give him a clip over the ear, Kev. He's not listening to a word."

Kev came over and did as he was asked, cuffing one side of my head so the other side banged into the wall.

I looked at the Administrator, who gave me a smile.

"There we go. You with me now?"

I nodded.

"Chris, what I was trying to explain to you was that I've been going easy on you. I could have had Kev here smashing your fingers with a hammer or slicing bits off your face. Instead, I've been letting you sit there nice and quiet with a bit of background music.

"But you need to play ball, buddy. There's gonna come a point where I'm gonna give up on ya—and then it's just gonna be bad.

"Hey. You hearin' me?"

But now I was thinking about what he'd said about cutting bits off and remembering the quote from the Roadbook that Pru and Trev had written on their wall:

What the road takes from you, I will return.
Whatever the road destroys, I will rebuild.

Could Central undo even that kind of damage? If they'd brought back the Envoy, I supposed they could. The thought made me strangely excited.

"… reckon he's lost it," said Kev. "Nine was too much for him."

"No, it's not that," said the Administrator. "You get this with some of 'em—they go off into their happy place and pretend none of it's real. Stumpy was like that: always talking into his hands like he had a radio in there."

"Maybe we should clip this guy too," said Kev.

"We'll give him a bit longer. But *not much* longer—you hear me, buddy? Give him something to go on with, Kev."

Kev grabbed my ear and scrubbed my face back and forth against the blockwork.

*   *   *

Len returned almost straight after they went. He switched off the noise, unlocked the gate and put the bowl down next to me.

"We've got a bit longer this time. This guy always takes ages. I thought you might like these."

I gasped as I realised what he was holding out to me. It was the little sheet of booster syrettes that we'd found at the light factory.

"Oh yeah," I said. "Yeah, that's what I need."

I snapped one free and broke off the cover that protected its tiny needle. Before I had a chance to doubt what I was doing, I stabbed myself in the side of the throat and squeezed—felt the cool spreading outward;

felt my mind growing clearer, my senses sharpening.

I snapped another free and held it out to him.

"Are you gonna have one?"

He shook his head. "I'm not a Traveller anymore."

"You must be," I said. "You wouldn't be doing this if you weren't. Come on."

"I went back on my oath—I took off my coat. I said what they told me to," He shuffled back and began turning for the door.

"Brother, I helped kill an Agent before I got to Crux. The Envoy'll pardon you—that's how it works. You just have to ask."

He shook his head again and closed the gate, leaving me alone with the noise.

CHAPTER 41

(Extract of the transcribed Records of Caleb Dox, Vol 1.36)

I was really excited after Phoebe showed me the photo, so I didn't really get any sleep. And I kept waitin' for Seini to show up, but she never did. In the mornin', they came and took me back to court. And the same people were all shoutin' the same stuff at me.

And then my lawyer got angry, cos he asked me if I was ready to change my plea, and I told him that we'd found something that meant we might not have to.

"If you will not take my advice, then you leave me no choice," he said. "As soon as the Mayor arrives, I will seek to withdraw as your counsel."

So he went and sat down and didn't look at me anymore. And I sat there lookin' round at everyone and wonderin' where Seini was and what the Mayor was gonna say.

But the Mayor never showed up. And after about three hours, some official lookin' lady came and said somethin' to the lawyers, and then they took me back to the Watch-house.

*   *   *

I was on my own for hours after that. I kept askin' the guard if he knew what was goin' on or where Seini was until he told me to shut up and stop botherin' him.

Then another guard took over, and she told me that she didn't know, but somethin' was goin' down, and Seini was involved, but she didn't know if it was good or bad or whatever.

So that made me kind of worried. I tried sendin' a signal to Central and doin' my sword drills—cos I could still remember most of 'em, even though I didn't have my sword—and when I had done that, I was pretty tired, so I lay down on my bunk.

And that's when Seini and her boss showed up. And Seini had a smile on her face—but it was a bit of a weird smile—and Chief Diritto was lookin' annoyed.

"Okay, Dox, you're free to go," she said. "The City has withdrawn all the charges against you. All funds forfeited in satisfaction of the terms of your bail have been restored to Seini—not that she will need them."

"Okay," I said. "What happened … ?"

"… Seini will be able to make everything clear to you," she said. "The only thing I need to explain is the stipulation that you leave the city within twenty-four hours … Again, Seini will be able to explain. Follow me, and we will retrieve your gear from the evidence room."

Then she walked in front of us up the stairs to a sort of cage with all these shelves, and a young guy gave me my sword and pack and made me write my name on a clipboard.

"Chief … I'm really sorry about this," said Seini.

"Don't be," said Diritto. "You did what you had to do. It's you I'm sorry about losing, not Gull. None of this was your fault. Just go and enjoy yourself. You've earned it."

Then she took us to a back door and buzzed it open, so we came out into the lane behind the Watch-house.

"I hope you'll send us a card now and then," said Diritto.

"Of course, Chief," said Seini.

Then she closed the door and we were by ourselves, and Seini was blowing her nose and lookin' like she was gonna cry. And it was all dark and pretty quiet, except there was a bit of light in the east and a bit of a smoke smell in the air.

"What's happenin', Seini?" I said.

"Let's go home, Ca. I can tell you on the way."

So she told me.

She said she'd got the photo from Phoebe and then gone to talk to Gus at the Shallow Dive to see if he knew who had been chasing Bren that night. And Gus said that he didn't know for sure, but he assumed that Bren had meant his parole officer. Cos Bren had been in trouble with the Watch, and they kept checkin' up on him.

So then Seini went and looked up who Bren's parole officer had been, and it was Detective Gull before he had become a detective.

So she went and told her boss about it, and they checked the records to find out what Gull and Swike had been doin' that night. And it turned out they were supposed to be over at the castle helpin' the Mayor's people with security.

So then Seini went over to the castle and asked the Mayor's secretary to check about that. And after he went away and left her locked in his office for like three hours, he came back and said Gull hadn't come that night cos he was feelin' sick and only Swike had turned up.

So Seini went back to the Watch-house and told Chief Diritto, and they got some cops to go around to Gull's place—cos this was still in the middle of the night. And when they got there, they found that he was dead and it looked like he'd shot himself. And there was all this stuff there, like a knife with blood on it and a shocker and a whole bunch of anti-Central books and stuff.

So it was like case closed. They reckoned he'd tried to set me up cos he hated Travellers, and then, when he found out that Seini was on to him, he killed himself.

Anyway, that's what she told me, except I only got about half of it the first time. And by the time she finished, we had got back to her place and were goin' up the stairs.

And I said, "So why do they want me to leave town then?"

"They want to cover it up," she said. "It's embarrassing for the Council, you being innocent and one of our own being the perp—especially after they made such a big thing about the trial. They'll probably try and say you cut a deal or something.

And then she said, "But it's not just you. They want me to go too."

"What? Why? You just solved the case for 'em," I said.

"Same reason. They don't want the embarrassment. It's coming from the Mayor. The Chief doesn't want me to go."

She opened the door and we went into her place. And I looked out of her window over the roofs and the streets and tried to understand it all, but I felt like my head was explodin' cos of all this stuff happenin' at once.

"So, do you want to come east with me?" I said.

And Seini looked up from the sink—cos she was makin' coffee—and said, "No, Ca. They're sending me to the resort."

"But what about your money?" I said.

"They've given it all back," she said. "But they're not making me pay for it."

"Do you have to go in twenty-four hours too?" I said.

"No, Ca … I have to go sooner," she said. "There's a shuttle leaving from the north gate in a couple of hours. I'm supposed to be on that."

"But I just found you," I said.

"I know, Ca. I know. I wish we'd had longer. I hoped we'd be going together."

"You could still come with me," I said.

She passed me a cup and sat down on the couch.

"You're my little brother, Ca … and I'm really happy that we got to see each other again. But we're not on the same road."

I sat down beside her and tried to work out what to say. I didn't want to make her feel bad, and I didn't want to make things weird between us, but it was the last time I was gonna get to say anything to her.

So I said, "I don't reckon it'll make you happy. Not forever. I mean even if it's really good … you'll get sick of it."

"I've got to give it a go, Ca. I don't see what else there is."

"There's Central. That's where everything comes from," I said.

"Yeah, let's not talk about that now," she said.

Then we were both quiet for a long time cos I knew there wasn't anything I could say to make her change her mind.

So in the end, I just said, "Well, thanks for solvin' the case and gettin' me out of prison."

"Hey, I'm glad I could help, Ca. I'm sorry that you had such a bad time in Addle."

"Yeah, it's funny how we thought it would be the best place when we were kids. I reckon I thought it was the same as Central—and like it would be like livin' in the old times. And you know, when I came in the gate—before I knew it was Story World—I kind of had that feelin' again for a while."

And Seini said, "It can be good sometimes. But I reckon it's like everything—it looks better from a distance. Most things turn out to be a disappointment when you finally get there."

And then we were both quiet again, cos I was thinkin' that about where she was goin', and she was thinkin' it about where I was goin'.

Then, when we'd finished our coffee, I rinsed the cups and Seini changed into her civilian clothes—which looked just like her work clothes. Then she got us both to stand next to her window and took a photo with her tablet thing so she'd have a picture of me.

Then she put her keys on the table—cos she was leavin' all her stuff to a friend from work—and we left.

We walked over to the place where she had to go, which was near the north gate—and that was where all the trucks and vans came and went, so there were all these loading platforms and stuff, and it smelled bad. Except the place Seini was goin' had its own office, which was really clean and new-lookin'. And it had glass doors and a big gold RR symbol— which Seini said meant Retirement and Restoration.

And when we went up to the doors, they opened up, and you could smell smells like fruit and coffee and stuff. And two ladies came out wearing yellow uniforms and hats, and one of them was holdin' a necklace made of flowers, and she put it on Seini.

And the other one said, "Welcome, Officer Dox, we have been expecting you. Our other guests are already here, so we are almost ready to embark. We have champagne and hors d'oeuvres waiting for you in the cruiser."

Then I was gonna go into the office with her, but the lady who'd given her the flowers said she was very sorry, but it was guests only from this point, so we had to say goodbye in the doorway.

And Seini gave me a hug and said, "Okay, Ca, I hope you get to Central like you want."

And I said, "I hope the resort is good and that you won't forget about Central if it's not."

And then the doors closed, and she was just a blurry shape behind the glass. And then she was gone.

But I still had two more places I wanted to go before I left Addle.

CHAPTER 42

As soon as I saw the Administrator, I knew something bad was about to happen. He was much too happy.

"How's things, Chris?" he said. "Still toughin' it out?"

I looked at him as Kev unlocked the gate and thought that it didn't seem long enough between visits. I wasn't sure what he'd had in mind when he'd said that I didn't have "much longer", but this felt like hours rather than days.

He gave a grin. "Resilient fella, aren't ya? It's okay. I can see you've found a way to handle the noise. That's why we're gonna try something new."

Kev came over and crouched down to unshackle my wrist.

"Think you're smart?" he said. "You're not gonna be feeling so pleased with yourself when we get upstairs."

"Don't talk to him, Kev," said Devlin. "Just get him to the lift. Get the camera for us, Stumpy. We're gonna need it set up in the operating room."

I saw Lenny appear in the background and give me a worried look as he began to unplug the equipment. Then I was trying to hold myself up as my legs got used to walking again, and Kev was half pushing and half dragging me by the scruff of the neck.

The Administrator followed us into the lift under his own steam and pushed the buttons to get the thing moving.

"I've got a surprise for you today, buddy," he said. "Couple of surprises, actually. I reckon they'll do the trick; give you a bit of perspective and a bit of focus."

I looked at him out of the corner of my eye and tried not to imagine what those surprises might be.

The elevator doors clanked open onto the same corridor I had come down when I'd first explored the place. Soon, we were passing through the lobby—this time, there was a receptionist at the desk and light outside. Then we were at the frosted doors of the clinic.

"Recognise this place?" said the Administrator.

I nodded.

"Know what it is?"

"No," I said.

"I guess you were just looking around last time, weren't you? No worries. All will be made clear."

He led the way through the doors into the white room with its machines and blinking lights.

"Anybody ever tell you where the Tox came from?"

"From the Corp doing experiments to make super-soldiers," I said. "And then it escaping."

"Yeah, well … I guess that's sort of right. The Council were trying to work out ways to use it on their soldiers alright, but the Corp didn't make it for that. They had much bigger plans."

"Like what?" I said. "Like making everyone kill each other?"

He chuckled. "Bigger than that, too. The Tox is what you might call a *purifier*—it boils a man down to his essence and strips away all the rest. For some fellas, that means they'll turn super-agro. Others will get focused on collecting or sorting stuff. Some blokes with skills get focused right in on that and forget everything else.

"Point is, Tox was designed to make people into one thing and get rid of the rest; to make everything simpler. Help you become your true self. I guess it's a bit like that stuff they shoot into you at Crux, except that stuff is trying to turn you into someone else."

My skin crawled as I listened to him. Where was this headed?

"Now you might wonder," he said, "Why anyone would want to make something that would do that. Why would the Corp want to help people with their personalities and hobbies and stuff?"

We'd come to the front of the clinic now—past the mechanical chairs and the white spider-machine that hung from the ceiling.

Devlin parked himself between a couple of the chairs and wheeled around to face me.

"Got any guesses?"

My mind went crazy as I noticed the ends of retractable restraints sprouting from the arm and leg rests. Were they going to shoot me full of Tox? Were they going to do something to me with that machine?

The world went dark around the edges of my vision. I didn't seem to be breathing.

The Administrator glanced over at me with a curious expression. "No idea? Well don't worry. It'll all be clear in a jiffy. Help him into a chair, Kev, so he can get the full experience. Remember to go easy on the face."

CHAPTER 43

(Extract of the transcribed Records of Caleb Dox, Vol 1.37)

I was pretty surprised how bad Fergus looked when I saw him.

His skin was all sort of grey and looked like it was a bit wet, and when he breathed it kind of sucked into his cheeks and made him look like a skull.

"I reckon he's been waitin' for ye," said Gaius. "Tis a good thing ye were able to come."

Then Phoebe put a hand on his cheek and said, "Caleb's here to see ye, uncle." And after a while, he opened his eyes and looked at me.

And I said, "Hey, Fergus, it's good to see you."

Then he coughed and grabbed my hand with his, which was all cold and clammy.

And he said, "Thank ye for comin' lad. I've had a bit of time to think, and I think I mighta been a bit harsh toward ye."

"You were just doin' what you thought was right," I said. "And you got me to think about the Roadbook more. I'm glad I got to travel with you."

"Aye … But I was … a bit too sure that … my way was the Pantarch's way … and I wanted to apologise for that." Then he coughed again and closed his eyes for a while, and looked like he was havin' a tough time.

"Gaius," he said, "After all my bold words, I am full of doubts about myself."

"Ye made mistakes as we all do, brother," said Gaius. "But ye served the Envoy. He's the one to fix yer eyes on now."

"Aye," said Fergus. "Aye … I'll go out as I came in—with my pockets empty."

"It's what's in yer veins, not yer pockets, brother," said Gaius.

Then Fergus gave a bit of a nod and took a breath and went still and let go of me.

And Phoebe closed his eyes. And Gaius crossed his arms into an X.

And we all just sat there for a while.

"I see they returned yer gear, Caleb," said Phoebe after a while.

"Yeah," I said. "Seini found out who really killed Thomas, so they let me go. I have to get out of Addle, though."

"That's a shame for us. We will miss ye," she said.

"Me too," I said. "When I was in prison, I was thinkin' that what I really wanted was to be able to stay and work here with you and Gaius. And now I can, I can't. And Seini's gone too."

Then Gaius put his arm on my shoulder because of the way my voice sounded. And told me to be encouraged.

"The Envoy'll watch over ye, lad. Get yerself some companions and ye'll do well enough."

CHAPTER 44

I tried to fight him—even managed to elbow him in the teeth—but Kev was too strong for me. In a couple of minutes, my wrists and chest were strapped down, leaving my head twisting around to glare at the Administrator, who was smiling and nodding.

"There you go," he said. "They're actually pretty comfy chairs, aren't they? And normally, we'd give you a shot so you'd be feeling all nice and dopey."

He rolled closer and leaned in as if he was about to share a secret.

"But not *you*, buddy. We need *you* bright-eyed and bushy-tailed so you can see your surprises and read your script."

I twisted my hands in the straps, trying to get at the buckles. What was he talking about?

"You see, this is the place, Chris. This is the place where the Corp gives everyone what they want. If you want to fight, we'll let you fight forever. You want to collect stuff you can do that forever too. This is the place where we finish what the Tox starts and where we free you from complications so you can focus on your fix. We even free you from your body.

"You want to know how we do it?"

"No," I said.

He gave a bit of a laugh and went on.

"What we do is … we bring you in here and strap you down—just like you are now—and then we get you doped up. And then we switch on Freddy here"—I screwed my head around to see that he was pointing his thumb at the spider machine—"and Freddy comes over and cuts out your brain and sticks it in a box. And then we send it away to Corpland, where they put it into one of their machines … You following me?

"So if you're a collector you might get turned into a Reaper, and if you're a sorter you might get shoved into a production line. A fella like you with a bit of Savage in you"—he gave me a wink—"you'd get made into a Hunter.

"And once they stick you in those things, they'll keep you going forever."

I strained and pulled against the straps. He nodded his head sympathetically.

"Sorry to dump this on you all at once, buddy—I know it's a lot to take in—but I needed to get you up to speed so we could show you the real surprises.

He looked up and over at the door.

"Okay, Kev. Go and give Stumpy a hand. I reckon we're good to go."

The guard went out the door, and the Administrator turned back to me.

"You look a bit peaky there. Don't worry; we're not gonna cut *your* brain out. That junk they stick in you at Crux makes 'em useless. Besides, we still need you to do your speech."

"Why are you doing this?" I said.

"You mean me personally? Fair question. Well, it's a job. And it's better than the alternatives. If you have to choose between being chopped or being the chopper, you go for the chopper. Simple as that."

He glanced up as the door hissed open and made a bong noise as someone kicked it. Out of sight, Kev growled and a woman gave an angry muffled groan.

My heart started beating erratically like it was about to explode.

"Righto, buddy," said Devlin. "Looks like we've got surprise number one. Bring her up front, Kev."

There was more scuffling, and Mallory appeared—held and restrained from behind by Kev. As they reached the wall, the guard jerked her round so she was right in front of me. The sight made the flame ignite in the base of my skull. I wrenched myself sideways, trying to break my restraints.

"Let her go!" I shouted.

"Easy, tiger," said the Administrator. "You'll get to save her in a minute. But we've got to show you surprise number two first. We wouldn't have found her without help from this young lady. So you owe her a bit of thanks."

"They found out about Cam," said Mallory, looking at me desperately. "I didn't have a choice."

I felt the earth spinning under me—felt myself falling out into space.

"Okay, Stumpy," called the Administrator.

The door hissed again. I heard Lenny's voice in the background.

"Boss, she says she doesn't have a son. I reckon we … we might have the wrong woman."

"You do," said a second voice. "My boy died years ago. Whoever you got there ain't mine."

It was older and rougher, but there was no mistaking my mother's voice. I fought to control my face and tried to play along.

"That right?" said the Administrator. "Well, bring her in anyway, Stump. Let's let 'em see each other just to make sure."

They came into view: the woman from the security feed and Lenny, holding her by the upper arm and looking like a hunted animal.

My mother was smaller than I remembered. I noticed the lines on her cheeks and the grey in her hair.

She glanced at me, just below the chin, and looked back at the Administrator.

"That him? Don't know him. Never seen him before."

"Alright," Devlin said, "And what about you, Chris? Do you recognise this lady? It says on her file here that she comes from Spillan. Says her name is Maz Prior. I reckon it'd be a bit funny if you'd never seen her before."

I opened my mouth to speak, but the Administrator stopped me with a hand on my arm.

"And if you lie to me again, buddy, I'll take your hand off when we're done. You'll end up like Stumpy."

I swallowed and tried to speak, painfully aware of the unevenness in my voice.

"I was only little when they sent my mum away. So I can't remember her that well. But she looked different from this lady. This is the lady I saw from a distance, and I thought it was her. But she looks different. I… I know some people from the Prior family. But my mum was a Walker like me."

My heart was thumping. I didn't know where to look. Was this what people did when they were lying? But I hadn't quite lied. My mum had obviously gone back to her maiden name.

The Administrator sighed.

"Alright. Okay. Well, that's a bit disappointing. But it solves one problem. I was trying to work out who we should do first, but if she's not your mum, that makes it easy. We'll do her first, and you can see how it works before we do your girlfriend. Put her in the other chair, Kev. I'll watch the chick."

As he spoke, he pulled out an automatic from an inner pocket of his chair and pointed it at Mallory.

"Take a seat, sweetheart."

She glared at him and slid down the wall to the floor.

I watched helplessly as Kev guided my mother, none too gently, toward the chair on the other side of the Administrator.

I looked desperately over at Lenny.

"Help us." I mouthed.

The man gave what was either a spasm or shrug and threw a terrified glance at Devlin.

But my mum was fighting now.

"Get off me. I'm not getting in that thing."

I twisted my head back and saw her try to kick Kev in the groin. But she missed, and he simply swept her off balance and manhandled her against the chair.

"Stop it!" I shouted. "She hasn't done anything. You do anything to her, and you'll answer to the Envoy for it."

I didn't know where that last statement had come from. But it had an effect on the other men in the room.

"Shut up, kid, or you'll get a clip over the ear," said the Administrator without taking his eyes off Mallory.

Kev didn't say anything. He just growled and looked up … and received a double-handed blow to the nose from Maz as she seized the opportunity. Before he had a chance to recover, she broke free and raced back toward the door. The big man swore and charged after her.

"What the hell, Kev?" Said the Administrator. "Go and give him a hand, Stumpy." But Stumpy was gone.

Meanwhile, there was more swearing—first from Kev, then from my mother. My hopes died as it was cut short.

The guard reappeared a moment later, carrying her over his shoulder. He dropped her into the chair and began securing her.

"Geez, Kev, you didn't kill her, did ya? She's no good to us dead."

"Nah, just knocked her out. Stupid dog."

Again fury, boiled and rose in the base of my mind. But this time, I fought it down. It was useless to me now.

"Stop it," I said to the Administrator. "Leave her alone."

"Sorry, buddy. We need to give you a demo so you can get the picture. We would have had to do this one before long anyway—she's pretty long in the tooth. Besides, she's not your mum, right, so why worry?" He gave me another wink.

Kev had her wrists secured in the straps now. He was working on her feet as she stirred and raised her head.

"Where am I?" she said groggily.

"You're in the clinic, love," said the Administrator. "Looks like you knocked your head, but we'll fix you up in a mo. Just lie there and relax."

"What? Who are you … Chris? Chris, what are you doing here? Chris?"

There was dead silence for a second.

"How about that, Chris? Looks like she recognises you after all. Do you reckon if we gave you a bang on the head, you'd remember her too?"

I turned my head to look at her, but it was hard to see with the tears in my eyes.

"Yeah, it's me, mum," I said. "I … I love you. I'm really sorry about …"

"Tha's all right," she said. "Tha' was a long time … Hey!"

She was cut off as Kev pushed her head back into the crescent-shaped head-wrest and pulled another strap tight over the bridge over her nose.

"Should I get one of the techs?" he said.

"No, I reckon we're good," said Devlin. "Just pull out the red button and push the black one with the two on it. Freddy'll take care of the rest."

There was a click and a hum; a series of short motor sounds.

"Okay. Stop it," I said. "You know who she is now. Just …"

The Administrator turned back to me. "What, you want me to swap her with your girlfriend? Do her first?"

"No! I don't want you to do either of them. Do me."

"No, buddy. I already told you. We need you to stand up and do your speech for the camera. How are you gonna do that without a brain?"

He paused a moment as the machine he called Freddy suddenly clicked three times and began gliding forward on the jointed armature that anchored it to the ceiling.

It positioned itself behind the headrest and raised three of its limbs.

One grasped my mother's face. A second stabbed a hypodermic needle into her neck. The third, tipped with shears, broke into a clatter and began sweeping the hair from her head in long strokes.

"Get off me!" she screamed.

"Leave her alone!" I shouted again.

The Administrator tilted his head away and gave a pained expression.

"Pipe down, mate. You know what you need to do. If you care about your mum, just say you'll do it and we can pull the pin."

"No, wait. Give me time to think!"

"You don't need more time, and you're not gonna get it. Soon as Freddy finishes shaving and swabbing, he's gonna start cutting. And then it's gonna be over-red-rover for Maz here. I reckon you've got about twenty seconds."

Maz half screamed and half groaned, but her head was held fast. Another of the machine's arms was spraying a pink liquid onto her now bald scalp.

I opened my mouth. What choice did I have? Was I supposed to just sacrifice my mum? Was that what Central wanted? I felt the rage rise in me like the shining edge of a whetted knife.

But it was an edge of decision too. Despite the chaos inside my mind, I saw that with absolute clarity. Whatever I did now would determine whatever would come next. But I didn't know what that meant, or what I was meant to do.

"Help me, Envoy," I said. "Help me."

I didn't even know I'd said it out loud in the moment, but again, it had an immediate effect. Freddy paused mid-spray. The Administrator reached over and struck me on the nose with the handle of his pistol, causing pain to explode in my face like a strange taste.

At the same time, Mallory seized her chance and leapt for the door.

I didn't see it, but I knew almost immediately from the sounds that

Kev had launched himself at her. There was a crash, a scream, a sound of cracking glass and a roar of pain.

My racing consciousness registered all of it alongside everything else: the pain in my nose, the Administrator telling Kev to get a grip, the high-pitched whine as a saw-tipped armature suddenly appeared behind my mother's head.

And then, in the midst of it, there was another memory: Eve, silhouetted in the headlights, singing through the megaphone with her sword in her hand.

And I knew what I had to do. I didn't have a megaphone—and who knew what had happened to my sword—but my singing wasn't going to be much worse than hers.

So I opened my mouth and sang. I sang the same song that she had sung on that night in the swamp—the song that spoke of the darkness as a vapour that would be consumed by the rising sun.

The Administrator leaned forward to shut me up with another pistol whipping.

And then everything went even more crazy.

CHAPTER 45

(Extract of the transcribed Records of Caleb Dox, Vol 1.38)

I found Gus workin' on his whisky still as I came up the lane behind the Shallow Dive.

"Hey, they let you out!" he said.

And I said, "Yeah, after what you told Seini about Bren, she went and checked out his parole officer, and it turned out to be him. So they let me go."

"That's great," he said. "Want to come in and celebrate? You can help me try some of this new stuff if you want."

"No thanks, Gus," I said. "But I need to check something. The reason why people were after Bren was cos he had a data stick from his sister—and it was meant to have some stuff about the work camps on it."

"Oh yeah?"

"Yeah. But do you remember how he was hangin' about behind the big pot plant, and you thought he had a lighter?"

"You reckon that was the data stick?"

"I don't know, but I was wonderin' if I could have a look."

"Sure, go ahead. I'll just be a few minutes."

"Thanks, Gus," I said.

So I went in through the back door past the kitchen. Most of the lights were off in the main bar, but I could still see okay cos there were lights over the counter and a bit of daylight comin' in through the front windows.

I started feelin' around the pot plant, and at first I didn't find anythin'—just bottle caps and cigarette buts—but when I ran my fingers through the soil, they hit something hard and kind of square. And when I pulled it out, it had a metal connector tab stickin' out one end, and "Maxydat" written in gold on the plastic.

And then I heard someone coming into the bar, so I said, "Hey, I found it, Gus. He left it in the potplant."

Except it wasn't Gus. It was the other detective who'd arrested me, Tina Swike, and when she came out of the shadows, she was pointin' a gun at my head.

And she said, "How about that? I thought the Mayor was wasting my time sending me after you, but you led me straight to it. Hand it over, Dox."

"What's on it?" I said.

"Nothing you or anyone else need to worry about," she said.

"I reckon if I do that, you'll just kill me like Gull killed those two kids," I said.

"Gull didn't kill anyone. I had to kill them because they knew what was on it," she said. "But if you hand it over now and clear off, we'll be good."

"So it's like a cover-up?" I said.

"What do you care?" she said. "Seini got retirement, and you got to go free and leave. Wasn't that the deal?"

"Nobody made any deal with me," I said.

"Well, how about this deal," she said. "You put that thing in my hand or I shoot you right now."

"I don't know what you're hidin'," I said. "But you can't hide it from the Envoy."

And she laughed and said, "You think I care about him? Trust me, I don't."

"You should. There'll be a reckonin' for stuff like you're doin'."

"Wow. I should have killed you in the square, shouldn't I?" she said. "Maybe I should do it now after all."

And she looked like she was about to shoot me. But then we both heard a floorboard creak back near the counter, so instead of doin' that, she sort of stepped sideways, and half turned her head and said

"I thought I told you to stay put, Bartender."

Except it wasn't Gus this time either, cos someone made a growling noise and jumped on her back so she fell over and fired her gun at the wall right next to my head—and for a second or two I couldn't see anything cos there was all smoke and dust in my eyes, and then I couldn't see anything cos of the shadow.

But I could hear Simha growling—cos I could tell it was her—and Swike swearin', and for a second, I thought maybe I should just leave 'em to it.

But then I heard a big crash, and Swike said, "Okay, now *you*, I'm gonna have to kill."

And Simha said, "How are you going to explain that to my dad?"

"I'll find a way," she said.

And then I got my eyes workin' again and came out from near the potplant, and I could see that Simha was lyin' on the floor in the middle of the room, and Swike was standing a couple of metres off to the left pointin' her gun at her.

And I said, "I reckon you've killed enough people, lady," and came at her with my sword. And she swung around and shot me, but it hit me in the thigh, and my coat caught it.

And then she lifted it up to point at my face, except that was when the sword knocked it out of her hand.

And then, before either of us could do anything else, Simha jumped on her again, and Swike gave this horrible scream and went down, and they rolled around for a second until Swike went still. And when Simha got up she had all blood around her mouth cos she'd gotten Swike in the neck.

And then I looked up and saw Gus standin' there, holding an old shotgun and lookin' freaked out.

"Does someone want to tell me what that was about?" he said.

And I held up the data stick and said, "If you've got anything that can show what's on this, we can find out."

So Gus plugged it into the computer on the counter, and he said there was a video file there and he made it play on one of the side walls.

And at first, it was all fuzzy, like the camera was covered, or maybe there wasn't enough light. But there was a voice—and it sounded like a girl—or like a young woman. And she said: "You want to know why people never come back from the camps?

"We thought it was just that they worked everyone to death or that they stopped handing out the suppressors. Well, it's not that."

Then it suddenly got lighter, and you could see she was outside in, like a courtyard, and it was still dark, except there were floodlights shinin' down. And she was goin' over to this brick building in the centre of the courtyard. And you could see that there was a tractor parked around the corner of it—and it was lit by a kind of orange light.

Then she came round the corner, and you could see that there was like a hatch in the side of the buildin', and there was all fire in there—and that's where the orange light was comin' from.

And the tractor had a trailer on the back, and there was a man and a lady in overalls liftin' somethin' off it and takin' it over to the hatch. And you couldn't see what it was at first, except when the camera came around the side of the tractor, you could suddenly see that it was a bunch of bodies. And most of 'em were dressed in overalls and had bare feet, but a couple were wearin' ordinary clothes and nice lookin' shoes.

Then she moved the camera up so you could see their top halves, and the tops of their heads were all missin'.

And the girl who was talkin' said, "We don't know what they're doing with the brains. But this is all that's left … And you can see what happens now."

Then, you could see her arms reach out and grab one of the bodies under the armpits. And one of the other people took it by the feet, except they took the shoes off first—cos it was one of the bodies that had normal clothes. And then the video got a bit jerky as they carried it across to the hatch, and put it on a sort of roller frame and pushed it into the fire. And the image froze as what was left of his head reached the opening.

And then it was really quiet in the bar. And Gus said a whole lot of swear words.

And Simha said, "What … the … Tox … was … that?"

And I didn't say anythin' cos it was like I couldn't breathe. Cos just where the video stopped, you could see that the dead guy had a flower necklace stuck under his collar—and that necklace thing was just like the one they'd put on Seini.

"Hey," I said. "I gotta go to wherever that is, and I have to go right now. How can I do that?"

And Gus looked at Simha and said, "If you knew someone with connections, they could probably get you a V from the motor pool."

And Simha said, "Yeah, okay. Come with me."

CHAPTER 46

I don't know why the machine did what it did. Maybe the song broke it loose of its captivity long enough to take some revenge. Maybe it was just trying to get at me.

What I do know is that the thing that was about to cut my mum's head open suddenly jerked forward and crashed into the Administrator. One moment, he was leaning forward to whack me with his gun. The next, he was jammed underneath the thing, making groaning noises, and Freddy's arms were flailing about and getting entangled in his wheelchair. I could hear the machine's servo-motors whining and straining as it tried to drag itself free.

I just kept singing. There was nothing else I could do with my arms strapped down, and I felt like, if singing was going to delay the extraction, then I was going to sing until my voice cracked and died.

Except now there was another voice—a better voice than mine. When I twisted my head, I saw it was Lenny. He had my sword and my pack and he was wearing the blood-smeared coat from my cell.

He used the *machaira* to slice through the strap holding my right wrist. He went to do the same to the other side, but I stopped him.

"I can do the others. Cut my mum free."

He nodded and kept singing. In fifteen seconds, I was out of the chair and helping him.

My mum was unconscious. She looked strange and scary with her hair shaved off and the pink stuff on her scalp, but when I checked her pulse, it was steady.

We got her out of the chair and began to carry her toward the lobby—Lenny at her shoulders, me at her feet. We went past Kev, who was lying in the doorway with blood all over his uniform and a large shard of broken door-glass sticking out of his side.

"Any ideas now?" I said. "I know how to get out the back, but that didn't go well last time."

Before he had time to answer me, there was a shout from Mallory in the lobby area.

"Come this way! There's a van coming in out the front!"

She had a pistol in one hand and a semi-automatic rifle in the other. As we got closer, we saw the receptionist and a guard lying on the tiles of the lobby with their hands on their heads. The front doors slid open, and she began shouting at some other people.

"Get down! Stay on the ground. Put your hands behind your head."

The newcomers froze in their tracks. There was a woman in a yellow skirt and blazer who was carrying a clipboard, another woman and two men dressed in casual clothes. A taller woman in a dark suit, with a face that reminded me of Caleb, brought up the rear. All of them, except the woman with the clipboard, had strings of flowers around their necks.

"I said, get down!" said Mallory, waving her guns at them.

They all did, except the tall woman.

"What's going on?" she said.

"We're escaping," I said. "You should too. If you stay here, they'll kill you."

"R&R is fake," said Lenny. "They cut out your brain and send it to Corpland."

The woman looked at Lenny and me. "Is that true?"

"Yes," I said. "They do it to workers as well. See," I nodded down at my mum, "they were about to operate on her."

"But what about the videos?"

"They're fake too," said Lenny. "They scan you when you come through and then use that to make the videos so it looks like you're still alive."

"We don't have time for this," said Mallory. "Someone's gonna set off an alarm any second. We need to get to that van."

The woman stepped out of our way, allowing us to move past her. But as we started down the steps, she had a last question.

"Hey, do either of you know my brother Caleb? He's a Traveller."

"Yes!" I said. "I was with him up to Addle."

"Are you Chris? I'm Seini." She turned to Mallory and pointed to the rifle. "You better give me that. You haven't cocked it."

Seini and Mallory ran ahead while Lenny and I followed, carrying my mum. Seini opened the sliding door and helped us lay her on the floor as Mallory got into the driver's seat.

And then the alarm went off.

Almost immediately, two guards appeared a hundred metres down on the road that encircled the hospital.

"Oi, what are you doing?" shouted one of them.

"Step out of the vehicle," said the other.

"Time to go!" said Seini.

"Driver's run off with the keys," shouted Mallory. "I'm going to need a moment."

Seini swore and fired at the asphalt in front of the men, causing them to pull back. Then another guard emerged from the lobby, raised a pistol and shot out the front windshield.

Seini swung about and returned fire over the passenger's seat, bringing him down. Then, the other two came back into view with their rifles up. There was a sound like a sledgehammer hitting a tin roof, and a ragged tear opened in the door post. Another hole appeared in the door panel next to Lenny and he fell forward over my mum's feet.

"I'm okay," he said. "Hit my coat."

He straightened up, rubbing his thigh, but he'd given me an idea.

"Hey, try to shield my mum and Seini," I said. "I'll cover Mallory."

I ducked around Caleb's sister, half falling between the front seats as I tried to make a wall in front of Mallory. I bumped her shoulder as she struggled with the wires under the steering column.

"Get out of my way!" she said. Then, as a bullet ricocheted off my shoulder into the dash—"I take it back. You can stay there."

Another window exploded. New holes were appearing in the side.

Between the shots, I heard the starter turn over and cut out.

"Come on," said Mallory. She tried again with the same result.

Seini fired a burst as other holes appeared. Lenny gave another grunt. "Still okay."

But suddenly, Mallory had the engine running.

"Hold on!" she called. She engaged the gears and shot us backwards out of the parking bay, braked and threw the machine into first. Clouds of white dust rose from the spinning wheels as the van fishtailed out into the driveway and began accelerating away.

But there was no time for relief. Because now, over the sound of our own engine, I could hear another sound—a sound that scared me just as much as the sound of the bullets. It was the deep and ragged roar of a massive diesel.

As our wheels caught and the dust thinned, I glimpsed the top of the machine burst into view above the trees behind us. Before we turned away from the hospital, I saw the guards leaping out of its way as the big painted skull smashed through the bushes that lined the driveway.

"What is that?" said Seini.

"They're Savages," I said. "That's the same machine that attacked our town before I left for Crux."

For a few seconds, I nursed a hope that they had come to attack the hospital. But they kept on coming. As Mallory went up through the gears, I kept on catching glimpses of the machine through the dust.

"Does someone know where to go?" said Mallory. "Cos I'm just driving away from that thing right now."

"Take the next fork to the right," said Lenny. "It winds around a bit and they won't be able to go as fast as us. Then there's a turnoff that'll take us near the Central road. If we get there enough before them, they might not see us."

She did as he said. Soon, we were driving through an avenue of gums, following the twists and turns of a dry creek bed. Through occasional gaps in the trees, we could see fields of green crowned with yellow flowers.

Miles passed, and we lost sight of our pursuers. When I stuck my head out of the passenger window, I could still hear the engine but only as a distant rumble.

"Okay," said Lenny. "Slow down now. That's the turnoff. There's a steep bit and then an old bridge."

Mallory braked and guided the van down over the old creek and up the other side to a low dusty ridge topped with gum trees. As we reached the crest, a broad horizon of golden canola opened out before us.

"What now?" said Mallory. "Should I just keep on this track?"

"No, this is just an old farm road," he said. "The road to Central is about three hundred metres away across that field. You can't see it now with the canola, but there's a raised roadway. We'll have to walk through the crop to get to it."

Mallory let the machine roll to a standstill and turned off the engine as Seini opened the hatch and jumped out.

"I'll go and check it out."

She slung the rifle and began pushing her way through the tall canola. A bird flew up, peeping, into the sky. For about five seconds, everything seemed absolutely peaceful; the haze of the sky blurring into the yellow and green; the smell of dust and the sound of the hot engine ticking and pinging as it cooled. Somewhere in the distance, the diesel droned and changed gear without getting any closer.

We had done it, I thought. We had made it back to the road.

Then there was a strange groaning noise from the back, and Lenny said, "Hey Chris, you better take a look at your mum."

CHAPTER 47

She was twitching—tiny spasms spreading from her fingers and feet as I bent over her. She groaned again and began to convulse.

"Is she epileptic?" said Mallory.

"I don't think so," I said.

"It's not that," said Lenny. "That's a toxin dump. Her anklet must have tripped."

He lifted one of her spasming legs and rolled up the trouser cuff. Sure enough, there was a spiderweb of purple veins spreading away from the device on her lower calf.

"What do we do?" I said, "Can we tourniquet it?"

"It's too late for that," said Lenny. "If she's fitting, it's already reached her brain. She needs treatment. Have you still got the syrettes?"

I did. I pulled the sheet out, broke one free and twisted off the end cap to expose the needle.

Down on the floor of the van, my mum's eyes were darting about under her eyelids, and saliva was dribbling out of her mouth.

I pushed two fingers into the side of her neck, stabbed the needle into where I felt the pulse, and squeezed until the ampule was empty.

For a start, it seemed to make things worse. Her convulsions became more extreme, and Lenny and I ended up having to hold her down because she'd arch her back and go rigid and then fling out her arm against one of the seats.

I began to worry that I'd killed her—that maybe jabbing the stuff into her carotid had wrecked her brain just like the Tox.

But then, it all began to subside. Her groans began to turn into muttering. Her limbs stopped thrashing. After another three minutes she was lying so still that I had to put an ear to her lips to make sure she was still breathing.

"She okay?" said Lenny.

"Think so," I said.

I glanced up at Mallory. But she gave me a strange look in return.

"So, would you have given me that stuff if I'd been unconscious?" she said.

"I don't know," I said. "Would you have wanted me to? If it was between that and having your brain fried?"

"I don't want anyone making my decisions for me," she said.

"Fair enough," I said. I gathered the syrettes off the floor of the van and broke another one free. "But if her tracker went off, we must be near the boundary. Why don't you just take one of these so you can decide for yourself."

She looked at it sitting in my hand.

"Still trying to save me?"

I shook my head. "I wasn't even able to save myself. But if you don't want it, don't take it."

I started to take my hand away, but she stopped me.

"I'll take it. But I'm not saying I'll use it. I haven't decided which way I'm going yet."

"What, are you thinking of going back there?"

"Not to *that* place. But maybe to the old city. I never got a chance to check out that factory for myself."

I thought there was something defiant in her voice—as if she was goading me into arguing with her—but I didn't have the energy for that.

On the periphery of my vision, Lenny was looking awkwardly around at the two of us.

"I think I'm gonna take a look and see what happened to that truck."

But before he had a chance to move, my mum suddenly took a deep breath and opened her eyes.

"Where am I?" She suddenly looked terrified as if she'd just remembered what had been happening. "Chris!"

"It's okay, mum," I said. "We got away. We're just near the Central road."

"I feel a bit strange," she said.

"I had to inject you with something," I said. "Your anklet went off, so I gave you the cure to stop it …"

"Okay," she said. She reached up and put a hand on my cheek. "I didn't think I'd ever see you again."

"Neither did I," I said—except when I said it, my voice went funny.

"Mum, there's some stuff I need to …"

I was interrupted by the sound of a gunshot. As I twisted about, I saw Seini standing knee–high above the canola with the rifle butted against her shoulder. She fired again as something big and black reared up about thirty metres away from her.

I guessed what it was even before Lenny said the word.

"Hunter!"

But suddenly, I felt completely calm. Maybe after all I'd been through, nothing else could scare me. Maybe I was just feeling so relieved about getting my mum and Mallory away from that clinic that I didn't care what happened to me now. Maybe it was something to do with what had happened to me when I was chained to the pipe, memorising those pages.

"I think I need my sword back, brother," I said.

Lenny drew it and handed it to me.

"And look after my mum, okay?"

Then I was running; down through the crop, following the trail of flattened stalks that Seini had left—toward the gunfire.

"Help me, Central," I said. "Help me, Tobias."

CHAPTER 48

It seemed to take a long time for me to make it through the canola. The stems kept catching my feet and flicking in my face, the scent of the flowers seemed cloying and sickly. By the time I could see the road, Seini had stopped firing, but she was still fighting. I could hear metal on metal, the whine of hydraulics. And I could hear Seini shouting.

"Get away from me, you stupid thing. Get away! No!"

I scrambled up the bank and saw them not more than twenty metres away. Seini was facing me, holding the rifle in both hands like a baton. The Hunter was between us with its back to me.

It was stockier than the Reaper that had attacked me back in the sugar cane, but that didn't make it any less terrifying. If the Reaper was a spindly daddy-longlegs, the Hunter was like a five-foot-high wolf spider, muscled and compact.

It was fast, too—it had been racing when I first saw it approaching Seini. But right now, it was advancing slowly and deliberately—forcing its prey backwards. Every few steps, one of its two front legs would lash out at her, and she would have to jump back and try to parry the attack with the gun.

And now I could see what it was trying to do. It was working her off the side of the road. Every lunge it made brought her closer to the edge. In a moment, her left foot was going to hit the crumbling embankment and she was going to lose her balance.

Seini could see it as well. The next time she stepped back, she tried to leap further and come back out into the road. But then the thing *did* move quickly—it immediately crowded her on her right side so again, she was forced back toward the edge.

Desperately, Seini stepped back and fired her weapon again at the thing's body, but it made no difference. She was right on the verge now.

But I was closer too, and the Hunter still hadn't noticed me. Before it had a chance to strike again, I dropped into a fighting crouch and brought my *machaira* down onto the armoured cable that looped over the top joint on its rear left leg.

It was a good hit. As the blade bit through the metal coil, there was a sound like a shotgun going off and a plume of orange fluid blasted up into the sky. The monster dipped slightly as the leg slumped.

And then it turned on me.

I had about a third of a second to rejoice in my achievement before I was fighting for my life.

It came straight at me, lashing out at me with its two front arms and forcing me backwards, just as it had with Seini.

But this was a very different style of attack. It had been playing with her, biding its time—maybe even enjoying its hunt. Now, it was just trying to kill. The curved claws at the end of its attack arms had turned into broad daggers that jabbed at my defences.

I parried the first couple of attacks with my *machaira* ... stepped backwards, and then locked my feet in the fighting stance that I'd learned at Crux. I parried and parried again.

Then it tried a high-low combination—aiming for my face and abdomen. I twisted and deflected the upper strike, but the lower attack gave my hip a bruising graze as it slid off the coat. Before I had a chance to regain my balance, it came at me again.

I suddenly had a sense that this was not a fight I could win. Whatever skills I had were outmatched by the Hunter's sheer power and speed. I was already tired, and in my present state, my strength wasn't going to last much longer. Sometime soon, it was going to find a gap, or I was going to fall.

But what else could I do? As I blocked and retreated again, I thought of singing at it, but I was panting so much that I could barely make a croak.

Then Seini gave me a moment's relief by attacking the thing from behind—firing her weapon right up against the thing's body shell. I don't know if the round penetrated, but it did cause it to spin about. Before she had a chance to hold up her gun, it struck her with the back of its hooks and knocked her right off her feet and down into the canola.

And now it came back for me. It aimed for my head. I ducked. It tried the high-low combination again. I dodged and parried again. It went for my legs, but my boots and balance held. I stepped out of the way.

Then it tried a combination attack on my body and got past my guard. As I rotated away from the first arm, the second slipped through and stabbed me through the flap of my coat. There was an explosion of pain from my side and a burning cold sensation.

I managed to step back, but I knew something bad had happened.

And now the thing began to take its time—as if it knew it had me and could take me apart at its leisure. It began probing, pushing me back toward the edge of the road.

I had another go at singing, but when I tried to fill my lungs, there was a sharp pain that made it impossible.

As I retreated, I saw something catch the light in the background. Something was coming up the road from Addle; something green and square and moving fast with a dust cloud behind it.

Then the Hunter came forward again, and there was no time to think about that. I tried Seini's manoeuvre—going back a step further and moving away from the verge—but it didn't work for me either. The monster simply moved further into the road to crowd me.

It attacked again and scored a hit on my thigh. I stayed upright, but I was right on the brink. It came at me high and low and struck my arm. I stepped back and slid, dropping my sword as I fought to keep from falling. The thing reared up over me.

And then the bus hit it. There was a massive crash, a sound of tyres slewing on the track and white dust everywhere. Then silence.

I found my sword and got to my feet, coughing and wincing at the pain in my chest. It was worse now. When I put my hand inside my coat, it came away soaked with blood.

I didn't probe any further. But when I tried to take a deep breath, I found that it wasn't possible—as if my lungs had shrunk. When I breathed out, the cold feeling came again.

"Well, that's fair enough," I thought. "It will be like what happened with the old Agent under the bridge." I wasn't afraid. I just hoped I would have long enough to deal with whatever was in that bus.

I began walking down the road in the direction it had disappeared. After a few metres, I found one of the Hunter's legs lying in a pool of hydraulic fluid. Then I came across the rest of it, twitching and fizzing on the gravelled verge.

I could hear voices up ahead—somebody calling and someone answering—but, at first, I didn't take it in because I was distracted by the sight of the bus. A long strip of its side panel had been ripped off like a strip of peel and was trailing on the road. The sight gave me a sense of *déja vu*, but I couldn't think why.

Then I saw shapes through the dust and began to recognise the voices: Seini's ... Lenny's ... all talking at once and someone saying my name—and then suddenly I found myself laughing because the third voice I heard was Caleb's.

"Who taught you to drive, brother?" I said.

And then they were all around me—and my mum was there too— and I had to stop them hugging me because I was worried about what that would do to me. And Caleb was saying, "Good to see you, bro," and thanking me for keeping that thing off Seini. And my mum had tears in her eyes and kept asking if I was okay. And Lenny was grinning at me and saying something about my sword skills.

And I laughed and coughed and felt like there was a little less room in my lungs every time I breathed in.

But I didn't care about that. I was just too happy to see them all together and to think they would be able to look after each other now. We were all back on the road. I'd come to the end, and it had worked out okay after all.

Except then the wind changed direction, and I heard it—coming faintly through the settling dust: the familiar sound of a big diesel engine.

"Hey, Seini," I said. "How many rounds do you have left in that gun?"

CHAPTER 49

It wasn't easy to persuade them to go. Lenny said, no way, we'd fight together. My mum said it was ridiculous. She grabbed hold of the sleeve of my coat like she would never let me go.

But I made Caleb understand.

"Listen, brother, that Hunter thing got me. I can feel my lungs filling—it's not something you can fix. If I come with you, you'll just have to watch it happen. But if you get back on that bus and drive, I can buy you some time. Maybe I can even stop them.

"You have to go, brother. And you have to go now because that rig's getting closer. And Seini isn't even treated yet."

And when I showed him the wound, he looked at it, and then looked in my face, and looked up the road, and put a hand on my shoulder and said, "You're a hero, bro. I'll look out for you in the City."

And then he got them all on the bus—even my mum, which meant Seini having to almost carry her—and he gave one big long blow on the horn, and they went.

Then I went down on one knee in the middle of the road and waited for the truck.

It would have been better for accuracy if I could have lain flat, of course. I thought of doing that—even of lying down behind the body of the Hunter and using its shell for a rest. But if my lungs were filling from the bottom, that was the last thing I wanted to do. I already had a sense that I was running out of time—that my breaths were getting so shallow as to be useless—so I needed to hold out as long as possible.

Besides, I thought, I didn't need to achieve any great feat of marksmanship. Seini had told me there were three bullets in the magazine, and my plan was to wait until they were almost on me and then fire point blank before they hit me. I didn't know if the bullets would get through the armour, but if I could wait long enough, I should be able to shoot through the slot where the driver looked out.

But they were driving so slowly. With the wheels of their truck spanning the road and resting on the embankment either side, the rig kept slewing back and forward, and whoever was driving had their work cut out for them.

I wondered what they thought as they saw me in the distance. Had the big man with the bones in his hair recognised me that night in the tunnel? Was he up there with the driver pointing and shouting?

Did they even have enough awareness to keep track of things like that? Back in Spillan, everyone talked about them as if they were nothing more than wild animals—barely capable of speech. But we'd been wrong about so many other things; how did I know we'd been right about that?

And now I was out of time. I was panting like a dog but it wasn't making any difference. The cold feeling was radiating out from the wound in my side, and shadows were creeping in from the edge of my vision. It was horrible feeling myself run out of air like that—but the worst part of it wasn't the feeling of suffocation but the thought that the thing would keep coming and catch my friends.

The truck was still about four hundred metres away but it was now or never. I raised my rifle and aimed it at the opening above the big white skull and fired and fired and fired and felt myself falling sideways into darkness.

*   *   *

And then it wasn't dark anymore. And it didn't hurt anymore.

Even as I felt my body hit the ground, I was suddenly watching it happen from above and behind. I saw my body collapsed over the rifle; the canola bending in the light breeze. I noticed a dragonfly pause over the shattered Hunter with the sunlight refracting into colours off its wings.

I tried to look up toward the truck and my view shifted—not like a head or eye turning, but like closing one eye and opening the other. The machine was still there; still coming.

But it seemed slower. In fact, everything seemed slower: a skylark escaping from the stalks of the canola flapped its wings at half speed; the dust billowing up from the truck tyres looked like it was moving through oil.

"Chris Walker, fancy meeting you here," said a familiar voice.

I looked around—skipping between faceted perspectives, but there was nobody there.

"Where are you, Eve?" I said.

"I'm in Central," she said, "I'm speaking to you through the network."

"And what about me? Am I dead?"

"Do you feel dead?"

"No, but my body looks like it and, you know, I'm not in it."

She laughed. "Yeah, that's a fair point. But you're not dead. Prax has got you in what they call bridge mode. It's how they preserve your consciousness until they retrieve your body. It's nothing compared to how it feels when they rebuild you, but it's not too bad."

"Am I in a drone, then?"

"You're in the network—the drone is just where your senses are localised. But if you wanted to, you could move to another node."

I tried moving down the road away from the truck and my view shifted. Again, it wasn't like flying; it was like suddenly being two hundred metres away from where I'd been.

I did it again and again until I was ahead of the bus. Now I could see Caleb at the wheel, staring down the road with a worried expression on his face. I could see Lenny, twisted in his seat to look into the dust cloud behind. I could see Caleb's sister with her arm around my mum.

I felt such love for them all—even Seini, who I'd only met an hour before.

"Are they going to be okay?" I said. "Are the Savages going to get them?"

"You know, you're really gonna have to stop calling them that, Chris," said Eve. "It's not nice and it's not accurate. But they aren't coming for your friends. They were only after you."

"Because of me shooting at them?"

She laughed again. "No, Chris, I don't think you've ever done them too much harm in that department."

"I guess not," I said.

I still had a whole lot of questions I wanted to ask her about that—mainly why they were after me—but I was distracted by another thing that had been in the back of my mind ever since I'd staggered out of the dust and found Caleb and the others.

"What about Mallory?" I said, "What's going to happen to her?"

"Sometimes you just have to entrust people to the Envoy, Chris."

"But couldn't he do something? Like he did with me up at Horeb?"

"How do you know he hasn't already? He doesn't work the same way with everyone—all you can do is do your best and leave the rest to him and Prax."

"I'm not so sure I did my best with her, Eve—or any of them—I made a lot of mistakes."

"Well, you might be surprised. He can do a lot with a little. Hold on, Prax wants to show you a couple of things."

As she said it, I was suddenly in another place. There was shadow and movement that I couldn't make out, but then I realised that I was gliding down a dark stairwell made of brick and concrete. We went further into the gloom, and the camera blinked to black and white. Now I could see the ruins of a factory basement: skeletons slumped over rusted guns; a barricade made of crates; overturned benches and spools of sheet metal and wire.

"This is the light factory," I said.

"Yes," said Prax in that huge voice. "And look."

The camera rose, gliding over the barrier to the place where we'd found the Traveller's gear. It hovered over someone standing in the middle of the space—someone wearing a dust mask, a pair of gloves and a well-cut suit. He had apparently just finished peeling back the layers of cardboard, blankets and sleeping mats, and was shining a torch onto a metal hatch in the concrete floor.

"That's the Professor," I said. "What's he doing?"

"He is about to discover the last cache of Hesper City Tox suppressant. And he is about to discover that the ingredients all came from Central."

"Is he doing that because of what we found there?"

"Yes, and because of what Rose saw while you were telling her about the Envoy."

"What *did* she see? Is she okay?"

But instead of an answer, the view changed. Now I was high in the vault of the old museum station and the camera was in motion, flying down toward a row of shelves. As we got closer, I could see someone rummaging around in a pile of electronic equipment—a familiar grey head, a set of round shoulders under a tartan dressing gown.

It was Trevor. He was dragging something out from under a pile of music discs—a box with dials and needles and a microphone attached by a short black spring cable.

"Do you understand what he is doing?" said Prax.

"Is he trying to do the SOS thing like I did?"

"He is."

"Will it work? Will you do something?"

"We will—not because of the radio, but because he belongs to the Envoy."

"And what will you do."

"Something that will force him and Prudence to leave their hole. It will be hard for them, but they will be glad in the long run."

I watched him dusting off the machine and felt a surge of delight.

Then I was back at the road—hovering above the old bus containing my friends.

"So you get the gist?" said Eve. "Nothing's wasted."

"I do," I said.

Down below in the canola, I noticed a bee at work in one of the flowers. When I focussed on him, I could see him scraping the pollen off his fur into little balls on his hind legs. Lower still in the undergrowth, I saw a skink stalking a millipede. And I thought how this was a Corp crop, but it was still so full of incredible things like that. What would it be like after the blue fire changed it all?

"So what happens now," I said. "Are you gonna stick me in that tank and test my memories?"

"Are you worried?" said Eve.

"No," I said. "I know about the pardon. But if you'd asked me when I was back in that cage, before Lenny helped me, I would have been worried then—I think I'd convinced myself that the cure hadn't worked on me."

"What changed?"

"Something—I dunno. It was like those bits of the Roadbook opened something up, and then something else happened when they had me strapped down in the chair."

"That's good, Chris—yeah, that's how it works. But keep your eyes fixed on the pardon. The other stuff comes and goes a bit.

"But in answer to your question: not yet. The Envoy's sending you back west; to Spillan."

"Back? Like this?"

"No. In your body," she said, "And with some friends."

"But … I'm dead … my lungs are punctured."

"Do you think that would be too much for the Envoy to handle, Chris?"

As she asked the question, I saw how ridiculous my objection was. I remembered how the man had cured me with spit; how he had anticipated my need for a knife at Wicket. And now, as I looked down, I suddenly realised that the scene I was seeing below me was the same one Prax had shown me at Prediger's house: a bus with its side panel ripped open, driving down a road surrounded by yellow flowers.

"No," I said.

"Exactly," said Eve. "In any case, Prax says to tell you that you're wrong about your lungs. You've got a tension pneumothorax, not a pulmonary haemorrhage."

"I don't know what that means."

She laughed. "I didn't either. But apparently, it means you've got air trapped in your chest cavity, not blood leaking into your lungs. Anyway, the Envoy has sent you someone who knows how to deal with it. Look."

And then I was above my body again. Except now there were people bent over me, and, as I looked at them, I could see they were people I recognised.

I could see Johnny crouched down at my side where my wound was. I could see Rose on the other side spreading antiseptic gel on a big adhesive dressing—they were both wearing Travellers' coats now.

And Mallory was there, kneeling at my head. I saw her shoulders rise and fall as she breathed into my lungs; watched her clamping my mouth and nose with her hands and giving orders to the other two.

And then suddenly I realised that these weren't the only people present. On the edge of the frame, I could see a pair of worn leather boots and torn trousers. As I willed myself to another camera angle, I found myself looking straight into the face of the big man with cysts on his face and bones in his hair. Behind him, other Savages were climbing down off their giant machine.

There was no panic—not even fear, really—as I saw them. The great calm was still there. But I knew what I was looking at.

"Can't you do something to stop them? Couldn't you use that beam thing?"

"Look at him again," said Eve.

And then I saw what I should have seen that night in the tunnel—what I did see but had been too terrified to process—that the big man was wearing a Traveller's coat over his rags.

"How did that happen?" I said. "How did any of that happen?"

"You'll have to ask them yourself, Chris. It's almost time; your friends have restarted your heart and got air back into your lungs. But it was good to talk to you again. I look forward to seeing you in the flesh when you get here."

"You too, Eve. Thanks for everything."

"You're very welcome. Now, brace yourself. It's going to hurt."

And everything went black and red.

EPILOGUE

(Extract of the Journals of Callan Vartry, Vol 1.2)

I guess it was a pretty good sort of funeral.

The Parson went out of his way—even wrote a sermon specially for the occasion about what a great man Mayor Stricton had been, and how such men were like trees walking around, giving shelter to everyone.

He talked about how the Mayor had been a man with a big heart— how he'd defended the town from without and within, and how he'd borne the burden of keeping the town free of the Tox.

"We must beseech the heavens that we should find such a man again."

Some of that was true, I thought. The Mayor had known how to hold the place together, and he'd been smart with his succession planning. The Council would probably manage to choose one of themselves to replace him without a big fight.

He'd been smart to leave me out of it too. After Chris left, I'd been his next pick, but he'd seen pretty quickly that I was never going to be a politician.

"I want you to oversee the defences, Stick. You'll never be Mayor, but you've got a sharp eye."

But he was a liar. I knew that now. Sally Menders, the doctor's daughter, had come and whispered the truth to me while I was fixing a gearbox in the shop.

"It wasn't a heart attack," she said. "Not a normal one anyway."

"What was it then?" I said.

"You have to promise not to tell," she said.

"I'm not going to promise that."

"Then I can't tell you."

"Okay."

She waited for almost a minute and then told me anyway.

"My Dad said he had a cyst on his heart, and it ruptured."

"What, like a Tox cyst?"

"Yes. And that's not all," she said. "He had another one in his armpit."

So he'd been infected. He'd been doing all that stuff to people like my sister, but all the while, he'd had one himself. Chris hadn't been totally crazy.

I wondered if the doctor had told the Council—and if the new Mayor would just keep on killing and exiling people.

I wondered what I was going to do about it.

The Parson turned to give his signal to the kid in the belltower, but then the radio in my pocket squawked and everyone looked around at me, because Billy T, my deputy, was shouting that he'd had a call from the patrol.

"It's old Ozzie. He says it's the truck. The big one! The big Savage truck!"

"Okay," I said. "You know what to do. Sound the alarm."

*Thank you for reading "The Blood Miles"!
If you enjoyed this book, and would like to help other people hear about it,
please consider taking a moment to rate or review the book on Amazon or
Goodreads. Such things make a big difference in this age of algorithms,
and will also encourage me to work on a sequel.*

(Andrew Moody)

ABOUT THE AUTHOR

Andrew Moody has been on the road to Sanctuary since his mother told him about the cure in 1974. Along the way, he picked up some degrees in design and theology and sometimes works as a designer, sometimes as a theological teacher. From 2016 to 2023, he was the inaugural Editorial Director of The Gospel Coalition Australia. Andrew travels with his wife, Jenny, and they have two grown-up children and a much-loved son-in-law. They have all been strengthened in their journey by the Agents and Travellers at Holy Trinity Doncaster (Melbourne, Australia). Andrew maintains a newsletter and blog at: andrewmoodywrites.com